THE MIRACLE MAN

a novel by
Todd Easterling

"Strong writing, strong characters, solidly researched, exciting novel. Great love scenes, powerful imagery. I think this is the best written book I've read for you. A very strong novel, and a good writer who, frankly, I think has more and quite possibly better books in him."
David Stein, Simon & Shuster

"The writing is good and atmospheric. Todd Easterling is an author with talent."
Joseph Pittman, as Senior Editor, Dutton Signet, a division of Penguin USA

"Todd Easterling certainly tells an intensely emotional story that features many sympathetic characters and he sets it convincingly in two vividly depicted, distinct locales. It has great cinematic potential."
Maggie Crawford, Senior Editor, Bantam-Doubleday-Dell, Random House Publishing Group, New York, NY

The Miracle Man
ISBN-10: 10:098898802X
ISBN-13: 978-0-9889880-2-6
Library of Congress Control Number: 2014904192

Virgin Iconic Entertainment
New York - London - Los Angeles - Sydney

ACKNOWLEDGEMENTS

First and foremost, I would like to thank Doctor Ian Wilmut, Professor Emeritus and Chairman of the Scottish Centre for Regenerative Medicine building, the first person to successfully clone a mammal, Dolly the sheep. He graciously assisted me during the creation of this story, helping with technical details. In addition, I would like to thank Dr. Raul Cano, the scientist who first extracted dinosaur DNA from ancient amber, which the late Michael Crichton's Jurassic Park was based on. I would also like to thank Yolan Friedmann, CEO of the Endangered Wildlife Trust. For his technical guidance on medical issues, I'd like to thank Dr. Hal Broxmeyer, professor of microbiology/immunology and co-leader of the program on Hematopoiesis, Microenvironment, and Immunology at Indiana University Simon Cancer center. Likewise, Dr. Edward Ball, Chief of Blood and Marrow Transplantation at Moores UCSD Cancer Center provided input. Last but not least, I'd like to thank my family for their support, including Emily, Hayley, and Sasha for tolerating lots of "I can't right now, I'm writing," and many attempts to open my locked office door.

DEDICATION

For my beautiful daughters, twins Emily and Hayley, and Sasha.

❧

ALSO BY TODD EASTERLING

The First Witness

- Over two years on 8 *Best Sellers in Suspense, Mysteries & Thrillers* lists, as high as #1.
- Top 1% in sales of all/4.2 million books February 2013 through June 2016+.

Hot new releases: #1 Best Seller
Techno-thrillers: #1
Political Suspense: #1
Conspiracies: #2
Travel adventure: #4
Genre Fiction, Political: #2
Suspense/military: #19
Assassinations: #29

Kilimanjaro is a snow covered mountain 19,710 feet high, and it is said to be the highest mountain in Africa. Its western summit is called the Masai "Ngàje Ngài," the House of God. Close to the western summit there is the dried and frozen carcass of a leopard. No one has explained what the leopard was seeking at that altitude.

Ernest Hemingway
The Snows of Kilimanjaro

PART ONE

CHAPTER ONE

At the first gesture of dawn, just a hint of pale sky peeks in from the window aimed eastward. An owl is heard and the flavor of autumn is in the air, solid and crisp. Her drowsiness evaporating, she rises to one elbow while stretching her neck and says to herself, "No use fighting it," as the hour hand moves over the five in the faintest of light. She draws her lips to his forehead and begs for a few more seconds, just a moment more of quietude, then picks herself up at once, dresses without showering, and blindly runs a comb through her tangled nest of hair. She moves down the hall toward the girls' rooms, blooming with the pink glow of a night-light. A quick check on Angela—she's cuddled up with her favorite doll, tucked in warmly. And a glance at Megan—sound asleep, flannel sheets gathered in knots at her feet, socks loitering about her delicate ankles. She then finds her way through the warm darkness to the kitchen where she scribbles a note on the pad attached to the refrigerator amidst a collage of crayon drawings, mostly horses bigger than barns and people with tiny heads, stick limbs, *David, I couldn't sleep, see you at the lab, don't forget your dentist appointment, Sis will be by to get Angela and Megan, love ya, Katie.*

She opens the refrigerator and pulls out a carton of milk, pours a glass smooth and white, then notices a piece of paper taped above the water and ice dispenser. Another poem Megan had discovered in English class. As Katie drinks the milk she reads,

> *Evolution*
> *by John Banister Tabb (1894)*
> *Out of the dusk a shadow,*
> *Then, a spark;*
> *Out of the cloud a silence,*
> *Then, a lark;*
> *Out of the heart a rapture,*
> *Then, a pain;*
> *Out of the dead, cold ashes,*
> *Life again.*

There, below the poem and drawn in purple and yellow, is a flower. An iris, a bearded iris. Megan's favorite flower. It's on the wallpaper in her room. It's on one of the blouses she wears each week, usually Fridays. It's everywhere Megan is. As Katie swallows the milk, she runs her eyes over it, from the drooping petals to the frail green stem which twists and loops upon itself until it becomes Megan's signature. Then she sets the glass down and puts the carton back on the top shelf, next to the orange juice, poppy-seed bagels and margarine. A minute later and she is out the front door.

She drives quickly down the sugar maple-lined lane that meanders from the gabled cape home they purchased four and a half years ago, white clapboards and black shutters, two chimneys with gray fissured grout needing repair. An antique iron lawn jockey keeps watch near the street, its paint crackled and rust peeking through around the face and belly and little stained buttocks—shades of jade mingled with turquoise that has bled down from its numbered iron jersey. One arm is missing, just below the elbow, though a metal ring still rests in the other as if it is awaiting a horse to be tied to it. Ahead, past the mailbox and two soggy newspapers, the road appears as a barren ribbon of black as it ascends several nameless rolling knolls, crosses Lauder's Creek and a narrow swath, then becomes one with the sky. Home slips away in the rearview mirror.

Meandering through the wooded hillocks for fifteen minutes, the headlights of the Mercedes SUV are eventually swallowed by a warm glow. The planet awakens, dawn arrives, animals stir, stables and farm buildings moan, and bright green John Deere's are warmed. Everything, everybody, is jarred back to life. Yet most of Kentucky still lay asleep, silent. Drapes drawn, shutters closed, not a soul to be seen. The sound of the tires is all she hears, save the muffled drone from the eight-cylinder. Mesmerized, time slips by as long shadows crossing her path become rounder then almost disappear. She feels alone, the only person on earth.

She arrives at the employee lot right on the hour, Steeple Chase Road, northwest of town. The closest parking spot to the entrance is hers, as usual.

She taps in her five-digit access code and enters the building. With heavy eyelids she strides purposefully toward the coffee room and realizes she forgot to put a bra on. Too late to worry about now. Making her way through the labyrinth of white walls and frigid metal fire doors, she switches on hallway after hallway of florescent lights she hates to no end. They flicker, spitting an austere bluish light, and buzz annoyingly until warmed for a few seconds.

❧

There are shades of silence, the chaotic chatter of finches the only exception, as the sun reveals itself in hues of yellow and hushed crimson above a white-washed cupola perched above the barn. A black crow is resting on the weathervane, its claws clenched about the back of a copper horse with a verdigris patina etched by sulfate, chloride, and time. Below, rays penetrate in through crooked crevices and knotted halos of aged oak and poplar boards, the light dancing hypnotically where nearby swaying tree branches impede its path. The horses are quiet, even Black Magic. Her nostrils flare as a sweet mist off the plains to the north secretes away and envelops her newborn's skin with the cool breath of fall.

A hundred yards away, across a sparkling carpet of bluegrass dotted with dew, a chill moves up Katie's spine as she turns toward a window. She senses a change. From within the stark cement walls and corrugated steel ceiling of the lab, she pulls a lock of her long red hair to one side, squints through reddened blue eyes. She leans forward and the windowpane before her becomes foggier with each breath. Minute ice crystals form and quickly vanish. Gazing outward, everything appears more still today, quiescent, except for the orange-red, crisp-yellow, and amber leaves floating haphazardly to the ground like butterflies gone mad. How could autumn come so quickly this year?

Her mind reels, *My god, could it have happened?*

The cup warming her hands and coaxing her from drowsiness is placed down on an oak table next to a copy of *Nature*. It tips over as she scoots her chair in too hard, the spill soaking the cover. She doesn't notice.

She rushes down another sterile passageway and exits the building. A thick security door slams behind her as she reaches down to her feet, ties her shoelaces more securely, then springs upward and runs toward the barn, white lab coat wavering like a cape. Misty air puffs from her chest, creating a trail of tiny clouds, dotting the way then quickly disappearing. She'd waited for this day for three years. And delaying the rewards of the lab's hard work even further, the pregnant mare was overdue. Until last night the staff had been afraid to induce delivery, wanting nature to runs its course, which seemed preposterous, Katie

11

thought, given the artificiality of the entire project and the life they'd created within the mare's womb.

Her slender fingers meet the iron latch of the gate and seem to instantly become frozen. They sting and she rubs them together to no effect, numbness already setting in. The gate clicks open and she pushes it hard. It rotates with a squeal and hits the fence, sending a shudder through her bones and the rails and posts that wander up the bank toward the frigid troughs, honey-colored hay bales, and muted pasture awaiting winter. Red buds and oaks stand partially green here, but upon the higher elevations the limbs of bare trees reach toward the sky and loom over the sweeping valley, presaging what will become of the farmlands and forests for the next five months. Brown and gray and other achromatic tones, little else.

"Let her be all right," a whisper leaves her lips. "Please, just let her be okay."

Dust rises as she makes her way down the first research corridor of the old barn. Damp, dank air smothers her face and sends shivers rippling through her small frame. Shooting up, shooting down. Shooting up, shooting down.

West of town on South Hampton Road David, in their blue Range Rover, winds his way through Smiley's Landing, just east of the river. He had slept in a half hour later than Katie, then gone to a dentist appointment. As he adjusts the heating controls, the Range Rover sways and its tires squeal as they cut through the hills—65 in a 45—and the vehicle rises and falls with the terrain and potholed pavement, unwanted reminders of last season's particularly wet spring. He leans forward and quiets the radio, raises a cell phone to his right ear and glances at his watch. He hits a memory button and the phone chirps to life. Two rings and he hears, "Good morning, Kentucky Thoroughbred Center, may I help you?"

"Hi Barb. David here." Still numb from the dentist, his tongue is heavy and he struggles to sound normal. "Could you patch me through to the conference room?"

"I'm fine. Thanks. How are you this morning, David?"

"Uh, sorry. I'm not in a great mood."

"Thanks for the warning. Hang on. I'll transfer you over."

Static, a couple clicks. Barb buzzes the conference room.

With his feet perched upon the mahogany conference table and right hand twirling a pockmarked pencil, one of the lab's brilliant up-and-comers, Ted Stanton, reaches with his left hand and hits an intercom button. "Yeah, Barb, what's up?"

"I got David coming your way. Line one. Be ready, he's grumpy."

"What else is new?"

"He's all yours." Barb hangs up.

Ted hits the speaker phone button then line one, "Are you there, David?"

"Yeah. Is everyone ready?"

"Everyone but Katie. Her car's in front but no one's seen her. I was about to run out to the barn. Where the hell are you, chief?"

"I'm about ten minutes away. May as well just wait for me, rather than yell over this thing. Find out what she's up to, okay?"

"Yes sir. Right away sir."

David was used to Ted's sense of humor and casualness, but he wasn't in the mood for levity, not after a dentist visit and rushing through the morning. David continued, "I'd cool it with the joking around. My mouth is swollen and—"

"Sorry, I'll see what's up," Ted interrupted. "We won't start the meeting until you get here, unless the call comes in from the investors— or should I say prospective investors." Ted paused, glancing across to the other side of the conference table. "But our able-bodied CFO apparently has his numbers ready. And we've all got our serious give-us-money faces on."

"Uh-huh...sounds like it. Okay, I'll be there in a few minutes or so."

"All right."

"Bye." David ends the call, sets his cell phone on the passenger seat, and then glances at the rearview mirror.

Katie approaches horse stall five. She hears stirring. "Are you okay, girl?" She slides a latch to the right and slowly pulls open the wood door. Her mouth drops, eyes widen.

"My god...we did it. We really did it."

She moves toward the newborn and its mother, who looks drawn out, sweaty. "You okay?" she asks again, wanting some indication of well-being from the weary thoroughbred she's spent countless hours worrying about over the past several months. On more than one lazy evening the thought had struck her that it seemed as if she was worrying about everything lately. And everyone.

The horse's big brown eyes blink laboriously and glisten with moisture, the rheumy secretions gathering dust and hay particles in a growing coagulation of puss which makes its way downward and leaves a trail on either side of its face. Katie rubs along the muscular neck, feels veins throbbing mightily, reaches lower and touches the damp, pounding chest.

"Calm down, girl. You're all right. Just calm down. In a couple days," Katie says in a hushed voice, barely audible, "you'll be out riding the trails again."

It was these trails, these rolling hills, these thick woodlands that Katie's family had settled on more years ago than anyone could remember. They came for the horses, as many do, for the world's finest thoroughbreds roam sprawling white-fenced farms throughout Kentucky. They live in massive barns that dot the hills and valleys, many adjoining Georgian and Federal homes and carefully groomed oval tracks where they train for the Kentucky Derby and lesser races each year.

Sprinkled between the farms, and proximal to the Ohio River, are rock quarries where gravel is mined, the many rivers and streams providing ample supplies.

One such operation, Clark Gravel Quarry, is quiet this morning. Most of the large trucks have picked up their first load and departed the forty-acre facility, headed to cement factories and other customers requiring the fine, pebbly rocks that have been crushed, polished, and distributed over millions of years of rambling, tumultuous water which has, every twenty years or so, blanketed the tiny river communities with mud and waist-high currents.

A bearded Dan Johnson, age forty-two and one of the quarry's eighteen drivers, ambles along whistling a cheery tune learned from Showboat tickets his second wife bought, third aisle, and makes his way from the foreman's building—a single-wide rusted trailer propped up on cinder blocks and positioned next to the quarry entrance where an antique backhoe with a yellow bucket stands proudly with its dinosaur-like mouth aimed at the clouds. A stack of termite-eaten shipping pallets lay to one side, piled seven feet high, maybe more.

"Running late today, huh Dan," a co-worker on a skip loader yells as he shuts down the massive diesel engine and locks the brakes with his steel-toed work boots. A few last puffs of carbonous soot belches from the exhaust, making the tin rain-lid clank and flap like the wing of a wild turkey. The vibrations beneath his feet dissipate and yield to tingling in his toes, arches, and ankles.

Dan nods and says, "Flat tire. Must have hit a nail coming in last night."

"They got a crew on it?"

"Uh-huh. Should be done by now. I was just going to walk over and check."

"Well, I can give you a ride." The driver climbs down from the dusty cab, his boots finding purchase with a series of staggered iron steps made of galvanized rod painted with rust. "I'm headin' over to maintenance," he continues.

Dan purses his lips, raises his brow. "Great. Thanks."

"Just give me a sec. I need to turn in my timecard from yesterday. Forgot all about it. Go ahead and hop in that red Toyota truck over there." He points toward a row of vehicles that have seen better days, tosses his keys over.

"All right," Dan says as he catches and slides them into his flannel shirt pocket. As he walks toward the truck he pulls out a pack of Kentucky home-grown tobacco and a lighter which he quickly thumbs to a dull flame, almost empty. He inhales deeply then opens the door and gets in. It'll be a long day, he tells himself, glancing at his watch. He has lost an hour, almost impossible to make up, but he will try. A load of quarter-inch gravel and sand mix is due in thirty minutes over in Louisville, a parking lot and loading dock going in at the new grocery store next to Target and the farm co-op his brother owns.

Five miles away from the lab facility, the Range Rover's transmission downshifts as David eases up on the pedal and nears a Mack truck and trailer loaded with oaks and maples and poplars stacked higher and wider than common sense would dictate, the vertical steel fingers of the flatbed bending outward and groaning with each curve. Black smoke everywhere. *Lately, there seems to be more of these than horse trailers*, David thinks as he shakes his head.

The truck driver grinds through gears, trying to find something that will tractor up the steep grade. More haze bellows into the mixed blue-gray sky from the noisy Cummins engine and its two exhausts which tower on either side of an air dam sitting high above the cab.

David picks up his cell phone again while peering around the steering wheel and hugging the double yellow. He crosses over for a split second to catch a view. Three cars are approaching, lights on. No way to pass.

He dials out and the receptionist answers once more, "Good morning, Kentucky Thoroughbred Center, may I help you?"

"Barb, it's David again. I'm stuck in traffic and—"

"Traffic where you live?"

"Yeah, I—"

"Can you hold for a second? I have three lines going."

"Sure."

The oncoming cars pass, whoosh, whoosh, whoosh. They disappear in the rearview mirror, fluttering leaves in chase.

David moves the wheel a bit more to the left. Looks clear. His heart picks up the pace as he sees the driver of the truck in front of him stick his hairy arm out the truck cab's open window and urge him to pass. David hesitates and thinks, *On a double yellow?*

The arm continues waving.

"Come on, come on," David says under his breath as he holds the cell phone's receiver a little further from his right ear. He looks to the side mirror. Still clear.

Finally, Barb's voice comes on, "I'm sorry, David. This place is crazy today."

"That's all right."

"You should be here by now," she continues.

"I know, I know. My dentist took longer than expected. And now there's a damn logging truck in front of me barely going twenty miles an hour," he says then cranes his neck forward. "Tell the staff not to wait. Just have someone take notes."

"Okay."

"Any news on the foal yet?"

"I don't know," Barb offers, then glances down at a security monitor with a video feed of the barn stables. "No one's come back from the stalls yet."

"All right. I'll be there shortly." David hangs up.

There was indeed news. And Katie is the only person who knows, at this very moment, what it is. This realization, this privilege, this honor, makes her smile as she continues rubbing Black Magic, then caresses the head of her newborn foal, its eyes not yet meeting, or at least not focusing on the world. Its charcoal-colored hair is wet and glistens like the pulsating neck of a stallion which has just won the Kentucky Derby.

Katie sneezes—dust particles still hang in the dewy air—and glances up at the mother then quickly back to the newborn as the pink fluids of birth begin attracting flies. They buzz and circle in a disarray of pleasure at the stench which is also derived from a night's worth of fresh dung.

"You're gonna make some headlines little boy," she whispers to the foal. "My lord, we actually did it." She smiles to herself and sighs. "Are you going to run like your daddy did?"

She strokes the sleek, long back, following the ups and downs of the rollercoaster spine till it becomes a feeble tail. "You sure look just like your daddy," she continues at length, her words trailing off.

A wave of guilt sweeps over her as she tells herself that all of the employees should be here; everyone should relish in the moment. Then she thinks of the two press releases sitting on her desk, a version for each contingency. One was tailored to play up a possible success: *Kentucky Thoroughbred Center Clones First Triple Crown Winner.* Another was drawn up to soften the blow of a failure: *Kentucky Thoroughbred Center Makes Progress Mapping Triple Crown Winner Genome.* The latter would eventually get around to saying that a foal had died, possibly even its mother, but progress had been made attempting to clone one of racing's finest horses. It was intended to be released to the press only in the event of word getting out about a failure. And such news would surely be leaked sooner or later. Two reporters, one from the *Lexington Herald-Leader* and one from the *Louisville Courier-Journal*, had already been bombarding her with questions about the Center's work, which she handled by stating that she was under a gag order due to the possibility of an initial public offering. She had grown accustomed to telling reporters, "I really can't say anything." It was a bit of an exaggeration, but not far from reality given the pressure to bring in venture capital, whether it is from private investors or an IPO. The company had struggled with cash flow for years, largely due to the expensive lab equipment essential for its sensitive genetics work.

With today's news, lack of money will no longer be a problem, she thinks as she stands and the mare gently moves closer to lick her newborn, closing her eyes with each stroke of her long tongue.

Although Katie doesn't want to leave the peaceful scene before her, she decides to go tell the others. Moving with caution, not wanting to startle either horse, she pries herself away.

The stall door closes behind her. One last glance through the gap between two rails and she moves stealthily down the corridor. A few tears grow from her eyes and cascade down her cheeks, drop to her denim collar and are quickly absorbed, becoming a blotch of indigo. The tears are not only for this birth, but for the painful years in which she had endured fertility testing and countless reproductive procedures, failing to become pregnant then, at last, succeeding with Megan and later Angela. She thought she had buried these feelings long ago, never to be dredged to the surface. Yet here she is, shedding tears as if *she* has just given birth. Her lack of control, at this moment, terrifies her. She trembles slightly and loses herself in memories, as she strides across the grass which connects the stalls to the main building. She approaches the security door, wiping her eyes as she switches to a more composed walk. Twenty feet. Ten. Two.

Suddenly the door swings open and Barb is standing there.

Out of breath, Katie tells her, "We did it. Everything's okay. It's a boy." She pauses to take a deep breath. Her flushed skin feels like it is boiling with excitement over the foal. She walks in, as Barb holds the door open. "Come on, let's tell everyone."

"They're all in the conference room," Barb replies. "The door is locked, I just tried to go in."

"Locked?"

"Yeah. And the speaker phone is turned up real loud. I think it's Flemming and those investors."

Katie turns and looks down the hallway toward the executive conference room. "I guess we could interrupt, and give everyone the news. What do you think?"

"Your call."

Katie pauses and wipes her forehead on her sleeve. "Well, maybe we better wait. I'm sure David will want to tell them the news himself."

Barb nods and says, "So, can I see the foal?"

"Sure, follow me."

"Hang on, just let me send the phones to voice mail."

"All right. I'll meet you back here. I want to grab my camera."

18

Katie swings around and heads toward her office, across from the coffee room. She pulls out the bottom left desk drawer and removes her Nikon camera. She closes the drawer and walks back to the main hall.

"Ready?" Barb asks, pushing her wire-rim glasses higher on her nose.

"Yep," Katie says nodding quickly, as she wraps the strap of the camera securely around her right wrist.

They exit the rear entrance, eyes squinting from the sun.

"So the foal's all right?"

"I think so."

"God, we can use this news."

"I know. This should spark some interest with those investors, keep us going until some business comes in. There shouldn't be any doubts about what the lab can do, not now." They walk for several seconds, neither saying a word, then at length Katie says, "Lord, when it rains it pours."

"What do mean?"

She slows, turns and looks Barb in her inquisitive hazel eyes.

Barb stops dead in her tracks.

"Look." Katie raises her left hand and a diamond ring glimmers brightly in the morning sun. Pear shaped with eight baguettes flanking the sides.

"No way! He finally popped the question?"

"Uh-huh, can you believe it."

"When?"

"Last night."

Barb reaches forward, says, "It's huge. It's just beautiful, Katie."

Katie smiles and replies, "Isn't it."

Barb moves her hands to Katie's chilled face and cradles each cheek. "Congratulations." A kiss on the left.

"Thanks."

"You've waited a long time for this, haven't you. I'm so happy for both of you. You two won't be able to sleep for a week, not with today's news to top it off."

"I know."

"So he asked you just last night?"

Nodding, Katie answers, "Yeah, about nine o'clock, after we put the girls to bed."

They start walking again.

Barb glances toward the barn. "I'm so happy for both of you." She pauses as they approach the gate to the stalls, looks at Katie with moist eyes, then continues, "See, I told you he'd ask sooner or later."

"You sure did. Probably twenty times over the past few years," Katie replies, nodding some more. She looks at her ring again before they walk in. "I was starting to wonder though... you know."

"Well, sometimes you have to be patient with the male of the species. They can be a bit slow at times."

"A bit?"

They approach the newborn and hear stirring within the stable, the other thoroughbreds waking up. A rooster is crowing in the distance, its shrill cry more indicative of some sort of peril than an acknowledgment of morning.

"I don't see her head," Barb says, craning her neck.

Katie walks faster then pauses and puts her chin atop a short dividing wall. "She must be lying down. I don't see her either."

They round a corner and arrive at the stall door. Katie slides the lever to the right and slowly opens it.

Black Magic is standing, head hung low. Tired.

Barb asks, "Is she all right? She looks weak."

"She'll be fine. Must have been a difficult delivery."

"Maybe we should put a blanket over her," Barb suggests.

"Good idea. Hand me that red one over there."

Barb walks over to a quilted blanket hanging on an iron hook, as Katie looks over to the newborn. It's trying to find its legs. The frail matchsticks are bent at crazy angles, body bumping into its mother.

They stare at the two horses for a couple of minutes, neither saying a word.

Barb finally turns to Katie and says, "Maybe you and David can take some time off now, go on a great honeymoon after the wedding. Venice maybe? Or Paris?"

"Sounds good to me," Katie replies as she pulls her hair behind her ears. "David's been working himself to death. We hardly have time to do anything lately."

And this was indeed the case. David was spending long days at the lab, eating takeout food he shouldn't, and traveling almost weekly to business meetings. For the past few months most of their conversations had taken place on the phone, usually with David in route and late to something critical to the lab, as was the case today.

Still stuck behind a truck, David sees the timber shift on the bed of the rear trailer. The entire rig and its cargo tilt toward the painted stripes in the middle of the road and each of the truck's tires heave over the plastic reflectors, most of them missing, cracked, or smashed into mere squares of glue. The horizontal beams marrying each axle, front and aft, bow in the center and seem to push the envelope of their operating capacity.

With the Range Rover following close behind the logging truck, the two vehicles wind their way up a narrow two-lane road from the lowlands. Signs move by in a blur of yellow and black—Trucks Use Low Gears, Falling Rock, Ice Forms On Bridges First, Watch For Deer.

The driver of the truck flashes his brake lights three times, clearly irritated by David's tail-gating. He sticks his arm out the truck's cab window again, urging David to pass.

David looks at his watch, exhales, then rubs his forehead as he thinks of the conference call that is probably going on at this very minute over at the lab. *They couldn't have waited this long for me.* Quietly, below the rumble of the engine and road, he says, "Maybe I can still catch the end of the meeting."

The only thing not putting his temper over the edge is the fact that the rest of the management team had been through these sorts of fire drills a dozen times over the past year. Lab tours, visits to the Advanced Breeding Center (a.k.a. barn out in the back). It had been one dog and pony show after another—*we're looking for some additional venture capital to expedite the introduction of services. We're trying to meet a window of opportunity in the market. We need to be seen as the leader in horse genetics and breeding. Break-even is expected within twelve months. The future is now, get in before the IPO.*

Everyone had the investor-elevator-pitch down.

He turns the wheel to the left and peers around the logs and the moiré of tree rings before him, dry years, wet years. He knows that after the next curve he'll be on a straightaway, near Graham's Nursery on North Pike. Two signs, one on each side of the road, fly by. *No passing.*

Dan Johnson tosses his cigarette to the ground and minces it with the heel of his right boot until it becomes a blackened porridge of gravel. He ambles toward the front left tire of his gravel truck and kicks it, as if this was a sure fire means of testing its repair.

"Don't worry, Dan, it's fixed," one of the mechanics yells over. He is washing his hands in a bright orange plastic tank bolted to the side of the main garage.

Dan nods and opens the door to the cab of the truck and climbs up the steps that are built into the left fuel tank. He fastens his seatbelt, makes sure the shift lever is in neutral, and twists the key. The engine struggles to turn over, as it usually does after being shut down for a short period of time. He presses in the clutch, knocks it in first, and the truck jerks to motion, its bed already filled with gravel. He drives toward the exit gate, and nods at the guard whose hat is promptly tipped. Seconds later and he is approaching the state highway.

David gives one more look around the left side of the timber-covered trailer before him. The hairy arm is still waving and he sees black smoke rising from the chrome pipes on either side of the cab. Adrenaline pumping, he nails the accelerator pedal to the floor and the Range Rover pauses for a split second then lurches forward, its V-8 roaring. He moves slightly into the oncoming lane.

He tugs the steering wheel to the left a bit more. Looks good. Should make it before the corner up ahead. And at least the diesel before him is slowing, its driver obviously wanting the Range Rover's shiny grill off his tail.

David continues to pass. "Come on," he says as he slowly makes his way along the wall of logs looming through the sunroof glass, and staring at him from the passenger window. The heel of the accelerator pedal is well into the carpet mat and padding. His knuckles turn slightly white, crippling the steering wheel, and he tries to ignore the fact that the passenger-side mirror is about ten inches from a shimmering chrome wheel rim of the truck. It appears more like a buzz saw from his viewpoint, the lug nuts cutting a kerf in the air.

"Get over!" David yells.

The truck moves suddenly to the left, crossing the double yellow line, and seemingly even closer to the right mirror. The Range Rover isn't even up to the truck's cab yet. David moves as far to the edge of the oncoming lane as he can without dropping onto the shoulder. Still holding the pedal down, he slowly makes his way alongside the cab. He can see a corner up ahead, winding from left to right, and he sees a BP gas station sign sticking up above the trees, glowing bright yellow and green. He figures he can surely pass the logging truck before reaching the curve, but it will be close. He tells himself he'll drop back if he sees a car coming, or if the logging truck moves even one inch closer to the right rearview mirror. It starts to sprinkle and he switches on the windshield wipers. The left one screeches and hops back and forth. He'd meant to change them six months ago.

Back near the gravel quarry Dan is cautiously shifting his way through gears of his gravel truck, making sure the plug in the tire is holding before picking up too much speed.

Traffic seems light today, he thinks as he approaches a fork in the road where highway 15 ends. Behind him are three cars, no doubt filled with angry, impatient drivers. But they are keeping their distance. All the locals know to stay at least a hundred yards behind gravel trucks, or risk having their windshields pummeled with pebbly shrapnel.

Dan reaches down and turns on the wipers and they jump to action dragging dirt, bird droppings, a few speckles of cement, and the first drops of tepid rain across the tempered glass. He tries to clean it but the bluish windshield fluid is all but gone, no help. He taps at the windshield washer button anyway as he looks to the left—all clear—then quickly right. He thinks he can see a logging truck coming up the grade. He doesn't notice any other vehicles. All he wants is to get onto the state highway in front of the logger. Without hesitating, he veers toward the left fork in the road and knocks the Mack down a couple gears as he makes his way onto the highway. Ahead, he sees the BP gas station and convenience store. Though he is running plenty late, and knows the logger will surely pass by and get in front of him, he contemplates stopping to buy a pack of cigarettes, cup of coffee, and maybe some windshield fluid if they have it. Figures it couldn't take more than a couple of minutes to run in and besides, *That damn tire plug should be checked*, he tells himself. *Gotta make sure it's holdin' air good and ain't leakin' none.*

He downshifts from fourth to third and the brakes squeal as he approaches the BP station and convenience store. He hears the gravel shift forward in the bed and feels a thumping vibration in the seat. Even though he's running late to his delivery, the coffee and nicotine are calling. He finds second gear and looks to the left, searching for a place to park the rig. He sees a spot that looks long enough, between a Chevy pickup towing an Airstream trailer, and another gravel truck from a competing quarry from up north, near Rabbit Hash. He starts to turn the wheel to the left to pull in but suddenly catches movement in the corner of his right eye—an indistinguishable smear of yellowish brown. He hits the brakes hard and is thrown against his seatbelt, its tension spring doing its job and keeping his face from smashing into the metal spokes of the gravel truck's steering wheel.

A deer? Dan silently asks himself.

He notices a school bus, parked across the street at the gas station behind the Chevy and Airstream. He doesn't see any kids around, but his heart races as he imagines a small child lying under one of his front wheels. This image had haunted him ever since he started driving these damn things. The driver's cab is so high it's hard to see what's ahead at times.

Please God...let it be a deer.

Sitting in the middle—dead center middle—of the northbound lane and directly in front of the BP gas station, he sets the brake, turns on his emergency flashers, and climbs down from the cab. As he walks around the front of the truck he sees the lifeless body lying there. He manages a breath. It isn't a child. Not this time anyway. He leans down on one knee, touches its neck, feeling for a pulse. It is dead. And it is probably a good thing, he thinks as he strokes the buck's head, as its back legs are twisted like a beer pretzel, bloodied to the point at which no tan, brown or white fur can be made out. Compound fractures in several places. His face mixes relief with sadness as he realizes he hasn't hurt a human being, but has nailed yet another deer. He had stopped hunting ten years ago because he couldn't squeeze a trigger without seeing the white of his daughter's eyes—a frozen memory of when he brought home a large doe in the back of the station wagon one day.

He glances around the right front fender, doesn't see any cars coming but knows he better move the rig and the deer over to the side. He reaches below the deer's neck with one arm and under its belly with his other, feels blood soak his flannel shirt.

What a day, first a flat tire, now this, he thinks as he carries the deer over to the shoulder of the road, next to the Airstream trailer in the BP parking lot. He sets it down and then shakes his head and says, "I'm sorry fella, I just didn't see ya."

David, just a half mile away from the gas station, the gravel truck, and the deer, is accelerating away from the logging truck and its driver's ballistic middle finger which is clearly visible in the rearview mirror of the Range Rover. David grabs his cell phone again and looks down, fumbling with the memory buttons. He hits the wrong one, "Dammit!"

More fumbling.

When he looks up, it is too late.

No time to rotate his foot to the brake pedal. No time to move both hands to the steering wheel. He starts to scream as the image of the gravel truck's tailgate fills the entire windshield and instantly washes over him—a wall of gray and black and brown, interrupted by a flash of yellow from the airbag. No time to think of Katie, or their girls.

Hearing the violent impact, Dan twists his body to the left, moving his eyes instantly from the deer before him and to his truck and the Range Rover wedged under its dump-bed. His mouth drops as he sees what is left of the vehicle that has just slammed into the back of his truck. Gravel pours smoothly through several cracks in the bed and spreads everywhere. He says, "My lord in heaven," then jumps to his feet and nearly falls on his face, catching a boot on the deer. He walks slowly toward the wreck and hears metal creaking and liquids of some sort sizzling. Vapor fills the air, and a tire blows.

People over at the gas station and convenience store run out the small green building, pointing, yelling. Dan hears one of them say, "Call an ambulance!" The clerk inside the station hits a safety switch to shut off all the pumps, just in case, and then reaches for a phone.

The throaty drone of a diesel engine is heard, probably the logging truck he had seen in the distance, Dan thinks as he runs toward the curve just before the gas station, waving his arms madly, hoping to get the driver to slow down.

The logger seems to see him, as he flashes his lights and Dan can hear down shifting and see smoke hiccupping from the truck's exhaust stacks.

Dan runs back toward the accident—what's left of the Range Rover—but hesitates as he gets close. He smells something. He smells gasoline. Then he realizes he is standing in it, his boots tan islands in a sea of swirling liquid rainbows and sparkling asphalt. Out of breath, he backs up some and stares, face red. He whispers, "What a mess."

The nose, the bumper, and some additional unrecognizable section of the vehicle before him are sandwiched under the rear of his truck, which if it had been dropped there from the heavens could not have landed more severely on its victim. The tail of the truck bed, gravel still seeping from it, is resting in what must have been the back seat. Rocks are sliding down and filling the open vehicle. The roof has been seared off and is wadded up in a crinkled knot of sheet metal over the rear cargo area, like a soda can creased and bent in on itself, ready for the recycling bin. He doubts anyone can still be alive. He prays that there won't be a fire, then moves closer, dreading what he will find. Looking for signs of life. Looking for the slightest spark.

CHAPTER TWO

It takes Katie ten minutes before she can stand on her own two legs. They had turned to rubber then tingled as the blood rushed from her head and the room began spinning like she remembered the carousel doing last summer over at the county fairgrounds. Around and around. Around and around.

The sheriff had shown up at the labs at eleven o'clock and told the news of David's accident to Barb first. Barb then called Katie and asked her to meet her in a conference room, alone. "I need to talk to you about something important," she said, trying to keep her composure, and stay calm. She didn't tell Katie why she needed to talk, and could barely keep from crying. Katie just assumed that Barb had been dumped again by her boyfriend over at the riverboat casino, an unfortunate bimonthly occurrence lately.

The news fell hard.

And then there was a void of words and emotion. That's what scared Barb the most. The deadpan response, the absence of tears, the sudden vacuum of life, of energy. She interrupted the silence and eventually said, "You have to stay strong, Katie," as she hugged her friend and employer, patted her back. When Katie's crying finally arrived it was a rhythmic panting, like a toddler's. It stayed for fifteen minutes then vanished as quickly as it came, all at once. Katie stared at her engagement ring, that's all she did, she just stared.

Barb gets up and cracks open a door to the room. Every employee is standing in the hall, not a dry eye to be seen. She asks a co-worker, Roger, to go get her coat so she can wrap it around Katie, keep her from going into shock, for she seems cold and clammy. When he hands it to her she covers Katie's shoulders, arms, and feels her head, then left wrist.

Barb says, "I think you're going into shock, honey. We should take you to the hospital. They can give you something, and then you can see David there. Okay?"

Katie slowly nods, her eyes not leaving her engagement ring.

They both walk to the front lobby of the lab facility. A sheriff is writing something on a clipboard, sitting in one of the black leather chairs. His wire-rim glasses are perched on his thick shiny nose, eyes peering through the wavy stripes of bifocals at the bottom. He looks up and grabs his hat from a table to his left, then pushes the wire bridge and rubber pads of his glasses rearward and closer to the drooped ledge of his forehead. "Are you okay ma'am?" he asks with a husky, weathered voice, tossed as gently as possible at Katie.

"Yes, I'll be all right," she replies, the pitiful words somehow finding their way through lips that scarcely move.

The Sheriff's beige Ford Taurus pulls up to the emergency room entrance at the University of Louisville Hospital. Katie and Barb are in the backseat, their first ride in a police car, people staring along the way, especially when stopped at intersections. The doors, which lack handles and locks, are opened from the outside and she and Barb are guided out, the sheriff even holding the tops of their heads down so as to not bump the roof. They feel like criminals.

After making their way through double doors that greet them by sliding away by themselves, and having their hair almost blown to shreds by an automatic fan that keeps cold air from rushing in, they enter the brick building, sheriff close behind, and meander through three hallways until reaching a reception counter tucked behind what looks like bullet-proof glass, thick and real friendly. A three-inch hole serves as the means to communicate with the nurse who is sitting on a stool on the other side, typing into a computer. The place smells like it has been doused in disinfectant.

They are asked to have a seat and told, "No news on David yet. Sorry."

The waiting room is the standard fair. Nothing fancy. The walls have colorful, cheery pictures that seem out of place. The ceiling has acoustic tiles to absorb the sounds of a busy ER, the crying, the consoling, the screaming, the soothing. Seated on a blue vinyl couch that is at least ten years old, Katie droops her head between her legs, rocks to and fro, and runs her fingers through her hair.

She mumbles to herself, "Need to stay strong, he'll be all right, please God let him be all right."

Barb rubs her back and the sheriff scribbles some more on his report, obviously waiting for Katie to calm down so he can ask some questions. What time did David leave home? Where was he going? When did he call into work? Who did he talk to? Was he under any medication? Does he ever drink and drive?

She surely won't be able to answer most of the questions. Hell, she wasn't with him. But they'll be asked anyway.

She had always been the strong one in the family. Like when Megan broke her arm in three places skiing in Vale. And when the lab was days, even hours, from being shut down by creditors three months after it opened. And when David's mother died and he fell to pieces. Always the strong one, Katie was.

And, somehow, she had even handled the prognosis from Megan's doctor three months ago—leukemia. "We'll just have to find a donor and get her a bone marrow transplant," she calmly told David that night, as if the cure was as simple as taking three aspirin, getting some bed rest.

Control, she'd always had it.

And, when Angela turned out to be a bone marrow match for her older sister, Katie reacted as if it was all planned out, a given, that she would donate the marrow when old enough, and save Megan's life. Just like that. Maybe her faith had something to do with it, David had often thought to himself. But Katie's rationale was more practical and down to earth. "Someone has to stay calm," she later told her mother when she said she was keeping her pain bottled up inside her, never letting her emotions be displayed, never blowing off steam.

The sheriff uncrosses his legs and his right boot lands on the floor with a thud as he clears his throat, and looks over. As Katie raises her head he says to her, "Ma'am, I know it's hard to talk right now, with your fiancé in there and all, but can you answer a few questions please? I'd really appreciate it."

Barb interjects and gives him a scolding look, narrowing her eyes, and says, "Can't it wait? She's been through a lot today."

"Well, ma'am, uh—"

"Look, her fiancé was just brought in here. Could you come back in—"

"It's okay, Barb. There's not much I can answer anyway," Katie interrupts.

And indeed there wasn't much she could say. Two minutes later, after a handful of questions, the sheriff stands and tucks the pen into his pocket, adjusts his stomach under his belt and says, "I'll check with you two later."

Brilliant idea, Barb thinks to herself.

As the officer walks toward the waiting room exit, Katie raises herself and asks, "Can I read the accident report?"

"Well, ma'am, we usually don't—"

"Please. I'm okay, really."

He sheepishly walks back over. "I'm really not done with it, and I don't think you should upset yourself further... if you don't mind me saying."

"Look, my dad was a cop for twenty years. I can handle it. Please."

Barb cuts in, "Maybe we should wait until you get some rest, honey."

"No, I want to see it. Please sir, let me read the report," Katie says firmly with swollen red eyes.

He pursues his lips for a second or two and his bristled gray mustache squeezes toward his nose and glasses. "Well, I guess it would be all right." He raises the clipboard, looks over what he has written, then hands it to her as if it is the Dead Sea scrolls.

Katie says, "Thank you."

"You're welcome. I'll give you some time alone." He turns and walks toward the exit, pauses, then moves his eyes to Barb, wanting some acknowledgment that she will look after Katie while she reads the report. Barb nods once and he leaves them alone, his head hanging low.

Katie struggles to read, her mind filled with thoughts and images of David. The first page has basic information: date of birth, name, type of vehicle, license plate number, driver's license, and officer information. The sections describing the accident were almost blank, except for a brief statement from Dan, the gravel truck driver.

Ten minutes later, a nurse walks over. Katie's head is resting on Barb's lap and her legs are curled up on the couch.

"Any news yet?" Barb asks the nurse.

"I'm afraid not. But I'm sure it won't be long."

Katie sits up. "What's taking so long?"

"I'm not sure, ma'am. The doctors haven't come out yet. I'm sorry. I'm sure they're doing everything they can." She pauses, managing a faint smile. "I just wanted to tell you that we have a phone call for you—a woman, she said she's your sister. You can take it right over here." She points to a phone in a nearby hallway.

Katie rushes over and picks it up, "Hello." Her voice is shallow, groggy.

"Katie?"

"Yes. Samantha?"

"Are you okay?"

"Yes, but David's apparently in pretty bad shape."

"I know, mom told me. An officer just left the house. Will you be all right until we get there?"

"Yes, I'll be fine. Can you stop by school and the sitter to pick up the girls?"

"Yeah, we already called to have Megan pulled out of class."

"What about Angela?"

A long pause then, "Uh..."

"Sammy, can you run over and pick her up?"

"You, you mean... you don't have Angela?"

"No, I've been here with David."

"Katie, Angela isn't at the sitter. We just called over there. The message on Mrs. Hansen's answering machine said she had to go out of town on an emergency."

"What?"

"Something to do with her mother."

"But I thought you picked both of them up, and dropped them off?"

"No, I couldn't come by. I called David and he said he—"

"My God, where is Angela?" Katie interrupts, voice shaky. There are a couple of seconds filled only with static from the poor connection. She starts to cry again, breathes hard into the receiver."

"I, I don't know, Katie. I thought—"

"Samantha! Where the hell is she?"

Katie begins to quiver uncontrollably as she grasps her forehead with her left hand, looks up at a galaxy of flickering, shooting stars. Faces—concerned, grave faces with heavy brows and bright eyes—drift by and float in from the hallway. Her mind fills with the most horrid of possibilities—was Angela with David?

The phone slides away and is yanked back to its base by the cord then dangles madly, flipping, spinning, and slamming to the floor. Katie collapses, seeing a syrupy wave of black behind bright rays, a fourth of July sparkler held against a moonless sky. She sinks to the floor and feels the coldness of tile under her cheek and her jaw, her temple throbbing. She smells pine, clean, fresh pine, the thick scent lingering over the floor. As she closes her eyes and darkness washes over her, mumbled voices become silence.

CHAPTER THREE

Katie and David rediscovered each other on the sort of summer day that can only be witnessed in Kentucky, a day fashioned from the whispers of birds, the laughter of horses, the quarrel of leaves wrestling with the sky. Since early morning, a gentle breeze had been tossed over the state, a gift from the gulf often not appreciated and always missed during the crisp days of winter. There were bright blue skies and not a single lumbering cloud from Indiana to West Virginia, nothing to steal away the sun's rays which jovially raked across the rolling hills of grass that thrive so well on soil laden with limestone and ample supplies of horse manure. From afar, the landscape appeared as one massive palette of green lying with its back to the earth and broad brushstrokes of blue hovering placidly across a vast canvas, punctuated only by miles of white and sometimes black wooden fences, pastures, and dabs of training rings and paddocks where horses were running or simply standing about. Some had their necks stretched down as they consumed the fast-growing bluegrass with the warmth of the sun sprinkling on their backs. It was a sweet, tranquil day. The day Katie and David found each other, again.

It was June of '06. Katie was working at the Kentucky Horse Park in northeast Lexington. During the warmer months, the park is one of the state's most popular attractions for tourists. They come to see the museum, roam through stables filled with all breeds of horses, and go for rides in carriages from an era fondly remembered and tenaciously clung to. They bring their digital cameras and they step in dung and rotting hay, and dream of owning a Tennessee Walker or Clydesdale or American Saddle Horse; they dream of living on a horse farm in Kentucky.

Katie had been working at the park for three months as a marketing and public relations manager, creating brochures, promotions, sending out press releases, and making sure the gift shop was supplied with plenty of horse-embroidered tee shirts, colorful books, coffee mugs, hats, and anything else a visitor might trade a credit card number for and take home. On her breaks she would often sit in the sun, feel the cool breezes sweep over her skin and linger over the scent of freshly cut bluegrass.

When David saw her sitting there, lengthy legs crossed and pale face wearing eyes tightly closed and angled squarely at the sky, he stumbled as he did a double take. How could God create such radiant red hair? Hair that on this day looked like it was ablaze from his viewpoint, under an Elm near the park entrance. He knew this woman. But fully one minute went by before this realization hit him. She, of course, looked different from the youthful picture of her in his mind, his memory. There was an air of maturity, poise, and sensuality. He couldn't help but notice her larger breasts, longer and curlier hair. And she had shapely legs that didn't seem even remotely possible for the girl he remembered.

But he knew this woman.

As he approached he said, "Katie, is that you?"

Tiny earthworm-like things were dancing somewhere between her eyelids and brain, as always happened when she aimed at the sun for too long, or rubbed her eyes too hard. His voice was what she recognized first, though deeper than she remembered. As her pupils adjusted and the worms left and the world became colorful again, he came sharply into focus. "David?"

They sat and talked and ran each other's eyes over one another for three, maybe four hours as the years of separation were erased. He the successful horse breeder, she the successful businesswoman, they the high school sweethearts who had grown apart.

I often think about you. How did we ever lose touch? You haven't changed a bit. How's your family? I heard you got married. I often think about you too.

That night they drove to Louisville and ate near the river at the finest restaurant David could find. The hour drive from Lexington gave them time to catch up, time to say they were sorry, and time to further break the ice.

When darkness fell they both gazed out a foggy window at a riverboat paddling its way across a mirror reflecting a million stars above, watched young lovers stroll hand-in-hand along the docks, sipped an oak and cherry inspired merlot recommended by the sommelier, and asked each other, What ever happened to us?

Yes, she had gotten married. Divorced. And now had two daughters. His marriage had ended in similar fashion, though no offspring to worry about. They told each other how their innocent romance seemed like another lifetime ago, both of them having dredged through the ravages of painful years of domestic combat and attempted reconciliation, prisoners yearning to escape but chained down by obligation and guilt and routine.

33

They ate and drank, each making sure to chew with their mouth closed, not drop their napkin or clank their glasses or silverware, and appear somewhat sophisticated and mannerly in their new selves. David had beef bourguignonne and she a grand-looking presentation of bouillabaisse, with bread served on the side on a tattered piece of wood shaped like a canoe paddle. Only once did Katie hear her mother's voice warning her as she had after David left her so many years ago—for what reason, she didn't know. And she hoped she wouldn't remember on this evening. Her mother had said, "Time heals all wounds, but the essence of someone never changes. Move on with your life."

And indeed she had moved on. Yet here she was, gaping at a man who had left deep, undefined wounds that were seemingly being cloaked by the smoke of the candle before her, separating her from the man she once loved. After dinner, as she leaned forward over the table and the warm glow, David told her how he had quit his job in West Virginia, moved to Lexington, and secured a position working for his father who owned one of the best horse farms in the country, so he said. It was obvious that he lived and breathed horse racing and breeding. With a sparkle in his eyes, he said he planned to start his own breeding center soon and even had partners lined up with seed capital. As Katie listened, she lost herself and remembered how they used to innocently dream of their future together, with eyes wide and wondrous, and speaking so fast their words were one.

As the evening and years slipped away they watched as a waiter wearing a ponytail gathered coins and bills sprinkled on nearby dirty tables. And soon the waiter twisted a key in the entrance door, and left it dangling. A sign it was time for David and Katie to go.

Without a curfew hanging over his head, and as he had many moons before, David took Katie home and for the first time as a man, kissed her. Standing there, in the faint light in front of her home, she felt like a schoolgirl again. Reaching up and touching his face with the palm of her right hand, and feeling a day's worth of beard she had never felt on the boy she had loved, she whispered for the second time that evening, "Whatever happened to us?"

CHAPTER FOUR

With the first sign of daybreak Katie's mother rose from her bed and tiptoed across floorboards tacked down with square-head nails, and made her way to the family room addition where Katie had finally managed to fall asleep, a couch purchased fourteen years ago on a revolving charge account and, since then, reupholstered twice, the latest fabric being some sort of durable bengaline that scratches one's skin and doesn't breathe but will last forever. Katie had always loathed it, but last night it was the safest and warmest and most comforting place in the world. The home she had grown up in.

Megan, who had cried until two in Katie's arms, was assigned to the guest bedroom, where she was used to sleeping when over-nighting at grandma and grandpa's house.

Yesterday, after passing out at the hospital, Katie had been aroused to consciousness with the assistance of a nurse and smelling salts. She then managed to drink a cup of de-caf tea and somehow calm down. Barb waited with her until her mother and father arrived with Megan and, shortly thereafter, another call came into the waiting room. The extension rang and Katie's mom answered immediately, "Hello."

"Is this Katie Ryan?"

"No, this is her mother, Nancy Ryan."

"This is Officer Johnson. I just went by the house, uh, daycare, Ms. Ryan said her daughter should be at and—"

"Can you hold for a second?" she interrupted, and then turned away from Katie who was lying on a couch, drowsy from a tranquilizer. A blanket was tucked about her shivering body. Her mother set the phone down on a table, then walked down a central hallway to a nurses station. She asked if she could pick up the line there, and the nurse handed her a phone and hit line four. She said into the receiver, "Sorry, I didn't want my daughter to hear."

"I understand. How's she doing?"

Katie's mom answered, "Not good."

There was silence then, "Well, I'm afraid what I have to say isn't going to help. The owner of the daycare confirmed that Angela was not dropped off this morning. In fact she wasn't home all day, didn't take care of any kids. I'm sorry ma'am, but she doesn't know where Angela is. Are you sure she was supposed to go there today?"

"Yes, that's what Katie told me. My youngest daughter, Samantha, was supposed to come by at eight, but came down with a cold. She said she called David and told him she better not be around the girls. He agreed and told her he'd ask a neighbor to pick both Megan and Angela up."

"I see. Do you know the name of the neighbor?"

"Mrs. Kroning."

"I assume you contacted her?"

"Katie called but no one answered. My husband is headed over there right now."

"And what about Megan?"

"We picked her up at school. She said that David still had Angela with him when he dropped her off this morning."

"And I assume that Angela still uses a child's car seat, or booster seat, and rides in the backseat of the vehicle?"

"Yes, Officer. Always."

"Okay ma'am." the Officer said, then paused for a couple of seconds before continuing. "Ma'am, did David tell Megan where he was going to take Angela? Perhaps Mrs. Kroning's house or—"

Katie's mom interrupted. "No."

"Is it possible that he took Angela with him to the dentist and then—"

"I, I don't know," she answered with a weakening voice, then suddenly felt her heart crawl into her throat.

The salvage yard is deserted when Sheriff Johnson pulls up to the front gate. An eight-foot fence stretches in either direction with a coil of barbed wire sitting on top. In the distance, between two of the ten rows of wrecked cars, a German Shepherd runs toward the gate, flashing its teeth, barking madly.

As Johnson stares at the dog he feels beads of sweat roll down his forehead. His chest pounds as he opens the patrol car door and looks around. He says to himself, "Where the hell is he?"

The owner of the yard, Sam Waters, is supposed to be here waiting. Before Johnson can reach for his radio handset to try and track him down again, he hears tires crunching through gravel and the sputtering of a well-worn engine. He pivots on one heel and sees Sam's rust-covered '98 Chevy tow truck. *What a piece of junk*, he thinks as he nods the brim of his hat.

Sam waves and says, "Afternoon," as he cranks down a window as far as it will go. He shoves the gear lever to *Park* and turns the key in the ignition, removes it, and hangs it from a hook attached to the rearview mirror. The engine chugs for a few more seconds then dies as if for the last time, backfiring and spitting smoke. Sam gets out, scratches his white beard and adjusts his suspenders which are covered in oil stains. There is a gaping hole in the right knee and, as he approaches, Johnson can see that he has a limp, favoring the same side.

"I thought I had missed you," Officer Johnson says.

"Sorry, the station got busy just as you called, and I had a tanker come in with a load of diesel. Busy as hell today. Haven't stopped movin' since I picked up that Range Rover."

Johnson nods politely.

They walk toward the gate, a ten foot section of the fence suspended from metal rollers and a guide rail. Rust everywhere.

"Now, why is it you want to see that-there wreck?"

"Just need to check something out."

Sam looks down and files through a key chain attached to his belt by a tiny pulley, one of those spring loaded jobs usually carried by janitors or security guards; there has to be a hundred keys attached to the thing. Somehow he finds the one he wants and inserts it into the padlock on the gate. He slides the lock out then drags the gate and his right leg to the side yard.

The German shepherd runs toward them.

Johnson points, "Uh, what about—"

"Oh...Sophie won't bite ya, don't worry."

Sophie? Johnson thinks as the brown and black dog approaches, eyes intense.

"She wouldn't hurt a fly," Sam adds as he pats its fury head with his stained fury hands. "All looks... no action."

Johnson gazes about the junkyard while keeping his arms crossed and fingers tucked in. "I don't see the Range Rover."

"I put it in the back. I didn't want anyone to get any ideas with that fancy stereo and cell phone inside, though I kinda doubt either of them work now. Haven't seen a wreck like that in a long time around here."

37

"Me either."

"Well, follow me. It's just a ways over," Sam says as he tosses a piece of candy to the ground near the gate and Sophie saunters up to it, lies down, and starts licking as they walk in the opposite direction.

The Range Rover is sandwiched between what is left of a Dodge van that had been cut in two by a freight train, and a cherry-red convertible Mustang with dealer plates.

Sam points to the Mustang. "Remnants of a DUI over the weekend," he says without the slightest indication of emotion. He pauses as they approach the Range Rover, sighs loudly as he shakes his head and says, "Now then, what did you wanna see?"

"I'd like to look inside."

"Sure. Help yourself. Not much to look at, though. And you best be careful. Those jaws-of-life things they use to cut roofs and doors off leave pretty sharp edges. Cut me up real bad over the years."

"Thanks. I'll take it slow," Johnson says as he climbs up onto where the hood should be, a twisted bumper wrapped around what is left of an eight cylinder engine. Most of the hood is now pushed back into the passenger compartment, save a piece that was removed to free David's body.

As Officer Johnson slowly crawls toward the passenger compartment, he cringes as he makes his way over the dashboard and steering wheel area, seeing dried blood on the deflated airbag. He steps onto the passenger seat, which is filled with a foot of gravel. He peers over the front seats and sees even more gravel, three, maybe four feet deep in the backseat.

Balanced on his knees and poised precariously on the passenger seat, with gravel digging into his kneecaps, he turns toward Sam and says, "You towed it in with all this gravel? That's a lot of weight. I'm surprised you didn't get rid of it, dump it on the side of the road or something."

"I thought about it, but I learned a long time ago that insurance companies don't want me messin' with wrecks until they see them. I just drag them in the way I find them."

Officer Johnson nods and then wipes his brow on his right shirt sleeve. His heart begins beating faster as he contemplates what he has to do. He bends over the front seats, toward the back, cups his hands together, and begins removing gravel. As he flings it out of the Range Rover's backseat, it rains down on the Dodge parked nearby, creating a machinegun-like staccato of noise, adding to the intensity. A few minutes pass as he removes more and more pebbly gray rocks, inching his way downward toward the seat cushion.

And then he sees it. More blood, the gravel caked together in a brownish glue. Now, leaning over the front seat and straining to dig toward the floor pan, sweat continues to drip from his face as he braces his left hand on the rear seat, and scoops gravel with his right.

He knows what it is even before he sees it.

The coldness. The stiffness. His eyes slowly focus on what he has just touched. What he knows he has just touched. His heart racing, Officer Johnson sees a tiny hand sticking up from the foot or so of gravel remaining on the floor pan of the Range Rover.

Katie had never liked carnations, not in the least. But that's exactly what most of her friends and family had sent. Yellow ones, pink ones, and some with various shades of baby blue had been placed around the casket and halfway into the middle aisle of the small church. Flowers everywhere. People everywhere. There couldn't have been more than a dozen seats left on the one remaining pew as the organist began to play and the floorboards vibrated beneath everyone's feet.

Sorrow everywhere.

She felt as though she was standing outside her body, watching grieving people enter, some old, some young, some she couldn't recognize or place. They offered strained smiles, awkward pats on her shoulders, a few whispering, I'm so sorry, honey. We love you, Katie. We'll pray for you.

When the service was over, she immediately stood and walked to the front of the church to the smallest coffin she'd ever seen, dropped to her knees, and held the coldest hand she'd ever touched, resting her head upon the silky padded lip of the mahogany that, she completely believed, would forever separate her from happiness.

Five minutes slipped away. Twenty. Everything was slipping away, she thought. And with only her mother and father still present, seated two rows back, she removed a handkerchief from her purse, wiped her eyes, then leaned in and kissed Angela's forehead.

"Goodbye my love."

After taking one last look at her baby daughter, she closed the casket.

She turned and angled her head at the light coming through the clear pieces of a stained-glass cross high above. She prayed that no other life be taken by the tragedy, yet deep down inside she heard the voice of fear and reason, that such a gift would only come about with a miracle.

With the cold reality of her precious Angela gone forever, her thoughts briefly turned to Megan, the bone marrow transplant Angela was going to provide, and the sinking feeling of what felt like the weight of the world on her shoulders. Without Angela, who would be the bone marrow donor now?

She lowered her head once more, resting it on the casket and began to weep uncontrollably. Minutes passed.

As she tried to compose herself, she raised her head and just stared at the casket, running her hands over its polished, smooth surface.

Suddenly she noticed a rainbow-like spot of light, a perfect triangle consisting of red, blue and green moving slowly across the lid of the casket, then over her left hand and fingers. She looked up at the stained glass again, seeing where the beam of light was coming from, a prism within the window. Bright sun was peering down on her, a warm and somehow comforting light.

Finally, she began to breathe normally again, taking in a deep, cleansing breath. As she lowered her eyes from the stained glass high above, to the lid of the casket before her, she watched as the light moved over her right hand and split into two identical but smaller beams of light. Seconds later, they became blurry and transformed from colorful spots into pure white light, then to faint specks of gray. And then they were gone.

Katie ran the images of the colorful prism-created light over and over in her mind, how beautiful they were, how delicate. Here one minute, gone the next.

She took another deep breath and began to rise to her feet, feeling an unexpected peace come over her. She heard a voice inside her, *You have to carry on and try to be strong—not for yourself, but for Megan.*

Katie made a decision at that very moment that she wasn't going to lose Megan, too.

PART TWO

Megan swings from the oak until the gnarled branch some twenty feet above her begins to creak and moan. Even the trunk of the tree sways slightly, and she can hear the knots in the nylon ropes, securing the swing's seat, loosen or tighten. She isn't sure which. One is shorter than the other, which makes her body lean toward one side. So she pulls harder on the right rope, like a pilot compensating for cross winds with forced stick and obedient rudder, her fuselage crooked in the air but nonetheless moving at a steady heading.

All the leaves are now gone and she can see an empty nest perched high, sandwiched in a V made of a dead branch and a thick and strong one. She asks herself, *Why would God let one branch die and one be strong?*

She then kicks her feet as hard as she can on the upswing, pointing her toes straight out like she'd been taught to do on the diving team, then tucks them back under the seat as gravity sucks her back down. She locks her elbows and tilts her face such that she can stare at the bare nest on each swing backward. She wonders what kind of birds will be born there this year. *Maybe they'll be robins?*

Six weeks had passed since David and Angela's car accident. Although goose bumps graced her arms and legs as of late, on this day the sun is out and the wind is out of the south. The sweat on her brow and dampness under her parka—evidence of a workout—are the only clues that she and time itself are flying, a sharp contrast to her more mundane hours imprisoned in the house, watching television, reading, and worrying about her illness. It was no life for a fourteen-year-old, or any-year-old...

"Yes, I hope they will be robins..." she whispers at length, gazing upward.

She likes cardinals too, with their bright red feathers and funny pointed heads that look like an Indian's or punker's Mohawk. And she also likes woodpeckers, especially when they pound their beaks against tree bark, sending a staccato beat through the backyard and chips flying. But robins are her favorite. Since last semester anyway. She had written a report on a poem by Emily Dickinson that for some reason had stuck in her mind. Some nights she says the words over and over in her head until falling asleep. On three occasions she became Emily Dickinson until her alarm clock mercilessly rattled her back to her mortal self. It was then, after the first dream, she had decided to become a writer.

Swinging faster, with the wind blowing what remained of her chemo-damaged thin hair—which when moving forward, slaps at the hood of her jacket, and when moving backward, flies over her eyes—she recites what had become her favorite Emily Dickinson poem.

> *If I can stop one heart from breaking*
> *I shall not live in vain*
> *If I can ease one life the aching*
> *Or cool one pain*
> *Or help one fainting robin*
> *Unto his nest again*
> *I shall not live in vain.*

Feeling a queasiness come over her, which she had often felt since becoming sick, she drops her feet and slows. Dust flies to the air from the tiny runway she has cut into the grass and she hops off on the final upswing.

Voilà, a perfect landing.

Without her weight the swing twists and jerks back and forth like a woodpecker's head, then quiets. She notices a dog calling in the distance, over near the fence and the toolshed, and upon further inspection sees that her friend Cindy is there as well, not fifty paces behind. She hasn't seen Cindy since being pulled out of school, though she did get a letter from her, trying to act all normal and everything. It was so obvious, Megan thought.

"Hi Megan!" Cindy calls out, cupping her hands about her mouth. She too intends to become a writer, perhaps Jefferson Junior High's up and coming gossip columnist, Megan had often thought. She approaches with her braces sparkling just between her ruby lips. Her Russian Wolfhound is panting, his head and long nose hung low and pink tongue almost dragging on the earth. Bentley is his name and he hasn't ever been given a bath as far as anyone can tell. He runs up and, as usual, promptly manages a sniff at Megan's crotch.

As she pushes the muddy nose away with her left hand, as nonchalantly as possible, she raises her right and waves politely to Cindy. Megan really doesn't want to talk to anyone from school, not yet anyway. It is just too soon, for several reasons now. Her cancer treatments.

43

Angela's death. There was just too much to avoid talking about. It had become too much work to steer conversations away from those topics. So she preferred to simply be by herself.

Cindy removes the hood from her head and says, "I haven't seen you in a while."

Megan nods, smiling ever so slightly.

"I noticed that you were swinging. Looks like fun."

"Yeah, it's pretty fun."

Cindy lowers her eyes. "I heard the news. I'm really sorry about your baby sister. And about David getting hurt."

"Thanks."

"Have you been okay?"

"Um...as good as can be, I guess," Megan answers.

Cindy swiftly changes gears. "Did you get my letter?"

"Uh-huh. Sorry I haven't written you back. I've been really busy."

This is a lie, and she knows Cindy sees it as such. Hell, she'd been bored stiff sitting around the house. Of course, she had been getting some reading done, but mostly she just went to the doctor for the chemo treatments and watched television and ate too much and got calls from grandma every few hours whenever she wasn't there with her.

"I've been busy too, with band and everything. Want to sit down?" Cindy asks, and then points over to a bench near the backdoor.

Megan says, "Okay," and they walk over and sit a foot apart, each pretending to admire the lovely view of the toolshed and Bentley relieving himself in the dormant rose bed.

"You'll never guess what happened at school."

"What?"

"Yesterday in the cafeteria Billy Murphy was eating a hot-dog and someone hit him in the back of the head with a milk carton, and he got up all pissed and turned around and threw his hot-dog over at Tom and Jim and Troy and it missed them and hit Mrs. Smith in the head and her glasses fell off and broke on the floor then Michelle said she heard her say Ah shit and That son of a bitch, but I didn't. Can you believe it, hit her right in her face."

"No way."

"Yes way, and Mr. Manning suspended Billy for a week and made him come back after school and scrub the cafeteria floor with a tooth brush and some soap."

Megan laughs. She hates Billy Murphy.

"I called Billy at home and he said he was glad he hit the old bitch

Mrs. Smith, and his mother heard him and yanked the phone away and slammed it down."

"Cool."

"I know."

"You know what he told me last week?"

"What?"

"He said he still likes you."

"Yuck!"

"He said he doesn't mind that you're sick or anything. He really likes you."

"I don't care," Megan says with a grumble, averting her eyes. "I like Tom."

"Who doesn't. But he's madly in love with Courtney Williams. He says she looks just like Taylor Swift."

"Oh God...you have to be kidding. Looks *just* like her? Yeah right, except she's got mega-zits, and she wears her makeup so dark she looks like she has two black eyes. And those clothes, please..."

"I know, I know, but he says he's going to marry her and have four kids. Can you believe it? Wednesday he bought her a glove for softball."

"How romantic. Maybe that's why she has the black eyes. She's probably been catching the ball with her face."

"Megan!"

"Well..."

"So do you want me to tell him that you like him?"

"No, I already have a glove."

Cindy manages a laugh and finally smiles a bit, her upper lip catching slightly on a rubber band. Her awkwardness is exactly what Megan had feared from her friends, but she says nothing. At least the ice is broken. *One down, ten wire-toothed gossips to go*, she thinks as she looks over at the bird's nest again, sighing and crossing her legs.

CHAPTER SIX

Katie arrives at the visitor entrance at ten o'clock, as she had every day since David took up residence at the hospital. But she hasn't come to see him—though she will probably stop by his room just in time to see him push his lunch tray away. She wants to meet with his doctor, Henry McCarthy.

"I'd really appreciate it if you wouldn't mention my coming by," Katie says as he shows her in.

"Certainly." He pushes his glasses further up his chiseled nose and moves behind a desk filled with folders, a keyboard, and LED monitor. He sits in a big overstuffed leather chair and continues, "Please, have a seat." He motions toward one of three guest chairs and Katie sits down. "What can I do for you?"

"Well, this isn't easy, I, I'm—"

"You're worried about David?"

"Yes," she says then fails miserably at an abortive attempt at a smile.

Doctor McCarthy nods. "Actually, I've been thinking of getting in touch with you. I'm glad that you came in."

"Oh? Why's that?"

"Well, I'm concerned about him too. As you know, David has complained about severe pain in his back, and also about headaches."

She nods slowly.

"We've done extensive x-rays and tests, and for the life of me I can't see anything wrong. He does say his legs are feeling better—no more throbbing under the casts—but this pain, I, I just—"

"Do you think he's making it up, Doctor?"

"I don't know, Katie. I really don't know. I'm just saying that I don't see anything, that's all. There are cases in which doctors cannot determine the cause of debilitating pain. It's not unheard of."

Katie looks briefly toward a window, blinds half closed, and says, "So what do you recommend?"

"I think it's time for David to go home, see how he feels there."

"Great," she says as her eyes brighten.

"I'm afraid he doesn't share your enthusiasm, Katie."

"You already told him?"

"Yes," Doctor McCarthy says as he pushes back from his desk a bit. "David said he doesn't think he is ready to go home yet, and asked for something stronger for his aches and pains. Just like that, one minute he seems fine, talking normal and even sitting up in bed, next minute he's lying there speaking slowly and asking for more pain killer."

"I see." Katie takes a deep breath. "What about his legs and his back? Are they healed enough, I mean, for him to get around at home?"

"Oh yes. They're healing fine. He should be able to get the casts off soon, and then he can start rehabilitation. I'd just make sure he avoids stairs for a while."

"So what do I do? I can't *make* him go home."

"I think you should talk to him. Tell him that we chatted briefly, and I told you the good news, you know, keep everything real positive. And see what he says."

"And what if he still says he wants to stay here?"

"Well, I think we should consider a psychologist. I know several. I'd be happy to recommend a couple."

"Lord, David will love that. He refers to them as shrinks."

"Katie, what he's been through—what you've all been through—would be trying for anyone. It's not a weakness to seek counseling. I mean, obviously there's a grieving period. That's normal. It could take a year or more. But this state of paralysis is obviously not good. He'll never get through it if he stays in the hospital. I really feel he needs some professional help."

Katie doesn't say anything for several seconds, then continues, "I think you're right, Doctor. It's crossed my mind too. Talking to someone, someone who can be objective and he can talk freely with, can't hurt. I'll see if I can convince him."

"Good. I also suggest he go into the office one or two days a week and slowly get on with his routine. Or, if he refuses, have some work brought home for him. The longer he waits, the worse this could get, Katie."

"I understand." She rubs her eyes hard then moves her fingers through her hair.

"What about you, Katie? Are you doing okay?"

She takes a breath, pauses, and says, "Oh yeah... hanging in there."

"You look tired. Are you having trouble sleeping still?"

"Yes, sometimes."

"Like *every* night sometimes?"

"Well..."

"I can give you something to take temporarily, if you think you need it." Doctor McCarthy stands and walks over to her.

"Oh no. I don't like taking anything unless I have to. I'll be all right... when David is all right."

He nods and smiles without showing any teeth, then seems to hesitate before asking, "How's Megan doing?"

"Better than humanly possible. I don't know how."

"Is there any word on a donor?"

"No," she replies and her eyes instantly become reflective.

"I'm sure they'll find a match soon." He stands and walks over. "Now, I want you to call me if I can help. Okay? Day or night. You have my cell number, right?"

"Yes. Thank you, I appreciate it. Really." She shakes his hand then turns toward the door as he pulls it open.

"You know, you don't have to carry all this on your shoulders."

"I wish that were true, doctor. I wish that were true." Her eyes move to his face once more. "But I'm afraid that, unfortunately, I do. For now, anyway."

He touches her back with the palm of his hand as she walks through the doorway. "Take care, Katie. You're all in my prayers."

"Thank you."

With that, she returns a strained but lovely smile and leaves.

Everything was peaceful. He saw the city lights below, their yellow glow diffused by a foggy haze between his body and the earth, and he looked at them, stared at their color and intensity, and realized he was soaring through the air, chin up, arms stretched outward, legs trailing behind like a horse's when clearing its hoofs over a bar, jumping with heart. Yet he could not sense speed, or distance, for the ground below appeared to be frozen in place. And there was no sound from the wind. Everything was still. Everything was silent. Everything was peaceful...

He thought of baby Angela, he saw her tiny body there, in the soft gray clouds, also flying, circling, and gliding, much higher than he.

Why is she here?

He calls out her name but she doesn't seem to hear. She just keeps circling, higher and higher. He reaches outward, into the mist, but he can't feel any moisture. He's swimming toward Angela, yet she just moves away from him. She doesn't hear. He sees death hover over her, grab at her, shake her in its cruel welcoming arms. He hears a voice,

"David, David, you're having a nightmare. Wake up, honey," Katie says as she rubs his forehead. She had been sitting beside the hospital bed watching him for twenty minutes, his eyelids jumping about, feet shaking, nonsensical sounds coming from his mouth. She now wonders whether she was right in rousing him, having once been told by someone that you aren't supposed to wake a person when they are dreaming. But he seemed distressed and she couldn't take seeing him like that—not in his sleep too—for his wakeful hours are dreadful enough.

David sees bright light, then Katie's face comes into focus and he slowly says to her with an air of confusion, "What happened?"

"Are you all right?"

He searches his mind, then says, "Guess I was having a dream."

"You looked like you were swimming across the Ohio River," she says as she caresses his left arm. "I was worried you would hurt your legs. So I thought I better wake you up."

CHAPTER SEVEN

"Katie, please, have a seat," Robert says as he motions to an empty chair at the end of the conference room table. She tilts her head in the affirmative and walks toward it, then looks at the faces which surround her, each one avoiding eye contact, everyone appearing jittery. Not a sound, except for the obnoxious blasts of the heater vent above her. "Gee, is this a dull party or what?" she says as she sits down and scoots in.

Finally, Ray Durning gives her a smile and she knows something is wrong, for he never shows his teeth except at the company Christmas parties after sloshing through a few gin and tonics. His usual expression is that of a captain whose ship is sinking fast, and as chief financial officer, this always gave everyone the chills. He just never smiles. Never.

Ray asks, "How is David doing?"

"He's doing better," she replies. "He likes being out of the hospital and back home."

"Good." Ray looks down, not wanting to probe too deep, and puts his frown back on.

She again glances around the room. "All right, so what's up guys?"

Robert clears his throat and turns the notepad before him over, then says, "Katie, I'm sorry for being so vague about the purpose of my calling this meeting, and for the short notice. We just wanted to talk to you first, you know, before David could find out."

He pauses, obviously searching for words. In his year as vice president of corporate development and sales he had never shown such reluctance in taking charge of a meeting. He usually dominates conversation and appears nervous, as if he needs to be somewhere else. But today he's different, almost pleasant and calm.

"Okay, what is it you want to discuss?"

"You know how much all of us here at the Center care about David and you, and—"

"Please Robert, just cut to the chase. Why are we all here?" She looks at the other senior executives. Jones and Thompson are tapping their fingers. In unison, they suddenly stop.

"Well, okay, I need, or rather *we* need your help."

"On what, Robert?"

"On getting David's approval for the merger, among other things."

"Ah, I see..."

"Now wait, hear me out, Katie."

She straightens her back and leans forward toward the conference room table. "You know, David doesn't exactly call it a merger. He says it's a hostile takeover. That Stanton & Hughes' board intends to simply push him," she says then again looks around the room, "along with all of us out, and then bring in their own management just like they have done at every company they've gobbled up. He says they'll turn this place into a corporate bureaucracy of checks and balances and they will be more focused on quarterly profit reports than on quality horse breeding and genetics R&D, and they'll—"

"Yes, I know very well how David feels," Robert interrupts as his face reddens. "But he's wrong, god dammit, he's wrong. He doesn't know what they're proposing or, for that matter, what's been going on around here. You know that. He hasn't been in since his car accident."

Katie clears her throat, trying to stay calm. "Robert, have you ever lost a child?"

"Please, I—"

"Or had a teenage daughter who'll die if she doesn't get a bone marrow transplant? Have you?"

"Come on Katie, you know I haven't."

"We've had a difficult year, Robert, to say the least." She feels her stomach tightening, face getting hot, the first time she'd shown any emotion since returning to work.

"Katie, we're all heartbroken over what happened with Angela, and the stress you've been under with Megan. And we're sick about how everything has affected David. I can't fathom how you cope so well, really. But the livelihood of every employee at this company depends on David. You know I've tried to be sensitive about this. Christ, we've all been walking on eggs around here. But he doesn't even answer the phone or return my messages, and he doesn't do anything with the documents and memos that I, or anyone sitting at this table, send home to him. He won't even sign a letter or contract, or review the financials. This can't go on. You must understand."

She lowers her eyes, pulls her hair behind her right ear. She knows Robert's right. Something has to change.

"Now, I'm not saying that David should come in. If he needs more time, so be it. Whatever it takes—another month, a year—that's fine. We all care deeply about him. But we also care deeply about this business, and the well-being of our employees. Just as you do. If we have to run things without him for a while, we can. But he can't sabotage operations by not allowing decisions to be made. We can't let all our work go up in smoke, not after the success of the first cloned foal, and just when we're about to start making money for a change. You know how many breeding inquiries we've gotten since the first foal. We're just *that* close to being profitable."

"I know, I know," Katie says as she wipes a tear from her cheek and exhales loudly. "I'm sorry..."

✿

When evening arrived Katie drove home slower than usual, even took a different route that meanders around on itself over near the racetrack and the thoroughbred club, its neon lights glaring at her. The car seemed to want to roam, and in her mind she could see horses running freely upon a lush spring hillside, and she saw herself as one of them, just running free. No one to answer to. No one to worry about. No one to grieve for. No one to save.

Just free.

She contemplated stopping at Restaurant Row and indulging in something fattening and tasty. A nice thick-crust, extra-cheese, large vegi pizza, perhaps. Or maybe some ice-cream—yeah, chocolate chip cookie dough—with a few glazed and frosted donuts on the side, the kind with those little sprinkly things on top that make a mess everywhere. Maybe a couple super-size McDonald's fries for dessert. But then, she told herself while shaking her head ashamedly, who would that help?

As she turned up the driveway she could see the lamp on in the bedroom and David sitting there looking out the window. She couldn't make out his face, but she was sure it was of stone, impervious to her arrival.

What does he think about all day? she whispered as the gravel crunched beneath the tires.

She could see him turn away, his arms kicking at the rubber of the wheelchair tires, as she neared the garage and pressed the button on the door opener clipped to the underside of the sun visor.

They hadn't slept together in ten weeks, as far as she could recall—two weeks before the accident, and eight, or is it nine, after. Of course, much of that time he was in the hospital, where she had, one afternoon, slipped her hand under the thin white sheet, lifted his gown, and stroked him for several minutes until hearing a nurse approach with a medicine cart. But even before the interruption David hadn't responded, remaining completely flaccid. And Katie couldn't feel the moisture that would normally avail itself, oiling her hands and soaking his briefs in anticipation of their lovemaking. Only she became awash with a glow, however fleeting.

"Just let me make you feel better, David," she had whispered to him. "Relax and close your eyes."

Something inside her also wanted to make sure *the thing* still worked, and that she too still functioned properly, though she wasn't sure what that felt like anymore. But she had hope. Perhaps something they once had shared and cherished could be retrieved, even take them away from themselves, their troubles. A few minutes would be glorious. A few seconds even.

But the response was tepid at best, *Like trying to light that wet fire wood last season*, she thought to herself later that evening. No spark.

As she waited for the garage door to slide up, she switched off the headlights of the Mercedes.

Inside the garage there were ten bags of trash over near the snow shovel, rake, hoe, and wheel barrel hanging on the wall. She had forgotten that each Tuesday she needed to take them down the driveway and set them by the mailbox. David had always done that. She'd remembered to do everything else though, at least she thought she had.

When she walked in the kitchen she noticed that the answering machine was, as it had greeted her each evening, blinking incessantly. She listened to all seven messages, jotting down numbers before the next beep, and stuck the note under a magnet on the refrigerator. She'd taken all the pictures Megan and Angela had made down. She wasn't sure why. They were now out in one of those damn bursting bags.

Katie raised her head from her pillow and stared at David. At two, when she had gone to the bathroom, he was still awake. At five, to let the dog out, he was still awake. It was the same routine each night since he got home from the hospital. Sleep much of the day sitting in the wheelchair, then toss and turn lying on the bed next to her—but emotionally away from her. Yet never complaining. That wasn't like him. He was the type who would rather hold everything in until exploding, or imploding.

She decides to go take a shower, and let him sleep.

She dwells on how she hadn't confronted him yet—about work—as she lathers herself with a lilac scented body soap under the warm water of the shower, about to start another identical day. She wanted to kick herself for chickening out.

Maybe he's not ready? Maybe I'll hurt him? What if he breaks down again?

She was just too exhausted to pick up the pieces of whatever her words would shatter. So she had put it off for tomorrow. Again.

As she rinses the shampoo out of her hair she feels the bubbles roll down over her breasts, her stomach, between her legs. She thinks about that night when he had opened the door, walked in, touched her with tenderness, and kissed her amid the steam and splashing water. And now she can feel him once again, running the tip of his tongue over her nipples as they became firm. And she can feel his hand, his fingers, reach down and gently rub at her.

With the pulse of the shower drumming at her bare reddened skin, and her hands guiding his, she feels a rare and brief moment of ecstasy as she tilts her head back, feeling the sweet contractions. And finally, the rhythm of her pelvis subsides, the bubbles carrying her away. Carrying the world away.

Over the past weeks she had showered with him each morning like this, while he lay asleep.

CHAPTER EIGHT

When Christmas arrived at the front door there were no welcoming lights on the house, no evergreen wreath with red holly berries encircling the brass knocker, no strands of garland streamed around the oak banister and spindly newel post that had typically treated visiting eyes which peered through the foggy windows flanking each side. Nor was there evidence of the annual Douglas fir in the living room. David said there was little reason to put decorations up, since they would be spending the day at Katie's parent's home over in Georgetown. He also said his legs were still weak from lack of exercise, the subtle atrophy one experiences right after having a cast removed, even worse with two. Besides, he said, what is there to celebrate *this* Christmas?

Katie knew, then, what tormented rationale had actually possessed him, but she said nothing. Sure, she had offered to bring home the tree and set it up herself, but his silent response had stopped her cold. And so the only overt sign of the holidays were a few neatly wrapped presents leaning against the wall near the front door, and four stockings tacked to the mantle with small nails. She had pinned three of them up while he napped one Saturday afternoon—one for her, one for Megan, and one for him. And when she returned from grocery shopping two hours later, he had pulled Angela's stocking out of a trunk in the basement and pinned it up as well, with its embroidered letters spelling out her name and a felt reindeer stitched below it, green, gold, and red. Katie cried when she saw it and quickly ran to the upstairs bathroom, then turned on the ceiling fan so her weeping would not be heard. She didn't think David noticed. In this rare moment of acknowledgment of the pain within her, she caught herself thinking, If he can so valiantly—or is it cowardly?—conceal his feelings, I can match him tear for tear, both of us hiding in the shadows. The thought sickened her. What were they becoming?

When Megan later asked at the dinner table why Angela's stocking was up, David placed his fork down, swallowed his food, and promptly excused himself. As Katie heard the bathroom door click shut, and the fan click on, she whispered in Megan's ear, "He put it up because Angela is still here, you know, watching over us. We just can't see her. I like to think she's an angel now, don't you?"

Megan nodded and gave a smile.

It's Monday. Katie arrives at the labs. David had asked her not to go in, for there was a doctor's appointment scheduled for Megan late in the afternoon. And if history was any indicator, Katie would fall into some project and lose all sense of time and place, maybe forget all about it. It had happened more times than she could remember. She had often caught herself wondering whether she was simply avoiding him, by not being home much, but deep down she knew this wasn't the case. She was just throwing herself at her work, taking her mind off things.

Although many of the employees are off for the day, Katie feels the need to try and tackle some of the paperwork and messages that have piled up. She walks in, flips on the lights, and sits down in front of her disheveled desk. Of first importance is the list she has compiled of various reporters and editors seeking more information, or rather an update, on the first foal. Some of the requests have been sitting here for two weeks. She spends the next three hours calling those she can, and reading the Private Placement Memorandum that had been prepared and circulated for comment, which in her case would essentially mean rewriting the entire thing. No decision had been made on whether to accept the investment from Stanton & Hughes, but two other companies had inquired to date—a large horse breeding firm located near Dublin, Ireland, and an entrepreneur by the name of Chris Rogers, representing a group of private investors specializing in biomedical startups. Katie had said at the last staff meeting, "Rogers wouldn't know the thoroughbred business from the hole in his ass." She almost regretted her words, given the shocked faces and nervous laughter that followed, but the truth was the truth, she thought.

By two o'clock she's made it through half the in-basket, returned fifteen voice mails by calling and leaving fifteen voice mails, and has red-lined her comments on the Private Placement Memorandum, the first being: David needs to sign off on this. This was futile, of course, as David hadn't signed off on hardly a thing since the accident. In response to her insistence, he had come into the office on four occasions to meet with Ray Durning on the operating budget, revenue forecast, and partner initiatives. But David stayed for just an hour or two and quickly drove home, having not stepped a foot into his office, and didn't even check on the horses or the lab's activities. For Katie, it was not only frustrating, but embarrassing. And each time she mentioned to him the possibility of going to see a psychologist, psychiatrist, or marriage and family counselor—hell, she'd be thrilled with a toll call to the psychic help line at this point—he dismissed it, saying he didn't need any help and, "I don't need anything."

"You don't need a lot of things lately," she told him the last time he ignored the suggestion to go talk to someone, but it didn't seem to sink in through the thick scars he'd developed since the car accident.

At three o'clock Katie realizes that she has a headache. Ten minutes later and it is getting worse, her head throbbing. She still has an hour to spare, but decides to go pick up Megan for her doctor's appointment. As she walks to her SUV, a mare running in the training circle catches her eye and she notices that someone must be in the barn, as the door is propped open with a brick. She decides to go make sure the horses are okay.

There is a foot of snow covering the grass and she can feel it soak into her shoes as she makes her way until finding a path that cuts a narrow swath of slush for her to follow. If it not for the indentations from someone's incredibly large boots, she would turn back. Instead, she places each foot in the white shadows of the last visitor, probably one of the trainers or vets.

Katie and Megan arrive at the Anderson Medical Building at five to four, the first time she has gotten Megan there without being late in a month. She almost parks in a handicapped spot near the entrance and in front of a row of newspaper vending machines, so the walk will be shorter to Doctor Carlton's office, but thinks this would be one more tacit acknowledgment, both for herself and for Megan, of the savage cancer invading their lives. To her, it would be one more step in the direction of surrender. And besides, Megan had made it clear that she didn't wish to be treated differently, no matter how bad it got.

They enter the building and wait in the reception area.

Twenty minutes later, Doctor Carlton enters the room and extends his hand. "Hello ladies. Nice to see you."

"Nice to see you, too," Katie says as she shakes his hand.

He then looks at Megan, greets her with a smile and brief handshake. "Hi Megan."

"Hello."

Moving his eyes back to Katie, he asks, "So, how's the foal doing that I read about in the newspaper, the racehorse clone?"

"He's doing great. Runs just like his papa," Katie replies.

"I bet. I'm rather surprised that there hasn't been more attention on him. The last story I saw was buried on page eight."

"Doesn't say much for my public relations skills, I guess."

"Oh, I'm sure that's not the case," Doctor Carlton says as he pulls his foot out of his mouth. He turns to Megan. "So how've you been feeling? You look good."

"I've had an upset stomach once in a while, but not too bad."

"Any throwing up?"

"Not anymore."

"Good." He turns and grabs a clipboard from his desk, then swivels back. "Well, we got the results of your last blood tests." He lifts a page, flips it over. "There's been some improvement in the white cell count."

Katie's eyebrows rise as she asks, "Could she be in remission?"

"I wouldn't call it that. Not yet. But we're winning the war for now. Obviously she still needs to have the transplant, no getting around that. The chemo has definitely helped though. But as you know, it won't do much for us long term."

Katie wraps an arm around Megan's shoulders and pulls her close to her chest.

"The good news is that we have time to find a donor."

Katie sighs then says, "Thank God."

After the checkup, Katie treats Megan to grilled turkey and cheese submarine sandwiches at a deli over at the mall, then they spend a couple hours touring clothing stores. Katie buys Megan a new dress—yellow with polka dots, spaghetti straps—and a pair of white sandals that she doesn't need now, but are too cheap to pass up. In the spring they will be put to good use.

It's thirty-five degrees outside, so they sit in the indoor food court, which is under the misty glass of a huge atrium, and watch people stroll by. For dessert they eat non-fat yogurts and sip diet Cokes and gossip like they used to do every weekend. Look at that woman's shoes! Can you believe the outfit on that girl? Check out this guy, what a hunk...

Their butts sore from the cheap plastic chairs at the food court, they drive home with full stomachs and empty wallets.

When night falls, Katie stands in the shallow darkness under the angled ceiling of the gable in Megan's room, her back to the bed and moist eyes aimed outside at the pond which is glimmering silver under a half moon. She had gone upstairs with David at eleven-thirty, after the local news and a cup of hot chocolate, but couldn't keep the night's bright sky from prying her eyelids open. As she leans against the window sill, feeling a draft creep in between the sashes, it suddenly strikes her that with each day sunrise seems to bleed into nightfall ever more quickly. She pulls her robe more securely about her chest and neck, silently turns around, then sits on the foot of the bed. She stares at Megan, watching her sleep peaceably, her chest gently rising and falling with each breath.

CHAPTER NINE

The milk, non-fat, was the first thing that Katie poured down the kitchen sink drain. Next came a couple ounces of orange juice, three Diet Cokes, and some applesauce. She decided to leave the bag of bagels and half-used tub of margarine, loaf of white bread, a banana—just one—and a jar of pickles which she couldn't remember when she had bought. The pantry came next. She hid all but two cans of chicken soup, some angel hair spaghetti, saltine crackers, and half a bag of chocolate chip cookies that were hard as a rock.

Her next stop was the rolltop desk. There, she pulled out two credit card bills that were due, a statement from Kentucky Utilities Company, and an AT&T phone bill. She set them out neatly on the kitchen counter, baiting with the chocolate chip cookies, and circled the due dates with a red pen. She left a note asking David to write out the checks and mail them, *And oh, we're out of stamps so you'll have to go to the post office. Need to go grocery shopping too. Thanks.*

Her last step was to go outside and turn on the water at one of the hoses. Since their house isn't on city water, all of the water comes from rainstorms and the gutters which send it to the cement cistern under the garage for storage. According to the long stick she had dropped down into the cistern, the water level was down to five inches. So the hose would likely spit this out within two hours, she estimated. Maybe less with a few showers and toilet flushes also using water. She then made sure the phone number for Johnny—the water deliveryman who was called whenever there was a drought—was in the address book near the phone. According to the Weather Channel, no rain was in the forecast for at least three days. David would have to call for a water delivery.

Friday. The US Airways Airbus A321 takes off at 1:30 in the afternoon. Katie and Megan are in business class, and the flight is not terribly crowded. They've spread out into four seats. It is Megan's first trip to New York, and Katie's second, though she can't recall much from the first time she had visited, back in high school.

As the flight makes its way, cutting through mostly gray sky, Katie wonders whether she has done the right thing. "You're going where?" David had asked yesterday, eyes wide.

"New York City."

"For god sake why?"

"Megan and I are going to see a play on Broadway."

"What?"

"I have the tickets right here," she said, then held them up for good measure. "We're leaving tomorrow."

He looked like she could knock him over with a good sneeze. She never did anything on the spur of the moment. Never.

He scratched his head, "What about Megan?"

"What about her?"

"I don't think it's safe for her to be flying. Her immune system is vulnerable. You know that."

"She'll be fine. Doctor Carlton said she's doing better. He okayed the trip, said it would be good for her. We should be celebrating."

He shook his head. "Well—"

"David, she'll be fine. You know how much she loves going to plays and musicals. You'll be okay, right?" Katie asked him, the picture of innocence.

"Of course I will."

As the plane descends into La Guardia Megan clenches her stomach. Katie tries not to look alarmed, turning away toward the window, but her heart seems to stop inside her chest. Megan's nausea had been better lately, and she assumed it was simply the flight bothering her daughter, but seeing her this way, the upset stomach, the discomfort, brings back too many memories of the past, and worries about the future.

As the plane levels off, Megan relaxes, placing her hands on her lap, then leans forward to see the skyline. She begins to feel better and asks her mom for some gum and says, "Is that New York?"

"That's it."

"Wow..."

They hear the flaps being extended, then the landing gear locking into position with a *clunk*. A few bumpy minutes later and they are on the ground.

When the sky became darker, and the city brighter, they ate dinner at a mom and pop pizza restaurant, sitting at a table next to a large window, and stared out at the lights and swarms of people moving quickly about. Later they took a cab over to the Empire State Building. Probably a mistake, Katie thought, as they piled into a crowded elevator on full, nervous stomachs.

On Saturday they visited the Statue of Liberty and walked around the theater district, waiting for show time. Katie took Megan's picture in front of the Ed Sullivan Theater, then stopped at a souvenir store and bought her a couple of tee shirts. At Times Square, Megan stood, eyes sparkling, and watched the traffic rush by, the hundreds of yellow cabs, the noisy trucks, the zombie-like passersby who stared at the sidewalk and not each other. Horns honked and sirens blared. Neon lights, blinking signs, sounds of someone speaking to a crowd, excitement and energy in the air—it was another planet compared to Kentucky horse country.

CHAPTER TEN

Her plan had worked brilliantly, at least for the three days following their return from New York. David was actually getting out of the house and running errands, as he had while they were gone. He went grocery shopping twice and took care of many of the chores that had piled up since the accident. Katie was feeling pretty good, that there was some hope on the horizon. Keep him busy, that was the trick.

But on Thursday David's mood changed as quickly as the weather, which turned to heavy downpours and high winds out of Indiana along with thunder and lightning which prompted riverboats and barges to remain docked on the sidelines of the Ohio River. Katie wondered whether his emotions had shifted because she and Megan had returned from New York. She was now home to take care of everything again. That had to be it, she thought. But she couldn't play more games, manipulating him into action and pushing to get him out of the house for the rest of their lives. And as it was, she felt a bit guilty for setting him up, even if it had worked for about a week. But why couldn't he stick with it?

Then it hit her. She found a letter David had opened while she and Megan were out for a couple hours, visiting with Grandma Ryan. It was from the National Bone Marrow Program, Office of Patient Advocacy. It was an update on the search for a donor. It was the third letter they had received from the organization. Katie and David had been told that the NBMP would assist them in the donor search process, choosing a transplant center, and working with insurance companies if problems arose. None had. Not yet anyway, though this was apparently a typical challenge once a donor is located and costs start to add up.

But finding the donor was the first obstacle. Katie didn't even want to think about the financial strain the transplant would put on the family, even with insurance assistance.

Acute Lymphatic Leukemia. That's what they said Megan had that rainy day they got the news. Cancer. The big C. The most common form of leukemia in children. To Megan it was frequent infections, fatigue, weakness, bleeding, bruising, blood blisters, pain in her legs and joints, swollen lymph nodes that she never knew she had, trouble running the bases in softball, and rigidness and discomfort when stretching for gymnastics. For some, it was a death sentence, a slow one at that.

The induction chemotherapy, the vincristine, the prednisone, the daunomycin, and other things she couldn't pronounce had, apparently, killed some of the rogue cells invading her body. But this was only the first step. And if she relapsed the chances for long-term survival would be zero to five percent. A donor had to be found. They were told that the NBMP had over three million volunteers willing to become marrow donors if a match occurred, and access to thirty-seven registries in twenty-nine countries through cooperation with Bone Marrow Donors Worldwide. Ms. Thompson had told Katie and David that recipients and donors are matched by comparing protein molecules called human leukocyte antigens. There are six HLA antigens considered important for marrow matching—two A, two B, and two DR antigens. A perfect match is a donor who has the same six antigens as the patient.

"Megan," Ms. Thompson said softly as Katie listened intently that day, "inherited HLA typing through the genes passed down from both you and your ex-husband. They're usually linked together in strands of three, a haplotype, or half one's inheritance."

Katie nodded politely, hanging on every word, though she probably knew more than Ms. Thompson about genetics, due to her work at the labs.

Ms. Thompson went on to say that there are twenty-four different antigens identified at the HLA-A site, fifty-two at the HLA-B site, and twenty at the HLA-DR site, and since each person has two antigens at each site, more than six million combinations of HLA antigens are theoretically possible in the general population.

Six million. A six with six zeros after it, Katie saw in her head.

"The NBMP allows no more than a one antigen mismatch between patient and donor, so Megan would receive a transplant if a six-of-six or five-of-six match occurred. The closer the match, the less chance of Graft Versus Host Disease there will be—her immune system attacking the new marrow." Ms. Thompson then explained that there is about a thirty-five percent chance that a sibling of a patient will be a match.

About a week after this meeting, Angela was tested, and indeed turned out to be a match. "But," Doctor Carlton told Katie and David, "she's too young to safely go through the transplant procedure. Unless there's a radical decline in Megan's health, it's best to hold off," he said calmly. To Katie, the onrush of relief she felt was soon abated by the news of having to wait for Angela to get older to serve as a donor for Megan.

And so the transplant, their lives, their happiness, were put on hold. Megan's bone marrow transplant would have to wait. Little did they know that tragedy would soon strike their family again.

After Angela's shattered body was found in the back of the Range Rover, there was a futile attempt to collect marrow. But the delay in finding her had destroyed any chance of her being able to save her older sister. And now, since a donor would have to be located in the general population, the chance of finding a match would be one in several million, given Megan's tissue type.

That first day with Ms. Thompson, the day that changed their lives forever, Katie wrote down everything she heard, not wanting to miss one single point. One thing stood out from all the statistics and medical jargon—the optimal donor would be an identical twin of Megan, or of Angela.

Katie pulled the letter out of the envelope and quickly scanned down. No wonder David was upset again, she told herself. It said that a three-of-six antigen match was the best found in the latest search of the registry. Unacceptable. Ms. Thompson's letter added, *We will all be praying for a match to turn up soon. Please be assured, the search will continue. My sincere sympathy for your family during this trying time. I'll be in touch if there is a change in donor status. Ms. Jill Thompson.*

Katie tried to tell herself that this was good news—at least some level of match came up...better than nothing—but found herself, just as surely as David had, facing the cold sobering reality of what was ahead.

When darkness eventually settles in, the house is still and quiet. Staring at the Broadway show poster they brought home from New York, while holding a stuffed animal she'd had since she was five years old, Megan says, "You know what, mom?"

"What?"

"I wish I could see Africa someday," Megan replies as she squeezes the well-worn tiger, which had been missing one eye for at least five years and had made far too many trips through the washer and dryer. Megan refused to part ways with it though, and so it had rested at the foot of her bed every night for as long as she could remember. She knew she was well beyond the age of having stuffed animals, but the tiger was part of the family at this point.

"Africa is a long ways away, honey," Katie says, pulling open the top drawer of the dresser. As usual, it screeches as she braces her knee on a lower drawer for extra leverage—another thing David hadn't gotten around to fixing. She puts a stack of folded underwear in and slides it shut, bumping with her right hip for the last inch, last screech.

Megan continues, "You went there, right?"

"Yeah."

"How old were you?"

"Oh, I don't know, maybe twenty or twenty-one. I was a sophomore in college."

"Did you like it?"

"Yes. It rained a lot, but we saw tons of wildlife. Elephants. Lions. I liked it."

"Will you take me there someday?"

"Well, I don't know. Maybe someday. It costs a lot of money."

"How much?"

"I have no idea now, but the airfare has got to be at least fifteen hundred dollars, maybe more. Why do you want to go there?"

"I just think it would be neat to see all those animals, you know, out in nature. Not locked up in a zoo. I remember Mr. Doyce telling the class last year that some of the animals are going extinct. He said if we want to see them we better hurry."

Katie sees in Megan's eyes an intensity and concern that wasn't there before. She sits down on the bed, pulls the sheet and blanket up to Megan's neck and says, "If you had one wish you could have come true, what would it be right now?"

She pauses, thinking for a couple seconds, then, "Not to be sick anymore."

Katie's heart seems to skip a beat, and she feels like kicking herself for asking such a dumb question. *God sakes, what else would she say?* She swallows hard then says, "Yes, I'm sure that wish will come true," as she strokes Megan's temple. "But besides not being sick anymore, would you wish to go to Africa? Is that what you would wish for?"

Megan nods twice.

"Well, maybe someday we can make that wish come true."

"Really!"

"Don't get too excited. Might take a while. David may want us to wait until the credit card bill comes and gets paid for the New York trip." She smiles and pats Megan's right leg.

"Yeah, probably..."

66

"Well, you better get some sleep," Katie continues as she picks herself up from the bed. "Good night, honey. I love you."

"Love you too, mom." She sits up and kisses her mother's cheek. "Thanks for taking me to New York. It was fun."

"You already thanked me, at least four times. But you're welcome. I'm glad you liked it." She walks to the door and tells Megan she'll see her in the morning and, "You sleep tight."

About an hour later, with Megan and David fast asleep, Katie descends the creaky wooden steps to the basement, alone in the silence and damp air. She's looking for a box. Inside the box, hand written on a piece of yellowed paper, are familiar words:

From a distance it appears as any other African tree I've seen really, such as a scraggly Ziziphus or Acacia. It is poised majestically near a cascading escarpment and centered between two opposing hills of golden green, neither of which is much to speak of, nor taller than the highest branch, twig, or leaf. And like everything else in the park—the vast plains, sweeping savannas, the beastly lions and lumbering elephants, the spotted hyenas, the birds of prey circling high above—the tree's crusted bark and twisted limbs are humbled by the presence of Kilimanjaro, towering further north, its white-capped shoulders standing squarely on the horizon. See its massive rooted trunk, thickened with time? Watch the swaying branches so stubborn and proud, undaunted by fire, nor flood, nor draught. What lives within its gangly arms? What dead lies beneath its roots?

This is where Katie had stopped writing, she now recalled. Page ninety-eight, pen in hand, journal cracked open and stretched over her sunburned, scarred knees. She seems to remember that she had been writing since noon, the sun at its zenith, and that her stomach had been growling, having been denied a proper lunch. That seemed like another lifetime ago now. She thinks to herself, *I was a different person, really...*

The journal was in a musty box filled with class yearbooks, papers, and stories and writings she had been proud of, along with a few report cards, diplomas and two tassels, graduation caps, and robes. Why, on this evening, she has ventured into the old memories...she isn't sure. Maybe, she thinks, it is because of the sparkle in Megan's eyes when she talked about Africa, reminding her of a time she also dreamed of far-away lands and saving the earth and its animals. A time of innocence and noble ambitions.

Where did that young idealistic woman go? she asks herself as she pulls each item from the box and brushes off years of dust, checking for mildew. Finally it comes to her, *Perhaps I'm trying to clear my mind of the present by thinking about, by reliving, the past?*

The peppery dirt that coats the journal's royal blue cover testifies to the number of years she hasn't tended to it. Years that now seemed so fleeting, so fragile. Lost in memories, she scarcely recognizes the girl who scribbled the words she just read. She indeed was another person. The journal was written back when she yearned to become a writer and studied literature with a reverence not often seen in college undergraduates, at least that's what one of her teachers had told her, "You have talent Katie, don't let it go to waste." How she wound up writing brochures and press releases rather than novels was a blur to her now. Something called life got in the way and had made her lose track of her dreams.

Funny how I never think about that anymore...

CHAPTER ELEVEN

Winter faded into spring, the chalky buds of the pear trees out back appearing first, each reaching for earlier dawns and later sunsets. Next came the English ivy that each fall presented itself in deep crimson, some yellow, climbing and spiraling skyward up the white oaks and maples along the south side of the house. Now, however, the ivy consisted of lime green spirally tendrils and tiny leafs beginning life once again.

For Katie these signs had, in the past, given lightness to her heart, a feeling of energy not found in the gray days between November and March. But this season it was not until she heard the high-pitched chirps of baby birds, tucked in safely somewhere under the eaves of the house, that forced her to acknowledge that even more time had slipped by their lives. The typical lightness of spring did not arrive.

As she moves her pillow to one side and rolls away from David, gazing out at the lawn through the gable window near their bed, she sees that the grass has seemingly turned from tan to green overnight. Why hadn't she noticed?

She watches the newspaper boy—actually he is forty-two and drives a minivan—toss the Sunday paper over to the mailbox, then loop his way out of the cul-de-sac and head toward Cold Hollow Road. As the tail lights disappear around a curve, she feels the bed jostle some, then David's body spooning against her back and legs, his warm arms sliding under her long tee shirt and his pelvis coming to rest squarely with her rear. They lay like this for ten minutes, neither speaking, just listening to the hungry baby birds outside.

An hour later she eats a bagel and bowl of hot oatmeal, then walks to the sun porch where David is sitting with Megan in a swing, he reading the newspaper, and Megan reading *Animal Farm.* Megan has a book report due on Monday which Katie will drop off for her, then make the rounds to all of her teachers and pick up her new assignments. The report is already written and proof-read, but Megan wants to go over the story one more time, this pass being the third.

"Where you going, mom?" Megan asks.

"I want to run over to work for a couple of hours."

David hears Katie tell Megan this, and puts the newspaper down to his lap and stops making the swing move. His slippers drag on the outdoor carpet of the sun porch, making a sound similar to playing cards being fanned. "On a Sunday?" he asks.

"I won't be long. I just need to check on a few things."

Katie arrives at the Kentucky Thoroughbred Center and there are no cars in the parking lot. As she enters her office, she pulls her purse from her shoulder and sets it on the desk. The zipper is tugged open and she reaches in and removes a folded piece of paper, a newspaper article she'd seen two days ago, but hadn't told David about. It is a story, or update, on a girl in Arizona who had been diagnosed with leukemia a few years ago. She was apparently doing fine, completely cured by a bone marrow transplant from her sister. But that in itself wasn't newsworthy. What made the girl's story unique was the fact that her parents had conceived her sister specifically to serve as a donor. Katie had already thought of this option, just days after Angela's death, but had put it out of her mind after discussing it with David. For them to even have a one in four chance of the baby being a donor match, Katie would have to become pregnant by Megan and Angela's biological father—Katie's first husband. That is, if he could even be found. He hadn't visited Megan or Angela since the divorce.

"You would actually consider getting pregnant by that jerk?" David had said, then felt stupid for letting his emotions override the big picture.

"Obviously," Katie replied, "I would use artificial insemination."

They tossed this back and forth for forty minutes until deciding that it would only be a last resort, if Megan showed signs of falling out of remission and no other donor became available. Knowing that time would be critical if that were to occur, they tried to track down Katie's ex-husband just in case, even hiring a private detective and exhausting thirty-five hundred dollars. The only thing he discovered was a bankruptcy trail, dozens of angry creditors, and three very irate girlfriends who thought he may have left the country. One thought he was working on a cruise ship in the Mediterranean. God only knows where the degenerate was hiding with his valuable sperm.

Katie puts her purse aside and studies the article once more, then turns on her computer and monitor. A minute later and she is on the internet, entering search strings and calling up articles and links to websites. Two hours pass in an eye blink and she's found seven websites, plus two articles from the *New York Times* on-line, that look promising. She takes the printouts and reads them over, while resting her feet on the edge of the desk, sipping a diet Coke. "I'll start calling in the morning," she says to herself in a hushed voice as she runs her hands through her hair. She scoots the chair back, folds her arms and rests them on the desk, then lays her head down, thinking and praying.

CHAPTER TWELVE

Katie sees the silhouette of a city emerging below a milky haze of ocean as the plane sweeps in over jagged mountains, snowless peaks reflecting purplish sky. There is rumbling next, the landing gear extending, she hopes. A tingling sensation moves up her spine and in her mind the ants that she watched climb up the sunny side of the barn yesterday are now fleeing over her skin. *Why does flying make me so damn nervous?*

It had been a turbulent flight, a storm near Dallas was the culprit, according to three announcements from Captain Ian Porter, "Apologize for the ride, folks, please keep your seatbelts fastened, we'll try for another altitude, thanks for flying Delta, enjoy the flight."

Enjoy the flight?

As the plane approaches Lindbergh Field from the east, she sees the San Diego zoo out the window to her right, the hills, cages, and enclosures scattered among thousands of eucalyptus trees, tourists streaming around on foot and in double-decker open-air buses. Nearby, the business towers of downtown appear as if they are rising from the Pacific, then seem to come much too close to the left wing and a delicate vapor trail bleeding from its tapered edge. *Great location for an airport*, Katie thinks as the plane seems to drop in from a hole in the sky.

She stretches her back, shakes off a few ants, and glances to her right. The thirty-something wavy-haired man with the laptop and tweed sport coat is still staring at her, as he had throughout much of the trip, which she rather liked...a man giving her attention for a change. She offers a shy smile and he instantly glues his eyes back to the spreadsheet he is analyzing, or pretending to anyway. Lots of tiny squares and tiny numbers that are so important he has decided to ignore a tiny flight attendant's request ten minutes ago to put away all electronic devices.

Katie looks down at her silken blouse, noticing that one of the buttons is undone. *Great, he was probably staring at my breasts the entire flight,* she thinks as she reaches up and covertly fastens the tortoise shell button. She feels herself redden with the sudden unexpected thrill of an exhibitionist then smiles slightly at the sensation and turns toward the window. She crosses her right leg over her left, lodging her high heel between the plastic wall of the fuselage and the seat in front of her.

She hears, "Please stay seated until the plane comes to a full stop."

The touch down isn't jarring, isn't bumpy, the tires don't screech, the seats and overhead compartments don't shake. Still, it is not pleasant. She again turns from the window. Though the seatbelt sign is still aglow with orange-red and the captain has given his direct orders, she unfastens her buckle and raises an armrest to her right, then twists her body sideways toward the aisle and quickly realizes that Mr. Laptop's eyes are rolling toward her and ascending up her skirt, which she has, no doubt, just opened widely. This time he does not turn away. His eyes move up to her face, of all places, as he says, "Rough flight, huh?"

"Yes, it sure was." She tucks her skirt under her leg. "Pretty bumpy," she continues. She feels his admiration, his wide pupils revealing his opinion of her. She reaches up and pulls her red swirls over her shoulder then remembers that she didn't wear her engagement ring. She didn't want to travel with it.

"Visiting San Diego on business?" he asks, stretching his arms forward.

She hesitates, questioning whether she wants to start a conversation, not really in the mood to talk. "Personal business," she replies. "And you?"

"I'm a business analyst, in town for some due diligence on an acquisition."

"Oh really? That sounds exciting," she says. She doesn't want to talk about the purpose of her trip. Keep the conversation on him, she tells herself. She reaches down and grabs her satchel from under the seat in front of her then places it on her lap.

"Ladies and gentlemen welcome to San Diego," the speaker above her head blares. "The temperature is sixty-eight degrees with partly sunny skies. We'll be exiting from the forward left door. Thank you for letting us serve you, and we hope to see you real soon."

Her admirer presses on, obviously preparing to make his move, "I'm Richard Gables." He extends his hand across the aisle, which suddenly seems as wide as the Pacific. Every bored passenger within five rows is watching.

"Pleasure to meet you. I'm Katie Ryan." Her hand meets his. Warm, firm. No calluses. Typical spreadsheet, analyst type. She suddenly feels awkward, as other passengers are indeed noticing them. Probably waited for him to make his move the entire flight.

They say nothing as the plane moves toward the terminal then docks next to a covered ramp. A minute later the door is opened and everyone stands and soldiers toward the front exit where the incessant call of a flight attendant emanates, "Goodbye, so long, goodbye, take care, bye bye..."

As tweed-clad Richard Gables departs the plane, he slows and turns slightly, then waits for Katie to catch up. He has no intention of letting this lovely woman slip away without at least some sort of attempt to get together, or at least obtain a phone number. "In town long?" he asks.

"Afraid not. Just a day or so, then back to Kentucky," she says as they walk.

"May I carry that for you?" he asks, noticing her struggle with a carry-on bag.

"Oh no. Thank you."

They reach the ticketing area.

"Well then, perhaps I'll see you on the return trip." His face offers clues to his sudden panicked feelings of how he will ever track her down. He takes a deep breath and decides to roll the dice, "Say, uh, would you like to have dinner while you're in town? Maybe the Marine Room over in La Jolla?" It isn't smooth, but he had to move quickly.

She pauses, smiling, and turns toward him. The ants again stream up her back, and this time they feel good. She feels an air of excitement. *What do you know, I'm actually getting attention from a man, a young and handsome one to boot.* The blood returns to her brain as she says, "That was rather to the point."

"Yeah, sorry. Just don't want you to get away, I guess."

She smiles at his boyish gaze. "Well, that would be nice. But I'm afraid my fiancé wouldn't appreciate it."

His face brightens further as he says, "Oh you're engaged, I'm sorry, I didn't see a ring."

"I forgot it," she says as her eyes move to her hand, her fingers fluttering upward, looking for the slightest trace of paler skin where her ring would be.

"Your fiancé's a lucky man."

He is? she thinks to herself.

"You're drop dead gorgeous."

She feels lightheaded. "My, well, thank you." She doesn't know what else to say.

Suddenly he has the need to be as far away as he can get. "Well, I better be going. Got to get to a meeting." He starts to turn. "It was nice talking with you."

"Same here. Take care."

She floats away from him, holding her shoulders back, swinging her hips just slightly more than usual. And he shuffles off with his head hung low. Just before rounding a corner, near the baggage claim area, she gives a last curious glance at him. He is standing there, watching her.

By the time Katie finally gets the rental car paperwork filled out and takes a shuttle bus to some distant parking lot, she's already feeling tired. She gets into a white Toyota Camry and heads toward an on ramp. Seconds later, she cracks the side window open and takes a breath of salty air, driving north on Highway 5. There are five lanes of solid traffic, barely crawling.

Finally, she pulls into the parking lot of Cooper Research, Inc., ten after seven local time. The company, she estimates as she glances at the orange sky to the west, can't be more than five minutes from the beaches of La Jolla. She had visited the area twice before, taking in the San Diego Zoo, Safari Park, Sea World, and Legoland in Carlsbad.

She aims the Camry into what seems to be far too small a parking space. On her right she can just barely see the black cloth top of what she guesses is a Ferrari, as she slowly comes to a stop. She opens her door, being careful not to hit the car to her left, slips out, then walks toward the huge glass doors of a shimmering office tower.

The building entrance is flanked by dozens of palm trees that gently sway back and forth in the evening breeze. A huge fountain sprays a calming, fine mist to the air. The peace and tranquility is only disturbed by the rumble of a helicopter taking off nearby at Miramar air base, and the resultant cry of some car alarm. Katie pauses just before entering the glass doors and wipes her sunglasses, straightens her blouse in the reflection of the mirrored surface.

The interior of the building looks similar to the outside: palm trees, fountains, mist. A marble reception counter is visible off in the distance and, behind it, a spiral glass staircase swirls upward past the man-made tropics then seemingly disappears into a modern-looking metallic ceiling with neon lights around the perimeter. She approaches the reception area. "Hello, I'm Katie Ryan. I'm here to see Mr. Lewis and Doctor Logan."

"Yes ma'am. Please sign in and, if you don't mind, would you please put this name tag on?"

"Certainly." She clips the tag to her blouse.

"If you will follow me," the receptionist says, flashing the whitest teeth Katie has ever seen. They had to have been purchased very recently, she thinks, just as much of the Barbie doll before her. "Care to take the elevator, or would you like some exercise?" she continues, then motions to the staircase.

"Oh, I'd like the exercise. After you." Actually Katie wants to take the elevator, but damned if she's going to admit it.

She almost trips twice on the beautiful but insanely awkward Plexiglas stairs; the steps are narrow near the point where they join a central support column. Miss one and you'll find yourself checking back into the reception counter head first, she tells herself.

"Here we are," Barbie says with not even a slight indication of being out of breath. "Quite a hike isn't it?"

"Yes," Katie replies, breathing heavily yet inconspicuously. "Quite a hike."

The meeting begins fifteen minutes later. Two men, mid-forties, walk into the conference room where she is waiting. One wears a white lab coat. She assumes he is Doctor Logan, the person she had read about in the *New York Times* article she had found online. She'd used the same trick at work, often asking personnel—from farm hands to doctorates—to wear pristine lab coats to impress visitors, make the company look more professional. The other man is clearly a marketing type. A wild red tie that screams for attention, Mont Blanc pen poised in a crisply starched button-down shirt, and embroidered initials on the cuffs. It would be his job to sell Katie on the company's services, and get a contract signed with that hundred dollar Mont Blanc pen. "Good evening, Ms. Ryan," he says, offering a broad smile.

"Hello." Katie extends her hand as he saunters around the marble table.

"I'm Chris Lewis, and this is Doctor Logan."

"Pleasure." She shakes both their hands.

"Please, please have a seat."

"Thank you."

"Would you like some coffee, water, or a soda?"

"No, I'm fine thanks."

"So you're from Kentucky?"

"Yes."

"Beautiful state," he says, but somehow his eyes reveal that he's never been there. He promptly looks down at a piece of paper folded in his left hand. He opens it and continues, "You work for a company involved in horse breeding and genetics, the one that's cloning thoroughbreds?"

"That's right."

"Well then…you're obviously familiar with biotechnology. So I won't bore you with our typical song and dance. But we do have one formality. We ask that every visitor, or prospective customer, sign a non-disclosure agreement. Do you mind?"

"No, that's fine, just let me read it over."

"Certainly." He stands and walks over to a small cabinet, opens a drawer, then pulls out a piece of paper and hands it to her, "Here you are. Please take your time."

She scans down the one paragraph—a bunch of legalese that simply means, Don't tell anyone what we're about to tell you. She had used a form with essentially the same wording a hundred times back at work. They were scarcely enforceable. She signs and dates the bottom, hands it back to him.

"Thank you." He leans back in his leather chair and crosses his legs. "Now then, I'm sure you're rather tired from your flight."

"A bit, yes."

"So why don't we talk about why you came all the way from Kentucky to see us."

"Okay, well, I'm interested in your capabilities, obviously, or what I think your capabilities are."

"Interested as a representative of Kentucky Thoroughbred Center, or on a personal basis?" He rocks back and forth.

"Personal." She decides to cut to the chase. A pause, then, "I'm trying to find a facility that can clone my daughter's DNA into one of my eggs."

The rocking stops as he says, "I see…"

Katie leans forward, "You *are* still conducting human cloning research, correct?"

"Yes, but not here. We have a lab across the border in Mexico. As you probably know, such work has been banned in the states."

"I think it's been banned in just about every country, including Mexico."

"True. But we haven't had any problems there."

Finally, Doctor Logan speaks, first clearing his throat. "Ms. Ryan, may I ask why you want to clone your daughter?"

"She has Leukemia."

His simple nod and steady eyes make it clear that he knows where she is going. He says, "I'm very sorry," then, "So they haven't found a donor?"

"No. My other daughter was a match, but she was killed in an auto accident last fall."

"My god, how terrible." He shakes his head and no one speaks for several awkward seconds, not knowing what to say.

"Well," Mr. Lewis says, "your situation would definitely fit with our requirements."

"Which are?"

"You're probably already familiar with them, if you've read the press we've been getting. They're quite simple. We only accept clients with leukemia. We don't take any cases in which invasive surgery would be performed on the clone given birth to—no kidney or lung transplants, things of that nature. As I'm sure you know, Ms. Ryan, a marrow transplant isn't a major operation, and is actually quite safe these days. So, aside from the assisted reproduction issues that will always be debated, we feel that public reaction won't be too terribly negative. We aren't offering our services in order to harvest major organs. And we're not going to jeopardize the health of the babies we will hopefully help create. We want to save lives, not take them."

She nods. She had read the exact same canned statements in the articles she'd found.

"But let me be frank. We haven't, to date anyway, succeeded with the cloning of a human being. We believe we're close, but there's no guarantee we can help you."

"I understand. Can you tell me just how close you think you are? I mean, have you succeeded to a certain point with human cells, or with cloning *any* animal cells?"

"No, not yet. We do, however, have a team assigned to cloning chimpanzees, and they're making good progress. As you may know, their DNA is about ninety-nine percent identical to that of a human."

"I understand there's a doctor in Chicago who has already cloned chimps."

"Yes, he apparently has, but from what we understand, he lost his funding and isn't conducting any research at the moment."

Another nod. She already knows this. "May I ask you how many cases you are working on right now?"

"We've only taken on nine cases since we started, about two years ago. Our investors have mandated that we take no more than twelve until we achieve a successful clone."

"So, are you saying that I could have one of the open slots?"

"Yes, assuming everyone agrees on the terms, and the contract is executed."

Translation: They get paid in advance, Katie thinks as she leans back in her chair. "And what are the terms?"

He scoots his chair closer to the table then pulls out his pen and turns it in his fingers. "Let me give you some background, first. When we formed the company we developed a pricing plan that would give early adopters of our service financial assistance. For the first six contracts we signed, we set a price of three hundred thousand dollars. As you might know from the work your company does, this doesn't come close to covering our costs."

"And for the next six contracts?"

"One million dollars," he says without blinking or hesitating one bit.

Katie reclines some more in her chair, blowing her cheeks outward. They may as well be telling her one billion.

"I know it's a lot of money."

She feels herself getting upset as she says, "Yes, yes it is..."

"And, again, there's no guarantee of a successful outcome. Even if we are able to create a clone with one of your eggs, and if it led to your giving birth to another daughter to serve as a donor, it's very possible it would be too late to save your daughter. I'm sorry for being so direct, but I'm sure you want the facts."

Her eyes turn to glass, still and reflective.

"Now, we do have some financing plans that might help, but our board requires fifty percent down, and the funds must be deposited in an offshore bank. This is for everyone's sake."

She wipes a tear from her cheek and says, "Lord, it sort of makes one feel like a criminal, trying to save their child's life."

"I'm afraid that our friends in D.C. only hear of the nightmarish cloning stories the media and Hollywood present. Hopefully this will change when lives start being saved." He moves a hand over his forehead and drags it down his face, finishing with a couple pinches of his stubble-covered chin.

It is getting late, and Katie is tired too. In her head she hears the words, *one million dollars* echoing over and over. Her temples begin to throb. *I flew two thousand miles for this? One million dollars... One million dollars...*

And her trip isn't over. Who knows what number she'll hear tomorrow, when she flies to San Francisco on another lead. Two million? Three?

Maybe David was right, I'm wasting my time, getting myself worked up only to be disappointed. What's worse, I lied to Megan about this trip, not wanting her to get her hopes up of finding, or rather creating, a donor—only to be let down. God knows she can't take much more. Katie rubs the nape of her neck, "So let me get this straight...May I be blunt?"

"Please."

"I sign a contract, give you five hundred thousand dollars down, which is placed in some offshore account out of reach of U.S. authorities, and of course U.S. jurisdiction, then trust that your lab in Mexico will succeed? No idea of when?"

"I'm afraid so, Ms. Ryan. And, if I may also be blunt, we turn down cases every month."

Later, in her hotel room, Katie walks in and the first thing she notices is the red light blinking on the phone by the bed. She closes the door, locks the security chain, then turns on a lamp.

There are two messages on the hotel's voice mail system: *Hi honey. Just wanted to call and tell you that I already miss you. Megan and I ordered pizza and are about to watch a movie. She says hello. I hope you aren't getting your hopes up too high. I'm sorry that I wasn't, well, supportive, but this just seems crazy to me. Call me in the morning, okay. Bye babe.*

Two beeps.

Katie, it's Barb. Sorry to bother you but I wanted you to know that I got a lead on Doctor Drake. Apparently he last worked at UCSD as a visiting professor and researcher, but he left a few years ago. An administrator in the biology department said she heard that he went to Johannesburg, South Africa, of all places. I'm trying to find out where. The other two company numbers you gave me are disconnected. Call me at home if you need anything else. Talk to you soon. Be careful out there.

Katie hangs up the phone receiver and slides off her shoes while simultaneously peeling her panty hose off. She then grabs a tiny bottle of wine, a fifteen dollar jar of macadamia nuts, and two imported candy bars out of the honor-bar refrigerator next to the desk, one of which—the white chocolate and almond bar—is half consumed by the time she turns on the bath and unsnaps her bra. *Probably just doubled the price of the room*, she thinks as she unscrews an aluminum cap and takes a long sip of chardonnay. She lowers herself slowly into the hot water of the tub, not knowing whether to laugh or cry.

CHAPTER THIRTEEN

A week, a very long week, has passed since Katie returned from California. She and Megan have just pulled up in front of school and Megan can feel the cool breeze washing over her naked, chemo-inspired scalp through the hat she is wearing as she slams the Mercedes SUV's passenger door shut. She feels her pulse quicken. How she looks is suddenly more important than how she feels. *Will my friends stare? Will even one boy talk to me?* she asks herself. Or might she find that her teachers or Principal Manning treat her differently, like some freak nearing death?

Last night, sleep had evaded her. She worried well into morning, gazing up at the brightening ceiling above her bed. It was stupid to worry so much about what people will think at school, she told herself at breakfast. *Nothing has changed. I'm still the same. Even lost a few pounds. But the hair!*

She swings her backpack over her shoulder and walks around the front of the SUV, her eyes not leaving the ground, then timidly looks up as her mom rolls down the window, peering from the SUV, and tries to put yet one more positive face on, smiling. In response, Megan tries to curl the corners of her own mouth upward but also has trouble, for she had sensed on more than one occasion that something hasn't been right since her mother returned from California.

Megan sees her mother clenching the SUV's steering wheel. "Mom, I'll be okay, don't worry."

"I'm not worried."

"Yeah...right."

Finally Megan raises her head and looks over at Smith Hall, the largest building at school, students streaming up the pockmarked and powdery brick steps, a few ornery kids passing time by sliding down the handrails. Everyone happy, no problems, bright futures, practice after school, dinner with normal families. Normal healthy families.

Katie asks, "Are you sure you have everything?"

"We checked three times." Megan motions to the over-stuffed backpack.

"Come here, honey." Katie raises her chin and puckers her lips which aren't wearing lipstick this early in the morning. Mother and daughter kiss as if this is the first day of kindergarten, It'll be okay, sweetie pie, mommy will pick you up right here, it'll be fun, Katie's concerned face says.

As Megan walks toward the flagpole at the base of the school steps her heart sputters as she notices Billy Murphy. He is leaning against the pole like he always does and talking to James Hemstead. All cool like, they are, Billy with one leg bent behind him, holding him as he spits the shells of sunflower seeds or something equally obnoxious into a flower bed. *What did I ever see in him?* the voice in Megan's head asks. As she nears, she hangs her neck low and makes sure that the hat obscures her face. Peeking her eyes under the brim, she sees that the oral-retentive delinquents are now turned away from her. And that's how she likes it, no staring, no attention. Incognito.

As her right shoe touches the first step and she reaches for the handrail, a gust of cruelty kicks up and blows her hat off her bare head like a Frisbee. It flies and spins across the school entrance, then rolls on edge. All she can do is look on, gasping, with her mouth open and eyelids peeled wide. Panic, sheer panic.

Katie, who is still parked at the curb and looking just as mortified, cracks open the SUV's driver-side door. She tells herself, *Just wait, she can handle it. Stay calm...*

Billy is the first to turn toward Megan. And the look on his face when he sees her bowling ball of a head makes her want to run back to the Mercedes SUV.

So she does.

Back home, as evening settles over the dormered cape, Katie makes thin spaghetti and a fresh tossed salad with cucumber, tomatoes, and alfalfa sprouts. There's also French bread with butter and parmesan cheese, just like Megan likes it. They haven't talked much since the ride home from school. Katie had told her to try and stop crying and relax. "Breathe, just breathe," she had said. "Tomorrow is another day. It was no big deal," she continued in the calmest voice she could muster. But inside, she was just as crushed. If she could have swapped places with Megan, she would have. If she could have climbed those school steps, holding down that hat, she would have.

"Dinner's ready," Katie yells, peeking her head into the family room where David is propped up in the recliner, watching the news. He nods and sets the remote aside, kicks down the footrest.

Not a word is spoken about the ordeal. And, after dinner, Megan helps clean off the table and does the dishes, silently, then says, "I'm tired, I think I'll go to bed."

When her door clicks shut upstairs David says, "I can't believe you brought her home just because her damn hat blew off."

"David, half her classmates saw her, just, just standing there bald. She was totally in shock."

"You should have made her put the hat back on. Just get through it, you know, get back into the swing of things. Now it'll be even harder."

This, Katie knows, is probably right, but in the heat of the moment she had told herself that Megan wasn't in any condition to enter that campus with tears smeared across her inflamed face, sobbing uncontrollably. She says, "I know, I know," as she stands near the sink and dries the tile counter. She begins to cry and soon feels David's hands wrap around her waist, his forehead setting gently upon her shoulder.

"Look, I'm sorry," he says softly, "It must have been tough to watch."

She sniffles and a few seconds go by then, "David, I've made a decision." She turns toward him.

"A decision about what?"

A long pause then, "I just can't sit around anymore, waiting for either a donor to turn up, or for Megan to get worse. Not knowing which will happen first," she says as she looks up at the light above the kitchen table, then pulls a breath of air in that stutters through her throat and chest. She wipes her eyes and continues, "I want to try and find a person who might be able to help, a doctor Barb and I have tracked down. He's apparently in South Africa."

"What? I thought you dropped that whole crazy idea and—"

"It's not crazy, David. *God dammit!*" She slams her palm down on the counter. Lowering her voice she continues, "*My* daughter, your soon-to-be step daughter, is *dying*. You understand? She's slowly—"

"She's doing fine right now."

"Yeah, right now. But it can't last. You know that. If the leukemia doesn't kill her the chemo and radiation eventually will. It can't last…"

He backs away from her and reaches for a napkin, hands it to her. He says, "They might find a donor. They might."

"And they might not. I'm not taking any chances."

84

He runs a hand through his hair, shaking his head, "I'm just worried that you're setting yourself up, and Megan, for a letdown. Yet another around this place…"

She wipes her eyes and blows her nose.

"Like I said, I thought you had dropped this whole thing, Katie. The trip you took—How many doctors did you visit or call?—you said it was all dead ends. And now you want to go chase some other doctor down in Africa of all places. Good god, Katie."

"David, he's not just some quack claiming that he has cloned human eggs, or that he's even working on doing so. In fact, he isn't even involved in human research at all anymore. His name is Evan Drake, and he's from the U.S. You make it sound like he's a voodoo doctor from the Kalahari."

Incredulous, David shakes his head.

"Based on what I've read," Katie continues, "he's the most experienced geneticist in the world, when it comes to cloning. He's cloned more animals than anyone else. His lab apparently does it almost every day. If anyone can help, I think he can."

"Have you talked to him?"

"No, not yet."

David rolls his eyes, sighing. "Then how do you know for sure?"

"I don't."

"This is crazy. It's just crazy," he says at length, shaking his head even more deliberately. "And it's illegal."

"I don't care about any damn laws," Katie says, then opens the refrigerator and pulls out some orange juice, "I care about my daughter. I'm not going to lose another one," she continues pensively, then suddenly wishes she could reach out and pull her words back into her big mouth.

David turns away, loses himself in the guilty thoughts that had haunted most of his waking hours since the accident and Angela's death.

Katie pours the juice and takes a long drink then says, "Look, honey, just let me give this a shot. You of all people should realize that what I'm talking about isn't that outrageous. Hell, even *we* have managed to pull the right people together to clone thoroughbreds. And the way I look at it, human clones are born every day. They're called identical twins. They aren't freaks, David."

Katie had read extensively about the use of siblings for a transplant, and even identical twins. She learned that there are three types of transplants: autologous, syngeneic, and allogeneic. Autologous transplants receive their own stem cells. Syngeneic transplants receive stem cells from their identical twin. And allogeneic transplants receive from their brother, sister, parent or an unrelated donor.

David continues, "You're not worried about the ethical questions, and the attention we will—"

"No, she interrupts, I'm not. I have no problem having one of my eggs removed and implanted with Megan's DNA, then put back. Not if it means I can give birth to another beautiful little girl—one that can save Megan's life. I have no problem with that at all," she says firmly, knowing that she is simplifying things.

"So it's a done deal?"

"Yep," she says as she closes the refrigerator door. "I'm going to save my daughter's life. I hope I have your support," she adds in a softer tone as she searches his eyes for a sparkle of understanding. But he doesn't say anything. She continues calmly, "I'm going to go to South Africa."

He purses his lips as he always does when he's tired of arguing. Just like when they quarreled over whether to postpone their wedding until next year.

"And I'm taking Megan with me," she continues.

"Oh you are..."

"We're leaving in two weeks. I've already booked the flights."

"Christsakes, Katie. We could have at least talked about it first."

"Yeah, look where that's getting us. My stomach is turning."

"You're just going to pull her out of school again? Drag a sick girl halfway around the world?"

"A minute ago you said she was doing fine," she says as she moves closer. "It's just Johannesburg. We'll be in a nice hotel, close to hospitals, perfectly safe."

He lowers his eyes to the wood floor and starts to walk away.

"David," she says demurely, then waits for him to turn his face toward her, "It will be okay. I promise."

"I think it's a mistake, Katie. A big...mistake."

"The worst thing that can happen is I give her her last wish. You know how much she has dreamed of going to Africa. Right? It's all she talks about doing, all she looks forward to."

The tears suddenly move to David's face, as Katie's. He nods slowly as Katie reaches up and wipes them away.

She wants to tell him that one of the reasons she has decided to leave for Africa is to heal him, too. But she says nothing.

Much to David's disappointment, Katie followed through with what she had told him that emotional night, and left for Africa with Megan. To Katie there really wasn't any decision to make. The donor search was continuing, of course, but something inside her told her that this—finding Doctor Evan Drake—could very well be Megan's last hope for a cure.

And so they made their way toward Africa.

As the plane banks slowly to the left, toward darker sky, Katie reaches up and turns on the light above her head. She then opens her purse, which is resting on the floor between her feet, and pulls out one of the newspaper articles she's brought with her. She tilts the page such that Megan can't see it and begins to read:

Africa, the Dark Continent—its vast plains, towering mountains, and thick jungles—is where genetics and assisted reproduction technology are, however discreetly, being put to daily use. The goal? Saving endangered species.

Far removed from the horrors of Hollywood thrillers, with their mutant creatures created in the form of modern-day Frankensteins, a handful of men and women have created what might be referred to as preservation outposts, scattered across the continent from Cape Town to Tanger, Dakar to Hargeysa. While scientists and entrepreneurs in the United States, Europe, and elsewhere tout their capabilities or plans for genetic engineering, cryogenics, and cloning, a quiet group of individuals have been working almost completely unnoticed.

Making use of live and dead animals, these individuals run regional Genome Resource Banks, collecting, processing, and storing gametes, embryos, and other biological material from rare and endangered species, essentially creating a third (frozen) population to preserve animals in the wild and in captivity. Their tools and methods vary somewhat, but in essence they collect embryos from live animals, and gather egg cells and sperm from live or dead animals, mostly rhinos and elephants. In-vitro fertilization is then used and the embryos are either stored or artificially inseminated. The objective is to maintain biodiversity and decrease the effects of inbreeding among animals that have been fragmented and isolated by humans, with little or no genetic exchange. Working against over-population, pollution, and constant pressure from elephant poachers whose tactics put their lives in danger, these men and woman are trying to save the African wilderness. One egg at a time.

And beyond this effort there are reports of an American man operating out of Johannesburg who is actually cloning endangered species and regenerating wildlife on the Kenyan and Tanzanian plains. For people in the small, primitive villages, many of which lack running water and electricity, these efforts have taken on almost a mythical, or spiritual meaning, as if God himself has come to save their land.

They call this god the Mwujiza Mwanamume—the Miracle Man.

Katie folds the article and slips it back into her purse, then reaches down and presses the button on the side of the armrest to raise her seat. A flight attendant approaches from the galley with two bottles of spring water, "Here you are ma'am."

"Thank you."

"And one for you." She hands a bottle to Megan.

"Thanks."

"Would either of you like some more ice for your glasses?"

"No, this is fine," Katie answers, not looking up.

Megan shakes her head no then takes a sip, not bothering to pour it into the plastic cup. She turns to her mother and asks, "Why do you keep reading that same piece of paper? I thought you weren't going to bring any work with you."

"It's just a copy of an interesting article I brought along, not really work."

"You swear?"

"Yes, cross my heart."

Megan moves her eyes through the small oval window to her left, to a fading chalky white cloud that looks like the head of a horse—a billowy nose that doesn't seem to be moving, and wispy streaks that make up the long, wind-blown mane. She yawns and mumbles, "How long before we get there?"

Katie reclines her seat, "You don't want to know, honey, you don't want to know…"

Megan sighs and leans her head against her mother's shoulder, dreaming of Africa.

PART THREE

It was a typical stormy day in April, sporadic downpours and furious winds. The type of day Doctor Evan Drake had come to know well in East Africa. A black and white picture, ripped precisely from the tattered glue binding of a book he'd saved from his university days, hung framed in golden bamboo carved at ninety degree angles and joined with grass-thin leather laces of gazelle skin, which he had tied with the tips of his fingers and teeth one rainy Sunday trapped somewhere in Tsavo National Park. Lying on his back under flapping canvas and claps of thunder, raindrops fell stubbornly and more vociferously than the staccato taps of a brown-eared woodpecker's beak on young, green bark. The "daraja," the only bridge built across a river in the direction he wished to travel, had washed out. The ground, the ruts, the tired road, were for wading, not driving. And so he took to passing time. The framed picture was the only art, if one can call it that, which he still owned. One of the few nonessentials shipped over from America in five four-foot wooden trunks of worldly goods: books, clothes, diplomas, a digital camera, lenses long and wide. It was a picture of Henry David Thoreau and upon its filthy protective glass he had taped four scraps of paper, actually portions of a brown bag one might encounter while grocery shopping in the states, but obtained in Nairobi whilst picking up medical and other supplies (syringes, gauze, darts, rope, and a dozen vials). There, printed boldly across the recycled parchment and scribbled in blue ink which had faded since his arrival, were words that had touched him. On many mornings, while he lay on the single prickly mattress of straw that served as his bed, he read one or more of the sentences to himself from Henry David Thoreau's 1854 book *Walden*.

A man is rich in proportion to the number of things which he can afford to let alone; most of the luxuries, and many of the so-called comforts of life are not only not indispensable but positive hindrances to the elevation of mankind; I went to the woods because I wished to live deliberately, to front only the essential facts of life, and see if I could not learn what it had to teach, and not, when I came to die, discover that I had not lived.

To Evan Drake, Africa was his woods, his Walden Pond. It was a retreat from civilization, from university teaching, from corporations which usually focused on profits rather than the greater good of mankind, the earth, and its animals. Africa was a place to learn from, to save, and to protect. And so it is that Doctor Evan Drake came to the wilds of Africa—and stayed.

This morning is not different from any other. After running his eyes over Thoreau's words, he sits up and gives a blurry gaze to the scene framed within the open thatched door of what had become one of his home-away-from-homes, a modest hut, ten feet by ten feet. The hut was about as far as he could get from California. It was here—the ravaged bloody heart of Africa—that he intended to *live*, before he came to die.

No cable TV, no satellite dishes, no telephone. Simplify, simplify, was his intent when he arrived on the vast continent. Of course, his research, medical skills, and his tools left nothing to simplicity, but to Evan Drake they were second nature to him at this point; they were a part of him.

His only luxury these days—necessities to aid in accomplishing his work and making his way south to Johannesburg and north to Marsabit on occasion—are a beat-up fuel-hungry '85 Land Rover on its second engine, and a Cessna 150 provided by the National Wildlife Federation and a German environmental agency out of Hamburg. The Land Rover has scarcely an indication of paint, white originally, some olive green now. But the plane is almost like new, bullet holes the only exception, courtesy of elephant poachers who didn't appreciate Evan Drake's work and would rather see him dead than saving Africa's animals.

Today he is tired, as it's the first morning back from the climb. He hadn't really wanted to go. The only reason he did was because he knew he needed to blow some cobwebs out of his mind, get away for a few days. Just relax. And when three of the village men said he should come and rejuvenate his "hungry soul" there was little argument. He had ascended Mount Kenya on two occasions, but Kilimanjaro, which is more costly to climb and requires crossing the border to Tanzania, had gone untouched by his thick rubber-soled boots.

And so they traveled south as far as the Land Rover could take them, where the village men arranged for a guide and two porters. After purchasing food for the trip at the Arusha market, they made their way to Marangu Gate where hundreds of chaggas were looking for work, offering assistance with the climb. How sad, Evan thought, and how desperate these men must be to want to climb such a mountain, time and time again, most not even wearing proper shoes or even shirts. They look so frail, their thin backs vertical rows of knobs.

The first stop would be Mandara Hut, which from their perspective down at the gate appeared completely veiled in a thick blanket of fog. Totally invisible. Baboons, monkeys, and birds not common at lower elevations rustled about the rain forest, providing a chaotic greeting as if to say *Welcome to our mountain*, as the men walked toward the soupy air and first camp area.

Their guide wore a smile bright as a young elephant's ivory and his eyes glistened when he talked of his family and of Kilimanjaro, perhaps one in the same. "There is no need to move quickly," he said, wanting the fast-paced American to slow down, find a comfortable stride, lest be worn-out when the real work began—ascending to the summit. Evan heeded his advice.

It took two and a half hours to reach Mandara Hut, nine thousand feet. The air was moist, cool, and coated everyone's skin. Evan's spirit soon soared with each footstep of higher altitude, the animal poachers in the valley left far behind, a million miles away, it seemed.

At dinner, other climbers carried on about their adventure, people from Denmark, England, Brazil, and Germany. The meal consisted of mushroom soup, potatoes, carrots, and fresh bread. When darkness came everyone sauntered wearily off, readying for damp sleeping bags, sharing the pit toilet that reeked of waste and urine.

Morning brought the first view of Kilimanjaro's Kibo Peak and another few hours of climbing brought Horombo Hut, almost twelve thousand feet high. Along the route, four guides making their way downward inquired of Evan's pale face, "U mwananchi wa wapi wewe?" to which he replied, "Mimi ni Mmarekani." I'm American. They were testing him, he thought. No doubt they could have asked him in English, but a white man who speaks Swahili is one not to be taken advantage of, and is best avoided. Robberies are not uncommon in East Africa and he had learned this first hand within one week of his arrival from Johannesburg, losing an Omega watch and a pocket full of shillings. He ended up with a bump on the head and ten stitches by a nearly toothless kanzu seamstress.

One of the men continued with inquisitive eyes, "Ah...America. Elvis Presley, yes?"

Evan nodded and watched as the obviously inebriated man promptly began to play an invisible guitar, gyrating his hips and grinding is pelvis until his penis plopped from under his leather skirt, hanging like a snake from a parched tree. Evan turned toward the guide, whose eyes were big and white with surprise, and laughed. When he looked back to Elvis he was cackling and had his manhood completely out and it was now the guitar. "Who would have expected such talent on the trail to Kilimanjaro?" Evan said, holding his stomach with one hand and patting the guide on his bony back with the other. They continued on.

The way to Kibo Hut was less eventful. Less bumping and grinding. As they climbed higher they could see their tired breaths. The view became vast and of another planet. Evan stopped to catch some thin air and let the Mawenzi peaks leave an impression on his eyes—seventeen thousand feet worth. Further still, at Gillman's Point, which lies at almost nineteen thousand feet, with half the oxygen available to his lungs at sea level, he felt he could reach up and touch the pallid sliver of a moon above his head. Just grab it, swing from it, toss it like a boomerang.

On his way to Gillman's Point he passed what is considered to be a dangerous spot. He had heard of the Saddle area from many of the villagers and what he saw surpassed even their grandest descriptions. It was easy to see why so many visitors died here each year, gaping at the peaks, walking for far too long and much too aggressively. Acute Mountain Sickness claimed as many as fifteen people a season, sometimes more. Nausea, vomiting, headaches were the precursor to a painful death. Kilimanjaro had no patience for the weak or overly confident it seemed, yet Evan's trip had gone without any problems. And when he reached the bottom of the mountain yesterday, he indeed felt refreshed and renewed, and ready to return to work.

And now, back in Kenya's Tsavo region, the morning sun is beckoning him to rise and get on with the day, regardless of how sore his feet feel. He stretches his legs and twists his neck left and right, aching from his journey. *It's good to be back in Kenya*, he thinks as he slips on a pair of sandals and squints through red eyes at the waking village in the distance, beyond which Kilimanjaro's iconic snow caps he had treaded upon loom.

CHAPTER FIFTEEN

By afternoon Evan's elbows and freckled arms are planted squarely on the Land Rover's spare tire mounted to the rear bumper, binoculars held between his thumbs and forefingers. He is steadying best as he can to witness the dark figure running toward him. He can't tell who it is. Just thin legs moving through the torrid waves rising from the ground, the sun already beginning to bake the Kenyan sand, silt, clay and its resolute inhabitants. He pauses, lowering the binoculars, and looks about; sweltering savannas for as far as his eyes can see lead to the east, a sloping ramp of virgin forest to the south, where bloodied hands of poachers lay temporarily idle; they masquerade as trees and rocks and still waters in the day, then rape the land when shadows are long and nightfall comes.

Evan knows something is wrong, for to run in such heat for the distance between the hut and the village is foolish and would not usually be attempted, especially by a dark-skinned man, or even a boy intimate with Kenya. What could be the matter?

He jumps in the Land Rover and turns the key in the ignition. The engine hesitates, as it always does on the first start of the day, even worse with the heat. Driving toward the slim male figure, the features of the person's face become sharper. It is Simu Mukuka, one of the young men he had hired last month to clear a new airstrip a couple miles away on ground less prone to flooding and washouts.

"Doctor Drake, Doctor Drake," he yells, the words barely escaping between heavy breaths.

Evan slams on the brakes and puts the transmission lever to PARK, climbs out. "What is it Simu?" He places his hands on the boy's shoulders, waiting for him to recover, "Take your time..."

"I, I saw them."

"Who?"

"Banda and his men."

"How many?"

"Six."

"Guns?"

"Three rifles, maybe more."

"Did they see you?"

"I think so, Doctor Drake. I think so." He wipes his brow and says, "Are you going to go after them?"

There is a long pause, then Evan answers, "No, they'll be gone by now. But thank you for coming to tell me."

"Maybe we can—"

"It's for another day. Don't worry, they'll be back. I have to leave soon, Simu."

"To Johannesburg?"

Evan nods. "Just a couple days, that's all."

This was not what Evan had expected when he left the states to go work in Africa. Certainly he knew there were still problems with poachers, and he'd read about the recent increase in illegal hunting which, ironically, was largely due to the success of earlier protective efforts. But things were much worse than he could have imagined, partially driven by growing and condensed populations of elephants in protective, often remote, portions of the continent. Now there were areas of vast reserves carved out of the landscape and dedicated to wild animals. In several remote places the number of elephants had actually increased, becoming attractive, easy prey for poachers seeking to reap the higher price driven by the ban on most ivory trade. For some, the profits to be gained were making the risks of getting caught worth taking.

But why is this beautiful, precious land so often one of violence? Evan had asked himself this countless times since returning to Africa. As a boy he had lived in Kenya for two years with his father. Since then, nothing seemed to have changed, except the color of the skin of the perpetrators.

His family had a long, bloody history in the shadows of Kilimanjaro and Mount Kenya. Charles Drake, his grandfather, was a safari guide, or "Great White Hunter," as they were once called. He worked at the Mount Kenya Safari Club for a short time, soon after being purchased by actor William Holden, American Ray Ryan, and Swiss financier Carl Hirschmann in the late fifties. Evan's grandfather who, by chance, had met Holden on a safari—actually they were temporarily held up in a torrential downpour, hunting drinks at a bar in Nairobi—eventually became one of the club's experts in tracking down wild game, and teaching such skills to the elite visitors who would grace the property for months on end. Royalty, aristocracy, and the rich and famous of the entertainment and business world, all came to this faraway place to live out their fantasies of the Dark Continent.

Years before this, Evan's great-grandfather, Jonathan James Drake, had been the first of the family to leave America and chase such exotic dreams in Africa. He was an employee of Abercrombie & Fitch, one of the companies that outfitted what came to be called the "Grand Adventure," Theodore Roosevelt's massive safari of 1909. Roosevelt had recently left office after two terms and wanted to let the American public forget about him, at least for a while. "To get out of the way," as he put it.

And so Roosevelt disappeared to Africa. He hired a small army of assistants and set sail. Evan remembered the tales his great-grandfather would tell him as a kid, sitting at the knees of the crusty old man, staring curiously at him as smoke puffed from a pipe and saturated his clothes, burned his eyes. It was these stories, Evan now knew, that had lit his imagination and driven him, too, to Kenya. The description of harsh but lovely landscapes. The wild and dangerous beasts. The way his great-grandfather described the train ride from Mombasa to Nairobi, the sun illuminating the smoke spitting at the sky from the cast iron stack. Mouth wide, chin raised, Evan used to dream that the mahogany pipe, cradled delicately in the spotted, arthritic hand of his great-grandfather, was the boiler of that train, painting gray swirls on a background of bright blue Kenyan sky. He couldn't, as of late, remember the details of everything he heard on those sweet evenings sitting on the porch, taking exotic trips in his mind, but on occasion he would pull out a page or two of notes, now kept at his office in Johannesburg, which his great-grandfather had scribbled down before his death.

The seas were rough and the drinks were stiff. It took over a month to reach Mombasa, but we had finally pulled into port on April twenty-first, I seem to remember. I can still see vividly, to this day, old Teddy, or "T.R." as we called him, standing at the rail and gazing out at the green hills which swept from the west and became gentle waves that met the bow of our ship. The truth be told, I welcomed those soft seas and green hills wholeheartedly. If only the other waters between our new land and America were equally calm!

As we arrived at the shoreline, the waves lapped against the side of the ship and, with my weary body not ten feet from TR, he said with somewhat a relieved voice, "By godfrey, that's a wonderful sight," as he walked across the gangplank. We came ashore, TR first, his son Kermit, then three naturalists from Smithsonian who had taken well to the voyage, better than the crew, better than I. Our legs had scarcely enjoyed firm soil when we boarded a six car train owned by Governor Frederick Jackson. I rode in the third car from the engine, peeking my head through a cracked and warped window I had slid completely open with some effort, pinching a finger all the while. A blood blister promptly erupted and I relieved the pressure by means of my pocket knife and some discomfort.

The heat was stifling, almost unbearable really, and if it not for the glorious scenery, which offered some medicine for my seasick heart, I surely would have fell ill. But as it was, I managed to aim my face at the slight breeze this place afforded me, and when we came upon a turn lending itself to the engine wrapping toward the right, nearer to my viewpoint, I happened to catch a generous glimpse of TR, in all his splendor. Prior to departing Mombasa, we had bolted a chair, believe it or not, to the engine's cowcatcher! What a sight it was to witness a President of the United States riding the tip of our iron arrow, chugging mightily and merrily along. He stared through thick glasses at the wildness of Africa, glasses whose lenses bore more resemblance to binoculars in my opinion. But he stared in a grand way, pointing, moving his head left and right quite purposely, and craning his neck like the giraffes we passed some ten miles from the point of our departure. What a sight! When we happened upon a group of elephants, ten maybe twelve, I came to think TR would step from that cowcatcher to get a better look and surely kill himself. How awful, I thought, to be involved, however remotely, in the untimely death of such a great man. I think I would not have returned to the states in such event, God forbid.

We arrived weary and not of pleasant scent in Nairobi, and I, after assisting with the unloading of boxes and tents, immediately took to helping Tom Black with organizing the porters, which came to number approximately two hundred, perhaps more. Cooks. Tent people. Men who said they could protect us from the wild, and from people who might not appreciate our visit. To me, this was of greater concern than the lions, tigers, rhinoceroses, hyenas, and other beasts. I rather thought it might be best to stay close to TR, as he often carried a gun that was of a sort I had never seen. He called it a Double Barrel Nitro Express Elephant Gun, Holland and Holland, I think, and it was apparently a gift from British friends prior to our departure, so he said. I asked once if I may hold the gun, and TR said, "By all means," handing me it with confidence and quite abruptly. I nearly fell forward, sticking a foot out just in time to save me from embarrassment. I gladly gave quick order to returning the gun. TR said I could shoot it, once we were a good distance into the bush, and I nodded my head yes, pretending this to be exactly what I would like to do.

As we finally made our way from Nairobi, I found myself in a conversation with a gentleman whose job it was to track our expenses. He told me fifty thousand dollars had been budgeted and that TR was paying forty percent, and those chaps from Smithsonian sixty percent. He said he expected the actual costs to double. I told him that the job of President must pay quite well and he laughed. I do not know why. I must say, even after two weeks of sweltering sun, that TR proved himself to be a nice fellow, even to the hands working for us under the most trying conditions. And although the entourage supporting his adventure left little to chance, or discomfort, he also proved himself ready for challenge, either by terrain, weather, or animal. Or Masai warrior.

Later, after our grand adventure, I happened across a book TR wrote, and the words impressed me, as had the man: 'I speak of Africa in golden joys, the joy of wandering through lonely lands, the joy of hunting the mighty and terrible lords of the wilderness, but these are no words that can tell the hidden spirit of the wild, that can reveal its mystery, its melancholy, and its charm. The thrill of a fight with dangerous game, the awful glory of sunrise.'

I rather liked those sentiments.

CHAPTER SIXTEEN

At the international airport in Johannesburg, Katie and Megan walk down what looks like a brand new concourse, heading to the baggage claim area. Their legs feel like rubber, backs are sore, eyelids heavy. Katie had worried about Megan since they changed planes in London some ten hours ago. All the stress of travel couldn't be good for her, but the doctor had said she'd be fine. And indeed this seemed to be the case, for she hadn't complained once, except when a man with garlic breath sat down next to her with his fuzzy gray caterpillar eyebrows and softball-size elbows hogging all the space. She couldn't even stick the headphone plug into the armrest. To top it off, he snored with his head turned toward her, mouth open and creating three chins, for at least a thousand miles. "Maybe we can upgrade to first class on the way home," Katie had whispered in her ear.

They arrive at the hotel, just five miles from the airport and three miles from downtown Johannesburg, where Barb had tracked down at least one of the offices and labs of Doctor Evan Drake; much of his staff had apparently recently moved to a new facility on the outskirts of town.

As Katie pops open their luggage to make sure everything is okay, Megan pulls open the drapes and discovers a small balcony with two wicker chairs, one blue and one white. She looks over the railing. They are on the fifth floor above a pool and tennis court where two plump men are batting a ball with little success. In the distance she can see the city. "So *this* is Africa?"

"Yep. South Africa anyway." Katie hangs up a tee shirt dress in the closet. "Not what you were expecting?"

"No...not exactly."

"Don't worry, we'll get out of the city and up to Kenya and Tanzania. That's the Africa in your mind, the one you've dreamed of. We'll stay here until I can meet with those people I told you about, then we'll move north. A real safari, right?" she says, then walks up behind Megan and hugs her. She doesn't like keeping the truth from her daughter, but she doesn't want her to get her hopes up. She had simply told her on the plane that there was a meeting set up with a group of geneticists and business people. Megan just assumed that it was to do with Kentucky

Thoroughbred Center. It wasn't unusual for her mom and David to combine business travel with a quick vacation.

Megan moves away from the window and over to a mirror. "God I feel gross. Just look at me." She wipes the shininess from her forehead.

"Why don't you jump in the shower. It'll make you feel better."

Megan enters the bathroom and turns on the water. After running it for a couple minutes she realizes the H and C on the chrome knobs are reversed. She dips a toe in but pauses, thinking she better grab some shampoo to wash her hair. She walks over to the door, which is cracked open, and starts to pull it but stops, hearing her mother's voice; she's apparently on the phone to work, which she said she wouldn't do. Megan listens in on the call.

"David, she'll be fine."

"No, I haven't called over yet. I thought we'd get some rest. We're both exhausted."

"Yes, probably in the morning. That's when Doctor Drake is supposed to come in."

"Yeah, hopefully."

"No, I didn't tell her."

"Dammit I know it's a long shot."

"For god sakes, calm down. I don't want to hurt her either. But this might be the last shot she has."

As Megan continues listening, her forehead wrinkles and her lower lip begins to quiver. She turns her head slightly, trying to hear over the sound of water behind her. Her mother's voice softens as she continues.

"If they haven't found a donor by now, they probably won't. You know the statistics."

"I'm not trying to be cold, David. That's the reality and we have to face it."

"Okay. I will."

"Right, uh-huh."

"Okay, okay, I said I will."

"Love you too."

"All right."

"I want to get off before she gets out of the shower."

"Okay. Bye."

Poking her head around a corner, Megan watches her mother hang up and shake her head with her jaw cocked to one side, just as she does when she grinds her teeth while sitting in the cafeteria at the

100

hospital, waiting wearily for her to reappear after a treatment session. She then seems to take a deep breath, sits down on one of the beds, and flops backward. With glassy eyes, she just stares at the ceiling.

Megan wipes the tears from her moist cheeks and slips silently into the shower.

CHAPTER SEVENTEEN

In the morning Katie and Megan leave the hotel and head down to the street, to a small cafe with a patio in front framed by waist-high painted wood lattice. There are plastic tables with colorful umbrellas, plastic chairs. A dog, a mutt really, saunters behind a flowerpot that yields him some shade and scarfs down someone's leftover bagel. He takes his time and seems oblivious to Megan and Katie, as if he eats here every morning among the tourists and locals. "Look at that dog, mom. Isn't it cute?" Megan says as she points to the right. Their table is ten feet away from the furry scavenger.

"Yes, in an ugly sort of way." Katie wipes her mouth with her napkin, places it under her plate so it won't blow away. She turns to Megan and says, "At least it made you smile. What's wrong with you today?"

Megan doesn't answer. She just sips through her straw, soaking up some orange juice. "Do you think he has a home?"

"I think *this* is his home, honey. Just a stray, from the looks of him. Just like us..."

Ten minutes and at least ten buses go by. Katie pushes her bottle of water away and says, "I'm ready, how about you?"

Megan tosses a piece of bread to the dog and says, "All right."

"He's only going to want more, you know."

She nods and promptly throws the rest of her food down and says, "Here's some more fella."

Shaking her head, Katie stands and pushes her chair in, "Okay, let's get going." She leaves a few coins on the table and mother and daughter stroll to the sidewalk. "Are you sure you'll be all right waiting back at the hotel while I go to my meeting?"

Megan nods.

"Well, I don't want you leaving the pool or the lobby area, got it?"

"I know, mom, I know."

Katie looks about the street, sees that the hotel is at least six blocks away. "Maybe we should get a taxi, huh."

"I don't see any..."

As they begin walking in the general direction of the hotel, Katie notices a taxi letting passengers out across the street in front of a bank. She waves her arms and the driver sees her as he opens the trunk of his car. First letting several trucks pass by, she grabs Megan's hand and they run across, get into the taxi, and head back to the hotel to drop Megan off.

With her mom waving as the car drives off, Megan heads toward the hotel lobby, room key in hand. She enters a large glass door and, as she glances over her shoulder, sees her mom's concerned face aiming back through the rear window of the taxi.

The cool air conditioning of the hotel hits her sweaty face and she feels like melting into the polished marble floor, just lying on her back, catching her breath, staring at the giant ceiling above.

She arrives at the room.

The pool, yeah the pool, that's where I think I'll spend my time while mom's gone.

She cracks open her suitcase and several pairs of socks tumble out, some shorts, a tooth brush, and a half dozen panties rolled in neat little balls, all smelling like fabric softener mingled with underarm deodorant from the travel case which she had barely gotten zipped. Something must have leaked, she thinks. Sure enough, as she rummages through her home-away-from-home wardrobe, transplanting articles of cloths to the mauve and teal floral bedspread, she comes across the damaged cargo. What a mess. She gathers what she can, tosses the deodorant in the trashcan near the television-clock-radio, then rinses out a sweatshirt that has taken the brunt of the spill. It is surely ruined. *Have to buy a new one. Oh well, it's kinda bulky anyway,* she tells herself.

She finds her bathing suit, a navy blue one-piece with a thin yellow stripe running diagonally. She doesn't really like it all that much, but grandma had given it to her with cataract-stricken yet encouraging hazel eyes before they left, "You'll look so pretty in it," she said, holding it up and stretching it into place. So in the stuffed bag it went. Before they left, Katie had told her that if she wanted she could buy a new one in Africa. Megan liked the idea of buying a bathing suit in a foreign land. Maybe they'd be different or something, more exotic and sexy.

She tries it on. First tugging the drapes shut a bit to avoid voyeurs in the opposite wing, she slips her sandals, shorts, panties, bra, and tee shirt off, then admires herself in the mirror bolted to the wall by turning slowly, sticking her chest forward, buns rearward, and raising her chin. There was one good thing about having leukemia, she often thought. She was thin.

And if it not for her head, which only has about one inch of hair on it—every strand of which is the exact same length—she would consider herself fairly attractive. David had told her she looked cute with it short. He had hunkered down and framed his hands like some sort of famous director, Stephen Spielberg or something, and took different angles at her saying, "Yeah, I like it, I like it a lot. Looks like a Paris runway model." Then he went on to say how sexy Demi Moore looked in some old movie in which she appeared bald, *GI Jane* she seemed to remember, which they had watched on Netflix. "Yeah, right!" she said, then ran to her room crying and slammed the door.

She slips each of her extremely white legs in and pulls the crotch up until it can't go any further, then bends over to secure her breasts in each cup, pulls the loops over her shoulders, which suddenly look more freckled than she remembers. With everything adjusted, tucked in, sucked in, lifted up just about right, she looks in the mirror. She had tried it on at home, but it was late and she was tired, just going through the motions for grandma, paying no attention, and she hadn't seen herself with it on in a mirror until now.

It's hideous, she thinks as she again twirls around, head cocked over her shoulder like a super model. *Yuck!* The yellow stripe makes her look like someone has squirted mustard across her chest and the crotch is pinching something it shouldn't and the lower back is a little baggy and her boobs are hanging out the sides near her underarms, which looks kind of sexy, she thinks, but everything there is supposed to be up front, on display where it counts. That's what they do with the models in *Cosmopolitan*, which her mom reads.

Not five seconds later and she has the suit off and tossed in the corner with a wet towel from her shower earlier this morning. "Sorry grandma, the suit sucks," she says as she paces back and forth.

The sun is streaming in and she peeks her head between the curtains and looks down at the pool, water shimmering, people lounging everywhere, faces angled up at the sun, that glorious exotic African sun. Men carrying drinks around on trays held balanced on their palms. And there are at least three hunks sitting alone, reading or just watching the world go by. And here she is, stuck in the room with Ester Williams' bathing suit from 1945. What's next?

More pacing.

There is only one option. Well, actually there are two. She can head out of the hotel and go down to the street where all those shops are and buy a new bathing suit—but she's been ordered to stay put, her mom will kill her—or she can go for option two. So she walks naked over to her mother's suitcase, pops it open, and searches for a bathing suit. Any bathing suit, any color, any style. She doesn't know which one mom's brought. But who cares. It may be any one of a dozen suits ranging from the downright slutty backyard-only variety worn just for David to the navy one-piece with yellow stripe granny-gift variety.

It is something in between, a bikini, thank god. She pulls it out and untangles the strings and slips it on. The mirror is next. She purses her lips, spinning around once. Looks pretty good, she thinks as she adjusts the bottoms a bit and ties the top a little higher to raise herself. It's settled. She's ready for the pool.

She slips her sandals back on and they suddenly seem out of place. She tells herself she needs something higher, *much* higher. Cover models on *Cosmopolitan* higher. She looks down to the floor next to her mom's bed, running her eyes over all the shoes brought on the trip and placed neatly in a row. There is only one pair of pumps, red. *Way cool*, Megan thinks. Why her mom brought them to Africa, she has no idea. She slips them on. A little big but not bad. She'd borrowed her mom's shoes before. Certainly she won't mind. Again the mirror. A spin. Her rear looks higher and calves tighter. Yep, a done deal. She grabs some suntan lotion, the key to the room, and is off to the elevator, towel wrapped around her waist and all sophisticated like.

In the hallway a maid says, "Good day, madam."

Megan returns a smile. *Madam?* she hears repeating in her mind. She then presses the Down button for the elevator, turns to the maid and confidently says, "Good day to you too." As the doors slide open, she gingerly moves the high heels she's wearing over the small open crevice on the floor, between the elevator car and the doorway, as if she is carefully walking across hot coals.

CHAPTER EIGHTEEN

Evan Drake, who had arrived in Johannesburg last night from the Tsavo region of Kenya, drives his rented Nissan sedan down the long drive that winds toward and overlooks his new animal genetics facility, just north of the city. He can see two vehicles parked in front, a Toyota Land Cruiser and a Land Rover, both with World Wildlife Fund letters and logos painted across their sides.

He enters the gravel parking lot, tires crunching loudly, and comes to a stop, then reaches down and sets the brake handle, switches off the ignition, and picks up a satchel which he had placed some notes and correspondence in. He steps out of the car and, not paying attention, places his right boot squarely in the middle of an anthill. Thousands of tiny brownish-red worker ants flee in every direction like thick Kenyan coffee spilled over the sand, some soaking in, and some streaming toward the front right tire, up the sidewall and across the chrome wheel and lug nuts, then disappearing somewhere within the wheel-well. He shakes a few stray ants off his boots and pant legs, then moves quickly away while slamming the car door harder than usual.

This is Evan's first visit to the new Wildlife Breeding Research Center. He had heard from Michael Jenkins, the facility's director, that it was truly impressive, everything from the outdoor animal stalls with their automated gates and feeding system, to the lab space and genetic engineering equipment inside. Some of it was purchased from a lab which had closed in England, but much of the equipment was brand new. There were four new extractors for incubating and shaking test tubes. Ultraviolet lights in every room, which turn on automatically at night to kill germs. Six Perkin-Elmer GenAmp 9600 thermal cyclers for performing polymerase chain reactions, analyzing DNA. Five Thermolyne Temp-Tronic thermo cyclers. An anaerobe chamber. And two Applied BioSystems automated sequencers with laser verification. Michael said the facility had also obtained ten computers for analyzing and aligning DNA sequences, predicting phylogenetic relationships, and designing primers. And one wing had a new scanning electron microscope, tissue culture facilities, and a darkroom for autoradiographs.

But what really stood out was the Cray Origin super computer that had arrived only a week ago, purchased by the University of Tokyo to support both the Center's wildlife de-extinction programs. Michael could barely contain his excitement when he told Evan that it had arrived. "Damn things can scale to over a million processor cores," he said over the phone. Evan knew there was reason to be exited. The Cray was the most powerful tool available for genome structure analysis, database management, and molecular visualization. Unfortunately, the Center would only have a small portion of the time available on the massive computer, the majority of its up-time going to the University of Witwatersrand, Afrikaans University, and graduate students from Japan working on thesis projects. All in all, the new facility was one of the best in the world for analyzing and manipulating DNA.

The last time Evan was this eager to see a lab and animal facility was back in 1996 when he traveled to Scotland to see the Roslin Institute, where Dolly the sheep was created. The University of California at San Diego paid for the trip. Dolly had stunned the scientific community, as everyone had thought the processes that lead to the specialization, or differentiation, of cells during growth of the embryo and fetus were irreversible. To Evan, visiting the institute lit a fire in his belly and drove him to imagining applications for cloning which were previously believed to be impossible—saving endangered wildlife. He knew that if he could replicate Dr. Ian Wilmut's success in cloning a sheep, and clone other animals in Africa, there might be hope for many of the vanishing species there. In the case of Dolly, some called the process the researchers used nothing short of a miracle. Cells were taken from the udder of a six-year-old Finn Dorset ewe and placed in a culture with few nutrients. They essentially starved and stopped dividing, switching off their active genes. While this was occurring, an unfertilized egg cell was taken from a Blackface ewe. At this stage of egg development the condensed chromosomes, which appeared as a tightly compacted spindle structure, were literally sucked out, leaving an egg cell containing all of the other cellular capabilities to produce an embryo. The two cells—one from the Blackface ewe and one from the Finn Dorset—were then placed next to each other. An electric pulse was then applied, making the two cells fuse together. And another pulse of energy encouraged cell division. And voilà, a clone. The accomplishment helped spark a revolution in biotech and genetic engineering, and led to Dr. Wilmut being made a member of the Order of the British Empire by Queen Elizabeth the Second; he was knighted in 2008. For Evan, meeting Dr. Wilmut and seeing his facility was one of the highlights of his career and he never forgot the night Dr.

Wilmut told him where the name "Dolly" came from. Since the cell used as a donor for the cloning of Dolly was taken from a mammary gland, Dr. Wilmut said, "We couldn't think of a more impressive pair of glands than country and western singer Dolly Parton's."

Later, in 2003, Evan heard the news that Dolly had died, and it was at a much younger age than a typical sheep, which can live to about twelve years. Dolly was diagnosed with progressive lung disease and was euthanized at age six. She also had arthritis, which wouldn't normally be associated with a sheep of that age. This raised the question of whether the cloning procedures accelerated Dolly's aging and possibly caused her health issues. At the time of Dolly's death, some experts on ethics and cloning said that the nature of Dolly's death could have a huge impact on the possibility of producing a cloned human baby someday.

The air is thick, the sort that you can crawl into and lose yourself in for a few hours, daydreaming and soaking in the heat until it warms the marrow of your bones.

Even the diseased marrow of your bones.

The last vacant chaise lounge is Megan's and its nylon straps and aluminum frame are nearly too hot to set her body against. A frail man in sandals and a shirt with the hotel's name embroidered across the front pocket approaches and picks up soiled wet towels and dirty glasses with lipstick prints on their rims, tiny pink umbrellas and long crooked straws resting inside. Megan listens to him as he softly sings in a monotone throaty voice a song she's never heard.

As he nears he says, "Hello, would you like a large towel, ma'am?"

There's that ma'am thing again, just like the maid called me. Megan adjusts her hat, not looking upward at the man. "Yes, please."

"Very well, I bring you two, maybe three, no. It is very hot today. And would you like something to drink?"

"Uh, do you have ice tea?"

"Yes...ma'am, with lay-mon," he says at length.

"That would be fine." She watches him walk off, humming and moving his head back and forth slightly.

Her eyes then take inventory of all the seemingly sophisticated foreign people gathered around the pool. Over near the diving board is a pot-bellied man with silver hair smoking a cigar and holding a drink in each hand as a woman wearing a loose floral blouse and white shorts, sandals, rubs white globs of lotion into his white globs of skin as he blows smoke like one of those buses she had seen chugging by the cafe this morning.

Megan can hear the couple talking. "Oh baby, that feels good," he says way too loudly, tilting his neck all around, and the woman says, "You're already burnt, Henry."

Megan is handed three freshly dryer-puffed towels and a tall glass of tea with a plastic flamingo floating in a sea of ice, slice of lay-mon, and a few escaped seeds. She paves the lounge chair with folded layers of terry cloth and when her rear hits the straps this time she can't detect the intense scorching heat.

"Thank you," she says, and the man whistles as he nods, heads over to Harry and his pale female companion.

When noon arrives the sun is pounding down at its brightest and hottest. It's the most intense heat Megan has ever felt. She's lying on her stomach when she hears a voice, "Ma'am, I have a drink for you."

"What?" She ties the strap of her mom's bikini about her neck, rises to her elbows. Squinting. "I didn't order another drink." She looks at the empty ice tea glass beside her.

"That man over there bought it for you. See? The one with the red bathing suit, with his feet in the water. See him?"

"Yes, yes. Please set it down on the table."

"Okay, yes ma'am."

"Thank you." She feels her heart throbbing in her chest, seemingly making her top tighter with each beat. *A man sending me drinks? Doesn't he know I'm just a kid?*

Hiding under the brim of her large hat, which suddenly seems too small, she tries to rally enough courage to take a peek and give him a nod of thanks, which she fears will then lead to him coming over to talk. *What then?*

He comes over to talk. He's at least six feet tall, bronze from his perfectly shaped brown curls to his perfectly manicured toes, not even a hair on them, she notices. Washboard stomach you only see in *Teen Magazine*. A red speedo bathing suit that looks like he has a sock stuffed in it, the big tube kind she used to use for soccer, she thinks as he sits down next to her, other side of the table.

"Aren't you going to drink it?" he asks with a smile made of what must be capped teeth; they catch fire and shoot a glare in every direction. More squinting.

"Yes, thank you for sending it over."

"No problem, I thought you'd enjoy it. It's a strawberry margarita with top shelf tequila. Do you like them?"

"Yes, oh yes," Megan replies as she reaches for the glass and the first margarita she's ever tasted. She had taken maybe two sips of alcohol in her entire life, Coors Light at a Christmas party when her mom said she could try a sip. She pushes the little umbrella to one side and takes a long drink of the margarita, which causes an instant chilling headache.

"Is it good?"

"Yes, real sweet." She licks the salt from her lips, attempting not to show any pain from the brain freeze.

"My name is Philip."

"I'm Megan."

"That's a lovely name."

"Thanks."

"Wonderful day isn't it." He looks about the pool.

"Yeah, a bit too hot though, I think."

"You are an American, no?"

"Yes."

"All foreigners say it is too hot in South Africa, yet they come during their winters anyway, they always come."

She nods, not knowing what to say, then, "Where are you from?"

"Brazil. I'm here on business."

Sure, she thinks, *business at the pool...*

"I have meetings this afternoon."

"What do you do?"

"I'm a buyer, a gold buyer, and I sell emeralds."

"Wow, really?"

"Yes, I come to Johannesburg several times a year. My company has an office here."

She takes another sip, stalling, searching for words.

"If you don't mind me saying," he continues, "I must tell you, you are an incredibly beautiful young lady." He runs his eyes over her, starting at her legs.

With this, Megan chokes slightly on the margarita and then clears her throat.

"Too much salt?" he asks with a concerned look.

"Yes, a bit."

The singing towel man approaches, sets a couple more down at the foot of Megan's chaise lounge. She smiles. He smiles. Then he and the song he's singing fade away behind a palm tree and disappear near the cabana bar.

Philip looks at her back as only a man who sells jewels and buys gold and lives in Brazil can, she thinks to herself as he says to her, "You know, I believe you're starting to burn. Would you like me to put some lotion on your back?"

"Oh, no, no thanks."

"Really, you look quite red, I insist."

"Uh, well...sure, I guess."

He scoots his chair closer and grabs the oil-free-banana-coconut-aloe-vitamin-E lotion, SPF-30, next to the sweating margarita.

Holy shit, holy shit, Megan thinks as she feels the cold lotion hit her back and the smooth brown hands of a stranger—who looks like that suave Latin guy on the soap opera her grandma watches—begin to rub in between her shoulder blades and down the tingling bumps of her spine.

His touch tickles her skin and makes her smile wider than she has smiled since becoming sick, and she feels lightheaded from the margarita.

He thinks I'm a beautiful young lady, she says to herself as she tries to manage a breath, *I'm a beautiful young lady...*

CHAPTER NINETEEN

Dust is swirling upward and a dozen people are gathered at the iron bars separating the elephant pen from the lab's rear entrance. Evan can't see what they are looking at, but he can hear a distinct cry, the cry of an African elephant in pain. He had heard such sounds before, once when he came across a baby on the Serengeti whose mother had been shot through the neck and left for dead, and once in Tsavo National Park, a matriarch which had apparently been rammed with the bumper and bush guards of a Jeep or Land Rover. Both legs broken on her left side.

The cries are louder.

He runs down the sterile central hall of the new facility. *Why would Rosie be crying?* he asks himself then sees one of the lab's employees, Michelle, and yells, "What's wrong?"

"Hurry!" is all she says in reply.

Other heads turn and several of the lab's personnel wave him over. He runs through a storage area and out a doorway to the back pens. Michelle sees him coming and runs to meet him halfway. "It's Rosie, she's got a foot stuck in the fence. George is trying to get her out but I think he's making it worse."

They run side by side to where everyone else is standing, pointing, some holding a hand over their mouth. Evan yells, "Get out of the way," then opens the gate, walks in slowly. At the far end of the pen, where a chain-link fence runs forty feet, from the man-made rocks at the left to the feeding troughs at the right, Rosie stands with her rear legs straight and her front legs bent at the knee, one of which is planted on the ground, the other resting on some drainage rocks on the other side of the fence. She has somehow managed to stick a foot through, or under, and get it caught. Evan sees blood pooling on the dirt. And George, a graduate student from Cape Town, is poking at Rosie's shoulder and neck, screaming, "No, no, no, get away, get away, away!" and now Evan can see what looks like a laceration running six inches near her knee, muscle or ligaments exposed.

Not wanting to upset Rosie any more than she already is, Evan moves slowly toward George's back. He sees Rosie's head turn toward him and tears running down her cheek from her glassy gray eyes, leathery eyelids. She lets out a cry that rattles the fence.

"No, no, no," George continues screaming, his face on fire and the stick in his hand thrusting at Rosie's side, her ribs, her back.

Evan yells, "Stop it god dammit, stop it!"

The stick continues to swing like a golf club and thuds against Rosie's thick wrinkled skin as she tries to pull her leg free, only getting the chain link wire further into her tissue. More blood.

George continues, "No, Rosie, no! Bad, bad—"

Evan reaches forward and grabs George by the neck and pulls him back. His face is covered in spittle and dirt and his eyes seem as big as Rosie's. He searches for the stick and yanks it out of George's hand, then pokes at his stomach just hard enough to get his attention, scare him a little but not hurt him, "How's it feel? Feel good, does it? How do you like it, George?" Evan asks. He then cracks the stick over his knee and throws the two pieces over the fence as George stumbles back, falling on his ass into what must be the world's largest pile of elephant dung.

"It's okay, girl, it's okay." Evan runs his hands over Rosie's left ear and feels the blood pumping. An African elephant's ears are made to cool its blood in the squelching heat, to serve as radiators if you will. They are larger than an Asian elephant's ears due to the extreme African temperatures. Rosie's feel like they will explode any second. Deep, thumping pulses.

"You'll be all right, you're okay," Evan says softly.

He hears her breathing and sees her chest heaving. As he leans down on one knee, he slips in some mud and struggles to stand. He grabs onto the fence.

Ten yards away, Michelle turns to Jim Watson, the maintenance supervisor, and asks, "Do you have any wire cutters?"

"Uh, I've got some clippers for the bushes, they might work. I might have some cutting pliers too."

"Good, get them."

As Jim walks into the main building, Michelle stands with a hand over her mouth, shaking, and watches Evan. She sees him rubbing Rosie's trunk, talking softly but not doing anything else, just rubbing. Then he walks around to her other side and, upon reaching higher ground, moves his hands over Rosie's head. More talking, more whispering. Michelle tries to hear what he is saying but cannot make it out. Rosie's eyes, which have been blinking quickly and darting about, seem to slow and her head drops some.

Jim returns, out of breath, and says, "Here, I don't know if they'll go through the fence though."

"Thanks." She holds them up above her head and yells, "Evan, Evan," and he looks over and nods twice. He pats Rosie a couple times more and then walks over, moving backward, never taking his eyes off the frightened elephant's face, then reaches behind his back and opens his right hand. Michelle places the snippers, blade down, into his palm and he makes his way back to Rosie.

"You're gonna be just fine, girl, just fine." Evan drops to his knees again, next to where her leg is stuck, and carefully places the blades of the snippers around a piece of chain link fence. Squeezing. The metal pops through and he quickly pulls a piece out of Rosie's flesh. She jerks her head back and forth but amazingly doesn't pull on her leg.

"Good girl, good girl, stay, stay."

A few more snips and he thinks the hole is large enough for her to pull her leg out.

"Careful now, careful."

She backs up a couple of feet and then pauses, sniffing her wound with the tip of her trunk.

"Okay, come on, come on, back, back, back, Rosie. That's a good girl. Little more. Back, Rosie. There you go, there you go..."

Her leg free, she sets her foot down in the mud and Evan moves a few feet away, then turns toward Michelle and yells for her to get some stainless steel staples, alcohol, and gauze bandages. He also says, "Get George out of this facility before I kill him."

Within ten minutes Rosie is tended to, and resting under a tree on the exact opposite side of the pen, as far as she can get from the hole in the fence. The sun crosses the blue sky some more, and there's finally calm in the air.

Katie had witnessed the whole thing. She had been standing outside the front entrance in the parking lot, peering through a fence. A taxi had dropped her off just as the accident unfolded, and she wasn't sure what to think when she saw the young elephant get poked with a stick and yelled at. She was stunned. Back home, any employee caught abusing one of the horses in that manner would be fired on the spot.

With the chaos over, Katie walks to the front entrance and makes her way to a reception area. No one around. Everyone still out back apparently. So she heads down a corridor where she sees people standing under an overhang. A few are shaking their heads. As she nears, she sees the man who had been so furious with the younger man just seconds ago, pat the injured elephant's back with absolute tenderness, say something

114

to it, then climb the fence where its foot was stuck. He carefully moves over the top and down the other side, takes a few steps, then bends over and picks up an apple. He takes a bite and the nectar rolls down his chin as he throws it over to the elephant's eagerly awaiting trunk, which is swinging back and forth like a clock pendulum. All the elephant had wanted was an apple on the other side of the fence.

Katie suddenly realizes that everyone is staring at her, except the man climbing back over the fence.

"May I help you," Michael says as he approaches. The tone of his words convey that he isn't happy about her just walking into the facility by herself.

"Uh, yes, sorry, no one was at the reception area and—"

"We had a bit of an emergency."

"Yes, I know. I was watching. Is the elephant okay?"

His voice softens somewhat, "She'll be fine." When he is within a few feet of her he continues, "Now, what can we do for you?"

"I'm here to see Doctor Evan Drake. Is he in?"

"Yes. Is he expecting you?"

Katie answers, "No," then pulls a business card from her back pocket. "I'm with a thoroughbred horse breeding facility in the U.S.," she continues, thinking she better come up with an innocuous reason for being there.

He takes the card. "Kentucky Thoroughbred Center?"

"That's right."

"I think I've heard of it."

She nods. "We've gotten quite a lot of press lately."

"I'm Michael Jenkins," he says with a forced smile, extending his hand. He was clearly still stressed out over the incident.

A man wearing a white lab coat approaches and Katie's eyes move to him as she asks, "Is that Doctor Drake?"

"No, Evan is outside."

"I see. Could you tell him I'm here, please?"

"Sure, but I doubt you'll want to talk to him right now. He's probably not in a great mood after what happened out there. But hang on and I'll find out if he'll see you."

Suddenly a door swings open and Evan walks in, covered in mud and worse things up to his knees. His face is red. Sweaty. He says, "Michael, keep these damn students away from Rosie. Did you see that idiot out there? Where the hell were you?"

"I was in the lab."

115

Evan shifts his attention, looks curiously at Katie.

Michael continues, "This lady would like to speak to you."

"Yeah, who are you?" he asks in a manner that tries to be pleasant but somehow fails. He wipes his forehead on his sleeve, then bends down and starts to untie his boots. "Not another newspaper or television reporter, I hope."

"No," Katie replies, looking down at his head, neck, as he continues to remove his boots. "I'm from the United States. I'm with a horse breeding and genetics facility in Kentucky."

The boots go flying over to a corner, sprinkling mud and dung across the tile floor. Evan straightens his back and starts to unbutton his shirt and says, "Horses?"

"Yes."

"I heard they cloned one up there."

"Yes, that's right. It was us." She pulls out another card and holds it out for him but he just keeps unbuttoning then slips off his shirt altogether. Katie immediately notices a diagonal scar running some six inches from his neck to below his left collarbone where it gets lost in swirls of brown and golden curls. As he looks down at her business card she studies his chest, his stomach, his arms, which have tan lines and freckles. Firm. Well-worked.

"Sorry about this mess," he says. "I don't usually greet visitors like this."

"I understand."

Finally he takes the card, holds it up. "Kentucky Thoroughbred Center, huh."

"Right, we're mapping the horse genome, and we offer breeding services, including cloning."

"I see." He sticks the card in his back pocket and says, "I'm Evan Drake, pleased to meet you. Pardon me for not shaking your hand, with all this dirt."

"Katie Ryan," she replies. "A little dirt won't hurt me." She extends her right hand and they shake as he offers an even but reserved, tight-lipped smile and his eyes crease at the corners.

"You're here to see me?"

"Yes, but I can come back later if this is a bad time, which it obviously is."

"Well ma'am." He clears his throat. "If you can hang on for ten minutes or so, I'll go clean up a little."

"Okay."

116

"Just have a seat over there," he says as he points to a glassed-in conference room near the entrance. He walks over and picks up his boots and shirt.

About fifteen minutes later she sees him making his way from across the main hallway. She watches him until he looks over at her, then lowers her eyes to the table before her. She feels guilty for using the Thoroughbred Center as an excuse for being there, *But what choice did I have? I couldn't have told him the real reason I'm here, not when he was so upset. Just stay calm, Katie. Work into it. Go slow.*

He walks in and says, "What a day," as he shakes his head.

"Is the elephant all right?" she asks.

"You saw what happened?"

"Yes. Terrible, just terrible."

"Yeah, Rosie will be okay. Just some stitches. Few mental scars. They'll be the hardest to heal." He sits down a few chairs away from her. "So tell me, what brings you to Africa, Ms. Ryan."

"Please call me Katie."

"All right, and please call me Evan."

She looks down, feels her skin becoming flushed, nervous. So much for going slow and staying calm, she tells herself, then suddenly decides to come clean, for she thinks if she lies or plays games it will surely damage any chance she has of obtaining his help. She clears her throat, looks up at him and says, "I must tell you, I am not here on behalf of my company. I—"

"You're looking for a job?" he interrupts.

"Oh no, no that's not it." She pauses then, "This isn't easy for me to say." Again she looks down at the table. "I need your help."

"Help? Help with what?"

"My daughter," she replies then glances over at the door to the conference room, which is open. "Could we have some privacy?"

"Sure." He gets up and shuts the door, then sits back down. He watches as she pulls some hair behind her right ear, and sees that her eyes are becoming moist and her hands are trembling slightly.

She continues, "My daughter, Megan, is very sick. She has leukemia." Another pause.

"I'm very sorry."

"Thank you. Anyway, we haven't been able to find a suitable blood marrow donor. She's in some level of remission right now, but we know it won't last forever."

"Ma'am, I mean, Katie, I don't know how I can help you. You

117

didn't come all the way down here *just* to see me, did you?"

She nods twice then looks up at him, "Yes, I'm afraid so." She studies him; his eyes are sparkling brown and his hair is parted from left to right, but pulled back some; short in back; a widow's peak defines his forehead.

He raises a hand and rubs downward over his face then says, "Katie, why are you here?"

She decides to come out with it, just get to the point. Taking a deep breath first she says, "I want you to save my daughter's life. She needs a matching bone marrow donor."

He leans forward slightly, his eyes confused.

"I know this may sound absurd, at least at first," she says with a shaky voice, "but I plan to have some of my eggs removed and, and then I want you to combine Megan's DNA with them so I can give birth to an identical twin of her—the perfect bone marrow donor."

His eyebrows raise as he scoots his chair away from the table, face going completely blank. Then his jaw moves side to side a few times and he shakes his head slowly.

"Please," she says as she wipes a tear from her cheek, "you're our only hope. We just need—"

"You want to *create* your own donor?" he asks, though he knows he heard her correctly. "An identical twin of your daughter?"

"Yes, that's right."

Not wanting to upset her further, he searches for what to say. "Uh, Katie, I appreciate what you and your daughter must be going through, really I do, but I no longer do any work in human genetics or assisted reproduction, as you probably already know. I only work with endangered animals."

"Yes, I know. But you've clearly been more successful than anyone else. You've cloned more species than any doctor in the field, by far."

Again, his head shakes, "I'm sorry. I really can't help your daughter. Megan is it?"

"Yes," she answers with a sniffle. The tears are streaming down now.

He reaches over to a credenza and picks up a box of Kleenex, hands it to her then says, "I just can't believe that you came all this way. I wish you would have called, first. This can't be easy. Did you come by yourself?"

She shakes her head no. "I brought Megan with me."

118

"Good lord..."

He runs a hand through his hair, looks at the ceiling, looks at the floor, and then at Katie, "I'm so sorry."

CHAPTER TWENTY

The note said, Mom, I went down to the pool, love Megan. Back from her meeting with Evan Drake, Katie changes her clothes, slips on shorts and a tee shirt, sandals, and wonders why her suitcase is open, with clothes strewn across the hotel bed.

She waits a couple of minutes for what ends up being a packed elevator, descends with silent faces all aimed the same direction, then exits at ground level. As she pushes a large brass handle attached to a glass door that leads from the lobby to the pool and patio, she doesn't see Megan anywhere. There are two men over near a bar. An older woman wearing a robe is reading a newspaper with her feet dangling in the shallow end of the pool. A couple kids are splashing about, throwing a beach ball. And over near the diving board there's a woman on her stomach with a man rubbing creamy lotion over her bright red back.

She's wearing a bathing suit just like mine, Katie thinks as she walks around the edge of the pool. Her legs feel heat rising from the cement, and steam floats over the areas where the kids have splashed water, which smells like chlorine.

She sits near a small round table with a glass top, metal legs. Her eyes slowly adjust to the brightness. The woman on her stomach turns over and Katie leans forward in her chair, trying to get a better look, the vinyl straps of the chair digging into her thighs. While squinting her eyes and raising a hand above them to provide shade, she whispers to herself, "Megan? No, it can't be..."

Katie is dumbfounded for several seconds, completely shocked. It is as if she's looking at a person she doesn't know. Not a girl. Not her daughter. Not a leukemia patient fighting for her life. But a young woman. A beautiful, dazzling, and curvaceous young woman. It suddenly strikes her that her little girl isn't so little anymore, and this realization almost outweighs the fact that some strange man is rubbing lotion into Megan's skin. Almost.

Katie stares from afar for about a minute, deadpan, just watching this lovely thing she had brought into the world seemingly yesterday. She thinks of the difficult delivery she had that rainy night Megan was born, and the way Megan ran her hands through the pink cake frosting on her first birthday, and she sees the Christmas tree tip over when Megan was three and tugging on a branch, then she hears the shrill cry on that first day of kindergarten and Mrs. Langdon saying, "Don't worry, she'll be fine," and she feels the quivering body of a girl who had just found out she had what could be a terminal disease. She starts breathing faster. *God I love her so.*

Katie stands and walks over as the man puts the cap on the bottle of lotion, sets it aside, next to four empty glasses.

Four empty glasses!

Megan hears her mother's voice. "Megan, is that you?" She tilts the brim of her hat up and her mother comes into view, her dark silhouette eclipsing a ball of fire high above. "Uh, hi," is the only thing she can pull from her mouth.

Katie says, "Nice bathing suit."

"Oh, thanks."

"I see you've met a friend."

"Yes, yes, this is Philip," she stammers, then sits up a little too fast and feels tipsy, the hotel drinks making an impact. Her eyes move to Philip as she continues, "Philip, this is my—"

"I'm Megan's *sister*, Katie," she interrupts as she leans forward and shakes his oily, thoroughly moisturized hand. She then looks at Megan, whose eyes seem as white and round as the paper coasters resting under the empty glasses.

"Pleased to meet you," Philip says warmly. "Would you care to join us for a drink?" His smile says, ménage à trois anyone?

Megan's head shifts to the empty glasses, then to her mom's eyes.

"No thanks," Katie replies, "I think I'll head back up to the room. Just wanted to get some fresh air for a minute."

"I'll go with you," the words fly between Megan's red lipstick-covered lips as she stands, and slips on the shoes that she'd tucked under the lounge.

"I just love those high heels on you, Sis," Katie says at length, in a voice at least half an octave higher than normal.

Megan doesn't respond. She just says, "Philip, thank you for the drinks. I enjoyed talking with you."

"Uh, you're both leaving?"

"Maybe we'll see you around the hotel."

"Yes, yes, of course," he says as he stands, mouth curled downward, his facial expression pleading.

"Nice meeting you Philip," Katie says as she starts to walk away. She turns to Megan, "Come on, Sis."

Megan follows at a distance, struggling to tame the high heels.

In the morning Katie and Megan go downstairs to the hotel cafe for breakfast. The buffet has scrambled eggs, hash browns, bacon, sausage, pancakes, waffles, and stacks of muffins and it costs fifteen dollars American. There are heat lamps, six of them, keeping everything warm and toasty. There are two dispensers for the coffee, regular and decaf. Both varieties are from Kenyan slopes. White linen napkins are piled at the end of the table next to the silverware which is stacked neatly. Orange juice is available, if you like, and there are also pitchers of milk, two percent and skim, and ice water.

"Looks good, doesn't it?" Katie says as they get in line.

"Yeah, I guess," Megan replies, trying to see what's left. They had slept in.

They load their plates with pancakes, some sort of fake syrup, and a few slabs of butter. Real authentic African cuisine, Katie thinks as she fills her plate.

"Maybe Philip will be coming down for breakfast, huh?" Katie says. It is the first time she has mentioned yesterday's charade.

Megan replies, "Yeah, maybe, Sis."

Katie smiles.

"Mom, I just want to thank you for not embarrassing me yesterday. I'm sorry I wore your bathing suit. Mine looked terrible. And that Philip guy, he, well, he just sat down and started ordering me drinks. I just wanted to get some sun, you know, and we got talking. Are you mad at me?"

Katie finds an empty table, sets down her plate. "No, I'm not mad. Don't worry about it. But you might want to cut down on the drinking. I'd hate to see you get locked up in a foreign country." She takes a bite of the pancakes and watches as Megan nods with absolute seriousness, then sips some orange juice.

PART FOUR

For the next three days they mainly took to running themselves over the texture of the city. Tourists in a foreign land, gazing, smelling, touching. They peered down from the observation deck of the Carlton Centre and felt the warm air drape over their wide-eyed faces, blow through their tangled hair and scalp, make goose bumps of their reddened skin. They visited a mine, Cullinan, and descended into the earth in a chilled and darkened shaft, vanishing under the sun and sand like nocturnal beings, seeing diamonds harvested then cut at precise angles and set in gold and silver. Rings. Necklaces. Bracelets. They set aside one day for a bus tour of Pretoria, Sun City, and Pilanesberg National Park, a crater of an extinct volcano. Strange trees. Birds. People from faraway places with faraway accents and words. Several times they were approached by young boys who asked if they would like to buy some *dagga*. Katie didn't know what they meant until one of them pinched his thumb and forefinger, raised his hand to his lips, and pretended to deeply inhale, then smiled. "No thanks," Katie replied each time.

Katie would call over to the lab and animal facility every day, May I speak to Doctor Drake please. I'm sorry, he's not here, may I take a message, no I'll try back, thanks. A call in the morning. A call in the afternoon. Same results.

Wednesday, nine o'clock, after breakfast. Katie watches as Megan—wearing the same bikini again but not the buy me drinks and rub lotion on me salacious high heels—heads down to the pool, the door clicking behind her. Finally alone, Katie wants to call home and check in with David. The raspy computer-chip voice of the answering machine comes on, beeps, and Katie says, "David are you there? David? Pick up the phone."

But David doesn't pick up. He's apparently not screening calls.

She hangs up and calls the office, wondering whether he could actually be at work.

Barb answers, "Kentucky Thoroughbred Center, may I help you?"

"Barb, it's Katie."

"Hey, we were just talking about you. How's the trip so far?"

"Wonderful, just wonderful. Really relaxing."

"Good, good."

"We're still in Johannesburg. The weather is beautiful."

"I'm jealous. It's been raining here for days. How's Megan?"

"She's fine. We've both been getting too much sun and too much food though."

"Well, it *is* a vacation, right?

"You got it. Say, I just called home and David didn't pick up. He wouldn't happen to be there would he?"

"Sure is. You won't believe it, but he's been coming in early and staying late every day since you left."

"You're kidding."

"No. It's like the old David is back. He's in practically every meeting, hundred and eighty degrees from the way he's been. Looks like your plan is working."

Katie takes a deep breath, glances at the rays streaming in from the window and says, "Thank God."

"Hang on a second, and I'll go get him. Okay?"

"All right."

Barb puts the line on hold and walks back to David's office, as he has his phone forwarded to voice mail and she can't ring him. The door is cracked open and she pushes it open. He's not there. She heads over to the main conference room, where she hears voices. He isn't there either but she asks, "Do you guys know where David is? Katie's on the phone."

Ted turns toward the window and says, "He's outside." He points toward the barn. Barb moves closer and sees David on horseback, meandering down the hill toward the south pasture. "Oh shoot, well, guess she'll have to call back," she says then walks to the reception area and picks up the phone, "Katie, are you still there?"

"Yes."

"David is out riding. He's heading down south hill. On Starbuck, I think."

"He's riding? Really?"

"Yeah. Like I said, the old David is back. Want me to send someone after him?"

"Um, no, no that's all right. I'll try back. Just tell him that I called and everything is okay. Be sure to tell him that Megan's having a great

125

time, and feels just fine, okay."

"Sure will."

And with that they say their good-byes and Katie hangs up and walks over to the hotel room's balcony. She rests her hands on the hot rusted metal of the railing and peers down, sees Megan sitting by the pool, legs crossed, reading a magazine. Good news, she's not drinking margaritas and no one is trying to pick her up. And the hat is veiling her face, so her red nose shouldn't get any redder.

Afternoon settles in. It's a thick one. It swallows the dry air whole. All at once there is humidity. Billowy clouds from the west dot the sky, pink vertical streaks below and white balloons on top. Thunderstorms crackle in the distance. Lightning shoots at the balloons and they *pop, pop, pop.*

A lovely, albeit wet, day in Africa.

When the rains finally let up, Katie leaves the hotel. The roads have more potholes than pavement, she thinks as she downshifts the sedan and turns left on Jan Smuts Avenue, heads through Parktown, Rosebank, and Dunkeld. She had rented the car yesterday and ventured out twice, purposely avoiding the main arteries and the heart of the city. Two previous hair-raising rides in a taxi had convinced her that perhaps she could handle driving on the opposite side of the road. So she had decided to take a chance with the rental car. If she got lost, well, she got lost. And so with credit card and Kentucky license in hand, Dolphin Car Hire had handed over the keys to an almost new sedan. Only three hundred miles.

Some fifteen minutes after leaving Megan at the hotel, she reaches the two-lane road that meanders to the Wildlife Breeding Research Center. Hopefully Evan Drake is in today. She figures that she's been given the brushoff each time she called and talked to their testy receptionist.

Better to just show up and make one last plea for Evan's help, she thinks. *He has to help, he just has to.*

The engine settles some as she changes gears and cranes her neck forward. Almost there.

On the side of the street, a woman in flowing white fabric, no shoes, no smile, turns and looks at her. She carries a canvas bag under one arm and a jug of something under the other. Large hoop earrings adorn her smooth shiny face. Her steps are more pensive as the soles of her feet meet the dirt shoulder of the road. Katie sees the white fabric billow outward from dark-skinned, taut, and shapely legs, a sail catching a breeze and ballooning out from its strong mast. Katie moves the sedan slowly by, carefully. The road is narrow. Still no smile from the woman.

One mile ahead a Land Cruiser is coming down a serpentine hill, though Katie can't see it, too many blind curves. A trailer is attached to its chrome ball, a safety chain, connections for brakes and lights too. Inside, a man and a woman are fastened and the windows are down all the way, permitting a sticky hot wind to enter. The woman turns to the man and says, "Better slow down, my love, we have a heavy load today."

He nods and moves the transmission lever to first and the engine whines as it slows the vehicle. The trailer gives a nudge to their backs.

"Do we need gas?" the woman asks.

"No, we're okay. I already filled the tanks. What did you think I was doing this morning while you slept in?"

She doesn't reply and just shakes her head.

They drive in silence for almost a minute, save the squeal from one of the trailer brakes. A few of the animals in back cry and growl and whimper to be let out. Although they are sedated, they behave nervously. Pacing and climbing. Clawing. They push on their bar and wire cages, some rusty, some new and painted green, which are tied with ropes to the flatbed, except the two lion cages bolted down directly over the two axles.

As Katie approaches a curve, left to right, three shirtless kids dart in front of her and the rental sedan's bumper just misses one of them. She slams down on the brake pedal, heart pounding, and watches as the kids laugh and point at her then walk away, kicking rocks with their sandaled feet. She puts the car in first and eases out the clutch while moving her eyes back and forth from the rearview mirror to the spindly gravel road ahead. The kids get smaller. One of them picks up a rock and tosses it toward the rear of the car, but she doesn't hear it hit.

As she reaches a hairpin corner, she's at least three feet on the wrong side of the road. There's no yellow or red or white line in the middle. No reflectors. No curbs or islands. Only a left side and a right side. She jerks the wheel to the left and tries to get back into her lane. Downshifts again.

And she sees it. A truck. No, a sport utility. And a trailer in tow.

Brakes screech. Both drivers yank their steering wheels to the left. The front fenders miss by inches. Maybe two. In a split second, Katie's off in a ditch, rolling down a hill, faster, faster. Bouncing. She grasps at the wheel and holds her foot down on the brake pedal. It doesn't seem to help.

Behind her, up on the road, the trailer is jackknifing, folding upon itself, moving sideways over the loose, pebbly road. Then it stops. The man, the driver, yells to his passenger, "Are you all right?"

"Yes, yes," she says, shaken. "Better get off the road. Can you straighten it?"

"I think so," he answers as he gives it some gas and the trailer unfolds, straightening out. "Did any cages fall off?"

"No," the woman answers as she twists her neck around. "Pull over there." She points to a clearing.

They park and jump out of the Land Cruiser and run to the side of the road. Below, they see a small yellow car and they see a woman standing beside it, looking up at them. "Are you all right?" the man yells at her. His voice sounds far too calm and collected given what just happened.

"Yes, I'm okay," Katie says, wiping her face on her sleeve. She closes the door and looks at the car. The front wheels are bent outward as if the vehicle were dropped, suspension probably broken. The front right fender is curled up, where it caught the rock that stopped her from sliding down the hill even further. When she looks back toward the woman and man on the hill they are already within six feet of her. "I didn't see you," the man says, breathing hard.

"I'm sorry, it was my fault. I'm so sorry. Are you okay? Is your vehicle okay?"

"Yes, dear," the woman answers with a slight but kind smile. "Now are you sure you're all right?"

Katie looks down at her left leg, bleeding at the knee. "It's just a small cut," she answers, "I think from the shift lever."

"Come, we'll take you to the hospital," the man says.

"No really, I'll be fine."

They all walk up the hill to the Land Cruiser.

"You are an American?" the woman asks.

"Yes, I'm just here visiting with my daughter," Katie replies, then watches as the woman looks at the man.

The man holds his neck, rubbing, as he peers down at the wrecked sedan and says, "That car is rented?"

"I'm afraid so. But I took out insurance."

"That's good but," he says then pauses as he shakes his head, "I think you'd be better off not reporting the accident."

"Why is that?"

"It will just mean trouble, dear," the woman cuts in. "The police may give you trouble. You are a foreigner. Guilty until proven innocent."

Katie pauses. Thinking, worrying. Then asks, "What do you suggest I do?"

The man walks toward the Land Cruiser and says, "You come with us, okay, you come with us. Hurry now." He quickly checks the cages, making sure the animals are okay, then hops in with the woman, who slides over to the front passenger seat. Katie climbs in the back seat. The engine is already running. He asks, "Did you leave anything in the car?"

"No. Nothing."

"Good." He knocks the Land Cruiser into gear, looks over his shoulder, and continues down the road. Katie suddenly wonders whether getting into a stranger's car is the wisest thing to do. She'd kill Megan if she did the same thing.

This couple seems sincere. And if they are caring for all these animals in back they can't be that bad, she thinks.

The man turns his head and says, "My name is Chamba and this is my wife, Dora."

"My name is Katie. Katie Ryan."

Dora rotates to her right and shakes her hand, says, "Hello, Katie, nice to meet you, though I wish it were under better circumstances. Where in America are you from?"

"The state of Kentucky."

"Oh yes, I've heard of it." She turns forward, speaks louder, "And what brings you to Africa, Katie?"

"Well, one reason is that my daughter is fascinated with the wildlife."

"Is she now..."

"She loves animals. And the other reason we came is that she is quite ill, so I thought it would be nice, you know, to show her a few countries, take in the sights."

"I see, I see..."

"I also wanted to visit the new animal facility. In fact, that's where I was heading. Is that where you were coming from?" Katie asks, then looks over her shoulder at the cages.

"Yes, that's right."

"So you both work there?"

"Well, we come down at least once a month, transporting animals to and from Kenya. We're leaving for Tsavo this morning."

"I hope I haven't delayed you too much. I'm really sorry about what happened. I'm not used to driving on the left side of the road."

129

"It's okay, Katie. No one was seriously hurt. That's what is important."

Katie looks left and right as Chamba turns onto a four-lane road and heads toward downtown. She asks, "So you probably know Doctor Evan Drake?"

Chamba's eyes move to the rearview mirror, "Yes," he says, "we work for him."

Katie feels something stir in her. She now has insiders. "Oh, you do," she says calmly. "I've read a lot about his work. My fiancé and I do similar work with horses back home."

"Breeding?" Dora asks.

"Yes. Facilitated breeding. And we've also begun cloning thoroughbred horses."

"Ah," Chamba says as his eyes widen in the rearview mirror. "For the Kentucky Derby?"

"Right, right..."

He changes lanes then turns his head and continues, "Who were you going to meet at the facility, if you don't mind me asking?"

"I wanted to see Doctor Drake one more time before we leave."

There is silence for a couple seconds then he continues, "Katie, Doctor Drake is not there now."

"What?"

"He left two days ago."

"But I thought he had just arrived."

"Yes, indeed he had. But there was an emergency at the field lab." She swallows hard. Throat feels dry.

"Did Doctor Drake know you were coming?" Chamba asks.

"No, no he didn't. I just thought he would be there."

As he slows somewhat, waiting for a truck to merge from an adjacent road, he says, "Well, maybe someone else can meet with you."

"I don't think so," she replies as she looks down at her knee. It's beginning to throb and the oxygenated red glow is turning to muted burgundy, dried blood. "I, I really don't think anyone else can help," she says at length, her words trailing off.

CHAPTER TWENTY-TWO

The map Megan studies is well-worn, almost completely tattered, in fact. Its edges, when folded, lack corners and there are fingerprints upon its surface. As she leans her head against one of the Land Cruiser's rear windows, which is cracked open halfway, she yawns as the sun bathes her face with warmth. Though she is coaxed toward sleep she continues squinting, staring at the map. It is of Kenya, and this is what it says at the top, KENYA, bold letters, all caps. Eventually she folds it and places it on her lap.

In four or five days, maybe more depending on whether there are rainy skies, blue skies, or windy skies, they'll be at the point in the middle of the map—near Tsavo National Park—she thinks as she unfolds it yet again and runs her fingers over its features. Aruba Dam. Athi and Galana rivers. Yatta Escarpment. The Kalinzo, the Serengeti, the Dika plains—all right there where she can touch them, right there where she can see them in her mind. They're clear, so perfectly clear. A few minutes pass and her eyes grow heavy and she is rocked to sleep by the motion of the Land Cruiser. Before leaving Katie had told her, "It'll be a long drive. Are you sure you're up to it?" and Megan had replied confidently, "Yes, mom. I'll be fine."

Earlier in the day, Katie had called the police and reported the wrecked rental sedan missing, "It isn't where I parked it, sir, here at the hotel." And the officer said, "We'll send a man right over." And so the car, the stolen car, still sat wedged atop a rock on one side and covered with brush on the other. She felt guilty for the deception. She'd never done anything like that before. But Chamba and Dora said it would be best. And the look in their eyes made her believe this to be the case. Immediately after filing the report, she notified the rental company, which offered to bring her another shiny yellow sedan. "No thanks," she said, "I don't want to risk having another stolen." Chamba, who was standing behind her, patted her on the back as she hung up and said, "That was good, Katie. Believe me, you are better off this way. And no one will know."

They then sat at the bar in the hotel lobby and Katie ordered ice tea for everyone.

"I can't thank you enough," she said. "You've been so kind,

especially considering that I almost ran you off the road."

"It's difficult being in another country, Katie, we know that," Dora said, then took a sip of tea.

"Well, I'm sorry I've delayed your trip."

"Quite all right. We'll be on our way soon enough."

"How long does it take to drive to Kenya from here?"

"Oh, about four or five days with steady driving and no problems, you know, with the weather, or mechanical breakdowns. If the winds are strong, or rains too heavy, we'll have to stop occasionally, more for the sake of the animals. It's a long ride, so we don't push ourselves—or our precious animal cargo."

Katie nodded then said, "Perhaps Megan and I will see you in Kenya. We're going to fly up, probably tomorrow."

Chamba took a long swallow of tea and said, "It's a big country Katie. Unfortunately, I doubt we'll see you."

"It's a shame we couldn't spend more time with you and your daughter," Dora said. "You seem like such a nice young lady."

Young? Katie thought as she smiled.

Chamba pushed his glass away. "Ah...that was refreshing." He licked his lips then swiveled on his bar stool and it squeaked.

Katie noticed that his eyes locked on Dora's and something unspoken seemed to be conveyed. Then he turned back to her and said, "Say, I know, why don't you and your daughter ride with us to Kenya?"

Bingo. Katie had hoped they would ask, and even considered raising the idea herself, but thought it would be too forward. *I almost ran them off the road and got them killed. Sure, I'll just ask them to give us a ride halfway across the continent. Great idea, Katie, just great,* she'd thought. She tried to look as if the whole thing hadn't occurred to her as she said, "Give us a ride, all that way?"

"Why not," Dora chimed in. "We have room. And you did say you wanted to see Africa. Believe me, we'll show you the *real* Africa. And when we get to our home in Nairobi you can stay with us."

Katie slowly shook her head, "We really couldn't—"

"We insist," Katie. "Chamba and I have to release the animals, then we'll show you some of the sights. We'd enjoy it," she said as she turned, "Right, Chamba?"

"Oh yes. It's not every day that we have visitors from America. You can tell us all about Kentucky."

And so it was settled.

An hour later, Katie and Megan had checked out of the hotel and loaded their luggage onto the top of the Land Cruiser. Chamba fastened it with rubber straps and braided nylon rope.

Now, as they make their way north with Dora and Chamba, Katie glances over at Megan, sun highlighting her hair. Her eyes are sealed. *She looks so healthy, so peaceful when she's asleep*, Katie thinks as she watches her blissfully escape the world, the leukemia. Katie wonders what Megan might be dreaming about.

"Yes, we've found a donor, Megan," Doctor Carlton says with a beaming smile. "And she's the same age as you and a perfect match. Six of six."

"Thank god. When can we do the transplant?"

"How about right now?"

"You mean, right this minute?"

"Yes, let's just get this whole thing over with. What do you say?"

"Uh, all right."

"Just change out of your softball uniform and put this on, and I'll inject the bone marrow."

"You already have it?"

"Yep. Right here. Okay now, just roll over. This won't hurt a bit. Just like getting a flu shot. No big deal."

"Okay."

"There, how's that?"

"What?"

"I'm done, Megan. See, it wasn't that bad. We just needed to find that perfect marrow match."

"That's all there is to it?"

"Yep. No big deal, like I said. Go ahead and change back into your softball uniform. What time's your game?"

"Four o'clock."

"Well, looks like you can still make it."

"You mean it's okay to play? I mean, shouldn't I rest for a while, make sure the marrow has taken?"

"Nah. You're healthy as a racehorse, Megan. You're cured."

"I, I just can't believe it..."

"Believe it, Megan. Here, look in this mirror. Your hair is growing back already."

"Oh my god, I just—"

"Now get dressed and go win that game. Okay?"

Chamba tries to avoid it but he can't. The front right tire lands squarely in a pothole and everyone is jarred forward.

"Sorry, I thought we'd miss that one," he says.

Dora shakes her head.

Katie loosens her seatbelt then looks at Megan, who is just waking up. "How was your nap, honey?"

"What happened, mom?"

"We just hit a bad spot in the road, that's all."

Megan yawns and stretches her neck. She remembers what she was dreaming about. Her head drops as she thinks to herself, *It was only a dream.*

She reaches up and feels her hair. It's still short, thin.

I'm still sick...It was only a dream, she repeats to herself once more.

"Are you okay?" Katie asks.

"Yes, I was dreaming, I guess."

"What about?"

"Um, can't remember really." Megan turns and looks to the rolling hills to the right, not wanting to upset her mother.

CHAPTER TWENTY-THREE

The city ahead appears as a jewel, like one of those diamonds back in Johannesburg, Megan thinks as she peers out the bug-speckled windshield. The sparkling lights dance in the cooler evening breeze. She asks, "Is that it? Is that Nairobi?"

"Yes, Megan. We're almost there," Chamba says as he turns his head and offers a relieved smile.

Katie stretches her back and leans forward, "It's bigger than I expected..."

The last four days it seemed as if they had bounced over every road between South Africa and Kenya. And Chamba was right. They did see Africa, as only possible from the ground. The dusty, bumpy ground. By the first night they had made it to central Zimbabwe. Second night, to the capital of Zambia, Lusaka. Third and fourth, to Tukuyu and Arusha, Tanzania. With miles upon miles of two-lane roads, some paved, some dirt, some in-between, there was little time for stopping. And since they stayed with friends of Dora and Chamba each night, who lived in populated towns and cities, there was little resemblance to a real safari, the exception being when, on occasion, animals were seen in the distance, or sometimes crossing the road, in which case all traffic came to a halt and engines went silent. Near Lake Kariba, south of Lusaka, hundreds, maybe thousands of zebras could be seen migrating, eating, running and playing. And near Serenje, Chamba pulled off the road and everyone hiked about a half mile to a water hole where he knew elephants liked to gather. But none were there.

The night's stars fade as they near the city of Nairobi and Katie thinks about all the stories Chamba told her about Evan along the way. She feels like she already knows him well.

"He saved my life," Katie, Chamba said when they were leaving Johannesburg.

"How?"

"I was working as a park ranger at East Tsavo, near Diandaza. It's a very remote area of the park. Not many tourists. I was checking the roads, you know, making sure they hadn't washed out from the rains we'd had. Anyway, as I came over a ridge near the Tiva River, I came upon a truck that was on its side, badly damaged. I pulled over, not knowing what I would find, you know, dead bodies, or injured people. I didn't know what I'd find."

Katie nodded as Chamba's eyes moved to the rearview mirror, looking at her reflection.

"I approached the truck and leaned over to see inside the crushed cab. No one was there. Then I felt a sharp pain, back of my head. I didn't wake up until three days later."

"My lord..."

"When I came to, Evan was by my bed at the hospital in Nairobi. He said he found me on the ground, face down. Bloodied. My car was gone. Apparently, a few hours later some other rangers found four dead elephants about a mile from the accident. Their tusks had been hacked off; they found them in my car, abandoned near Manyani Gate. Poachers had basically tried to kill me, then stole my car"

Chamba then told Katie about how Evan hired him and Dora, a month or so after the accident, to haul animals back and forth between Tsavo and the facility in Johannesburg, "He's been real good to us, Katie. And he's been good to the village we work out of."

The village Chamba spoke of is on the Serengeti Plains, in the shadow of Kilimanjaro to the west. Evan had worked the region for three years. There are only ten buildings, mostly private residences and a couple of markets to catch tourist vans passing through. Most of the buildings are owned and leased out by a woman named Emily Stafford— or Miss Emily, as she likes to be called—who arrived in 1985, another *Out of Africa* Karen Blixen inspired transplant, wanting to grow coffee and searching for her own Denys Finch-Hatton, Blixen's lover and a big game hunter she wrote lavishly about in her book.

Miss Emily owns seven of the ten buildings in the village, all colonial designs, painted white, sweeping porches, light with an air of sophistication. Very stately British. And her home, central to the village, is the finest. Plaster walls. Wide planked floors. Overstuffed chairs covered in English chintzes. And each table always has cut flowers sitting upon it, grown in the lush gardens which are maintained by her bibis and shambamen. Flowering vines frame the twelve-over-twelve dual-pane windows. Surrounding these buildings are thirty-five or so traditional Kenyan huts, shelters for the harvesters of coffee, the keepers of gardens, the lawns. And the cooks, the hunters, the gatherers, and growers, most barely scraping a living out of the soil, dirt, and sun-scorched land. A few dollars a day on average.

Chamba went on to tell Katie that Miss Emily, most of the villagers and visitors might say, is a large woman. Full-figured, she calls it. Her hair is golden with only a smattering of gray flecks, especially at her temples. When the noon sun hits her silky long strands, which she ties in a ponytail most days, one can see darker roots lurking below the surface. Miss Emily, the locals claim, has many things lurking below the surface.

Not that she's a fat woman, Chamba added, or even remotely obese from a medical perspective. No one would say that. She simply is, well, full-figured, rounded out a bit, feminine, at least by the standards of some other century long gone by. But she is easy on the eyes. Real easy. Soft, supple skin void of wrinkles, a rarity for anyone living in remote Kenya. Piercing green eyes that can look through you. For the few who meet her—the tourists passing through or perhaps a lonely game warden—it's clear that she takes care of herself, her skin and hair anyway.

She also dresses well. Chamba told Katie that she wears long, paper-thin cotton skirts, usually yellow or blue or rose and green, which she purchases in Nairobi, and she wears no underwear ever since she passed mid-life just before her move to Kenya. Yes, no underwear, that's what she is famous for. She likes the way the breeze blows up her freshly shaven full-figured legs in the morning and she likes the way her housekeeper, Toma Zho, rubs shaving cream over her porcelain skin, across her calves, thighs. Floral blouses, also of cotton, are always worn, usually tucked in neatly even when no one is around to see. She wears bras when it is hot, to keep the sweat from her fleshy sunflower-size breasts contained, and she goes loose when temperatures are below eighty. Or when a particularly handsome passerby is in the village.

Chamba went on to say, "You see, Katie, Miss Emily is known to seek men. Tall men. Short men. Skinny men. Full-figured men. There are nights when her voice, a voice of passion which—to the less informed be mistaken as torture—may be heard emanating from her stately home and it is these nights she has met a lonely passerby who has caught her fancy."

Chamba went on to say, "They all tend to catch her fancy."

She usually sets her trap when she sees a Jeep or Land Rover or any other make or model of vehicle or manned beast making its way down the mountain toward the village. Like clockwork she then makes her way to the front garden, which is surrounded by a white picket fence, perhaps the only one in Kenya. It is there, near the fragrant red roses, she bends over and picks weeds, deadheads tired blooms, or just mills about until her victim rolls in seeking water or directions or a stay for the night, or a voice of passion. Often, on breezy days, Miss Emily's floral skirts flitter about and catch the wind like an untethered sail of a boat while she tends to her garden for hours. On breezy days many men have visited with Miss Emily.

🍃

It's nearly eleven in the evening when Chamba, Dora, Katie, and Megan arrive in *Karen*, a suburb that lies twelve kilometers to the southwest of Nairobi, where the air is thin yet moist and sweet. Everyone is tired. Chamba is hanging on the steering wheel, Dora is half asleep and leaning against the sweaty, streaked passenger window. Even the animals on the trailer are quiet, no stirring, Megan notices, ready for this journey to end.

They drive past Wilson, a commuter airport, and past the main gates to the National Park, down Langata Road toward the center of Karen. Thorn trees guide the way, dappled moonlight leaking through their branches onto the pavement which is noticeably void of pot holes, road kill, and beggars. Tonight will be spent, finally, at Dora and Chamba's home.

The first thing that strikes Katie as strange is the size and quality of the houses as they climb higher up a hill. Most are guarded by formidable gates, many with guards on duty. They stare curiously as the Land Cruiser and long trailer of animals go by.

A few minutes later and Chamba raises his boot from the accelerator pedal and the vehicle slows as he pulls alongside a rock retaining wall that, upon rounding a curve, becomes a guard house. A man approaches wearing a uniform, blue or black, hard to tell with the glare off the insect-speckled and smeared windshield. A flashlight, long and bright, dangles from his hand. No gun visible. As he nears he says, "Jambo, Chamba."

"Jambo."

"Another long ride, yes?"

"Indeed, too long."

"I'll open the gates."

"Thank you."

As they swing open, Chamba pulls in slowly and parks on a wide, smooth lawn, just mowed and painted silver by the moon. Headlights are turned off and the engine follows. Silence. Everyone gets out and stretches their arms and legs. Megan yawns but suddenly feels a burst of energy, *We've made it.*

"In the morning," Dora says, "my mother will cook us a good breakfast. Fried tomatoes, bacon, and eggs. And we'll show you the grounds."

"This is so kind of you, I just—"

"Katie, if you say thank you one more time..."

"I know, I know."

Chamba checks on the animals then walks over and says, "You won't believe the view in the morning, Megan." He points through some trees. "The Ngong Hills are lovely at dawn. And we'll show you the gardens," he says as he unties one of the bags on top of the Land Cruiser's roof. He continues, "There are bottlebrush trees with red flowers, cape chestnuts in pink, roses, and bougainvilleas."

"Sounds wonderful," Katie says. Megan nods in the darkness.

"And then we'll take the animals out to the park, and find Doctor Drake for you."

The village was full of activity when Evan arrived earlier in the day, cars and people bustling about, shoeless kids kicking soccer balls in the street, men guiding animals from one place to another alongside all the chaos.

The Land Rover and its trailer jerked to a stop as Evan locked the brakes, then turned the engine off. To the right there were yet more kids kicking a ball around; he recognized the ball they were playing with, which he had brought back on his last trip up from Johannesburg. He was surprised they hadn't worn it out yet, and that it still appeared to have air inside despite the heat and the abuse it was getting.

By noon he had hired ten men and two boys. All from the village. Some climbed atop the metal cage bolted to the top of the Land Rover's roof. Some clung to the rust-ridden fenders and bumpers, holding their dry and chapped fingers tightly about the tubular brush guards. And some rode on the trailer where there was room. They drove toward the northwest, to Tsavo River, happily singing and swaying, proud and appreciative to have work on this day.

"Under the African sun, under the African sun,
My heart lies open, my heart lies warm,
Not a worry to be found, not a sight or a sound,
Under the African sun, under the African sun..."

139

"It's a good day to build a new home, Doctor Drake," young Simu said. He was chewing on an acacia leaf and reclined in the passenger seat with his feet up on the Land Rover's dash—as if he were riding down a main boulevard on a Friday night in 1950's America, cruising with confidence in a Thunderbird or Corvette. He was wearing cutoff blue jeans and leather sandals, a blue tee shirt with a Coca Cola logo. His lips were full, cheeks soft—a handsome boy if ever there was one, Miss Emily had told him one recent day.

Simu's primary job, when working with Evan, was to round up the others and offer a day's pay, perhaps two or three days depending on the site Evan was to pick and work needed. For some in the village, it would be the only money they'd earn for weeks, the only means of purchasing food for their families. And for this reason, Evan tried to provide such work as often as possible, and spread the tasks to as many villagers as he could.

Evan had already picked the worksite for the day. It had caught his eye almost eight months ago, quite by accident. He just stumbled upon it, tracking a family of elephants, one of which had a transmitter he wanted to put a new battery in. Although they all got away, crossing the river at twilight, the pursuit wasn't without its rewards, for the cliffs and trees which lie near the river seemed the perfect place to build a camp someday. Someday was today.

Evan followed the river for ten miles as the tires cut rifts through the sand. Half their air had been taken out such that they would not sink too deeply into the earth and get stuck. The equipment and the men were heavy but within an hour they reached the spot he had chosen, "We'll call it Camp Baobab," he said as he leaned forward, peering through the dusty windshield of the Land Rover.

"Baobab? You name your camp after a tree, Doctor Drake?"

"I think it is appropriate Simu, don't you," he said, then pointed toward the base of a cliff.

There, dwarfed by the shear vertical rocks and hills rising majestically some four hundred feet, painted yellowish pink in the afternoon sun, stood a tree. One tree. A baobab. An ancient cathedral boxed in by skyscrapers. It was the biggest one Evan or Simu had ever seen, though they all tend to be huge. Evan figured that the radius of the trunk on this one had to be at least thirty-five feet in diameter. And the canopy, well over one-hundred feet, each limb larger than the trunk of any other species in the world. Evan had read that the largest living

Baobab found was in Modjadjiskloof, Limpopo, with a height of seventy-two feet and diameter of one hundred fifty-four feet. That one was carbon dated to 6,000 years, the oldest tree in the world. Its trunk, which was hollowed out by a fire, was turned into a bar and wine cellar. Most Baobabs, though, are treated with far more reverence and considered sacred by the locals, a place of social gathering.

"You'll have lots of monkey bread, Doctor Drake," Simu said with a laugh, referring to the pulp of the baobab fruit, usually used for making drinks. The fruit is filled with big black seeds and surrounded by tart cream, a powdery pulp. Monkeys can often be seen eating the fruit.

Evan nodded at Simu while searching for the best path to get the Land Rover and trailer as close as possible to the Baobab without bouncing every wide-eyed Kenyan off the roof, fenders, or trailer, and onto their rear-ends.

He found a good spot to park and turned the engine off, set the brake. Bodies jumped from every corner in unison. There were confused expressions, staring at the tree, the cliffs, and Evan. The men's faces said, Why are we here?

"Everyone ready?" Evan asked.

Heads turned left and right. Mumbling, lots of Swahili mumbling.

Simu stepped forward, scratching the back of his head, "Ready for what, Doctor Drake?"

"Have you ever heard of Swiss Family Robinson?"

"Uh, no, I don't think so. They are friends of yours? In Johannesburg?"

Evan smiled, turned toward the men, and waved an arm for everyone to follow. "No Simu, never mind. We're going to build a new home for me. A new home in that tree," he said, nodding with the brim of his hat, which was made of straw, never washed and well-worn.

This was not the first time he had considered building a treehouse. He had seen one three years ago when passing through Francistown. A film crew from Italy was making a documentary on lions and created two ten-by-ten platforms in a tree near a water hole. Their perched position kept them almost entirely invisible to wildlife, provided a great spot for observation, and afforded some degree of safety, especially while sleeping. It also stayed cool and sheltered the crew during strong rain and wind. To Evan, it also seemed enticingly romantic, perhaps eccentric, the notion of living in a tree, even just occasionally while he stayed in the bush to collect DNA or release animals. He told himself he would build one someday if he had the time, and that day had finally come.

And so the men, and Simu, marched toward the great tree, the barefoot army clueless but ready to work.

Bamboos make good posts. They are round, and strong. They don't rot, at least not for a dozen or more years. They are easy to work with, and they are plentiful near this treehouse that is taking shape under the boiling African sun. *Why does it always have to be so bloody hot when work is to be done?* Evan had thought on many occasions.

There are three main sections to this treehouse. See the twisted limb jutting horizontally from the right side of the trunk like an aged man's arthritic arm, fingers, each inch curled and knotted? It is here, where the larger branches first divide into smaller, that the men are preparing to attach the largest platform. They are tying each piece of bamboo with thin strips of calfskin, supple, compliant, yet strong, and creating walls made of smaller bamboo sprouts to protect from the winds, the rains, and the likely dust storms that will come through once a week, maybe more often.

If my dad could only see this, Evan thinks as he hoists another piece of bamboo upward, then gazes as it is swallowed by lacy leaves. When he was ten he and his dad made a treehouse in the backyard, in an old oak tree. Like most projects, his dad took it quite seriously. "How many square feet do you think you need?" he had asked young Evan.

Evan, who was eight at the time, replied with confused eyes, "Square feet?"

The oak in his backyard at 1134 Shady Grove Avenue had a large V where the main platform was attached and, above this, a canvas roof provided shelter. To some degree anyway. Now, dozens of years later, as Evan hands a long piece of bamboo to Simu who is dangling from a branch, he remembers the day he and his dad built that treehouse, first the platform—the beams, the joists, and flooring. And then they used two-by-two boards for the framing, as two-by four boards would have been too heavy for the tree. His dad had bolted just one end of each main beam to a custom vice clamp-like structure surrounding the tree. The other ends were secured by a cable wrapped in garden hose so that the house could give and sway, rather than break apart and fall when winds stressed the tree and the aerial fort they'd built. Evan learned about

142

headers and cripples and jack studs, king studs. He also learned to avoid damaging the cambium layer of a tree, which conveys the flow of nutrients. And he discovered what an arborist does and thought that such a line of work would be a nice job to have—getting to climb trees all day. "What do they pay arborists, dad?" Evan had asked.

His dad, always one for brevity, answered simply, "I don't know, son."

Today Evan can't help but think that his father is smiling down on him and this fine treehouse in Kenya, Africa. No two-by-twos, no tape measures, no hammers, no screws and bolts. He'd be proud, real proud.

CHAPTER TWENTY-FOUR

An open window, the rustle of shrubs swaying in the morning breeze, the whistling of exotic birds, the smell of rich Kenyan coffee—all Katie's senses seem to be heightened as her eyelids peel open. It is dawn in Nairobi, pallid orange and yellow-blue. Soft rose-scented air. She had even had a comfortable bed for a change—handmade quilts of cotton, over-stuffed pillows filled with feathers, delicate webs of lace sewn onto the sheets at the edges. She lies still and soaks in the sensations, bathes in it, relishes in it. After long days on the road trip from Johannesburg to Nairobi, it was pure heaven.

On any other day this would be the time she would start thinking and worrying about work. What spin to put on a press release. How to educate, manipulate, or motivate the next reporter, customer, or investor. What should be in the presentation to the board of directors this month. Will payroll be met on Friday for the employees. And, more recently, whether David will come into work. But today it strikes her as strange that she hasn't thought about work since she and Megan left the states. Not once. And it feels good. No hollowness. Nothing missing.

I could get used to this, she thinks as she rolls over and looks at Megan, asleep on a wooden cot near the door.

Katie was the first generation of Ryan women in her family to go to college, first to have a career, first to have ulcers and migraines. And as such, at least according to her mother, she was entitled to the typical conflicting feelings of being torn between family duties and the goal of independence, and self-growth. Society expected her to work eight to ten hours a day climbing ladders while keeping a clean house and creating and raising happy and healthy and computer-literate kids, not to mention being able and willing to wear the pink nightie on Saturday nights, firm breasts, no cellulite. But as she lay here under the gentle breeze, she is a million miles from her old self. And it feels good.

By ten o'clock they had eaten breakfast, which Dora and her mother had made far too much of, and gotten on the road. As Chamba reduces speed, approaching the sleepy sun-flooded village, Katie points and says, "My, what a lovely house that is."

"Yes, yes indeed. That's Miss Emily's house I told you about.

That's her over there, in her rose garden."

"So she lives here year-round?"

"Oh yes. She grows some coffee, not a lot, lives here all the months," Chamba answers. "Dora and I work for her when Evan doesn't have any projects for us. I'm sure she would like to meet you and Megan. As I mentioned last night, she likes to meet *every* visitor to the village."

Katie nods.

"I think I'll stop. Perhaps she knows where Evan is. I don't see his Land Rover in the village. He must be out in the bush," Chamba says as he brings the long vehicle to a halt. A loud squeal emits from the trailer brakes, sending shivers up stiff and aching spines. He continues, "My goodness, those brake pads will definitely have to be changed this year. They don't last long in the dust and heat."

Miss Emily sees a man approaching and she rises at once, turns on one heel, "Well hello, Chamba. I didn't know you were coming up from Johannesburg this week. Looking for work today?"

"No, no thank you, not today. I have to release some animals. I might be able to work tomorrow though, if Evan doesn't need us."

"I'm never your first choice, am I."

He smiles then says, "The animals are my first choice, Miss Emily. Always the animals."

"Yes...you and Evan are of like minds, aren't you. No time to spend with a nice middle-aged lady." She feigns a slight frown then returns a toothy, straight grin, nodding and brushing her palms together to shake off soil from her somewhat callused and spotted hands. A loose gold bracelet shimmers in the sun and her dress billows up as the breeze settles in, seeking shade among the healthy roses. Bees, big full-figured African bees, swirl about her knees but she doesn't care. They, too, work for her, pollinating and singing in the garden all day, all spring and summer. As she pulls her hair to one side her eyes give way to creases at the edges, not deep wrinkles, but just a hint of age and distinction. Well-worn badges of a hard working woman who has lived life to the fullest.

Chamba continues, "Speaking of Evan, have you seen him today?"

"Yes, early this morning. He picked up some men. I don't know where they were going. I told him if he'd bring me back some monkey fruit I'd make something for dinner for him."

"I see..."

Miss Emily turns toward the Land Cruiser, "Who did you bring with you, Chamba?"

"They are Americans and—"

"Really?" she interrupts, her tone rising.

"Yes, ma'am. They're looking for Evan. Dora and I gave them a ride from Johannesburg."

"My, that was nice of you."

"It was no trouble really. They're nice people, Miss Emily. Would you like to meet them?"

"Yes, of course. But give me a minute to freshen up, okay. Then bring them up to the house. I'll prepare something cold to drink."

"Yes, ma'am, I'll tell them. Thank you."

Ten minutes later Chamba knocks on the screen door and Miss Emily approaches and says, "Come in, please come in," and when everyone is inside she emerges from the kitchen with a tray of ice teas and slices of lemon cut into precise wedges, some goat's cheese and crackers.

Katie smiles. "I hope we're not intruding."

"By no means, please sit down," she replies as she sets the tray on a butler's table then walks over and extends her right hand, clean and scented with moisturizer reminiscent of lilac. She continues with a hint of southern drawl, "Most people call me Miss Emily around here."

"I'm Katie Ryan, and this is my daughter Megan."

"Pleased to meet you. Hello Megan."

"Hi. Nice to meet you too," Megan says as she senses a hand that feels clammy but moderately soft, supple.

"Chamba tells me that you are from the U.S.?"

"Yes. Kentucky."

"My, my...what brings you all the way to Kenya?"

Katie hesitates, wiping her brow where beads are developing, and says, "It's a rather long story. We're trying to track down Doctor Evan Drake." The curious raised eyebrows on Miss Emily's face make Katie think that more questions are surely coming, but before they do, she continues with, "You certainly have a lovely home."

"Thank you. I enjoy it. Lots of work though. It's over a hundred years old."

Small talk continues as the light coming in from Miss Emily's windows overlooking her garden casts shorter shadows, the sun nearly at its zenith. The air is void of movement and seems to annoyingly make clothes stick to skin. Faces, arms, and legs grow shiny. Afternoon slips by.

Evan's back muscles are tight and his skin is red where dirt doesn't cover it. A long day. Sore feet, sore hands, sore everything. Who would have thought he'd work years on a Ph.D. and end up hacking at tree limbs and hoisting bamboo to the air in hundred and ten degree weather.

The tree platforms nearly complete, he drives the men back to the village and drops them off near the beer barrel where they will douse their troubles, their aches, and celebrate a day's pay while they sip noisily from long straws and lose themselves in dizziness until their wives holler and scream for them to come home, gather something to eat, You have a family for god's sake.

Blisters on the bottom of Evan's left foot, and the front of its big toe, become a limp. A few groans escape between his chapped lips as he climbs the steps to Miss Emily's house, exhausted. He can almost taste the ice tea or lemonade or whatever she has waiting for him and he hopes she doesn't get mad that he forgot to bring her the monkey fruit he had agreed to. Maybe tomorrow, he'll say, I promise to bring some tomorrow.

The door creaks open and his eyes attempt to adjust, squinting, as he hears a familiar voice but only sees silhouettes of human forms, all seated about Miss Emily's living room. *It can't be them*, he tells himself. *It just can't...*

"Hello Evan," Miss Emily says as she gets up and walks over, "You have visitors. Katie and Megan Ryan have been waiting for you."

His mouth drops as his sunburned head tries to calculate how this woman, this gorgeous and brave and fragile woman named Katie, and her sick child have managed to track him to the heart of Kenya, all the way from Johannesburg. There's only one explanation, and it's sitting on the couch, eyes averted, "Hello Chamba," Evan says as he focuses in on Chamba's innocent face.

"Hello Evan."

"Made the trip okay, I see."

"Oh yes. Animals are fine."

"Good, good." Evan walks toward Katie and says, "What a surprise to see you here."

"Yes, Dora and Chamba were nice enough to give us a ride."

"I see," he says reservedly, trying to contain any outward appearance of dismay, or disapproval. He then looks at the equally lovely girl next to her. "And you must be Megan?"

"Yes."

He offers his hand. "You look just like your mother."

147

Uh huh. Just like her but without hair, Megan thinks as she smiles politely.

Miss Emily chimes in, "Would you like some ice tea?

"I would kill for some."

"Great, I'll be right back."

Katie settles into the cushy protective arms of a wing-back chair and tries to calm herself. All morning she had worried over what she would say to Evan, how she would make another plea for his help. But she couldn't find the words and had decided to not say anything until they came to her, lest she ruin her last chance by saying something wrong, or too hastily.

She thinks, *Well, at least he didn't just turn around and walk out. Probably assumes that I'm some crazy lunatic, following him halfway across the African continent. Good lord...*

As afternoon yields to evening and Kilimanjaro looms purplish-blue and tosses pale clouds at the horizon, there's no talk of why Katie and Megan are in Tsavo. No questions. No messy scene. No embarrassing inquiries in front of Dora, Chamba, and Miss Emily. And when dinner is served outside on the porch—grilled chicken, potatoes, beans, fresh sun-baked bread sprinkled with poppy seeds—everyone eats and tells stories as a family who has been reunited after months of separation. Miss Emily talks of her roses, "Just planted twenty-five Mr. Lincolns," and Dora complains about her sore back, exacerbated by the arduous drive from Johannesburg, "Feels like it's tied in knots," she says as she stretches from a wicker chair and Evan says, "Mine too, we made some tree platforms today, down by the river. They should make excellent observation decks."

All in all it is a pleasant feast, good food and kind strangers forced together amidst the African wilderness, if tamed somewhat by Miss Emily's fine home. Evan's obvious passion for this land and all its inhabitants, Katie thinks as he rambles on about the tree platforms and the giraffes he saw today, becomes evident in his brown eyes. As unexpectedly as everything else in her life this past year, they sparkle and radiate and fill her heart. *Here is a person who loves what he does, and is trying to make a difference in the world,* she tells herself.

Seven-thirty arrives. Evening is approaching. It's cooler, much cooler, yet still warm enough to keep faces shiny, arms and legs sticky. Chamba takes one more bite of cheese from his plate then rises from a chair and says, "It's time to release the animals.

Megan perks up and asks, "Can I go with you. I'd really—"

"Megan, I think we've inconvenienced Chamba and Dora enough, don't you?"

Chamba grimaces, "Now, now, Katie, you haven't been of trouble at all. None at all. And I'd love to show Megan how we release the animals. Would you like to come along too?"

"Well..."

Evan approaches from the kitchen, where he just washed his hands and leaned over to smell a rose tucked into a small white vase behind the sink. "Why don't we all go? It's a beautiful evening. Fresh air would do us some good."

Miss Emily yawns then says, "You all go ahead. I'll stay here and clean up a bit, and have coffee and dessert ready when you get back.

Katie turns to her, "Let me stay and help. I can always—"

"I won't hear of it," Miss Emily interrupts as she walks over to the screen door, opens it wide. "Go, everyone, go. Have fun."

Minutes later Chamba starts the Land Cruiser's tired engine.

Evan is sitting in the passenger seat, Dora is in the middle, Katie and Megan are in the back seat. The animals seem to know something is up. One of the lions rocks back and forth in its cage and the baby rhino sniffs at the soft air as Chamba nudges the trailer forward in low gear.

As speed is gathered Katie asks, "Do you always release them in the evening?"

Chamba replies over his shoulder, "Yes, it's safer that way. After such a long journey the animals are often lazy, you know, their muscles are somewhat atrophied. They're very vulnerable, especially the babies. And there's still sedative in their blood. So the cover of darkness gives them a better chance to avoid predators and the hot sun."

"I see."

As they pull away from the house, Chamba catches a blur of Miss Emily in the left side mirror. She's running as best as she can toward the rear of the Land Cruiser, waving her arms. "I think Miss Emily changed her mind," he says as he pokes his head out the window and looks back at her while applying the brakes.

Heads turn as she comes to a stop near the door where Megan is seated.

"Room for one more?" Miss Emily inquires, breathing hard.

"Of course," Katie replies as she scoots over some and Megan

149

slides into the middle spot of the back seat, making space.

"I decided to come along. I'll clean up later."

And so off they go, headed toward the escarpment. Purple still lingers in the sky to the west and clouds void of light, save a lightning strike every few seconds, hover over the east.

"Looks like there's going to be a storm," Katie says, leaning forward so as to see through the windshield. Dust covers every inch of it except for two smeared fan-shapes where the blades last scraped.

Twenty minutes later and they are at the water hole where Chamba and Dora usually set the animals free, making sure they have a chance to drink before wandering off. There are also some trees on one side for refuge, and smaller game can be found for a quick meal.

Evan is first to jump out and start unstrapping the cages. With twilight, the stirring picks up, the cages rattle and squeak; the tranquilizers are slowly wearing off. Time to let us out, the nervous eyes of the animals say.

"Are they all okay?" Megan asks, turning to Evan.

"Yeah, looks like it," he answers, running his eyes from cage to cage. "We haven't lost one in two years." He motions to Chamba, "Give me a hand with this one, she's a bit agitated, ready to hit the road."

The cage Evan is unstrapping is that of the young rhino. Her mother and two other adults were found dead near a water hole at Ngulia Rhino Sanctuary six weeks ago. When Chamba found her she was dehydrated and had two days left, tops. After a week back at the village holding pen, where she was fed and regained her strength, Chamba and Dora drove her to the facility in Johannesburg. Evan and his staff then removed an egg, which is still frozen and awaiting fertilization. Now, having regained her strength, the rhino should have a fighting chance, if she can avoid poachers.

As Chamba finishes untying the cages, Evan drops a metal leg down near the trailer hitch, then disconnects everything from the Land Cruiser's rear bumper. He then drives in a circle and comes to a stop, such that the wench on the front end is opposite the ramp of the trailer.

He engages the clutch on the wench and pulls some cable out, holding a large metal hook. An eyelet on the rhino cage is latched onto and a button is pressed on the wench. The cage slowly slides rearward until it meets the ramp. Gravity helps do the rest, as he and Chamba slow the wench and guide the cage down to the ground. The rhino lets out a cry and bangs the cage left and right.

"Okay, that should do it," Evan says, "everyone get back in the

Land Cruiser. She may be a little testy after being locked up for so long."

With everyone safe inside, he pulls three pins from the latches on the cage. A door swings open and he stands back, next to the left wheel well of the trailer.

Megan whispers, "She's not moving."

"Shoosh," Katie says, "she'll come out."

Evan says, "Come on girl, time to hit the road. No more hitchin' a ride." And with these words and a tap on the cage from Evan, the rhino charges forward. As she clears the cage she gives a strong kick at the door with one of her back legs.

"Did I say something wrong," Evan says under his breath as he closes the door, watches her run off toward some bushes.

And just like that, the rhino is gone.

Katie and Megan get out of the Land Cruiser, Dora and Chamba follow.

"Wow, that was cool," Megan says.

Katie looks at Evan, "She sure ran away from you fast."

"Yeah," he says as he bends over to pick up a pin he has dropped. "Just like all the females in my life."

Katie smiles and walks around the other side of the trailer to help Chamba slide the empty cage off the ramp, so the others can be lowered.

Dora yawns, leaning against the Land Cruiser. Her rear gathers dirt and, after she steps away, the chrome appears shiny on the upper lip of the bumper. Nothing new, her face seems to say, same old routine we go through every few weeks.

Other animals follow, first a relatively rare, at least in Tsavo, bohor reedbuck antelope. A fringe-eared oryx that Megan thinks is cute. Then a timid klipspringer whose left front leg had somehow been broken just before Evan found it a few months ago. He could have simply put it out of its misery, but they too are less common in Tsavo these days, and he couldn't bring himself to shooting it when those soft brown eyes had gazed up at him.

Next to be released are two strikingly beautiful cheetahs which, he tells Megan, the facility nicknamed Ricky and Lucy. They are clones of another pair over in South Kitui National Reserve.

"On the next couple trips," he goes on, "we'll be letting go the Big Five—a buffalo, leopard, lion, another rhinoceros, and a baby elephant—all created in petri dishes back at the lab. Their eggs and sperm were gathered from animals over at One Tree Hill," he says proudly as he points to his left.

"Amazing," Katie says as she watches him hoist a cage back onto the trailer. Chamba helps, grabbing the opposite side.

"Chamba and I will probably release them a hundred miles or so away. What do you think, Mudanda Rock, Chamba?"

"Yes, I think that would be good. We haven't gone there in some time."

A window is rolled down all the way in the back seat of the Land Cruiser and Miss Emily yells out with a flushed face, "Is it safe to get out now?"

Evan shakes his head a couple times and rolls his eyes, facing Katie. He turns toward Miss Emily, "Yes, yes it's safe. They're all about a mile away by now. Much too far to bite you."

"Funny Evan," she says as she gets out. "You know I don't like to be that close to the animals, not since that hyena ran toward me a year ago and—"

"You were carrying a dead chicken. He just wanted some dinner."

"Uh-huh. And I was going to be dessert. He chased me all the way to my front door."

"Maybe he just wanted some ice tea, Miss Emily," Chamba joins in, smiling. "Everybody loves your ice tea."

A wave of laughter fills the evening air.

With the empty cages secured, everyone piles back into the Land Cruiser and Chamba asks Katie, "Would you like to see the overlook before we head back?"

"Overlook?"

"It's a spot," he says pointing, "over there. The view is quite good. You can see for miles in every direction."

"Well, I guess," she says, then looks to Evan for confirmation that it is okay.

He leans forward, stares at the darkening sky. "I guess we could head over. It is rather spectacular this time of day, especially looking toward Mount Kilimanjaro. Might even see an elephant or two."

"Really?" Megan says excitedly.

"Fifty-fifty chance. Go ahead, Chamba, head over. If it's okay with Miss Emily."

"Fine with me," she responds with only a hint of reluctance in her voice.

As Chamba aims the Land Cruiser east Miss Emily decides to pepper Katie with questions, about one every hundred yards or so. "What do you do? Are you married? Oh, I see. Why isn't your fiancé—What did you say his name was, David?—here with you and Megan?"

Katie, feeling a little shell shocked, tells her that David couldn't come on the trip, "He's swamped with work right now." Tells her that she called David while at Dora and Chamba's house in Nairobi, and that he missed Megan and her, but was glad they were having a good time. "He's really a great guy," she adds.

Miss Emily keeps the questions coming. "How long are you staying? Is this your first trip to Africa? How did you hear of Evan's work?" she asks, assuming that Katie's interest in tracking him down was somehow connected to what she had told her about Kentucky Thoroughbred Center.

Finally, thank god, Chamba interrupts the inquisition and points out three giraffes off to the right. He slows and lets Megan stick her head out the window opening to catch a better glimpse.

"Wow, they're so tall," she says as the soft, warm air bathes her face and she smells something sweet.

They loiter for a couple of minutes, then drive on.

When they arrive at the overlook there are no elephants, no cheetahs, no animals at all. Just twenty or so people sitting or standing near a fire pit. Evan recognizes several of the men. One of them is Chamba's father. "Did you know they would be here, Chamba?" Evan asks.

Chamba doesn't answer, and instead turns to Katie and says, "Isn't the view nice here?"

"Yes, very nice, Chamba. Who are all these people?" she asks.

"One of them is my father," he replies, "and the others are from the village."

"Oh really. Why are they way out here?"

"Well, they—"

"Looks like they're preparing for a dance," Miss Emily interrupts.

"Yeah, looks like it," Chamba says innocently as Evan turns to him, gives him a contemning stare.

Having figured out why Chamba wanted to drive to the overlook, Evan just shakes his head then turns away. Chamba had used the same routine about ten months ago when a husband and wife from London came through the village. The woman had AIDS, a blood transfusion gone awry, and wanted to see Africa before she died. Chamba had brought the woman to his father and the dancers, too.

153

It was on the way to Africa, on the first flight between Atlanta and Amsterdam, that Katie had pulled down the leather bag she'd placed in the overhead compartment before takeoff. She then shuffled through its contents, eyes wide, as if opening a long awaited Christmas present.

Megan asked, "What are you getting?" and Katie replied, "I have a gift for you."

It was the journal. The same dust-covered journal Katie had taken with her to Africa so many years ago. She hadn't ever mentioned it to Megan. Only about half the pages were filled in—mostly descriptions of the landscape, trees, animals, a few poems, and even a dozen or so sketches.

"What's this?" Megan inquired, fanning the pages as Katie replaced the backpack in the upper baggage compartment, sat and fastened her seatbelt.

"It's a journal I took on my last trip to Africa. I want you to have it."

"Really?"

Katie nodded, then stroked her palm over Megan's temple.

"Isn't there like, like, personal stuff in here, stuff that you don't want me to read?"

"Oh, I thought about that, but I don't think there's anything I can't share with you. Right?"

Megan smiled, "Thanks mom. Wow, you drew pictures too?"

"A few, not that good really."

"Yeah they are," Megan said as she looked up at her mother's glistening eyes. "I promise I'll take good care of it," she continued.

Katie reclined her seat. "Well, it isn't meant for a museum, no stuffing it away in a drawer. I want you to use it. Okay? Finish it. I did the first half. You do the second."

"Are you going to read what I write?"

"That's up to you. I don't have to. It can be your personal diary if you want. I just thought it would be neat for us to have our memories of Africa all in one place, side by side."

Megan leaned her head against her mother's shoulder, closed the journal, and held it to her chest with both arms crossed over it.

🌱

It is Thursday, I think, and I'm not sure what the date is. We're in some village in the middle of Tsavo National Park, in Kenya. Mom is inside helping Miss Emily with breakfast and I'm outside sitting in Miss Emily's rose garden, in a big wicker chair that swallows me whole. The roses are sparkling with dew and I can smell them. I want to plant some when we get home. I really like them a lot and Miss Emily really likes them too. She has hundreds of them, I think. Maybe thousands. Miss Emily must be very wealthy, but she doesn't brag or nothing. She has several men here who help her with the house and the grounds. She treats them well, it appears.

Everyone seems real tired today. I am too. Last night was, I think, the strangest night I have ever seen. It really was. I'll never forget it, no matter how old I live to be, and what ends up happening with my cancer. I don't know why I call it, my cancer. I don't own it. I think it owns me, really. Anyway, everything started out normal last night. Chamba, Dora, Evan, Miss Emily, mom, and I went and released some of the animals that we brought from Johannesburg. The rhino was my favorite, as it scared Miss Emily the most, kicking and making a weird noise, kind of like when David blows his nose in the morning back home. I'm happy that all the animals survived the trip. Chamba told me that they don't always make it, but that they have been lucky lately. He says that Evan's work is helping to save Africa's endangered species. I still don't understand how he gets the egg and sperm from dead animals, or live ones for that matter. I think I'll ask him about that. I think I'd like to be whatever kind of doctor he is, after I go to college. If I go to college. Or maybe I'll be a writer, like I planned.

After we released the animals, Chamba drove us to a hilltop where there were a lot of people standing around a fire. He told us not to worry and that they were from the village. He introduced me to some of them. One of the men was his dad. He didn't have any clothes except for a wrap made of some sort of leather, fastened around his waist. He was real skinny and I could see his ribs. Every one of them. Chamba said his dad was born in Tanzania, another country in Africa, and that he moved him to the village just one year ago, because his mother had died, Chamba's grandmother, and he wanted his dad to be near him.

There were about ten men and ten women around the fire. We sat down on the soft, cool sand and Chamba pointed to different places

155

around Tsavo. We could see the village way below and people walking around the huts and Miss Emily's big white house. The people looked like ants. Real small. I then talked to Miss Emily for a while. She asked me about school and whether I had a boyfriend and other typical questions. She didn't ask me about the leukemia, so I didn't tell her anything. I don't think she knows. At least I don't think so. And I really hope she doesn't find out. I just want to be a normal tourist, visiting Africa. Chamba and Dora know. I heard them asking mom about it one night on the way from Johannesburg. They thought I was asleep, I think, but I was really just leaning my head against the window with my eyes closed. I just wanted to hear what they would say. Mom said I was sick and had leukemia but that I was doing better. I felt relieved when she said I was doing better, I really did. And I just kept my eyes closed. Anyway, as Miss Emily pounded me with questions, and I denied having a boyfriend about a million times, I saw Chamba ask mom to follow him. They went back over to the Land Cruiser and talked for a few minutes. I couldn't hear what they were saying this time. I just saw mom look over at me, then nod at Chamba.

We watched the stars and the bright white moon come up and the sun go down over what Chamba said was the highest peak of Kilimanjaro. It seemed as though all of Kenya was rising into the sky. I've never seen such bright stars in all my life, much brighter than in Kentucky, except on the clearest of winter nights. Mom said it was because there isn't as much air pollution in Tsavo, and not as much moisture.

About ten minutes later something kind of weird started to happen. A few of the men near the fire started walking in a circle around it, and some women started singing African songs of some sort. I couldn't understand a word. But it sounded kind of good, whatever they were singing, and the men stayed with the rhythm. I asked what they were doing and Evan said, You're about to be treated to a traditional African dance. I was excited, at this point anyway. After all, how many girls my age get to see real Africans dancing around a fire right in the middle of Africa. The closest thing I've seen to this was when mom and I went to see The Lion King. But this was different and a little scary, being out in the open with all the wild animals.

There is a bird, a yellow-throated sand-grouse, sitting in a tree, claws clenched about a thin dead branch. Keen eyes peeled open, it sees a bright spot flaring in the distance, like a small sun, only with movement around it in every direction. Its wings shuffle a bit and it spreads them wide and leaps from the branch, swooping downward to gain speed. The wings flap smoothly as it flies toward the bright spot, the movement in the darkness.

Megan hears a shrieking sound. Her mouth drops and she intones, "What's that?"

"A bird. See it?" Evan says, pointing high at a mere dot in the sky, just barely distinguishable.

"It doesn't seem frightened by the dancing, or the fire."

Evan nods and sits down next to her. Katie is still talking to Chamba, over near the Land Cruiser.

"Megan," Evan continues with a serious edge to his voice, "I'm afraid I didn't tell you everything when I said you would get to see a traditional African dance."

She turns and looks up at him. She sees the reflection of the fire splashing across his face. She asks, "What do you mean?"

"I'm afraid Chamba has taken it upon himself to ask these people to come here, and dance for you."

"For me?"

"Yes, just for you."

"It's a healing dance, Megan."

She looks down at her legs, which are crossed and resting on a layer of moist sand and grass that tickles her ankles.

He goes on, "I'm sure that's what Chamba is telling your mother over there. Just so you know, she had nothing to do with this. You see, Chamba's father is what's known as a master of healing, a *mganga*, they call them, and—"

"Can he really heal?"

"He believes so, and his people do too. They take this, the healing dance, very seriously. And when Chamba learned that you were sick, he probably just thought he would try and help. But I wish he would have told us about this."

There is silence for several seconds as Megan stares off at the fire and the blushed bodies moving around it.

"If you want, we can leave," Evan says, rubbing his hand over her back.

"Won't they be offended?"

"You're worried about them?"

"Well..."

157

"You're amazing, Megan," he says softly. "No, I'm sure they won't mind. We can just say that you are tired, and then we'll head back to the village."

Katie and Chamba approach with Dora, who is shaking her head, obviously irritated with her husband. As they near, Evan says, "Megan and I have just been talking, you know, about the healing dance. I told her that the dancers won't be offended if we head back to the village."

Katie leans down on one knee, holds her right palm up to Megan's face, "Do you want to go back, honey?"

Megan's gaze moves from her mother's eyes to the sky, where she again sees the bird, now circling the fire and the dancers as if it is joining in. It crosses her mind that maybe it is just riding on the rising currents of warm air. She then hears the singing getting faster, louder, and sees that one of the men is tapping a long walking stick at the ground. A rut seems to have formed in the sand, for the light from the fire drops away, creating a black ring where the dancers move clockwise.

I decided to stay and watch the dance, or at least I thought that was all I would be doing. I was a bit frightened that all these village people had come all the way out to this hilltop in the middle of Tsavo just to dance for me. Afterall, I'm not even African and don't even know them. When mom asked whether I wanted to leave or stay, I hesitated, not knowing what to say. I didn't want to hurt Chamba and Dora's feelings, since they've been so nice to us, and gave us a ride all the way from Johannesburg. They didn't have to do that. I was kind of upset that Chamba had told all these strangers that I was sick, without asking me first. I mean, that's one reason I came to Africa, to get away from my old life, and get away from people who know I'm sick. But, and I don't know why, I said I'd like to stay and watch the dance. The words seemed to just leap from my mouth without my thinking or saying them, almost effortlessly, kind of like that bird that floated over the fire without even flapping its wings.

Evan tried to explain what we would be seeing. But first he told us we should move closer to the fire and the ring of dancers. So we all walked over and sat down together, facing the warmth, just out of reach of the embers that were floating up over the dancers and then down to the ground. Everyone seemed so worried about me, like I was going to freak out or something. Chamba kept saying, "Megan, this is nothing that can hurt you, you understand, nothing that can hurt you." Actually, all the fuss made me a little nervous. I thought, hey, it's just a dance, what's the big deal. But Chamba and Dora acted like I was about to have a bone marrow transplant or something.

Anyway, as the dancers moved faster around the fire Evan told me that they were working themselves into something called "kia" and that they were trying to raise their spiritual energy, or what they call "num," to a point which they can heal people. He said they do these dances about four times a month, and sometimes they last all night. At this point I was already sort of tired, and didn't want to hear that, but he said this one wouldn't be that long. He then joked, "You can go home and tell your friends that you learned the dwa—the giraffe dance." Evan then smiled. But then he became more serious when Chamba looked over. Evan then said, "But this is very important to these people, Megan. The healing dance is vital to their spirituality, right Chamba." Chamba nodded without moving his eyes, which looked all glassy and wet. Right about then I heard a loud yell from one of the dancers and I thought my heart would stop. It sounded something like, "Zai—i! Kowhadididi!" Then the man who yelled looked right at me.

There are ten men and five women dancing around the fire now, all led by Chamba's father who chants and taps a long, well-worn stick, its bark stripped off, smooth as river rock. He pokes at the earth, yet looks at the stars and every few steps glances over at Megan. Smoke spirals upward, catching the thin hesitant breeze slipping down from Mount Kilimanjaro.

Dora sits next to her Chamba, then leans over and whispers to Katie, "They're getting closer. The num is beginning to boil. See their sweat?"

"Yes." Katie is mesmerized by what she is witnessing.

"That's the first sign of num. It's very close now..."

Katie swallows hard and feels her pulse quicken, not sure that staying was a good idea after all. She thinks, *If David could just see us now...lord, he'd kill me. But it's too late to leave.*

Chanting, more dancing.

The night air becomes heavy and sky even darker, clouds from the west lingering closer and peering down on the healing dance. They gather then break apart, circle, hover, and gather once more.

Suddenly the mood of the dancers changes, becoming jovial and loose. No frowns, no wrinkled foreheads, no blank transcendental stares at the abyss inside the fire and smoke. There are lighter taps of the walking sticks and lighter taps of the naked feet. Megan thinks the dance must be over, everyone relaxing, it seems, but Chamba rises at the sight and asks Dora to dance with him, "Come Dora, dance, dance," and she begins to pick herself up, as an elephant waddles back and forth, gaining momentum. A knee. Another knee. A palm on the grass, and her grand figure slowly conquers gravity, the moon, the stars, the clouds helping lift her to the air.

"Come, my precious love," Chamba continues, smiling, as she gives him a contentious stare.

"Oh my back..." she says at length, clutching her lower spine.

"We'll heal your back," he says as he takes her hand and they walk toward the fire ring where only the women are singing now, their words faint and floating like feathers upon the smoke.

Evan gets up, his lean, muscular frame not making work of it, and he says, "Katie, would you like to dance?"

At first she thinks he is joking, and her face does nothing to conceal this. "I, I don't know—"

"Ah, it's easy, just do what they do," he continues as he motions toward Chamba and Dora and the fire.

"Well, okay," she says as she gets up then turns to Megan. "Do you mind?"

"No, go ahead," she replies as she crosses her arms across her chest, "I'm looking forward to seeing this."

"Yeah, I bet." Katie offers Evan her arm and says, "Okay Evan, lead the way. Don't be offended if I step on your toes."

"You can't. See? Everyone goes the same direction."

She looks over at the dancers, "Well, then don't be offended if I nip at your heels."

"Ah...you'll do fine."

"I take it you've done this a few times?"

He nods, "Oh...four or five. The last time was about a year ago. I had the flu and Chamba made me get up and boil some num."

As they near the fire the dancers slow and open a space for them to join in. The singing intensifies, arms swing and touch the clouds, necks bop like wild turkeys, and bodies become rubber.

Katie is stiff at first but starts to enjoy moving about as she watches Evan try to copy all of Chamba's moves, which are much more graceful, purposeful. The circle becomes one, everyone somehow in sync. Evan looks over to Megan and sees her laughing, shaking her head. He waves his right arm, tries to get her to join in.

Megan points at herself, as if to say, Me?

Evan nods then runs over to get her. The circle opens and invites her in, envelops her. She's right behind Evan who is right behind Katie. Dora and Chamba are in front. Miss Emily is in the Land Cruiser.

More laughing. Louder singing, the village men now joining in again,

"Zai—i! Kowhadididi!"

"Zai—i! Kowhadididi!"

"Zai—i! Kowhadididi!"

Lightning rips across the lowering sky and Katie looks up, startled, and trips. She falls to her knees, her face somehow mingling embarrassment and joy. The dancers don't stop, they just move in place as Evan extends a hand, "Are you okay?"

"Yes, not watching where I'm going, I'm afraid." She dusts off her legs and wipes her face, which transfers some dirt to her cheeks and gives the appearance of a warrior. Diagonal streaks.

Smiling, Evan says, "Wait, you've got something on your face." He reaches up with both hands and gently brushes each cheek with the back of his fingers. His eyes lock onto hers, which stirs feelings inside himself that he doesn't expect.

She is somewhat taken aback at the touch of his skin to hers. It's as if all the world has just shut off. No singing, no lightning, no breezes moving over her.

He says to her, "There, I think I got it."

"Thanks," she replies and the singing is turned back on. She begins moving again with the rhythm and everyone follows.

I wasn't sure I wanted to be in the dance. I mean, I've never danced like that before. But there didn't seem much to what they were doing. And I think just about anyone could dance better than mom. So

when Evan asked me to come over I thought, what do I have to lose? It's not like Billy Murphy or my other classmates were there watching me or something. And just about everyone dancing had very short hair, so I didn't think I'd stand out too bad.

We all must have gone around that fire a hundred times. You would think it would be boring, but it wasn't. Chamba's father kept changing the pace and did different weird moves with his arms and legs, and we just followed as best as we could. I've never laughed so hard in my life, especially when mom fell down.

Then everything started to change. Chamba's father started shaking a lot. I mean really a lot. I thought he was having a heart attack or something. Sweat was dripping from every inch of his thin, frail body and he looked wobbly. When he turned toward me his eyes were glassy and blank. Everyone stopped dancing except him, but the singing continued as he moved around the fire and stared at each of us. I thought I was going to freak! I think Chamba saw that I was getting nervous. He came over and put an arm around me and said, "Don't worry, Megan, my father is struggling with the gods because it is from them that sickness comes to us."

I nodded as if everything was all right, and I wasn't worried. But I sort of was. Chamba's father was now falling to the ground occasionally and having to be helped back up by the other dancers. He was trembling badly. Chamba leaned down and whispered in my ear, The spirits are attracted by the beautiful singing and dancing. They're above us, and all around us, and my father is in battle with them. He's going to see the sickness in us, and pull it out.

Again I nodded. I thought, hey, cool with me, you can pull out all the leukemia you want, I don't mind one bit. And as I thought this to myself Chamba's father began to approach me and a chill shot through my entire body, tingling from my spine to my neck, like when a teacher asks a question no one knows, then turns to you for the answer. As he made his way over, Chamba said, "Don't worry, Megan, don't worry." This sort of made me worry a whole lot more. His father was four feet from me now and he was holding his hands out, fluttering them up and down. I turned and looked at mom, and she seemed just as nervous as I was. Then I looked at Evan and he just nodded, as if to say, hang in there kid, he'll be done in a minute.

Something about this nod made me calm down some, and I looked back at Chamba's father. He was chanting loudly and looking up at the dark clouds. As if on cue, lightning instantly lit up everything, and he looked back down at me. He was still trembling and his skin seemed like it was covered with Vaseline or something. He was real shiny and must have smelled terrible, but I couldn't smell anything. He came closer suddenly, and I jumped back a bit but felt Chamba's hand on my back, steadying me. I felt like turning around and running for the Land Cruiser, but I knew it would create a big scene. So I stayed put, and Chamba's father started fluttering his hands above my head, then down my neck and arms. He then moved to my chest and just kept on fluttering downward, even over my boobs, then to my legs. As he came back up, shaking and yelling something, I started feeling kind of dizzy, then real hot, and the fire was just a big orange and yellow blur with the silhouette of a thin man moving in front of it. I heard the singing soften and my mom's voice saying something I couldn't understand.

CHAPTER TWENTY-SIX

In a dream early in the morning hours, quietly, she came to her, the slight figure draped in loose graveclothes. A yellow sun dress awash with crisp white daisies. She wore a blue ribbon, woven neatly, tied in a bow about her golden hair made of sunlight and silk. All around her were flowers. Angela loved flowers.

Spinning round...

Behind Megan, to her left, to her right, the dancers, even Chamba's father, stood silently looking on with eyes speckled with compassion.

And near them, was her baby sister. Angela.

"Angela, what are you doing here?" Megan asked, confused and lost in a blurry nightscape. She looked around, spinning round, she saw where she was. It was Boone Park, a few minutes from home, next to school. Under the maples and poplars and oaks. "Why are the dancers here? They can't be in Kentucky, they just can't."

Spinning round.

"I miss you, Megan," the soft voice came, a whisper of an angel.

It can't be Angela, Megan thought, she's dead. And it doesn't sound like her. She didn't talk like that.

"I miss you, Megan," she continued. "Do you miss me?"

"Yes, yes, of course. But...I thought you passed away. The car accident. You died, Angela."

"I didn't die, Megan, I'm here with you. See? Look at me. Touch me. Smell my hair."

"It can't be you—"

"I miss you, Megan. I love you."

"I love you too."

"I'm sorry I couldn't give you the transplant, I'm so sorry. Do you forgive me, Megan? Do you?"

"It wasn't your fault."

"Do you? Do you forgive me?"

"I don't blame you, Angela."

"I could have saved you..."

Megan shook her head, dizziness, everything blurred even more. Again she looked about her dream world. "Why are you here? Why are these people, the dancers, why are you all here?"

"They brought me, Megan. They brought me here to see you, to talk to you, to let me tell you how much I love you. And how sorry I am. Do you understand?"

"I, I..."

"You must believe. They want to heal you, Megan. Let them heal you. Believe, just believe..."

And then, as suddenly as they appeared, the tender sparkling eyes of her baby sister, staring out of death, slowly faded like stars greeting dawn. Then they disappeared entirely.

And indeed the sun was rising, seemingly at that very instant. Megan opened her eyes and a breeze swam over her face from the open window above the black iron bed she was in at Miss Emily's house. She sensed the scent of roses, clean and crisp and exquisite.

Megan sighs, as she remembers her dream. Once again, only a dream.

CHAPTER TWENTY-SEVEN

Miss Emily is cooking eggs and bacon this morning. Megan smells the enticing aromas as she finishes writing in her journal, her hand tired. Her whole body tired, really. What a night, she thinks to herself, exhausted. She folds the journal and places the cap on the pen, walks down a long hallway with black and white pictures staring at her, and moves toward the welcome aromas of breakfast.

"You're finally up, huh sweetie?" Miss Emily says, hovering over the kitchen sink, clanking glasses and knocking pans together. Both her hands are moving at once and in every direction except where her eyes are pointed, an experienced conductor leading a familiar orchestra. Grease is spitting and heaving itself from a frying pan and the air smells of coffee so thick and potent a finger might be used to take a taste from the air.

"I kinda slept in," Megan finally replies.

"You passed Kinda an hour ago, honey," she says with a belly laugh that makes her rear jiggle beneath her flowered dress; the tapestry of white carnations dance over a rolling blue field, from her tanned knees to her waist. "That's all right," she continues. "You needed a good rest. It was a long night wasn't it."

Megan nods, wipes the sleep from her eyes. She gives a glance about the kitchen then says, "Where's my mom?"

"Outside. On the verandah. She's on her third cup of coffee already."

"I'm sure she is. She lives on the stuff."

"You're probably too young to like it, aren't you."

"I drink it once in a while. I'll have a little, if you don't mind. Anything to wake me up."

As Miss Emily pours a cup piping hot with lazy steam rolling over the lip, Megan hears singing leaking in from the open window above the sink. A high pitch, melodic, and as sweet as her grandma's voice in the choir on Sunday mornings. Megan listens intently:

"Little lady, little lady...
so lovely your flowers grow.

Little lady, little lady...
by God's breath you sow."

Megan walks over to another window glazed with moist morning air, then peers outward as Miss Emily approaches.

"Here you go, honey," she says, handing Megan a cup and saucer. Blue with white carnations, just like her dress. "She has a lovely voice, doesn't she," Miss Emily continues, also looking outside.

"Yeah, real good."

"That's Marta. She helps me tend the garden once a week. I just can't keep up with it anymore. Not with this back of mine."

Outside on the verandah, Katie is sitting in a wicker lounge whose arms are bare of paint and seat worn through in spots, giving it the appearance of leopard skin. She is taking in the view of the coffee fields and they are taking in her. The air is fresh and clear as crystal. *Such a beautiful place to live*, she thinks as she runs her eyes over the horizon again. *If only David could be here to see it.*

David?

With the exception of Miss Emily's inquisition, she hadn't thought of him since she called home from Chamba's and Dora's house in Nairobi. He was asleep, groggy, answered after the fourth ring just before the Sorry we're not at home message.

"Hello," he said, as the static hissed and popped on the line.

"It's me, honey."

A long pause then, "Gee, I thought you ditched me, decided to stay down there or something."

The words hit her dead center in the gut, and she didn't know why.

"Are you and Megan okay?"

"Yes, we're fine. Everything's fine. I just wanted to check in. We arrived safely in Nairobi last night. It was quite a drive."

"I still can't believe you got in a car with complete strangers and drove all that way and—"

"David, let's not start that again. All right? We're fine. And Dora and Chamba are the kindest people I think I've ever met. They're taking good care of us."

"When are you coming home?"

"Well..."

"Katie, you can't stay down there forever."

"I know, I know. I'm not sure how much longer. They're taking us

167

to Tsavo National Park today. Megan's really looking forward to it."

"Is she doing okay?"

"Yes, she feels fine. Looks great, her hair's even coming back."

"Good, good. Well, is she around? I'd like to say hi."

"She's outside with Chamba. I'm sorry, I should have waited to call."

"Just tell her I love her, and miss her. I miss you too."

"I know honey, we'll be home soon, I promise."

"When are you going to check in again?"

"I'm not sure. I doubt we'll have access to a phone or cell signal at the park. If I can, I'll call you in a couple of days, okay?"

"All right."

"But don't worry about us, you know, if I can't check in. It could be several days. Well, I better get off here. I'm not paying for the call. They insisted."

"I love you."

"Love you too. Bye."

"Bye."

She pensively hung up, stared at the wall in front of her covered with family pictures, most yellowed or tattered and resting in thin wooden frames without glass, then thanked Chamba for letting her use the phone.

And now, amidst the varied scents of roses floating up to the verandah, David and work and doctor appointments and bone marrow waiting lists seem a million miles away from this little remote village sitting before her. She stares at the vast green blankets of coffee resting at the feet of Kilimanjaro off in the distance. She yawns and stretches her arms over her head as Megan walks from the house carrying two cups of coffee. "Good morning, mom."

"Hey...you're up, huh. Good morning."

"Here, Miss Emily said you'd probably like some more coffee," Megan says as she gingerly hands her the simmering cup.

"Thanks. Here, sit down. Just look at this view."

"I know. I can't believe I'm really here. Mom, do you think we'll get to see some elephants today?"

"Maybe. You never know. Evan told me that they move around a lot. But he said he'd take us out today to have a look."

"Cool."

"Are you sure you're up to it?"

"You mean after last night?" Megan asks.

"Yeah. We stayed out pretty late."

"No big deal. I'm fine. I had fun. It just got kinda weird at the end, you know, when Chamba's father came over to me."

Katie takes a sip of coffee then says, "I know. I almost tried to stop him, and make everyone stop singing and dancing, but I didn't want to cause a big scene."

Megan nods.

"Well," Katie continues, "I guess not many Kentuckians get to take part in an African healing dance though. Right?"

Megan looks pensive, distracted. Her head turns away.

"Megan, did you hear a word I said?"

Megan turns toward her mother, her face long and serious. "Mom, do you believe those dancers can really heal people, I mean, really cure a disease?"

"I believe *they* believe they can."

"But you don't think they really can?"

Katie pauses, trying to find the right words, then looks her daughter straight in her wide eyes and says, "Yes, I believe they can heal, with God's help. I really think they can heal, Megan. That is, if the people they are trying to help believe they will be healed."

"What if you're not African?"

Katie moves her eyes to the horizon, "I think we're all the same, don't you? Chamba, his father, Dora, Miss Emily, Evan—we're all the same."

Megan looks down at the white boards of the verandah where a stream of ants are pouring through a crack. As she follows their trail she sees that they are coming from a flower pot near the verandah's hand railing.

Katie moves her attention back to Megan. "Don't you think we're all the same?"

Megan nods slowly, then scoots the chair she's sitting on closer to Katie, places her head on her mother's shoulder and reaches for her hand.

CHAPTER TWENTY-EIGHT

A pale limpid moon bows in the noon sky as Africa veils itself beneath cascading waves of shimmering ashen heat. From the village, the landscape appears as if massive bodies of water have suddenly formed across the plains, vast oceans connecting and reflecting continents of green and brown. A mirage. An invitation to move toward easy, refreshing waters, lapping waves of blue.

It is twelve-thirty when Evan aims his Land Rover down the serpentine, graveled drive of Miss Emily's house. He tells everyone, "Better fasten your seatbelts. It'll be a little rough where we're going."

He had decided to take his vehicle rather than Chamba's so they wouldn't have to disconnect the animal trailer. Evan's old Land Rover wasn't much as far as looks are concerned, but it had almost become a friend to him over the years. A reliable friend.

A lunch has been packed—bacon, lettuce, tomato sandwiches and potato crisps, watermelon and white wine from a store in Nairobi, courtesy of Miss Emily who said it was essential for a proper outing into the bush country. The picnic basket tied to the roof with bright orange bungee cords is the only luggage for the journey. Evan had said to keep the weight down, which Miss Emily laughed at then responded to by returning a wry grimace and tugging at her dress fastened tightly about her waist and said, "I'm retaining water right now, hope I don't sink the boat." She then feigned another half laugh and half smile, climbed into the backseat of the Land Rover and rolled the window next to her down.

Cameras, sun block, sunglasses, and a small box of tissue were all Evan allowed inside his four-wheeled, rusted vessel, except for a book which he saw Megan reading when he entered Miss Emily's house. *Out of Africa*. Megan had seen it sitting on a shelf in the living room bookcase and inquired of Miss Emily, "Why do you have three copies of *Out of Africa?*"

"Three, that's all?" she replied, then went on to say that she thought she had six and must have given a few away. She told Megan that over the years friends had given them to her, but when Megan picked each one up she found stickers on each binding with the same exact price from the same exact store. So her friends, Megan thought, must have bought them all at the same place and at the same time. Miss Emily said she could have one of the three and Megan thanked her, "I really appreciate it," and removed it from the shelf where it was cradled by books with the name F. Scott Fitzgerald emblazoned on their well-worn cloth covers. She ran her eyes over their titles and found several of them very intriguing: *Bernice Bobs Her Hair, The Diamond As Big As The Ritz,* and *The Great Gatsby*.

I'll have to read those someday, she thought to herself then said, "You sure do like this Fitzgerald guy. Does he write really good?"

"Yes," Miss Emily replied seriously but with a hidden grin, "I think he's an up and coming author, lots of potential...but he hasn't published anything lately. He indeed writes really *well*."

Save the one and only book, the cameras, and other small items, the only other cargo is an extra container of African rainwater tied, as always, to the rear bumper in a can intended for gasoline or diesel, simply for an added measure of safety. Evan once walked sixty kilometers without water, his only friends the thorn trees and acacias which loaned him shade to defend himself from the burning air. A fuel pump had broken down near the foothills of Mount Kilimanjaro, a lesson that almost cost him his life. Always carry water. Always. On that wretched day a maelstrom of vultures circled high, reconnoitered, and followed his path, apparently patient and waiting to pick at his thirsty, tired bones. Chamba later said that the *Sheitani*, the devil, was out for his soul, and Evan agreed that it was so hot on that journey he indeed felt like he was in hell.

There will be no vultures today, Evan says to himself as the Land Rover makes its way, tires crunching across the pebbles and larger stones. Chamba is sitting shotgun with Dora by his side and in the back seat are Miss Emily sandwiched between Katie and Megan. Miss Emily fans herself with a piece of cardboard she found on the floorboard and wears an expression that mingles a hint of lasciviousness with arrogance, like an old-time southern bell waiting to be asked to dance while poised on a ballroom floor of some grand mansion or plantation. She even throws in an accent on occasion, along with a "y'all" here and there. Katie wonders whether she's really from the south or if she simply picks up the dialect of whomever is around her, for when they first arrived she spoke with a heavy forward tongue reminiscent of Dora and the locals. And now she's gone deep south, all in one night, as every sentence ends on a high note and her i-n-g endings don't have g's. Katie ponders how many weary foreign travelers have wandered into Miss Emily's nest and found themselves suddenly conversing with someone from their faraway home.

Y'all goin' on a safari?

As the earth heaves itself at the moving watercolor that is the afternoon sun, and the cool shade of morning fades along with the dusty image of the village and Miss Emily's house in the Land Rover's rearview mirrors, Megan catches a glimpse of a hippo and asks Evan if they can stop and see it up close.

He says "No, They're too dangerous," and goes on to tell her that hippos kill more people—Africans and tourists—than any other animal. The one she has spotted is one which Evan has known of and tracked for over a year, nicknamed Fat Albert. "He's not a happy camper, Megan," he says as he slows somewhat and nudges slightly closer, "That hippo is three tons of flesh and teeth, and overturned two canoes last year."

"Did anyone get hurt?" Megan inquires, leaning forward and on the edge of the seat.

"No. But it left four German canoeists with some very expensive and very wet Leica cameras. They stayed with you a couple days, didn't they Miss Emily?"

"Yes, yes they did. Real nice fellows," Miss Emily says as she swats a fly on her round, bronze kneecap.

Evan goes on to tell Megan how he was almost attacked once in Zambia, "We were stupid, real stupid. I hadn't been here that long and we were paddling down the Zambezi River near Victoria Falls, not paying an ounce of attention to anything but our conversation. All the sudden a hippo rose from the water right before the boat, even picked us up some. It was pretty shallow. The hippo just stood there and stared at us, trying to decide whether we were dinner or not, I suppose. He started biting at the water, tossing his head back and forth, slashing violently. That's their warning sign. If you ever see one do that, get away from it fast."

Chamba nods and chimes in, "There's a saying in Africa, the most dangerous place is between a hippo and its route to water."

"So what happened," Megan asks with eyes that meet Evan's as he turns his head toward the back seat. She sees the skin of his neck crease and fold upon itself. Reddened and tan.

"Well, the hippo came at us. We jumped out and ran to the shore," he says matter-of-factly then continues after a pause, "I looked over my shoulder and he was slamming his chin down on the boat, smashing it to pieces."

"Wow..."

"I remember my friend saying, Welcome to Africa."

"And then what?"

172

"Oh, we just walked back to camp, real fast like. No more boat."

Evan had promised Megan that he'd find her at least one elephant on their ride and picnic into the wild. Male or female, baby or adult, any kind of elephant by three o'clock would do. Yet no one, not even Miss Emily with her rubberized hunter-green grand safari binoculars that cost her two hundred dollars via mail order, had laid eyes on a single animal, except the one hippo, and two hyenas loitering around a ravaged carcass of some sort. Their bones shown through their skin like a playful child's fingers aglow with the beam of a flashlight, and they snarled with crooked teeth, which Chamba had pointed out were "as yellow as a scorpion's tail." The hyenas' cheeks, necks, and front paws had rusty red flakes and smears, dried blood. A successful day of stalking, preying, scavenging for protein.

So at five minutes till three o'clock, Evan is surrendering his natural hunting abilities. He pulls to a stop and hops out of the Land Rover with nary a word, then flops down the tailgate and reaches underneath a blue tarp to remove a gray plastic case. He opens it up, still not saying anything.

Megan intones, "He brought a laptop computer?"

Evan doesn't reply. He's apparently in deep concentration, she thinks. So she looks at Chamba, who nods.

Evan tilts his sweaty wrist, glances at his watch. "Three minutes," he says quietly.

"What are you doing," Megan finally asks.

"Looking for elephants."

"On a computer?" she replies incredulously.

"Yep, hang on one sec," he answers then types in something.

The laptop beeps and then he plugs in a small black box, four by four inches square, with a chrome antenna on one side.

Beep beep beep.

"There we go," he continues as he looks at the liquid crystal display, hits a couple more keys. And with that, he closes the laptop and secretes it away, back under the wrinkled tarp, and closes the tailgate with a clunk.

A few seconds later and his foot is planted on the accelerator pedal and he says as he points, "There are a couple elephants over this ridge."

The Land Rover is moving so quickly toward this ridge no one manages to say anything until he slows down near some thick bushes tattooed with tiny white spots.

The engine coughs then hushes completely.

"Okay, everyone get out, slowly," he says. "Try not to make any noise. Leave the doors open."

Heads obediently nod yes.

"All right, this way..."

They walk over to the bushes and Megan sees that the little white spots on them are actually bulbous seed pods waiting to drop or fly away or be picked up by the wind or by some furry legged animal.

As Evan pulls some branches aside, making a little window for everyone to peer through, he whispers, "There's one of them. Here Megan, scoot closer."

She moves in front of him.

"See it?"

"Yeah..."

"I don't see anything," Katie says as she leans her head toward Evan's shoulder.

Chamba says, "Next to that big tree, see?"

"She's right there, mom. Can't you see it?" Megan whispers as she pulls the branches down.

"Oh...there. I see it. Wow..."

Evan turns to her, "That's *Mrembo*, which means beautiful."

"You've seen her before?" Katie asks.

"Yes. Many times. I tagged her. Look on her back, around the neck. See that black strap?"

"Yes."

"It's holding a radio collar."

"So that's how you tracked her down, with the laptop."

He nods and whispers, "We have GPS collars on almost all of the larger game in Tsavo."

"Interesting," Katie says. "So why didn't you just use the GPS when we arrived, to help find them sooner?"

"Well, I like a challenge once in a while. All this technology can take the fun out of things. Don't you think?"

"I agree." She then thinks about how many times she had tried to make her smart phone get a signal on the drive between Johannesburg and Nairobi, as if she couldn't live or breathe without being connected to the internet for a few days.

"What I don't understand is," Evan continues, "where's the other one."

"Other one?"

"I saw two ID's on the laptop. Mrembo and her baby girl, Daisy."

"There, I think I see her, over to the left," Katie points.

"Yep, there she is."

All eyes follow the two elephants walking about in the distance, their bodies glistening in the heat of the day.

"Can we move closer," Megan asks. "Would it scare them away?"

"It might," Evan replies. "Why don't we wait a couple minutes, then walk down this ridge. These two are pretty calm, I seem to remember. They might let us get close."

"Cool," Megan says, then tosses a steady stare over to Daisy, who is slowly coming into full view, swinging her trunk and bouncing left and right.

And then it happens.

A shot.

Then another.

From the hill to the left? No. The bushes near the stream? Perhaps. The sound echoes, bouncing off every surface. Trees. Rocks. Shocked faces.

"Get down!" Evan yells urgently, but trying not to be too loud. "Everyone stay quiet..."

"Mom," Megan starts to speak, "what—"

"Quiet, honey. Stay down."

Evan's face mingles anger with fear. He holds Megan's head down with one palm and with the other Katie's back as he raises his eyes to the elephants once more. Only Daisy is standing. Her mother is lying on her side in a growing pool of blood which reflects the sun. He says under his breath, "Those sonsofbitches." He feels his temples throbbing, his face getting hot. He asks himself, *Did I bring a gun? No. Left it at the village.* "Chamba," he whispers, "Did you bring a gun?"

"Yes," Chamba replies and slides his hand into his shirt, then into a chest holster, and pulls out a small Taurus .38. Rusted but loaded. He hands it to Evan.

As if the scene before them isn't enough, Katie is surprised that Chamba had a handgun strapped to his chest. But she tells herself that it must be for protection when releasing the animals every few weeks for Evan.

They apparently haven't been seen, for there are two men cascading down a rock-strewn embankment two hundred yards to the right of the kill. A trail of dust and stones chases them, envelops their black boots, and tries to bury them. One man carries a rifle, the other a steel machete that twists and turns and gleams in the sun like a mirror. Both are dressed in khaki clothes, shirts and shorts that stick to their sweaty bodies. One of them has short facial hair, a beard. Evan recognizes him. He had worked Tsavo for the past year, making quick runs into the park then vanishing over the Tanzanian border. Word in the village was that he carried a laptop and GPS receiver in his truck, which Evan found hard to believe. Until now. The man and his partner had almost been caught three times over the past few months, but had gotten away. And here the two men are, just sitting ducks. Yet what the hell can Evan and Chamba do about them, with Katie, Dora, Megan, and Miss Emily present. Too dangerous. Plus, all there was to protect everyone was Chamba's dated and dilapidated .38 pistol.

Megan begins to shake. She slowly raises her head but Evan whispers urgently, "Stay down!"

"What do you want to do?" Chamba inquires apprehensively. Dora and Miss Emily are ducked down behind him, knowing not to move or say a word.

A pause, then Evan says, "We gotta sit tight, I don't want anyone to get hurt."

"But it's—"

"I know, Chamba. I know who it is. I've wanted to catch these two poachers for a long time. But not today. We'll let them take the tusks and get away...this time. Don't worry, they'll be back and we'll be ready."

Chamba shakes his head and peers toward the two murderers. They've reached their target and with a few swift swings of the machete a tusk and sizable chunk of the mother elephant's nose is severed and falls away like the limb of a tree, cherry-red blood gushes out at once and is swallowed by the earth. Another swing finishes the job and takes the other six-foot tusk that will soon be trinkets and tourist junk sitting in some roadside store, or shipped off to Asia.

The killers seem to talk, and one of them aims a hand with African blood on it to the hazy horizon where the baby elephant, Daisy, escaped to seconds ago.

CHAPTER TWENTY-NINE

The battle between elephants, poachers and game authorities began long before Evan arrived in Kenya. It was 1947. The British colonial administration set aside seven thousand acres, and Tsavo National Park was born. Almost immediately the conflict between man and animal was set in motion. The Wakamba tribe, traditional elephant hunters, lived in the area, their huts nestled and camouflaged among the commiphora shrubs. They carried long-bows with arrows dipped in poison strong enough to stop an elephant's heart within minutes, sometimes seconds. Park officials battled against the Wakamba people, for the elephants were increasingly being pushed to the fringes of the hillsides and more protected areas. As the war raged on, rifles replaced bows and arrows. Most of the tribe was ousted from the park and the elephant population increased from about fifteen thousand to over forty thousand.

Elephants don't have any natural predators. Man is the species' greatest enemy. So as Tsavo implemented tactics aimed at stopping poaching, the elephant population swelled to such an extent that the landscape became trampled and devastated, for an adult elephant can consume five hundred pounds of forage a day. Trees and plants necessary for other wildlife were ravaged, the park was dying. And dying fast.

Some called for a culling program to reduce the number of elephants. Others suggested that the best thing for the park was to let nature take its course, learn from it. Good or bad. But culling proponents argued that this, Tsavo, was not a natural situation. Rather, it was a confined habitat, forcing animals which were used to roaming hundreds of miles into a relatively small area where they could wreak havoc upon the entire ecosystem. What ensued was indeed the classic philosophical dilemma of conservation, one which Evan knew all too well. On one side you had people who believed that nature knows best and that wildlife should just be let alone. And on the other you had people who believed that wildlife is a resource that needs to be managed, controlled. Mastered.

The hands-on verses hands-off argument was still being hotly contended when a great drought struck Tsavo in the early seventies. It seemed that nature couldn't decide whether to make the park a barren desert, or make its valleys a vast sea. The climate always varied widely from year to year, season to season. But during this drought, over six thousand elephants perished as the ground and everything growing on it shriveled up. To naturalists it was proof that leaving the park alone was the best action—the strongest, fittest animals survived and the weak succumbed to thirst and starvation. To the proponents of culling, it was proof that man should have intervened and thinned out the population beforehand.

Ironically, after the drought, it was the thousands of tusks lying about the park that caused a revived wave of poaching. Six thousand elephants can leave behind a lot of ivory and it was easy picking for rebel Somalis who entered in droves, escaping their country's civil unrest. But these poachers, or *shifta* (bandits) as the Kenyans called them, came not with poison arrows but with sharpened *pangas* (machetes), loaded AK-47s, large trucks, and radio communication capabilities. Their targets were not only the tusks left behind by the drought, but over thirty thousand elephants that remained in Tsavo. Having depleted their own supply of ivory, the Somali government was sending men next door to raid the neighbor's, Kenya's, supply.

For the most part, it was easy money. After a few days lying in the sweltering African sun, an elephant's tusks can be pulled from the skull by hand, whereas those from a recent kill must be hacked off. The top prize: the tusks of an old bull, which can be six times the weight of a female's. Hampered by lack of funding for park staff, who were out gunned by poachers, the carnage continued through the seventies and eighties until fewer than five thousand elephants remained. Even these precious few had waiting customers willing to pay almost any price to satisfy their insatiable demand.

The increasing affluence of Asian nations during this time fueled poaching to new levels. Ever smaller populations of elephants sent the price of ivory higher and higher. Although trading was supposedly regulated by CITES, the Convention for International Trade in Endangered Species, wildlife inspections and customs paperwork were easy to get around. Tusks were often smuggled into countries with higher quotas on export. Burundi, with no elephants whatsoever, applied for high export quotas and served as a clearing house for other countries.

And the importers of ivory carried out equally deceptive practices—doctoring papers, paying off officials, lying about the contents of incoming crates. Dummy corporations were set up in Hong Kong, Macao, Singapore, the Philippines, Thailand, and Taiwan. Finally, CITES tried to take action. It passed a law permitting only *worked* ivory, enhanced by artisans, to be exported. To circumvent this, poachers simply had a couple rings carved into the tusks before being crated and shipped.

Where were all these crates headed?

Japan is where most of the ivory was shipped. And, at the time, Evan became entrenched in the effort to shed light on the issue. The distribution channels were flowing, hemorrhaging really, in cold elephant blood. For every hundred poached elephants, the prized tusks of about forty were ending up in Japan. Another twenty-five in Europe. And fifteen in the U.S. At its peak, Japan imported over a hundred tons of ivory each year and had over ninety companies involved in processing it.

In 1985, Evan flew to Tokyo with a contingency from the African Wildlife Fund. It was his first trip to Japan and he had actually looked forward to it, having admired many of the culture's achievements, philosophies. For Evan, it was ironic that a people who seemingly nurtured nature and spirituality could be involved in the slaughter of such a majestic animal. Weren't these the same people who cared for and meticulously trained the roots and branches of bonsai trees into beautiful representations of nature, many of which were passed from generation to generation? Wasn't this the same country that worshipped fine gardens with plants tenderly cared for and sparkling clear water, colorful and exquisite fish?

Then it hit him. Was it all about improving and controlling nature, whether it be shaping the branches of a foot-tall bonsai, or raking gravel into neat rows in a garden—or carving the tusks of a six-ton elephant? Couldn't they see what they were doing?

Evan had arrived in the bustling, awe-inspiring city of Tokyo on a crisp autumn morning. He took deep breath-fulls of everything he could see, then with a team of ten colleagues met privately with government and business leaders who claimed ivory was critical to the Japanese culture and economy. Later in the day, in a carefully orchestrated presentation, Evan and other visitors were shown examples of how ivory was used.

"We consider ivory a sacred object and one which must be cared for and cherished," one official said solemnly. Evan replied, "I'd imagine the elephants whose faces were hacked off would have felt the same about their ivory." As flashbulbs popped and cameras aimed at Evan's head, he finally knew what it was like to be snared in a cage with no way out. Fortunately, the conference ended shortly thereafter, but only after a public relations video played in which various so-called beneficial uses for elephant tusks flashed across the white screen that had magically slid down behind the Japanese officials and members of the Tokyo Arts and Crafts Cooperative. First, a stringed instrument called a *shamisen* was shown, plucked by a *bachi*—a very large pick made of ivory. Next came the *biwa*, a guitar-like instrument with shiny white frets also made of ivory, played by a lovely young woman with silky black hair, wearing a black kimono. She dissolved into shots of carvers making figurines after samurai and the Seven Gods of Luck.

The video then presented what its narrator referred to as, "The finest example of Japanese carving, the *netsuke*." Since kimonos don't have pockets, people wearing them carry objects in the sleeves or sash around the wrists. That is until the *inro* was invented. At one time it was made of leather and held flint or tinder. Later they were made of silk and contained tobacco or herb. The *inro* would be tied to the person's sash and, to keep the string tight, a *netsuke* was placed on the end, made of finely carved ivory, of course.

As Evan fidgeted in his tiny metal folding chair like a kid at church, the video continued and showed an artist creating a traditional Japanese wood-block print made with ivory paint. When the video ended, and the screen disappeared into the ceiling, one of the artisans presented another use of ivory, a *hanko*, essentially a personal signature seal used to imprint important papers. One is often carried in an *inro*, secured by an ivory *netsuke*. The presenter said that many Japanese have two, one plastic and one ivory, and the mayors of each city certify them for use on marriage certificates, real estate contracts, and other important documents. "It represents the fidelity to one's word," the man said as he held several up for the audience to see, then asked if there were any questions.

Big mistake.

Evan stood, innocently scratched his head and asked, "Can't you just sign your name or, or use a rubber stamp or something? Shame to kill a seventy year old animal—with a bigger brain than yourself—just to put some ink on a piece of paper."

And with that the press conference ended, angry looks tossing back and forth, the clicks of Nikons sounding, and blinding flashes firing everywhere. Evan half expected to be poached then and there.

Evan returned to Africa, frustrated with what he'd seen in Japan. Within a few days, he took a series of flights to Gonarezhou Park in Zimbabwe and, after gathering supplies, set out on a three-day hike to clear his mind, blow off some steam. Spend time with *living* ivory. But every time he saw an elephant, he pictured that damn video on ivory, or the shop windows he gazed in as he walked down the back streets of Tokyo, storekeepers trying to sell him ivory bowls, key chains, even tiny statues of tiny penises and flowering renditions of women.

It was astonishing really, Evan thought, that a country about the size of California could so drastically expedite the extinction of an entire species. And even more astonishing, some seventy percent of their ivory went to produce goods simply made to increase status and show affluence. In the nineteen-eighties alone, the costs of this exhibition were the souls of seven hundred thousand elephants vanished from the face of the earth forever.

For weeks following the trip to Japan, as Evan hiked through the valleys of Gonarezhou back in Africa, he couldn't help but dwell on a statistic he had read in *Nature*—that ninety-nine percent of all species that have ever lived are extinct. How long would it be before the last one percent, including elephants and man himself, succumbed to a similar fate? It was then that he realized the purpose of his life and the legacy he wished to leave behind. If he had to, he would save Africa's wildlife one animal at a time by preservation work and by cloning endangered species. He made it his goal to become *the* expert in the new field of "de-extinction."

CHAPTER THIRTY

A sickening silence pervades the air as the Land Rover moves slowly through the bush, leaving the blood-stained wastelands behind. Evan had insisted they wait at least two hours before driving on, for he had heard stories of poachers threatening tourists—witnesses—who happened to be in the wrong place at the wrong time. If it not for the worsening weather, he would have suggested everyone stay put even longer.

Without notice the sky has darkened. Drops of rain big as bees swarm about the vehicle and pummel the windshield, mixing earth-colored putty and buttery grime. Startling thuds upon the roof are heard, more like hail.

Megan's head leans against a window halfway down and the rain, blowing from the opposite side of the Land Rover, does not hit squarely on her face but merely scathes it, soothes it, and moves on. A fine mist, however, mingles with teardrops leaving her eyes, the image of the shooting still fresh and repeating, over and over. Over and over.

This is not the Africa held so dearly in her mind. This, too, is not the Africa Evan wished to convey.

"And surely this is not the way the Gods meant it to be," Chamba tells everyone as he rubs his forehead with vigor and sighs contempt through his supple, thick lips. "Something has to be done about the poachers."

"Yes, I know, Chamba. Something indeed has to be done," Evan says, turning to him.

"But what?"

"I think it's time we also take up hunting," Evan says below his breath, trying to only move the words into Chamba's ears.

This fails, and Miss Emily says, "You mean, go after them?"

With scornful eyes he replies, "Yes, that's what I mean. It's obvious that this, this reactionary mode we're in, isn't working. And the few honest game officials are spread too thin. I think it's pretty clear, I'm going to have to go after them myself, you know, just take matters into my own hands. At least for those two crossing over from Tanzania."

She shakes her head, "You could be arrested."

"Well, I'm not going to sit around and watch those bastards kill my elephants."

Chamba starts to say something but pauses, staring straight ahead at the barren landscape for several seconds, then firmly avows, "I understand, Evan. And I will help you. I understand..."

Once again they drive on in silence.

Soon, though, the silence is broken. The Land Rover seems to misfire, a sputter, then another.

"It's that damn carburetor again," Evan says. "When it rains hard like this the air filter gets saturated. Sometimes I have to sit and let it dry. But I don't think it will be drying anytime soon," he continues as he tilts his head upward, aiming at the clouds.

Katie clears her throat then says, "It's really starting to come down. I've never seen rain like this."

More sputters, as the Land Rover bucks and jostles everyone to and fro. Seats squeak, though only slightly evident over the pounding on the roof.

Suddenly Chamba leans forward, wearing a concerned face.

Evan asks, "What is it Chamba?"

"Look," he says as he points straight ahead into the cloudy image sitting before them.

"What is it?" Megan asks, finally managing to speak. "Elephants?"

"No, Megan. Probably Cape buffalo," Chamba replies then turns to Evan and says, "I don't like this."

"I know..."

On the horizon a blurry line of dots rises from left to right, appearing and fading, then reappearing.

"They're headed right for us," Evan says.

"But why?" Katie asks, sitting on the edge of the back seat.

"I don't know."

"I think they are running from a wall of water," Chamba says. "I saw this once before, many years ago, as a boy."

"You mean a flashflood?" Evan asks just as the Land Rover backfires.

"What?"

"A flashflood?" he repeats loudly. He downshifts to first gear.

Chamba nods, "We should turn around."

Evan steps hard on the brake pedal, the clutch, throws the shift lever in reverse, backs up while turning, then drives in the opposite direction.

The rain becomes vicious, with sheets of rain pummeling the Land

Rover's roof. The windshield wipers aren't helping. Evan can't see a thing.

"What do you think, where should we go, Chamba?"

"What about Tambulu?"

"Too far," he says, shaking his head no.

"Uh, maybe—"

"What's the highest elevation around here?"

"It's all valley, Evan."

"Yes I know that, but—"

"Perhaps the new tree platforms, the north canyon?"

There's a pause then Evan nods and says, "But which way from here. I can't see a damn thing."

"Wouldn't it be to the right?" Miss Emily yells from the back seat.

"No, I think to the left," Dora puts in. "When we left the area of the shooting the escarpment was on our right. So the north canyon must be on the left."

"I think she's right," Evan says and immediately pulls hard on the slippery rubber steering wheel. The Land Rover coughs and hisses some more. The earth beneath the tires turns to liquid.

Whether it was the experience of seeing the elephant get shot and its face dismantled before her eyes, or the threat before her now— being swallowed by rising water—Megan doesn't know. But suddenly she realizes death is looking at her more deliberately than ever before, more swiftly than leukemia yet equally traumatic and cruel.

Why am I not scared anymore? We could be washed away any minute. Why am I so calm?

And then it hits her.

I'm the same as everyone else. I'm not different. We're all facing death. All of us. We're just waiting to die, together. I'm not alone.

She feels ashamed for reaping such confidence and peace at the expense of the others. *It's not right*, she tells herself. *Wonder if drowning would be less painful than dying from cancer?*

Her mind reels. *Maybe this is for the best, just get it over with in one swoop, no more chemo, no more radiation, no more hiding under big hats and running from friends, no more missing Angela, or seeing mom and David cry, no more worrying about my future, who'll I'll marry, what I'll be, whether my kids get sick too. It will be over just like that. Probably real fast, won't feel a thing. Just let everything go, drink in death, swallow it whole.*

A wall of water is indeed chasing them, a half-mile back at most, Evan calculates as he works the accelerator pedal, trying to find a smoother RPM. He thinks the flashflood might be even closer now. Though he keeps checking, each glance to the side mirror yields nothing but a blur. The sky is one with the ground and, if it not for gravity, up and down would be one in the same, water in every direction. The downpour is so strong that it almost seems that the rain is rising from the earth, as if Lake Victoria has suddenly decided to give back its watery world to the clouds which lent it to her with one fell swoop.

"I think we're finally heading up hill," Evan says over his shoulder, which is damp with perspiration. He glances to the back seat, checking on Katie and Megan. Their wide-eyed faces are silent, concerned but controlled.

"Yes, I think so," Chamba agrees then motions with the flattened sweaty palm of his right hand in a sloping movement away from his chest. Dora grabs his other hand and squeezes it as if she's ringing out soiled laundry, then turns to Miss Emily, Megan, and Katie and says, "Don't worry, everything will be all right."

Don't worry, everything be all right, Megan repeats beneath her breath. *How many times have I heard that lately? Doctors, mom, David, teachers. Everyone's always telling me everything will be all right—yet everything just gets worse.*

Evan downshifts the Land Rover and says, "See that large rock, Chamba?"

"Yes."

"We're headed the right direction. I remember noticing it when we came back from the tree platforms. North canyon should be just a couple hundred yards ahead."

"Good, good..."

Katie's head throbs and wants to explode. The thought of her exposing Megan to danger hadn't occurred to her until now. She begins to question her reasoning, her decisions. Maybe reason had already left her when she decided to bring Megan to Africa. Maybe reason was now coming forward and stripping away such grandiose illusions of curing her daughter, of giving her hope, of challenging and defeating the wickedness terrorizing Megan's delicate young body. Jostling up and down on the slippery vinyl seat with the sound of rain beating at her ears, she suddenly hears David's voice above the clamor, How could you endanger Megan like this? We'll be all right, David, I promise. All right? Hell, you're all about to drown in the middle of East Africa. God will take care of us, David, we'll be all right. Like he took care of Megan's leukemia? How could you endanger her like this?

Katie grabs her head and rings out the moisture from her hair, rings out the voices.

"Mom are you okay?" Megan asks.

Her hands come down, chin raises, "Yes honey, just a headache that's all."

Megan grabs her hand, wet and shaking, "Don't worry, we'll be all right, mom," she says as she moves her eyes to her mother's.

Katie nods, and manages a smile between her tightened lips. *A pillar of strength*, she thinks to herself. *That's what I am all right. My daughter calming me down...when I should be the one comforting her.*

Courage had never failed her before, yet at this moment she scarcely recognizes herself. She tells herself to be strong, *We'll get through this*, and glances back through the rear window. Impossible, completely fogged over. It's like standing in the shower at home, trying to see through that outdated pebbly privacy glass she'd wanted to replace for years but David hadn't let her.

"We're almost there," Evan says loudly. "I think I see it."

"Yes, there, there it is." Chamba points forward.

The towering baobab tree reaches its long arms toward them, waving, heaving, creaking in the downpour and wind, bowing to a higher power.

"You can slow down, Evan," Chamba continues.

But it is too late. Everyone in the back seat hits their head on the roof. Megan's mouth begins to bleed. She's bitten her tongue and crimson drops slowly traverse down the curves of her chin and neck.

Then another hard bounce.

"Slow down, Evan," Chamba pleads, then looks at Megan and hands her a handkerchief. She takes it and blots her chin.

Finally the Land Rover stops and Evan yells, "Everyone out. Hurry!"

Miss Emily unleashes her door, Katie hers, and Chamba and Evan also jump out. Dora and Megan follow. All four doors are left open.

Evan pulls his hair and some rain out of his eyes and says, "Come on, over to the tree." He takes Megan's hand, Katie's as well, and they run under the mighty baobab. The rain softens, as if someone has turned down the faucet. No more stabbing at their heads, backs, bare arms. They gather at the tree trunk and turn around to get a good look at their pursuer, water rising up from the valley.

"It's getting closer, Evan," Chamba lets out, then motions with his head to the platforms Evan and his workers had built to observe wildlife.

186

The treehouse.

Evan nods and says to Katie and Megan, "We need to get higher. There's a rope ladder on the other side. Follow me."

Everyone moves around to the other side of the trunk.

"Okay, Megan, you first..."

Fifteen steps up the rungs and she is finally atop one of the bamboo platforms. The others follow. Katie, Dora, and Miss Emily, who slips and nearly falls to the ground, then Chamba. Only Evan remains at the base of the ladder. He wants to move the Land Rover closer, to higher ground under the tree canopy. And he knows he should grab what few supplies are in it. He sees a flash and, a second later, hears thunder rumble and echo off the nearby cliffs. The ground shakes beneath his boots. Then another strike, and another. It feels like he can almost touch the lightning strikes, smell them cook the earth. He struggles to see through the rain, trying to make out the Land Rover. And as he steps out from under the canopy of the tree it comes into view, a mere splotch of green amid vertical smears of gray rain.

As he starts to move toward it, the image changes. The daub of green gets smaller, shorter, then disappears in an instant—the liquid glacier sweeping over everything in its path.

He turns around and runs for the ladder.

High above, Katie sits down on the main platform, leans against the prickly tree trunk, and pulls Megan close.

PART FIVE

Early morning. David is smiling at the gorgeously clear blue and green Kentucky day. All remnants of yesterday's high humidity left the state at dawn when cool dry air descended from Canada, entering his and Katie's master bedroom through an open dormer window and soothing his face, urging him to rise early. And now, an hour later and standing under a forest of maple trees, he bends over to pick up a well-worn shovel, then carefully places the heel of his right boot on the upper lip and shoves the blade at the heavy clay soil. He had wanted to work on the flower bed of irises for almost two years, but hadn't found the time. Or hadn't made the time.

Irises are lovely, especially purple bearded ones such as the *Violet Tiger* or *Serene Moment*, but they are demanding and seek attention every two or three years. Eventually, clumps of roots choke off nutrients from each other, crowd together as one, and before you know it they get stingy with blooms and just as soon throw their energy at spreading themselves beneath the earth in ever increasing masses of twisted fiber tubers.

"They have to be divided," Hank Farley, at Hank Farley & Sons Nursery on South Pike, told David over the phone. "Oh, You can throw some 6-10-10 fertilizer on them if you want, but I personally, well, I don't think there's any use fertilizing them until you divide and separate them. They just need some space, that's all. Gotta give them some room and they'll come back. Don't you worry none, you'll get plenty of nice growth next spring."

Space. Room. Growth.

They'll come back, David thinks as he moves a few weary Irises a shovel-handle's length away. He straightens his back and wipes the droplets from his forehead thinking, *Katie will come back, too. Maybe she just needs a little space.*

He covers the tubers with soil.

I wonder if Megan is all right? They should have checked in by now...

They hunkered down like weary soldiers on the front, held on, and awaited daybreak. After the rains surrendered, a colder mass of air moved in and hovered over the tree platforms, sandwiching their wet bodies between the sky and the newborn lake at the feet of the grand tree they remain perched in.

On this island—this refuge among broad velvety leaves, sprawling branches and floors of bamboo—they huddled closely and held hands and spoke calming words to each other. It would be all right in the morning, they said, the waters will recede back to their channels. And they will descend to dry ground. These were their words.

But the water hasn't receded.

All are asleep, except Evan who barely closed his eyes for more than forty-five minutes all night. And as the sun pours ruddy burnt orange over a ridge to the east, its reflection shimmers on the flooded basin. Evan watches as the warm colors descend and are slowly cradled by the valley.

Trying not to disturb Katie, whose head had somehow found his lonely shoulder in the darkness of the night, he draws himself away from her while gently moving her toward Megan. He then takes in a long view of her mangled yet strikingly lovely hair cascading down her slender neck, flowing downward over pale ridges of collar bone and into the valley of her breasts. Surprisingly, even after the stress of the poachers and the storm, her face appears calm, rested, and beautiful.

He smiles to himself as he remembers their conversation last night, which seemingly ended only minutes ago. With everyone else asleep, and the sound of the rain making its way through a maze of leaves above, they had huddled close together in their private, inky black world and talked about any and everything. There were words of sorrow initially—leukemia treatments, talk of poaching, and worries about what Megan had witnessed...the mother elephant being shot. But eventually they moved on to more positive topics—the work being done to save endangered species, how Megan had been feeling better lately, and how stunning Africa and its wildlife are. And finally they settled on lighter subjects—horse breeding, family, vacations they had taken. Hopes and Dreams.

Evan rises to one knee and stretches his arms over his head, hears popping in his knees and feels his back spasm slightly. Every muscle in his body feels as stiff as the stubborn bamboo which supported him through the trying night. He surveys the tree platforms, determining whether anything had shifted in the storm, came loose, dropped or washed away, then takes inventory of the bodies strewn about him. Chamba and Dora are flat on their backs and a sheet of tattered twigs and lost leaves blankets much of their bodies. There's a parade of ants making their way up and over Chamba's left leg, then disappearing into the crevice between two bamboo beams. Miss Emily is propped up against the baobab trunk a hundred and eighty degrees from Megan and Katie on the smallest but perhaps most secluded platform, joined to the main section by a narrow gang plank with ropes loosely serving as safety handrails. For Miss Emily to seek her own private room, even on a wildlife observation platform, doesn't strike Evan as odd. He tells himself that if they're stuck here for more than a day there will be drapes made of woven leaves or animal skins, or privacy blinds consisting of sticks twined together to perfection, all hanging neatly from a branch.

His eyes have trouble leaving Katie. They linger over her once more and beg to be left alone, if only for a few more minutes—to relish in her exquisite cheeks that reach for the sky and branches high above, her supple white skin hiding age and worry well, her flowing curves from head to toe. But the thought that this woman—this engaged woman—is calling on his heart unsettles him. He manages a blink, then another, and finally pulls himself away from her with a deep breath of fresh Kenyan air made for the morning before him.

His only consoling thought is that perhaps she hasn't said everything there is to say about her relationship with David. *Why isn't he here with her, taking care of her, protecting her and Megan? And why would she leave her fiancé behind on such a trip?*

He feels like a complete idiot even thinking about such things, but he can't help it.

What is it about her? he asks himself as feelings and images of her float through his mind—her sense of spirit, the life in her voice, her undeniable rare beauty, the love she shows for her daughter, the way the left corner of her mouth rises just slightly higher than the other when she smiles, the sweet angles and curves of her long legs when she climbed up the tree ahead of him, the way the fabric of her wet blouse rests upon her breasts, the smell of her skin and hair, touch of her slender hand when they met in Johannesburg, the shades of mystery surrounding her pupils. Everything about her.

He had wanted to touch her last night, to hold her close, if only to caress her temple, stroke her hair. He wanted to make her feel that everything would be all right. Everything. Her head on his shoulder, he'd felt more compassion this morning, and more passion that moment, than with any woman who had ever graced his life, pressed soft lips to his, or lied naked against his body.

But it was more than this. It was the hundred questions that were born under the clouds and under the stars and began vaguely, unobtrusively, and ended with concerns, passions, reasons for living and dying—from where have you lived to *what* do you live for.

It was the remembered feelings of childhood and veiled realities of adulthood—of fears, goals, of falling in love for the first time. It was the first kiss at a dance, the last tear when going off to college. It was the soft spoken words of his soul reflecting in her moonlit eyes once the skies cleared. And it was the unexpected pauses, nuances of silence, neither awkward nor dull. It was all this that lived between the unceasing rain of evening, which eventually turned into a starlit sky sometime around midnight, and the serenity of morning—while everyone else lay fast asleep and blind to their private world. They had talked for hours, but it seemed to pass in a heartbeat.

Evan walks carefully over to the edge of the platform and looks down. Water. Everywhere, water. Glancing about the horizon he sees an ocean before him with just the wind whipped and soaked tips of bushes and trees poking through, like tattered sails of sunken ships. It takes his breath away and makes his mouth fall open in disbelief. He's never seen anything like this before. Never. Not even the flood at Kanderi two years ago, which he had flown over, comes close. The only things not covered with water are the baobab he is perched in, a sheer cliff three hundred yards away and, in the opposite direction, the village and some hills to the west. And, of course, mighty Mount Kilimanjaro far off in the distance.

"Good lord..." he says at length.

His voice coaxes Katie from sleep, from a dream, and she raises her head, but says nothing. Startled, she slowly pieces together why she is sitting thirty feet up in a massive tree of platforms Swiss Family Robinson would have been awed by. She looks up and fingers of light dance among the branches in soothing motion. Then she remembers her dream. Or was it a dream? A whispery conversation with Evan until the brightening sky arrived. A sweet, cool breeze painting her face after the downpour eased. Finding herself leaning against his damp shoulder, then melting back to sleep.

Yes, it all had to be a dream. She tells herself this three times before saying, "Good morning Evan," to the strong back of a figure silhouetted against water as far as she can see. He pivots toward her and her eyes adjust to the shallow silky light making its way to his face.

"Good morning," he returns.

"I guess we made it."

"It appears that way. Welcome to Tsavo."

She smiles and tiny frail lines at the corners of her eyes surrender her age. She suddenly feels self-conscious of how she must look after such a rough night. She looks at herself. Her hair is in knots, her skin is creased where it snuggled against the tree, against Megan. And against the shoulder in her dream.

Evan approaches and sits down next to her, whispers, "Guess everyone's wiped out from yesterday. I'm surprised you're awake already, after our, well, lengthy conversation."

His words send her spine tingling and she thinks, *If the conversation actually took place, was the feel of his shoulder also real? Maybe he doesn't remember...*

"Did you get cold?" he asks with concerned brown eyes that radiate specks of green and amber light, the morning sun's rays refracting magically.

"Uh, no, no, not too bad."

Make-believe or not, she thinks to herself, *his shoulder was warm. Wonderfully warm.*

She leans forward and takes in the horizon then asks, "What are we going to do?"

"Well," he says then pauses, "I'd guess that the water will recede quite a bit in the next few hours. Probably not enough to let us drive out—If we can even find the Land Rover—but enough to get down from here."

Katie nods. "It could be worse, I guess."

A pause then Evan says, "I don't know how."

"Well, we have plenty of water."

He grins and nods, pats her knee a few times then rises to his feet. "I'm going to check on Miss Emily," he says, then disappears to the other side of the huge baobab trunk, to what he has decided to call "the suite."

He finds the mountains and valleys that make up Miss Emily's body resting on their side—the humps and bumps creating a rollercoaster of voluptuous curves. Her dress is pulled up just high enough that half her bare underwear-less rear is hanging out and is getting bathed in morning light. What a sight. The alabaster cheeks are almost blinding. He thinks, *Maybe an airliner flying high above will see them and send for help. Save us all, they will.*

He feels a twinge of guilt for the thought and shakes his head, lets her be, then makes his way over to Chamba and Dora, both still in their nighttime worlds, sound asleep.

"Lively crew we have," he says softly as he makes his way back over to Katie.

CHAPTER THIRTY-TWO

The sky fell for three straight days. On occasion, when it seemed the water was retreating, Evan would glowingly say, "Looks like low tide again," yet within a couple of hours the waves would come about and rise toward the single-treed shoreline once more. A never ending staccato of nature trapping them into their leafy moist cage high amongst the branches.

"This Africa is an impostor," Miss Emily said dramatically one afternoon when the downpours started up again. It's angry and void of compassion for all its inhabitants who love it and call it home, including me."

Or were they all simply guests of Africa now? It surely didn't feel like home at this point. The landscape seemed so distant, ethereal, and ever changed. Would it ever be the same? How could the lions, the elephants, the Cape buffalo and giraffes survive such chaos. What corner of this watery catastrophe of nature were they hiding in, if they had survived at all?

Evan contemplated what it must be like to be a wild animal, used to roaming freely and then suddenly thrust into a tiny corner of the world—locked up in a small cage at a zoo, the train car of an aged circus, or backyard of a pretentious suburbanite seeking attention and admiration through ownership of some exotic species.

There was little to do during the daylight hours. Eat baobab fruit until even the thought sickened them. Collect raindrops in their mouths from the crusty elbow of a branch. Wring out the rain and perspiration from their clothes. Tell stories to each other. Watch bugs. And stare at the horizon from their brown and green abandoned wooden ship, their tree house in the baobab tree which was now their temporary home.

Then something strange happened.

A slivery gold ray of sun poked through the gray moisture, as if the most lovely finger of God were reaching down. Not shedding much light or warmth or indication of day, but nevertheless spreading hope. Eventually it blossomed into a broad hand then, just an afternoon later, yielded to exquisitely clear skies as if nothing had happened at all. A rebirth. Crisp, thin air, air you could drink deep into your lungs, was everywhere. The Africa Evan knew was returning but she was still a stranger, for the water line continued to rest circuitously about the baobab tree and the nearby cliffs.

The next morning, much to their amazement, the murky liquid that hadn't budged for days was suddenly an eighth of a mile away, having retreated during the night. It left behind mushy brown earth, lost trees, and orphaned thorny bushes strewn about as if a tropical hurricane had blown through. There was scarcely a recognizable feature. Finally, they could descend from their leafy, verdant home which had protected them from the storm, fed them, and inadvertently made them all grow closer together. It was time to set their feet to dry, or rather, dryer ground.

Evan climbed down first, eager to try and find the Land Rover, or what was left of it. Just before leaving the last ladder rung at the bottom of the trunk he jovially said, "One small step for man, and one giant leap for mankind." And with that he pushed away like Neil Armstrong, his boots squashing three inches into the dark humus and mud.

The others followed, first Megan, then Katie, Dora, Chamba, and Miss Emily last. With frail legs and arms approaching faint atrophy, they limped away from their humble temporary home, emerged from its shade and into bright sunlit ground, stretching and yawning with faces that mingled joy with weary discontent as reality settled in. They were still trapped.

Running their eyes quickly over the terrain revealed their landlocked position, sandwiched against cliffs on one side, and a half-moon piece of earth on the other which was met by miles of water that stretched toward what seemed another continent—the tiny village and Miss Emily's big white house.

"Looks like the water didn't make it up to your home at least," Evan says, pointing.

"Thank god, I rather thought it would just be a memory now, Miss Emily said, squinting and staring off in the distance."

"I see smoke rising in a couple places, people cooking probably. Everyone must be all right."

Megan walks away and surveys their position with eyes wide and amazed. She rounds the baobab, skirting its perimeter of branches such that her feet follow the cool shadows yet her head never loses the warmth of the sun.

"Don't worry, honey," she hears her mother yell out with a strained voice reaching valiantly for calmness.

Megan knows what this means. Worry, and worry a lot. She approaches and coyly says, "Who said I was worried?" and Evan smiles and rubs a hand atop her head, pulls her close for a hug.

"I think we better look for some food," Chamba says, "you know, before it rains again."

The thought of rain, even hearing the word rain, deflates everyone's expression.

Dora says to the sky and her God above, "It's not going to rain anymore, that's enough."

"Amen," Katie joins in.

"Nevertheless, we must find some food, some protein. We can't live on baobab fruit forever."

"Chamba, I'm not planning on living here forever," Miss Emily chimes in and then quickly throws a glance toward the cliffs hovering behind her. "Can't we climb out of here? Or make a raft or something."

Evan shakes his head then cranes it upward, "Those cliffs are way too steep. We would need climbing gear, and I'm not sure if even that would help. Plus, what would we do when we get to the top? We'd still be stuck, just higher up."

"Well then," Chamba says, "what about a raft? It just might be possible."

"Yeah Evan," Miss Emily puts in, her face lighting up as it always does when someone confirms her ideas. "We could take down one of the bamboo platforms from the tree and—"

"Just sail on over to the village?"

"Yes, why not?"

"Look, if you and Gilligan want to paste together a boat out of twigs and bird droppings, go ahead," Evan replies with only a hint of a grin, head still shaking. He pauses. "I'm sorry, that was uncalled-for. I just can't believe this. Just, just look at our valley. How many animals died over the past few days? Look at this," he says as he waves an arm across the horizon.

Chamba nods once and with sorrowful and calm eyes says in a measured tone, "Yes, Doctor Drake, but it is nature. It is God's will. It's not for us to understand, or control."

Evan raises his brow at being called Doctor so coolly, collectedly. He tightens his lips slightly then averts his eyes as he walks away, knowing that Chamba is commenting on more than just their current predicament and inability to control and protect and love Africa. Chamba was commenting on Evan's genetics work, too.

Standing in the shadowy islet of one of the baobab's branches, Katie feels embarrassed for witnessing the exchange and in the recesses of her mind senses something collapse, if only for a moment. These seemingly perfect, kind people are human too.

She sits on a rock and pulls her hair from one side to the other, angles her face at the vague daylight moon hanging discreetly above. The smooth opalescent surface of the rock feels cool and soothing to her thighs, her rear, her dry legs, like lotion applied after showering, shaving, then slipping on silk pajamas on a crisp fall night.

CHAPTER THIRTY-THREE

"Kilimanjaro is a snow covered mountain 19,710 feet high, and it is said to be the highest mountain in Africa. Its western summit is called the Masai "Ngàje Ngài," the House of God. Close to the western summit there is the dried and frozen carcass of a leopard. No one has explained what the leopard was seeking at that altitude." And with that Miss Emily's voice softens as she continues, "Isn't that beautiful, Megan?"

"Yes, what's it from?"

"Have you studied Ernest Hemingway in school yet?"

"No, I don't think so."

"Well, you will. That was the first paragraph of *The Snows of Kilimanjaro*."

"Oh wait, I think Mrs. Sullivan read part of it to us in English class. But it's been awhile. Can you tell me the rest of the story?"

"I'm afraid that's all I memorized, honey. But maybe tonight I'll tell you how the story goes...to the best of my memory anyway."

Megan looks out at the sunlit slopes of Kilimanjaro far in the distance. Each morning and evening she had asked Miss Emily to tell her a story. Something, anything, to pass the time, especially when the others were off looking for food or scouting around. She turns to Miss Emily once more, "So why *did* the leopard go up to the summit?"

"Oh...I think simply to die, to be close to God."

"You mean, like suicide?"

"Well, I've never thought of it like that, Megan. I prefer to think that the leopard wanted, for whatever reason, to leave this world with dignity, you know, to reach the summit and just fade away, all alone. Much more romantic, don't you think?"

"Yeah, I guess."

"But come to think of it, Ernest Hemingway did end up taking his own life..."

Megan seems to ponder this for several seconds then says, "Maybe he just wanted some dignity too. Was he sick or something?"

"I don't know, honey, I don't know."

Megan turns away as her attention is stolen by the image of her mother and Evan walking near the water.

Miss Emily continues, "I wish we had something—anything—to read, how about you?"

"Huh?"

"I said that I wish we had some magazines or books to read, you know, to pass the time." She picks at one of her long fingernails, removing some mud. She continues, "Actually this would be a good time to do some writing too. No interruptions or distractions."

"Do you like to write?" Megan inquires.

"Oh yes, every night usually. I'm working on my third novel."

"Really?"

She nods and says, "It's about half done."

"And you've completed two others?"

"That's right."

"What are they about?"

"Well, I guess you could call them romance adventures. Mostly about people falling in love, and vice versa, breaking up. Something I'm somewhat of an expert on. The vice versa part, that is."

"Was it hard, I mean, writing the first one? That's what I want to do when I get older. I want to be a writer."

"Good for you. It's not easy though kiddo. Lots of hard work. And you have to have patience and self-discipline."

"How long does it take to write a book?"

"It depends. Sometimes the words and feelings pour out of you and beg to be put down on paper. Other times it seems like torture."

"You mean writer's block."

"Right."

"Yeah, Mrs. Sullivan told us about that. She said you just have to stay focused and put something down each day. And eventually you'll have a story."

"Well, I'm afraid I don't agree with that philosophy. My experience is that you have to feel the passion, you know, the yearning to write in order to create something you can be proud of. Whenever I don't have a clear idea of where my story is going, I stop and live with the characters for a while, take some time off."

"What do you mean, *live* with them?"

"Believe it or not, the characters in your stories become your friends. You think and worry about them day and night, even dream about them. And when you're finally done with your book, you cry because they've left you, or don't need you anymore and have to stand on their own."

From a distance, looking back at the baobab tree, it appears as just a lonely bush sitting at the base of commanding tan and orange cliffs with striated taffy grooves painted perpendicular to the horizon. Katie glances over her shoulder just before the image fades behind some rocks.

Evan, several steps ahead, calls out, "Come on, I think we can get through over here." He begins climbing a sloping boulder which is blocking the way, sandwiched between the cliffs and water. "It's not that steep," he continues, then lowers a hand to help pull Katie up. "I think once we get over this we can walk around to the other side of the cliffs. If we're lucky there'll be higher ground so we can get out of here."

She reaches up with her arms and feels his hands take hers, then suddenly senses the breeze billowing her blouse outward. She feels his eyes on her as she surges upward, places a foot atop the boulder and heaves the other in the same direction.

Evan loses his footing. "Wait, I'm—"

He slips and Katie heaves toward him. Losing his balance, he falls backward and she follows, covering him like a blanket.

"Are you okay," he inquires with concerned eyes, moving the hair from Katie's reddened face which is inches from his.

"Yes, I'm sorry. I guess we both slipped."

"I guess?" he says, then laughs.

Katie smiles and joins in, "Are you all right?"

"I'll live, I guess."

More laughter. She feels the back of his hand gently stroking her left cheek, then her forehead. She finally locks her eyes onto him and for a split second feels a connection that ripples from head to toe, squeezing the breath from her. A moment later and he's pulling his hand away and swallowing hard, apparently also lost in the unexpected moment. Entwined and lying here strewn atop his body, she feels him beneath her, the hair on his legs tingling her pallid skin, the muscled ripples of his stomach rising and falling against her. She goes weak, paralyzed, yearning for more of him. Every bit of her wants to live here in his arms, stay here in this moment.

He touches her blushing cheek once more and with glassy eyes his smile changes to hesitant words, "We better get going, it'll be dark soon."

She nods and gently removes herself, sliding off to his right side but moving slowly enough to taste more of him. She senses his palm once more upon her head and then she is free.

"Why don't we sit here a minute and catch our breath."

"Good idea," she says as she swings herself around to the view and sits beside him.

"I think if we just climb up a little further," he continues, pointing, "we can drop back down and make our way around to the other side of the cliffs. If you're up for it, that is."

"Oh, I'm fine," she assures him as she brushes off some dirt from her elbows. Running her eyes over the horizon she continues, "You know, I hate to say it, but Tsavo looks even prettier with all this water. At least this time of day."

He nods.

"I wonder how long it will last."

"Hard to say. The water line hasn't gone down much in the last few hours. The rivers and streams must be backed up," he says, watching her comb locks of her hair through her fingers, trying to undo days of uncombed tangles.

"David must be very worried about you and Megan," he goes on. He had wanted to bring up the subject of her engagement numerous times since getting stranded, especially the nights they would stay up talking. He couldn't wait any longer.

"Oh, he probably just thinks we're off on some safari out in the middle of nowhere. And spending money no less. At Chamba and Dora's house I called and told him we may not be able to contact him for days at a time." She pauses, looking down. "And besides, he's probably working himself to death at the Center again," she says with a tinge of animosity in her expression.

More untangling of her hair.

She continues, "He loves his work—the horses and, of course, the races. Or at least he's getting back to loving them again. He sort of shut down after the car accident. Wouldn't go into work or do anything around the house. It was like living with a ghost, this brooding figure passing through the house and not saying anything."

"But he's coming around now?"

"Yes. It's kind of funny," she says as her eyes become moist, "he seems to get along better when I'm not around."

Evan struggles for words, "I, I don't believe that for a minute."

"Well, all I know is that when I leave him alone his mood changes.

He actually shaves, gets out of his sweat pants, and goes to work. He manicures in the yard. And he talks with Megan more. My mother told me that I must be enabling him, you know, codependent or some silly thing. Either that or he thinks he made a mistake."

"What do you mean?"

"He asked me to marry him just before the accident. I think he basically caved into reality—you know, that this was as good as it was going to get. We had lived together for several years and, well, I'm just afraid he thought it was time to pop the question or move on. Sometimes I think he flipped a coin and it landed with *get married* on the up side. I always wondered whether we moved in together too quickly, and set things in motion that would be hard to stop."

"But you still haven't gotten married," Evan says, more as a statement searching for confirmation than an open question.

"Nope, the wedding's postponed until things get back to normal. Whatever normal is."

A long pause.

"Katie, do you love him?" Evan asks, his eyes meeting hers. This was the other question he had wanted to ask a dozen times over the past few days. She obviously wasn't the type to go off and get engaged without loving a person, but he sensed that a lot of proverbial water had passed under the bridge since then.

"Yes, I love him."

Turning away, something inside Evan collapses.

Her words continue more gradually, "I just don't know whether I'm *in* love with him anymore. Do you know what I mean?"

He nods, manages a consoling, slight smile.

"David's not the same person he was before the accident, even he admits it. And I feel so damn guilty for having these feelings, this distance from him. It wasn't his fault that Angela died, or," she says as a tear rolls down her cheek, "maybe it was. Maybe I'm treating him differently, and somehow blaming him. And maybe he's sensing it, you know." She looks up at Evan and he wraps an arm around her waist and pulls her close.

"I'm so sorry Katie," he says then feels his shirt gathering the drops from her eyes. "You don't deserve this pain, not one bit of it. You're a wonderful, sensitive person. A great mother. You're full of love. I knew it the instant I met you."

Sobbing somewhat and shaking her head she whispers, "I don't know anymore..."

"And maybe I shouldn't say this—you are engaged after all—but you're the most beautiful woman I've ever laid eyes on. David's lucky he has you. He has no idea what he has in you."

A slight breeze picks up and laps against their faces. Katie's tears chill then slowly fade away. Neither says a word for several minutes. They just sit, side by side, absorbing all that is Africa. Billowy clouds shaped for active imaginations that look far too heavy to stay up in the air. Mountains and hillsides newly greened with life, their upper edges contrasting against strikingly blue skies. Mount Kilimanjaro staring majestically down as if all below it—the usually parched plants, the starving animals, the struggling people in the villages, the fleeting tourists and their fleeting dollars—are here solely to adorn it like ornaments placed about the branches of a Christmas tree, never overshadowing its presence but merely serving to highlight its glory.

Finally, Katie breaks the silence and says, "I feel so stupid for rambling on about myself. Why don't you tell me more about *you*."

Evan turns away briefly and says, "There's not much more to tell. And it's not all that different from what you've experienced—falling in and out of love, struggling like everyone else. I had sort of a messy breakup a few years back. And then I came to Africa."

Katie senses a pain, or damage, that goes deeper than his words, revealing itself in snapshot glances he gives her between sentences, thoughts. She stretches her legs out upon the warming surface of the rock and yawns as subtly as possible. "But you're over that, right, the breakup?" she asks.

He shakes his head slowly, "I don't know."

His voice has an air of redemption, as if he is still atoning for some pain he'd inflicted in his past, a miscarried relationship perhaps. Katie senses a bruised soul beneath his tanned skin exterior that neither wisdom, the passing years, or his true love—Africa—has completely healed.

There is a long pause as they soak in a column of light, faces angled as one, flower blooms following the arc of the sun.

Evan finally says, "Well, I guess we should get moving and—"

"I'm sorry," Katie says softly, "I didn't mean to, you know, get too personal."

"That's all right," he says then drinks in the warmth that pours through him as she caresses his arm.

She says to him gently with a smile, "Come on, let's see what's over this ridge."

CHAPTER THIRTY-FOUR

Angela's things have gone virtually untouched since the car accident. Her toy chest still overflows with furry bears with funny names, some scraggly and stained by dirty fingers, peanut butter and jelly mostly. And others seemingly brand new. Grandma had been asked on more than one occasion to limit the gifts to Christmas and birthdays only. "You're spoiling her to no end," David had told her each time the tiny fuzzy beasts arrived. But they just kept on coming, some forced to hide in the closet and under the bed and high upon the dresser in front of a faded, antique silver mirror.

David enters and surveys the room, as usual during his once a week ritual. Tiny plastic button eyes stare at him as he walks slowly over to a chest of drawers painted with pink and green flowers. He drops one knee to the floor and places his fingers around the handle of the second drawer from the bottom, slides it outward and, as he does each Saturday morning, pulls out a pair of Angela's pajamas, lemon yellow with red poppies. The ritual progresses as usual: he first places them on the bed, carefully eases the wrinkles from the terry cloth, then grabs a tattered book from the night stand, a story about rabbits chomping through a spring garden and hiding from a frustrated Australian shepherd named Kenya. It was Angela's favorite book. Each Friday night he would read it to her while sitting at the foot of the bed in the glow of the hall light, partially obscured by the half-closed door to her room. He wasn't sure how much she actually understood of the book, but the colorful pictures made her smile contentedly and wafted her mind toward sleep.

Katie had never seen David's routine with the pajamas, the early morning visits to Angela's room carried out with precision and grace, however one day Megan walked in while he was folding the pajamas and securing them for next weekend.

"What are you doing?" Megan asked pensively.

"Just straightening up, that's all," David replied as he pushed the drawer closed and gathered his emotions before turning around.

Megan felt it best not to inquire further and kept the encounter to herself.

Today there will, of course, be no interruptions. The house had stood as a lonely, forgotten monument since Katie and Megan had left for Africa. Even the squirrels seem to be gone from the expanse of lawn framing the unpaved driveway.

He flips the pages of the book, one by one. Angela wouldn't like it if he skipped a page. A minute later he closes the cover and places it back on the nightstand, then runs his fingers over the pajamas. In his mind they come to life. Little fingers tug at his hand. A soft cheek nuzzles against his nose. Tiny ticklish toes wriggle and kick. And marbleized eyes look up in wonder.

Then, with the stories read, the prayers said, the kisses made, he carefully gathers her up, holds her in his arms, and lifts her to his face. Even after all these months after her death, he still smells her—the baby shampoo and powdery fresh scents of childhood. A last kiss and he folds the pajamas neatly, and places them back in the drawer until next Saturday.

That is, if he's back in time before next weekend.

There was really no reason to wait any longer, he had decided yesterday afternoon. Everything at work was settled—the investment from Stanton & Hughes was a done deal, the signatures placed neatly at the bottom of the last page of the contract. A signing ceremony had been held near the big paddock, under a bright blue Kentucky sky, all of the employees pretending to be happy. But they'd lost two board seats and some equity, and there was little choice in the matter. They needed cash in order to finance expansion and compete with two new facilities in Lexington and one out in Santa Barbara, California.

David's bags were packed. He would only take two, just enough clothes to last a week, and maybe a couple extra days if it came to that. The return ticket was for next Thursday. Surely by then he would find Katie and Megan—somewhere in Tsavo.

CHAPTER THIRTY-FIVE

Evan and Katie amble along the muddy terrain side by side, sticky arms occasionally brushing, eyes on eyes, talking about everything and talking about nothing. Have you ever thought about leaving Africa? No, never. Isn't it lonely at times? Yes, sometimes. Is Kentucky as beautiful as I've heard? Yes, it's lovely. Wonder why those mountains over there are so purple? I don't know, seed-heads from the rains maybe. The mud feels rather soothing on the feet, doesn't it. Yeah, especially when it squishes between your toes. Do you think you'll ever get married? I'd like to.

Evan's reddish-blonde stubble, lengthening with each lost day, glistens in the sunlit shafts which every few steps permeate the natural skyscrapers to their right. Shadows long and dark stretch over their heads, envelope them whole, and travel well into the water like long piers along a neglected, storm-battered beach.

"I'm afraid we've run into another barrier," he says, pointing to some rocks that once more obscure their path, a pink and tan wall running from the base of the cliffs to the water's edge. "They look taller than the last ones, I don't know if we'll be able to get over these."

"Don't know until we try," Katie says. "I'm game."

Reaching the rocks he says, "You know, I think it might be easier to just wade around them. Might get a little wet, but the water doesn't look very deep here."

As they round the tiny peninsula, waist deep in slimy liquid and clay, Katie suddenly stops and whispers urgently, "Wait, look."

About two hundred yards ahead they see a truck with its hood open and two people hunched over the fenders, heads tucked into the engine compartment like ostriches with their necks in the sand. No shirts, no shoes, nothing but cut-off shorts and butt cracks.

"Get down," Evan whispers as he gently touches her lower back and pulls her close.

"Maybe they can help us get out?"

"Maybe..."

She sees the concern in his eyes. "What's wrong, Evan?"

"Doesn't that truck look like the one those poachers had? See, it has a canvas cover on the bed, olive green."

"You think it's them?"

"I don't know. There are a lot of old trucks in Tsavo. Even the game wardens drive junkers like that. But we better be careful. If they are poachers, and they know who I am, they'd just as soon shoot me than give us a ride to the village. Let's sit tight for a minute and see what they do."

"Okay."

After ten minutes one of the men pulls himself from the engine compartment and jumps into the cab of the truck. The starter cranks clangorously but the engine doesn't turn over. He hops down, slams the door, then kicks it. He yells something at the other man, whose face is obscured by long, ratty black hair. They both look toward the rocks Katie and Evan are hunched down behind.

"Down!" Evan whispers again. He watches as the two men appear to contemplate which direction to take. Scratching their heads, nodding, pointing. They suddenly swing around and start walking away.

"Looks like they're moving on," he continues.

Katie doesn't say anything for several seconds, then, "I think it *is* those men who shot that elephant."

"I'm...I'm not sure. These guys look kind of scraggly—all skin and bones. Younger too. But I'm going to find out."

"How?"

"I want to run over to the truck and see what's inside. You stay here."

"I'm coming with you," Katie says as she touches his arm.

"No, I'll be fine. I can move faster without you."

"You've never seen me run."

"Please, Katie, just stay here. I'll be right back, I promise."

She nods and says, "All right, but be careful okay?"

"I will."

He makes his way with slight, purposeful movements, not too fast and very careful, then stops about fifty feet from Katie and waits a couple of minutes.

Is something wrong? she wonders.

Evan swats flies with green eyes and huge wings of gossamer that buzz his head like tiny biplanes circling King Kong atop the Empire State Building.

God, I have to be smelling pretty bad for all this attention, he thinks. *Maybe I'll take a dip in the water tonight, and freshen up.*

He watches, hunched over and hands on his knees, as the two

men move around another ledge of rocks and disappear into a haze of shadows. Quickly, he leaves the flies behind and runs as fast as he can, making sure to keep the truck between himself and the men, and staying in the shallow water such that no footprints are left, if the men return. The forced breeze feels cool to his skin, bathes his hair and rinses his back.

The truck is at least twenty years old, a Mercedes flatbed converted with warped wooden rails and a wagon-like canopy of canvas torn in several spots. Metal loops, appearing as the ribs of a slain giant resting on his back, protrude through fibrous green skin. The vehicle is camouflaged by tan and gray spray paint, the work of amateurs. Well-traveled tires are nearly bald, retreads missing pieces here and there, rims void of chrome. There are no fenders. A windshield with spider web cracks adorns a hood of quilted metal with shoddy welds and faded graffiti.

It's amazing, Evan thinks, *that they even made it this far into the park in such a jalopy.*

A zigzag rope loops left and right and skyward through brass eyelets riveted into the canvas flaps at the rear of the truck. The eyelets sparkle in the sun and are the only things not rusted, not cracked, not peeling or spray painted.

Flies! More flies!

They're everywhere as he unties a sloppy knot at the base of the bed and tugs the rope loose, which is stiffer than he expects, perhaps containing a thin strand of wire. A good yank and it slithers free as if it is alive, drops to the moist ground and coils as a snake until it finds itself in a neat and tidy twelve inch loop as if it was just removed from a shelf at a hardware store. He peels one side of the tarp back and suddenly feels as if he's riding a motorcycle at high speed, bugs spraying at his body amidst a self-generated wind. He swats them frantically and leaps back, spitting imaginary intruders from his mouth, rubbing his squinted eyes, scratching his shiny skin. The flies vacate instantly and spread into the air above the truck, wings creating a buzzing noise.

He moves close, but he already knows what is inside.

The smell. The smell of bloodied tusks and severed skulls, the smell of African death. It's everywhere. And on closer inspection he sees shards of ivory rising from the mass as weathered tombstones, spotted light filtering down upon them through holes in the canvas above. A graveyard born of greed. He counts the pairs he can lay eyes on. Ten. Twenty. Forty pairs, resting on maybe another forty pairs. Eighty elephants, dead just like that. And if each one had lived to be about seventy years old, the typical life expectancy for the species, then there were more than five thousand years of elephant lives piled before him in a mangled heap soon to be handles for letter openers and knifes, flower vases, ashtrays, jewelry boxes, and trinkets. No matter how many times he sees such a sight it never gets easier, the stomach tightens then heaves, the brain boils.

Vengeance. That's the next thought that enters Evan's mind and he even starts to run around the side of the truck, toward the direction the two men headed. He envisions cutting half their faces off and letting them lie where they fall, like what they did to the elephants. Slow and painful. This thought, too, makes his stomach turn. But the bastards would deserve it.

As the reality of the situation settles in—he can't jeopardize the safety of the others—he stops and calms himself, moves to the rear of the truck, closes the canvas flaps and loops the rope back through the brass eyelets, then ties the ends in a knot. He turns and runs from the truck. His mind reels. He wants to scream but can't.

This is not the first time Evan has felt such emotion, such disgust over the way elephants are often treated. He was just a boy the first time. It was the second, and biggest, circus he'd ever been too. A circus train had rolled in to town just before his tenth birthday. He watched, staring out his bedroom window, the bright lights showering men with a golden glow as they hammered long stakes and hoisted polls taller than any building in town until the red and white circus tents magically appeared. He couldn't sleep, for it seemed as though a city had sprouted with scarcely anyone noticing, except himself, in his nighttime world. With a paperback of *Catcher in the Rye* in his rear pocket along with a pack of candy cigarettes and a comb missing half its teeth, Evan rode his new ten speed Schwinn over each afternoon immediately after school getting out and watched the final touches being installed by shirtless men, most with tattoos. They put up colorful flags of countries he had never visited, signs with words outlined with colorful light bulbs, and built ticket booths that looked like jail cells, bars on windows behind which women sold tickets. Evan loved watching the circus come to life. Upon seeing a man drop his hammer, Evan ran over and picked it up, held it securely and aimed the handle toward the darkened silhouette. He thought he saw a tooth sparkle, ever so slightly, as the silhouette grunted, "Thanks boy."

"You're welcome mister," Evan replied, then nearly gagged as he swallowed a whiff of body odor emanating from an arm made of muscle and veins. The man's hand appeared massive as it grasped the hammer, making it look like a toy.

As the man turned and walked away, Evan heard a buzzing sound.
Flies!

They buzzed and swarmed through the dank air. One landed on his nose and he swatted at it frantically, shaking his head. More flies circled his head but they soon left as quickly as they had appeared.

When seven-thirty and Friday night came, his dad said, "You wanna come with me?"

"Where?"

"The store, we need some milk."

"Okay," Evan answered.

Maple Avenue moved by the passenger window, as did the store and as did its milk.

"Where you goin', dad?" Evan asked.

His dad just grinned and patted Evan's knee while tapping a Camel cigarette loose from a box tucked in his shirt pocket, then turned the huge Mercury sedan to the right, into an open field filled with cars and people walking quickly toward a big sign, one made of light bulbs—ENTRANCE.

Cotton candy in hand, the show started, lights dimmed, a drum thundered from somewhere hidden and the clamor of the crowd settled into whispers. Places where no one was sitting suddenly filled with bodies, and a fat man in a red suit and black top hat appeared out of nowhere, waving his fat arms. It was exactly as Evan had imagined from his bedroom window, even better. Cotton candy.

There were lions and tigers that jumped through hoops of fire and horses that pranced in precise circles with people standing on their backs and elephants that picked women up with their trunks and dogs that pushed baby carriages and a tiny van out of which came tiny men and skinny people who swung and flipped from cables and motorcyclists who drove upside down in round cages and a helmeted man who got shot from a cannon and clowns that looked scary, not happy. "All of that was there, it really was," Evan told his mother the next morning while eating Cream of Wheat and drinking chocolate Ovaltine, eating two pieces of toast.

After school Evan set out to take a closer look at the circus, behind the scenes you might say. With Smitty Taylor at his side they hopped a fence and pretended they belonged with the circus, "We'll tell them we are there to help tear down the tents," Smitty said to Evan, picking his nose. They had made it just in time, for the tents were being taken down and the ropes were being coiled into neat little boxes then tossed into bigger boxes.

It was fun for a while, sitting atop the branch of a grand oak tree and in their minds ordering workers to do this and do that, move faster, be neater. But then they heard a whistle blow and their heads spun around until their attention locked on a jowl of a man with two eyes the size of those lights that make up the bright signs. He yelled, "You boys get the hell out of here!"

"Who, us?" Evan asked in a shaky voice.

"Doesn't he know you're a payin' customer?" Smitty said with eyes mingling terror and anger.

Evan shook his head, climbed down from the tree branch and began to run in the opposite direction of the whistle. He wanted to, as the man suggested, get the hell out of there. As he and Smitty rounded a group of trailers that were fashioned like wagons in a big circle, they stopped and ducked underneath one of them and stayed still while the man with the whistle moved by. Smitty must have been pretty scared, Evan thought, because when he scooted out he noticed that Smitty's shorts were all wet. But Evan didn't say anything about it. "Come on, Smitty, let's look around some more." That's all he said.

Over near the back of the Five and Dime store there were eight train cars but no engine and judging by the color of them, Evan thought, they had to be part of the circus train. He hadn't noticed the train cars before.

"Maybe it was brought in just to pick up all of those boxes and tents," he told Smitty.

So they sauntered over to them and, as they got closer, heard yelling. It was coming from the other side, in between the railcars and the back of the Five and Dime. Evan dropped to his knees and looked underneath. He saw two huge black boots shuffling about in dirt and hay, and he saw four giant gray feet, elephant feet. He stood up and looked at Smitty, whispered, "Come, this way..."

They crawled on their bellies below tons of train, which didn't seem too scary, Evan thought, because there wasn't any engine, so how could it move. As they crawled, the gravel sanded their scrawny legs and stomach like sandpaper, but they hunkered down in the darkness and atop the tar-smelling railroad ties, watching with not even a blink as a man tossed foreign words at the elephant and hit the poor thing with a whip, which didn't seem too terrible but then he seemed to get real upset and went to pick up a board, a big board, five feet long at least, Evan thought. He noticed little spikes or nails sticking from one end.

More shouting came, but louder, and it became clear that the man was trying to make the elephant back up into a cage about twenty feet away, door held open by a little kid with long hair and no shoes, and a dirty face with two white and blue marbles for eyes. The elephant just swung his trunk back and forth as if to say, No, I'm not going in that cage, then dropped his head as if shamed or something. The man got more mad, spitting and screaming, screaming and spitting, then held the board with nails like Hank Aaron readying for a home run.

Swoosh!

Evan had to squeeze his eyes shut when he heard it hit, and when he opened them he could see blood leaking from the shoulder of the elephant. It streamed down its front left leg until the thick gray skin was completely red. Then it puddled for a few seconds and soaked into the dirt and hay. Smitty started crying and shuffled out from under the railcar and ran in the general direction of his house. Evan waited until the elephant was in the cage and the man with the stick was long gone, then pulled himself out. As he ran away, his mind raced. He wanted to scream but couldn't.

CHAPTER THIRTY-SIX

It was a deep ruby red Megan was using, visualizing. She holds her legs up in the air and spreads her toes far apart, trying to catch the billowy clouds that look like cotton balls, and imagines dabbing a brush and stroking each nail to perfection. No need to blow, the breeze does the job just fine. Then, one by one, she removes the clouds separating her beautified toes and crosses one leg over the other, closes her eyes and floats peaceably off to another world, one with showers and shampoo and curling irons and blow dryers. And ruby red fingernail polish.

Almost two weeks have passed since they left the comfort of the hotel in Johannesburg. She was never one to enjoy camping, let alone forced survival training activities in the middle of Kenya. But how many leukemia patients got to do this? Not many, she assumed. And at least she was getting a decent tan now that the rains had moved to another country, having completed their path of destruction in Tsavo. Even her hair is feeling healthier, adding silky length daily, though she can't see it to confirm. A far cry from the scraggly strands that graced her head just weeks ago, like the first brave weeds after a harsh winter.

The sun looms low on the horizon, painting a pointed shadow on her face—her skyward-aimed nose acting as a sundial. The shadow moves right to left, longer, shorter, long again. She falls asleep, soothing afternoon sleep...

Thirty minutes go by. Finally, something awakens the nerves of her skin, now reddened. She senses something touching her left arm. "Go away, I'm asleep," she whispers. Her arm's peach fuzz tingles and tickles. *This can't be a dream.*

She tries to open her eyes but the sun presses her eyelids down. She slowly pries them open, her pupils adjusting to the bright light. Everything appears bleached white and she struggles to discern shape, color, depth of field. She tries to swat away whatever sort of gargantuan alien-like African bug is crawling over her arm, coaxing her from a pleasant dream she's already forgotten.

And then she sees it. Standing a few feet away is an elephant, staring at her with baseball eyes and butterfly wing lashes, dragging its trunk slowly up and down her arm. She screams and the trunk jerks quickly away. The elephant stumbles backward, equally scared no doubt, turns, then runs as fast as its legs can carry it. Megan leaps to her feet, breathing hard and staring. She licks her dry lips and follows the elephant as it makes its way around some trees several hundred yards away, near the water. She calms somewhat as she realizes what has just caressed her arm—a very small elephant, probably the orphan of the mother they had seen shot days ago. It must be Daisy.

But why was she touching me?

At least she survived the flash floods, Megan thinks as she wipes sweat from her forehead. She starts to walk back to the baobab tree, a mere twig on the horizon.

The sun sinks into a crimson bowl of sky cradled by the open hands of Kilimanjaro's tallest two peaks, Kibo and Mawenzi. The warm glow reaches out and hovers over Evan and Chamba as they wade through waist-high muddied water that has decided to recede enough to unveil the shimmering windshield of the long-lost Land Rover. They had seen it two hours ago while hunting along the north canyon.

"Do you think it will start?" Chamba says as they near what must be the hood and front bumper.

Evan shakes his head, "I doubt it. I really doubt it. But we won't know until this water goes down some more."

"At least it looks like it's in one piece," Chamba says as he drags his feet through slimy earth. It pulls at his legs and he struggles to move forward.

With little choice, they hesitantly leave the battered vehicle where it lies.

"With any luck the water will drop below the level of the carburetor and electrical system within a couple of days," Evan tells Chamba. "That is, if no more rain comes."

When they arrive back at the baobab tree, Dora and Miss Emily are scattering dried leaves, twigs, and pieces of bark on a fire outlined in a circle of smooth tan rocks. Black smoke is curling into the air, climbing up the side of the nearby cliffs.

Dora sees Evan and Chamba approaching. Their faces appear aglow, shadows of flames flickering across their serious expressions in the darkening twilight.

215

"Is the fire ready?" Chamba asks, making his way closer.

"I think so," Dora answers.

Miss Emily's ears seem to perk up. "I'll get the meat," she says eagerly.

Everyone gathers around the fire as the meat is laid out on a pinkish rock, the thinnest they could find. The white flesh sizzles and sends steam upward. Megan winces and turns her head as the scent drifts over her face.

"Scoot over here, honey," Katie says as she tugs on Megan's arm.

Megan moves closer then looks at Chamba and asks, "How did you kill it?"

"A lot of luck, Megan. A lot of luck."

"Oh, I don't know about that," Evan cuts in. "I think it was more skill than anything. Chamba used a vine to tie his pocketknife to a long stick. We waited on top of a boulder up in this canyon," he says as he motions with his head, "until we saw three bush duikers get within, what was it Chamba, twenty feet?"

"Yes, maybe thirty."

"Anyway, he cocked his arm like he was about to win the gold metal for javelin throwing—like this. Then he let it go. It swooshed through the air and the next thing I knew there was a dead bush duiker in front of us."

Megan's face suddenly saddens. "Was it in any pain?"

"Nope. He got it right in the chest, probably the heart. I don't think it felt a thing."

She nods though she doesn't believe a word of it. Pain or no pain, she wasn't looking forward to ingesting what in her eyes appears as Disney's *Bambi* on a stick. Her face angles down at the fire.

After a long pause, Katie says, "Megan, we have to eat something. We can't live just on baobab fruit, berries, and roots. You're doing so well, I mean..."

The words seem like ice water hitting Megan in the face, drawing her back to reality. It was the first time her mother had brought up her illness since they had gotten stranded.

Evan, who has been sitting Indian style, legs crossed, unfolds himself and grabs a small pointed stick. He pokes at the meat, flips it over. More sizzling. He tries to change the subject, "So...tell me about this elephant you saw."

When Megan had returned earlier in the day, she told everyone of her experience and Chamba had asked, "Are you sure you weren't dreaming?" to which Megan replied, "Here, touch my arm, there's still elephant snot or something sticky on it from the trunk."

"Indeed there is," Chamba had said as he brushed his palm over her skin, then offered a hearty laugh until he turned red.

Dora slapped his back to try and make him stop. "Chamba, you're embarrassing the girl."

Megan, in fact, hadn't been embarrassed and rather liked hearing the laughter, anything to spice things up during the long days and nights. She turns to Evan and tells him about the encounter with Daisy.

And now, after hearing the words, "It tastes just like chicken," at least three times, dinner concludes with Chamba closing his eyes and tilting his head at the salted night sky. Megan also looks up but she doesn't close her eyes. She sees what appears as millions of fireflies blinking furiously earthward, then hears soft words seemingly floating from Chamba's mouth, which hardly moves at all.

"God, thank you for this meal you have given us and for protecting our dear friends gathered around this fire before you. Though we don't know for what purpose, we do know that we have been brought together before you and by you, and we pray we shall go home when the waters recede and you are done teaching us what we are supposed to learn here in your glorious wilderness of Tsavo. Amen." Chamba opens his eyes.

Dora also says, "Amen," then looks at Katie, hands her a slight but pleasant smile that reveals no teeth.

No one says a word for several minutes. They just stare fixedly at the fire and listen to the mysterious voices of Africa calling in the distance, cackling, shrieking, squawking, growling, howling, and whooping. "Perhaps the animals praying...in their own way," Chamba comments.

Why Katie can't sleep, she doesn't know. Maybe it is the incredibly vivid and brilliant stars tonight, a string of luminescent pearls stretching from horizon to horizon tied in haphazard knots that connect faraway worlds. When she squints they diffuse, first making her think of lighted Christmas trees, dripping with icicle and draped with silvered ornaments; when she blinks, they rearrange themselves and settle into new patterns.

Why can't I get to sleep?

She turns to her side and the bed of fresh leaves Evan had made for her. Days ago they felt supple and light to her skin, but now they provide little comfort. They crunch and some crumble into pieces. Below the leaves, she feels the bamboo platform conforming to the shape of her back—or maybe it's her back conforming to the shape of the bamboo. For ten minutes she watches the low sky rotate by, east to west. Her attention shifts. She looks around the largest of the bamboo platforms. Megan is asleep. Miss Emily is out of sight but within snoring distance. And Dora and Chamba are curled together as one.

Where is Evan?

Evan would normally be draped across a pile of baobab leaves near the edge of the platform where he too could often be seen touching stars and juggling planets. But he's not there. She hadn't heard him climb down the ladder but he surely must have at some point during the night. She picks herself up at once and steps carefully around the baobab's trunk, eyelids peeled wide to let as much light in as possible. She sees Miss Emily, stretched across her private "suite," the east platform, mouth hanging open and two rows of teeth reflecting bits of starlight.

But where is he?

Finally she remembers. *The waterfall. That must be it.*

He had mentioned it fireside while Chamba and Megan skimmed rocks toward the distant and pale torches dotting the village and Miss Emily's house and the shimmering slopes of Kilimanjaro standing sternly behind. "The waterfall is at least thirty feet tall," Evan had said while pointing, "It's just up the canyon over there. I may go take a shower tonight, if it is warm enough."

It's definitely warm enough, Katie thinks as she imagines standing under tepid fresh water, rinsing her hair. *God only knows what I smell like.*

She gingerly climbs down the ladder of the baobab treehouse and into the darkened abyss beneath the platforms, beneath the broad canopy of leaves, beneath the watchful moon. Evan said that the waterfall was about a ten minute walk. The thought of ambling along in the night amidst strange nocturnal beings isn't comforting in the least, but she starts toward the canyon, the one Megan had nicknamed Gray Beard, as at night a prominent mouth-like ledge protrudes below caved indentations that appear as eye sockets and down below, where the chin meets the valley floor, striated vertical columns of granite droop and curl themselves into a massive beard, unfolding upon sandy outcroppings of small thorn trees. The effect is most striking when the moon, especially one as full and luminous as the one hanging in the sky tonight, stares down just shy of vertical, and the shadows of rocks scatter clearly over the ground.

There are noises; Katie hears animals stir as she makes her way along trickling water. Bushes rustle and invisible hoofs or feet thud by in the distance, somewhere on the steep slopes. Evan had said, "Just follow the stream. Stay on the right side, for better footing. Eventually you'll feel mist coating your face, then, another fifty yards or so, you'll hear the water."

She hears the water. And as she nears the waterfall she sees tremulous light cascading down the shear face of a majestic cliff above. The glowing liquid juts outward in a horizontal spray then gives way as gravity pulls at it, drawing it to a small misty pool where it breaks apart, beads, and reforms. Shiny rocks wearing a thin veil of moisture bounce moonlight deep into the V of the canyon, revealing what appears to be fountains of water dancing at the base of the fall. As she gets closer, the noise becomes more intense. Spattering, crisp sounds float upward on the humid air.

It is here, amidst a foggy hollow, that she sees Evan. Turned away, face aimed at the waterfall.

She moves closer with the sudden adrenaline rush of being somewhere she's never been, stalking in silent shadows, no one knowing where she is—a child sneaking out of her room Christmas morning and surveying before anyone else is up.

She wonders how she'll let him know she is here without scaring him half to death, for the way he moves, slowly and gently, he is surely in another world all to himself. She pauses, sits down on a rock near the water, somewhat concealed by a bush that smells like crisp pine mingled with some herb she can't quite identify. She watches him soak into the mountain. The muscles of his broad shoulders, his long arms and back, the small bumps of his spine, the rounded pale flesh of his rear, and the crisp line where his bronze legs begin. Her breath fails her. She scarcely draws any air at all, as if she's the uninvited guest at some sort of sacred vigil. Then at once she sighs with pleasure and drinks in the warm wet breeze made from the waterfall.

As Evan turns toward her she feels her pulse quicken. She hunches lower, elbows draped on her knees.

Should I just walk over, tell him I couldn't sleep? Hi Evan, nice evening isn't it? Just happened to be out for a little stroll in the dead of night and noticed you bathing butt-naked under the waterfall, thought I'd stop by.

She raises her head just enough to lay her eyes on him once more.

219

He's still facing her direction but his head is angled down and he's scrubbing his stomach, armpits, and chest. Then he spreads his legs apart slightly and reaches down and with his left hand holds himself while his right seems to splash water and rub gently. She suddenly feels light headed as he lets go and a shadow slings lower beneath him, swinging somewhat, then his legs again close together as he runs his hands over his forehead and through his hair.

Feeling both exhilarated and a bit ashamed for watching, Katie rises to her weak legs and backs away, behind a ledge of rocks. She leans herself against the cool smooth surface of a boulder and inhales deeply.

It could be so easy, she thinks, *just walk over there and take him in my arms, all of him. Just take him in. What's holding me back? I'm not married for god sakes, not yet anyway*, she tries feebly to convince herself. The way she and David's relationship had been going, she wasn't even sure if she was still engaged.

She realizes that she is breathing hard. Dropping her chin, she sees her body crisp in the moonlight, her blouse wet and glued to her breasts. She reaches up and touches them, feels them engorge and heave with each intake of air, imagines Evan's hands on her, right now, right here.

As she leans forward the cotton fabric at her lower back sticks to the rock, as if something, someone, is telling her to stay put, *Don't do something you may regret Katie...*

And so she just dreams of him, standing there, other side of these cool, smooth boulders that separate her from him, reality from fantasy, frustration from ecstasy, restraint from self-regard. Alone in her desire and guilt, she pulls away and walks back down toward the valley, straddling the winding stream—all the while, in her mind, feeling him touch her.

As she nears the floodplain, she feels a sharp stinging sensation under the arch of her left foot. Then a bird shrieks as it chases its shadow skimming across the water before her.

Back at the waterfall, Evan makes his way over to the edge of the basin and pinches at various plants he sees. He holds up each piece and smells it, and tosses away three handfuls of leaves and twigs before finding something that smells better than he does, a severed frond from a raffia palm. He tears off a portion and rips it into shreds, then smears the extract under his arms and all over his body. Another fresh clump, he uses for shampoo. He starts to laugh as he envisions waking up in the morning all sticky and covered with ants. But at least he'll smell good.

His first clue that he has been under this waterfall for far too long is the new position of the moon. His second is that his hands and feet are wrinkled like a kid who's spent his first day at the beach. He rinses his shorts, socks, and shirt out then kicks himself for not doing so the instant he arrived. They'd be almost dry by now, no doubt. But instead he has to slip them on wet. He ambles down along the stream, feeling refreshed, reborn.

And then he sees her sitting there, a ghost of a figure draped in thin gray moonlight at the end of the stream, feet dangling in the current where the water meets the floodplain.

"Katie?" he says softly.

She jumps up, heart thumping profusely in her chest, as when she saw him under the waterfall. "Evan?"

"What are you doing up?"

"I, I just went for a walk. Couldn't sleep. I cut my foot," she says. "Is it bad?"

She sits down once more and holds her left leg crossed over her right. "Looks like it's stopped bleeding," she answers.

"Let me see."

"It's nothing, really."

He sits down next to her and picks up her foot, runs the tips of his fingers over the arch. His touch sends a chill shooting through her, "Hey that tickles..."

"Sorry," he says as he tries to get a good look. "Yeah, the bleeding has stopped. You'll live, I think."

"Lucky me," she says. "So what are you doing up?" she asks, all innocent like.

"Oh, I hiked up to the waterfall," Evan answers, pointing with his chin, "and took a little shower. God I feel better, you should try it."

"Is the water very cold?"

"It's not too bad, once you get used to it. You want to go, I'll walk you up there?"

She looks for words in the shimmering pebbly earth beneath her feet, knowing that the answer she would like to give may change her life. With every ounce of her she wants to say, *yes.*

"You'll feel a lot better...believe me," Evan continues. "But you can hike up tomorrow if you like and—"

"No," she interrupts. "I would like to rinse off. You don't mind heading back up?"

"No, not at all. Come on," Evan says as he stands, then reaches

221

down to take her hand. He looks at her eyes and sees tiny stars mirroring back at the sky.

As she stands, Katie feels a stinging sensation in her foot but it quickly fades away.

"Are you sure you can walk okay?"

"Yes, it feels fine now. Just a tiny wound from a thorn or something. I think I got it out."

They follow the stream, Evan occasionally grabbing Katie's hand to help maneuver her over and around the rocks or branches.

Unscathed, they reach the waterfall. He tells her, "I'll stay here by these rocks while you jump in." He turns around, averting his eyes to give her privacy.

"Okay," she replies then steps down across several flat stones seemingly placed in a perfect arrangement for entering the natural pool. When the water rises to her knees, she glances over her shoulder to see if he is watching. He's not. So she unbuttons her shorts and slides them and her panties off, then quickly descends to her waist while holding them above the water. She tosses them over to some purplish boulders, then slides her blouse over her head and does the same.

"Okay," she yells as she drops to her neck. The chill takes her breath away and she feels goose bumps all over her body.

"Can I look now?" he calls out.

"Yeah."

Evan walks around a smooth outcropping, moves to the edge of the water and sits down on a polished stone. "Doesn't it feel great?"

"Wonderful!"

"Move over to the waterfall. You can go underneath and pop up on the other side in a little grotto." He watches as Katie bops over to the cascade. He knows she can stand up, as the water is only thigh-high there, but she stays low and manages to get underneath the waterfall. She disappears for an instant then he sees her face behind a watery curtain, shimmering silver.

She must think I can't see her, he thinks as he watches, for she slowly stands, suddenly uninhibited. Then he remembers that, from the other side, the water appears as a solid streak of gray and a mist fills the air, blurs the eyes. He almost feels guilty for not telling her. Almost.

And so he gazes at this gorgeous woman who has dropped into his life as suddenly and profoundly as the torrential rains that swept through the recent long and dreary days—days he knows he will eventually look back on as intermittent messages of longing in her eyes, and waves of her red hair shimmering in the breeze, and whispers from her lips as she lay facing him in the night.

Evan struggles to define Katie's shape, which is blurred like an impressionistic watercolor, liquid and smooth with soft edges outlining the curves of a perfect hourglass figure. As she turns sideways, the faint tapered slope of her breasts angles down, then upward slightly. Turning a bit more, he sees the chrome-like outline of her more clearly, the curves of her body catching moonlight which is seemingly amplified by the sheet of water before her.

My god, he thinks as he swallows some moist air, *she's absolutely beautiful.*

A minute later and her face pops up in front of the waterfall with a tranquil half smile. "This feels so...good!"

"I told you."

"I wish we would have discovered this days ago."

"I know, I know..."

"Are you coming back in?"

Evan pauses, somewhat surprised at the invitation and as her words linger and mix with the spray of mist over the pool he finally says, "I think I will."

She turns her back to him and he slips off his clothes, which haven't dried yet. Even his hands are still wrinkled from his last swim and shower this evening. He dives in and surfaces near her, about four feet away. At first he tries not to look down, but soon finds his eyes managing a glance at Katie. He can't see anything but small waves sprinkled with stars, lapping against her chest, her neck, her rounded yet defined shoulders.

Katie wipes her eyes, then investigates in every direction as she asks, "Do you think this has always been here, or is it from all the rain?"

He looks at the gully surrounding them. "Oh, it's definitely been here. Feel how smooth the rocks are?"

She nods.

"This reminds me of Lugard's Falls over near the Galana River on the Yatta escarpment. It's incredible, much taller than this. But not too good for a bath, we'd be washed away," he says then cups his right hand, scoops up some water and takes a sip. "But the prettiest falls I've seen are on what's called the Chogoria Route on Mount Kenya."

Katie smoothes her hair back, wipes her eyes, "I wish I could see more of Kenya."

"I wish I could show you more. Maybe I can, once we get out of here. Then again, you'll probably head home right away," Evan continues, his words trailing off as if floating away on the current.

Katie's chin drops and she studies the water for a few seconds, then she looks up and says softly, "Part of me would like to stay here forever, you know, not go back to my responsibilities and worries. Pressures at work. The constant doctor appointments, never knowing if they'll tell me terrible news about one of Megan's tests."

"It must be very hard."

There's a long pause as Katie again lowers her eyes. When she raises them again, he can see a tear tumbling down her left cheek, then vanishing into the wet skin of her neck where it hides, absorbed by the waterfall's mist.

Katie starts to say something but the words, the feelings, get caught in her throat, her chest tightening like a vise.

"It's okay, Katie," Evan utters beneath his breath then moves closer, raises his hand and erases the salty trail of the tear. He sees her take a deep breath, sniffle, then close her eyes as he brushes his palm slowly over her temple. He desperately wants to hug her, hold her in his arms and wring out the pain in her heart. And god, just the thought of her wet breasts pressing against his chest makes his mind intoxicated, and knees feel like rubber. If he held her now, here, naked in the moonlight, there surely wouldn't be any turning back, no chance for rational thinking or the typical assessment of ramifications his scientific brain was used to.

And so he simply touches her face.

He traces her lips with the tips of his fingers, glides his palms through her tangled hair, and gently holds her chin. All while she keeps her eyes—those piercing blues that make him smile inside—tightly secured as if she wants to feel, but doesn't want to see what is taking place. She hadn't been touched by a man in a long time.

When Katie finally opens her eyes they glisten and call for him to move closer. But he stands still, not wanting to push her, for she hasn't shown any affection toward him. Her arms are still down at her sides, beneath the inky black water. She hasn't said a word since he touched her. And she hasn't reciprocated beyond the starry message contained in her eyes. *Her life is surely complicated enough without my presence*, Evan tells himself as only the sound of the waterfall splashing at the pool fills the night air.

With her cheeks, her temples, her chin tingling with each caress of his fingers, she finally reaches up to his face with both hands and cradles him, admires him. Then she slips her right hand behind the nape of his neck and pulls him toward her, eyes closing once more. When her lips feel his, she tilts her head, he tilts his, and the world goes away, just like at the healing dance when he helped her up after she tripped—there is sweet, sudden silence as if someone reached over and turned off a massive faucet above their heads. Complete silence. There's no water about their bodies, there's no flood in the valley below them, there's no sickness in the world. There are no worries whatsoever. Only silence.

When Katie opens her eyes again and the waterfall comes back on, and the water rises to her chest, and the blood returns to her head, she waits for Evan to pull away from her lips slightly, then manages a deep breath.

Evan doesn't know what to say, though words seem to want to burst from him. Breathing hard, he again reaches up to her face, her head, and combs through swirls of wet hair.

Before he can think clearly he whispers, "Sorry..." He doesn't know why he said it. It just comes out. Sorry he's making her life even more complicated? Sorry he's falling in love with her? Sorry she'll be leaving soon? Sorry that Megan has leukemia. Sorry for all the pain within her?

Just *sorry*, and he doesn't know why.

As Katie touches his face again he moves his eyes lower, yearning to explore more of her. Apparently feeling his gaze, his obvious craving for her, she raises herself somewhat and he sees the tops of her breasts, which rhythmically rise and fall with the small waves lapping against them. And as more of her emerges he feels himself engorge, coming alive beneath the water. *My god, just the thought of her pressing against me.*

Then, as if Katie has read his mind, she moves closer. Her smooth silvery skin layers against him and he instantly feels her warmth.

Katie faintly says, "Evan..."

All of her problems, all of her concerns, all of her scars wash away. She angles her face upward once more and senses his mouth press against hers, lets the tip of his tongue outline her lips, her teeth. Then she feels him beneath the water, against her. Firm. Slippery. She reaches behind his back and slides her hands down his spine to his rear which feels muscular and rounded, yet as cold and as smooth as the polished pebbles beneath her feet. She gently squeezes at the soft flesh, pulls his pelvis closer, and imagines him within her.

Again, the sound if the waterfall grows faint and Katie loses herself in his arms.

CHAPTER THIRTY-SEVEN

Yet another day arrives, trapped in the heart of Africa. Near the campsite, Evan pulls aside some thin Acacia branches which serve as a natural wall between his position and an open area, a sloping escarpment becoming dryer with each hour. He shapes the twigs and spindly shoots such that a porthole is formed in the bushes. He then peers through and sees waves of heat rising like ghosts from the rose-stained sand and mud. He's amazed at what he sees. Almost every elephant orphaned before the age of two dies. And even those between the ages of two and five have less than a thirty percent chance of living. And this is why his mouth is agape and his eyes are fixed on the baby elephant before him, which is about three hundred feet from the baobab treehouse.

The only explanation for it to survive the storm and floods, he thinks as he watches it move toward the water, *is the presence of nearby allomothers. That has to be it, but where are they?*

Allomothers are the immature females of an elephant family which help take care of older females' young. They are baby sitters, in effect, and if a young elephant has more than four of them nearby it will enjoy a survival rate of more than eighty percent. Aside from feeding, the baby may spend more time with its allomothers, learning and playing, than with its mother. But as Evan glances at the horizon he doesn't see any other elephants. Not one.

Megan approaches. "Do you think it's the one whose mother was shot?" she asks with a whisper, hunched over with her hands on her knees.

"Yes, I'm afraid so. It's Daisy, all right. I tagged her about six months ago. And she's probably the one you saw in that dream yesterday," Evan says, then looks at her with a wry grin, pats her on the back.

"You're the only one who believed that I saw her. I could tell."

Evan nods then says, "Well, everyone will believe you today. I'll make sure of that."

Megan smiles broadly. "Cool. Thanks."

They watch as Daisy frolics in the water, tosses streams of it over her back and rolls in the mud. Evan tells Megan that the mud serves as sunscreen lotion, and also helps keep flies away.

They head back to the baobab tree and find Katie and Dora cleaning fish, Chamba's morning catch. It seems that with each passing day their diet is improving and the food is actually starting to taste good. With the sun nearing high noon, they approach carrying twigs and pieces of whatever branches they can carry. Firewood for cooking lunch.

"Mom, we saw it," Megan says as she drops the wood near the fire pit, brushes off her hands.

"Saw what?"

"The baby elephant."

With an incredulous stare, and her head tilted slightly, Katie says, "You're kidding," then looks to Evan for confirmation.

Nodding slowly he says, "She's right. It's taking a mud bath, not far from here."

"The one whose mother was shot, Daisy?"

"Yes."

Nearby, Dora removes the spine from a fish she is preparing and asks, "How old is it, Evan?"

"I'd say three to four years old."

"So it's feeding for itself?"

He nods again, "We saw it eating acacia branches."

Dora's face assembles into a grimaced expression as she raises her head and continues, "Those men should be hung for what they did to the mother."

Evan nods twice. He then turns toward Katie. The longer than usual look in her eyes reaffirms a secret—or one of the secrets—they had agreed to last evening. They hadn't told the others about seeing the poachers, or finding the truck loaded with elephant tusks. Although Evan figured that the two men would probably become lost for days in the eastern canyons and, if they kept going in the direction they were headed, the Kalinzo Plain, he didn't want anyone worrying about them possibly coming back through their area. So he and Katie had decided not to say anything. There were enough things for the others to be concerned about.

This was but one of the secrets they now shared, and each time their eyes met this morning an unspoken closeness occurred between them which felt assuring and exciting. It was he who said they should take it slow. "I don't want you to do something you'll regret in the morning." Yet he had wanted to make love to her with every touch of her soft lips to his, every inhale and exhale, every rise and fall of her chest pressing against his skin.

For Katie, she could find as many reasons to surrender to her desires as there were glowing stars in the evening air. Yet she had worried that his words held deeper meaning, that perhaps he didn't want to make love to her at all. Perhaps their passion was borne of the unexpected romantic atmosphere they found themselves in, the beauty of the waterfall and the calling of each other's bare skin. So with just a sliver of control gathered between them as they placed their backs upon an area of smooth grass near the waterfall, they had simply run their hands over one another, held each other, and spoke few words until the first trace of pale clouds on the eastern horizon stared back at them before sunrise—it was time to go back to camp before the others awakened.

Now, seeing her stand here with the breeze washing through her wild hair, and seeing the way her blouse clings to the valley of her back as she leans over to start the fire, Evan dreams of what she would have felt like if they had gone much further. To swim wholly in her curves, to feel himself linger within her after hours of uninterrupted pleasure with only the sound of the waterfall and light from the stars and moon.

As the dry brush beneath the twigs and branches catch fire, Katie hands a plastic lighter back to Dora then looks over and notices Evan's admiring eyes, which quickly retreat when meeting hers. A sudden rush of blood moves to her face and she too turns away, blushing like a schoolgirl. She hopes Dora and Megan don't notice, but just to be safe, she turns away and walks slowly toward the edge of the water, which has dropped at least four feet today. Even the Land Rover, which she sees in the distance, has completely revealed itself and she notices Chamba with his head buried in the engine compartment, apparently trying to see if the engine will ever work again.

Miss Emily, who has been napping since eleven, climbs down from the baobab treehouse looking more disheveled than usual. "Do I smell something cooking?"

"Yes. Fish. Just about ready," Dora says over her shoulder.

"Wonderful! I'm starving."

Dora grins and says beneath her breath, "What else is new?" She instantly feels guilty though and continues, "Forgive me Lord."

After lunch, Megan, Evan, and Katie go for a walk. Katie wants to see the elephant she's heard so much about. Along the way they see a pair of numbian vultures riding invisible roller coasters high above, a waxbill hang gliding near what Evan says are hyenas scouring about a temporary island further north, and several black-breasted bustards meandering aimlessly through muddy terrain.

228

"There are over four hundred different species of bird in Tsavo," Evan says as he picks up a flat rock, cocks his body and right arm sideways, then skips it across the water as his eyes brighten as if he is thirteen years old again.

"Good one," Megan confirms as the rock hops five times before sinking. Ripples widen on the still water and subtly fade away into each other. She surveys the ground for just the right shaped stone and also sends one sailing. Three hops and a big plop.

Within minutes they reach the area where Evan and Megan had seen Daisy. At first they scarcely see a thing, the sun's rays also skipping across the water, bombarding their eyes, but as they squint and struggle to define the monochrome, sun-drenched world before them, a large shadow rises and the plump silhouette of Daisy takes form.

"There she is. See?" Evan says in a hushed voice, pointing.

Katie places a hand above her eyes, "Yeah, I see her..."

Daisy moves toward dry ground and eventually reaches an acacia that's all but bare. They watch as she uncoils her trunk, all fifty thousand muscles within it, and reaches for branches that still have leaves.

Evan turns to Megan and tells her that elephants in zoos often learn to toss objects onto trees in order to make the branches drop to within reach. "They're really quite intelligent," Evan says as everyone moves nearer, skirting behind a boulder so they won't be seen by Daisy.

"Do you think she'll let us get even closer?" Megan asks. "Maybe we can knock some of those branches down for her."

After wiping the sweat from his forehead, Evan answers, "She'd probably run off, once she sees us."

"But she wasn't scared when she came up to me, smelling my arm."

"True, but you were asleep, or half asleep. You weren't threatening to her."

"Wonder why she wanted to smell me."

"Oh, she was probably just checking on you, that's all. Elephants seem to have a sixth sense. Daisy wanted to make sure you were okay, I guess."

CHAPTER THIRTY-EIGHT

With each shade of gray that folded down over the land Katie became more nervous. She had planned all day about what she would say to Evan, and how she would say it. The dialogue had played in her mind over and over. She wanted to apologize for tracking him down to Tsavo like an animal, interrupting his work, and pressuring him to help Megan when they were back in Johannesburg. She wanted to let him off the hook. Her worst fear was that he might take her attraction to him last night as some sort of seduction aimed at getting his help. She felt ashamed for even contemplating that he might think she was that manipulative or shallow. But she couldn't shake the feeling. If she could get him alone tonight, she would tell him how sorry she was and that this, being stuck out in the middle of Tsavo, was all her fault. Not his.

Dinner was on Chamba. He had buried it in the sand with bark and leaves and it had cooked all day, the luscious taste of smoke pouring into the languid air. When Megan had asked what it was, Chamba replied with a smile, "Pavu la paa." She just shook her head, afraid to inquire further. Stomach growling, she took a piece of meat between her thumb and forefinger and nibbled at it as if it would come alive at any second and nibble at her.

When the last bit of sun flung itself over the horizon, everyone sat around the fire and stared at it as if it were their favorite TV show. Eyes became glassy, reflective, and private worlds took over weary sun-strained minds. Everyone was worn out. The "safari" was getting old.

Finally, after dozing off three times, Chamba picks himself up, yawns and utters slowly, "I'm tired...time to hit the leaves. Good night."

Megan moves her attention from the fire and says, "Lala salama, Chamba."

"Hey, you remembered. You'll be speaking Swahili fluently before you know it."

She smiles as Dora also rises and wishes everyone good night. And within minutes Miss Emily is on her feet mumbling, "See ya'll in the mornin'."

Katie's senses her pulse speeding up, her heart seemingly wanting to thump out of her chest. *Evan and I are almost alone*, she tells herself.

She almost wishes Megan would stay up awhile, and give her more time to make a decision that she knows is coming, as deliberately and as surely as the moon rising in an encore appearance of last night. But five yawns later Megan, too, gathers herself and heads to the baobab treehouse. "Good night mom. Good night Evan."

"Sleep tight honey," Katie replies.

Then Evan, "Night Megan."

Evan and Katie watch as Megan climbs up the ladder and disappears into the canopy of leaves. Their attention then moves to ground level and they stare at the fire. There is silence for at least a minute, as the flickering light scatters over their faces. "Lovely night, isn't it," Katie finally says, mostly wanting some sound, any sound, to break the quietude.

"Yes. It's beautiful."

The years slip away and suddenly Katie feels like she's seventeen and leaving the high school prom and Joey Miller is waiting for a clue as to whether they're going to make out. She's nervous at first, but realizes that the butterflies in her stomach are the exact ones she had dreamed of gathering once again at some point in her life—the energy, the unknown, the excitement of being near someone who makes her feel alive.

Eventually, she starts to feel more relaxed. *This is silly*, she tells herself. *We're adults here.*

"Did you say something?" Evan asks.

"Uh, no, just thinking that's all."

He nods, waiting for her to fill in the blanks. But she doesn't, so he asks, "Thinking about what?"

"Oh, everything I guess," she continues, reaching for words. "Say, there is something I wanted to talk to you about and—"

"About last night?"

"No, no, not about last night."

Relieved, Evan nods again, slightly too fast.

"I wanted to apologize."

"Apologize for what?"

There's more silence as Katie searches for the right words in the blue and orange flames dancing before her. Then she moves her eyes to Evan's face and says, "It was crazy for me to impose my problems on you, you know, just show up on your doorstep and ask for help. I didn't mean to—"

"Katie, you didn't impose. You just—"

"Wait, please hear me out. Please," she says softly but with

231

deliberate measure. "You wouldn't be sitting out here in the middle of nowhere if we hadn't followed you up from Johannesburg. It wasn't right. I'm truly sorry, Evan."

"You were just trying to help your daughter. I respect and admire you for that."

As Katie moves her attention back to the fire, Evan stands and moves closer, sits down next to her.

Katie continues with a lower voice, "Anyway, I just wanted to tell you that I understand, you know, about your not agreeing to help. Being out here with all this spare time on my hands has given me a lot of time to think. To think about things I haven't wanted to face back home. Things that, well, are painful. But I guess reality can be painful, can't it."

"Katie, look at me, please look at me," Evan whispers just above the crackling sound of the fire. "You're the most incredible person I've ever met."

"Please..."

"No, really. I can't imagine how you've managed to handle everything that's been thrown at you over the past year. I mean, my god, most people would either be basket cases or would have locked their emotions up and become bitter. But...but you, you're a miracle, Katie."

Again, her watery eyes meet his.

"And if I had a daughter who had leukemia, I'd do everything possible to help her too."

Katie looks down, crosses her legs. "You know, David thought the whole idea of having one of my eggs removed and, with success, later giving birth to an identical twin of Megan was, well, crazy. Lord, the arguments we had. But I just thought, if all these doctors are out there doing reproductive cloning on sheep, cows, and monkeys, and now our breeding center is starting to do thoroughbred horses, what's the harm in cloning with one of my eggs, giving birth to a twin of Megan, and saving her life? It's not like I would have two daughters who are exactly the same. Their environment and experiences would make them unique, not to mention the age difference," she says then rubs her forehead. "I mean, how is that any different than the women who take fertility drugs and give birth to identical twins?" She pauses then asks, "Did you hear about that couple from Alaska last year?"

Evan shakes his head no.

"They had identical quadruplets. Four beautiful, healthy babies. All the same. The media made it sound like they were going to have to share one soul or something—that God wouldn't love them just as much as any other child of his," she says then takes a deep breath. "I don't know, maybe it is crazy…"

Again Evan shakes his head and while staring at the fire says, "I've had a lot of time to think out here too, Katie. It's not crazy. In fact it may be one of the only ethical reasons to clone a human being—to *save* a human being. I think people are just afraid of the unknown. That maybe some billionaire somewhere is going to start making little copies of himself or something. People don't seem to realize that every time they see identical twins they're looking at clones essentially. No, their eggs weren't created in petri dishes, but they are clones—exact copies—in every sense of the word."

She nods slowly. She came to the same conclusion months ago, but nobody would listen.

"Look, I'm not promising anything," Evan continues intently, eyes fixed on her face. "But once we get out of here, I promise I'll try and do what I can. Okay? And if I can't—"

"Evan," she interrupts, "I didn't raise the subject to try and convince you to help. I meant what I said, I'm sorry for putting you in this position, both personally and professionally."

He reaches up to her face, strokes her cheek with the back of his hand. "I know you're sorry, Katie. But I'm not. I've never felt as alive as I have these past days with you," he says deliberately. "I want to help Megan if I can. Please, tell me you believe me."

The water is even warmer than last night when Katie dips her toes in, but it still makes her exhale loudly and shiver for several seconds. She wiggles her toes and tiny pebbles wedge between them, then she looks at the waterfall, shimmering under another full moon that looks so close she can reach up and grab it.

"How's the water tonight?" Evan asks.

"Feels great! Little warmer even."

"Great," he says as he unties his boots, peels off his socks. He looks up and Katie is pulling the tail of her blouse from her shorts. He waits for her to tell him to turn around, but she says nothing, and lifts the blouse off in one motion. Or almost off, that is. The collar gets caught on her necklace and she's stuck, her arms dangling in the air above her.

"Evan, can you give me a little hand here?" a muffled voice

emanates from beneath the blouse which is now completely covering her head.

"My pleasure," he says with a laugh. He moves cautiously over the slippery stones, toward her.

"It's caught on my necklace."

"Uh, huh. I noticed. I rather like it like this."

"I'm sure you do," she says then feels him place his hands at her bare ribs. It takes her breath away. Like a million other things she had gone over in her mind today, especially the emotional intimacy which had occurred between them last night, she'd thought of him touching her again.

Evan takes his time, admiring her for several seconds. Stalling.

"Hey, what are you doing?" she asks.

"Oh, nothing..."

She feels his hands move to her breasts, softly cupping them. Then she senses delicate kisses, outlining her pink flesh, and his tongue sliding over her. Every ounce of blood in her head seems to drain to her feet, to the trickling water. Her mind wanders through a field of euphoria, picturing him touching her, loving her.

Then he says, "Okay, let's see here," and his fingers find the necklace, which is snagged on a loose thread. "There you go," he continues as he helps her pull the blouse up and over her head.

A smile develops at the corners of her mouth as she says, "You're a tease."

"Who, me?"

She closes her eyes and presses herself against him and they hold each other, rocking back and forth to the rhythm of the waterfall.

When she opens them again he's staring at her admiringly, peacefully. He smiles, she smiles, they move their lips together and become one.

He slides his hands lower as if he's touching delicate china, barely laying the skin of his fingers on her back. And as he works his way around to her stomach, the first button of her shorts is already undone. The rest follow with slight twists. And again he works his way to her rear, slides his hands over the softest skin he has ever touched. No underwear, he thinks. He feels her unbuckle his belt, a button, and slowly lower his zipper, then she reaches inside his underwear and gently cradles him as her mouth firms itself to his once more. After a few seconds, she lowers herself and drags her lips down over his chest, his stomach. Then, dropping to her knees, she pulls his underwear down. Unleashed, he dangles before her in the moonlight, breathing faster, feeling the cool breeze of the fall until her lips again find him. Warm, wet, he feels her drag her tongue over him.

When Katie senses his hands on her head, swirling her hair but slowing her, she rises and smoothes herself over his body, which is now lathered with the nectar of the falls.

He picks up his clothes and takes her hand, then sits down on the grass at the edge of the water and watches her place herself next to him.

"God you are beyond gorgeous, Katie," he says softly as he follows the curves of her, from her legs to the stars.

A row of teeth revealed between slightly parted lips, barely discernible in the dim light, is her only reply as she smiles slightly.

They lie down facing each other, stroking each other, marveling in the moment.

We have tonight, that's all that is for certain, Katie thinks. When the sky turns pale, and the sun returns, their private little world will all be over, just like last night. Their passion would wither in the brightness of day as they would once again hide what has developed between them.

And so the waterfall, the sounds of the African night, again slip away.

In the renewed silence around them she whispers in his left ear, "You make me feel so good." Evan pulls back some, locks onto her eyes and they tell her the same.

He runs his hands over her and gazes, mouth cracked open a bit, then leaves kisses beginning with the firm bulge of her calf and ascending to the supple skin of her neck. Pausing at her left ear, he softly says, "Are you sure, Katie? Are we doing the right thing? Are you sure?"

"Yes. Yes, I'm sure..."

The touch of her inner thighs sends them apart as he lingers over her, smearing his wet cheeks to hers. He feels her hand bring him closer. And finally, he enters. The muscles of his back ripple and swirl and he senses a sudden primal rush of breath from her mouth.

Strewn upon the untouched virgin grass of a darkened Africa, under a blanket of galaxies, they discover what each had believed impossible in a relationship—a mutual craving and reverence for each other that neither had ever experienced with another lover. And a tacit understanding that was born of arduous relationships, dreams placed on hold, and undaunted appreciation of the fragility of life in all its forms.

Being here, being together in this moment makes them both feel that it was all meant to be—their hearts, minds, and bodies completely void of hesitation. This is their only connection to certainty, except dawn drawing near.

CHAPTER THIRTY-NINE

"Gee mom, you look tired this morning," Megan says as she walks over with two handfuls of pasty baobab fruit. "Want some breakfast?"

Katie yawns and mentally shoves her eyelids open. The dreadful sun is staring back at her, that needful thing she had desperately wanted to stay away while resting in Evan's arms very early in the morning, before returning to the treehouse.

Another yawn and she grumbles, "I'm not hungry. Thanks. Where is everyone? What time is it?"

"Evan and Chamba are working on the Land Rover. Dora went for her morning walk, and Miss Emily's is sleeping in, as always. And does it really matter what time it is, mom?" Megan says, quivering her head for a split second then rolling her eyes dramatically as she turns away. "It's not like we have anywhere to go, or something to be on time for."

Katie turns over, her bed of leaves crunching, and suddenly remembers what happened last night. As if trying to recall a pleasant dream, she goes over everything in her mind. Meandering along the stream with Evan, hand in hand. The touch of his fingers, his tongue, his moist lips on her as he helped her take her blouse off. The feel of him inside her. Swimming together and moving through the waterfall, then hiding in its recess where no one could see or hear them.

Her tired body, the tenderness between her legs, is the only proof that it in fact was not a dream. As she soaks in the memories of him, the images before her closed eyes make her sigh and feel warm all over.

A routine settled in. Three dawns and clear nights passed before Evan's and Katie's eyes, each identical to the other with the only exception being the migration of love making from darkness to light. Indeed, they still ambled each evening to the waterfall, in what had become a ritual of sorts. But their passion had erupted numerous times in the heat of the day, on the rare occasions they found themselves alone.

The first occurrence was not planned, or terribly long. Chamba,

Dora, Miss Emily, and Megan had set off to see Daisy, with Evan and Katie left behind to tend to the day's mystery meat—as Megan now called it—which was cooking for lunch. When a gust of wind kicked up, sending smoke and ashes into the air, Katie managed to catch some of the gray cloud with her eyes.

"You should probably go rinse it out," Evan said, seeing her baby blues turn watery, then red.

Katie nodded and made off toward the canteen in the baobab treehouse, the main platform. There, Chamba had fashioned what looked like an upside down umbrella, made from canvas discovered under one of the Land Rover's seats. With each brief shower the rain would funnel into the canteen and, even when it didn't rain, morning dew would form, aided by the canopy of leaves above which added a surprisingly sweet splash of flavor. The nectar became an unexpected delicacy, something to look forward to. At times, when the canteen became empty, everyone would take turns running off to the stream for refills, then promptly place it back under the canvas such that the exotic flavors would continue to drip throughout the hours of the day.

Katie was gone longer than Evan thought she should be, so he headed off for the treehouse too. "Are you okay up there?" he asked as he began climbing the ladder.

"Yes, just got something in my eye."

By this time he was halfway up the ladder. Upon reaching the main platform, he walked over to her. "Here, let me help. Tilt your head back."

He trickled some of the nectar over her eyes as she blinked rapidly, her long lashes flapping like butterfly wings.

"Better?" he asked.

"Yes, I think so..."

As they climbed down the ladder, Evan first, he glanced up and saw her long legs straddle down the rungs and the white flesh of her rear peeking from her ragged-looking shorts. That was all it took. "Hey, why don't you head back up there for a few minutes?"

"Why?" she asked.

"I forgot something," he said with a smile.

At the top of the ladder, she turned to him and he reached up to her face without a word and drew her to him. What followed was unlike their nighttime encounters. Perhaps it was the lazy sunshine filtering through the branches and leaves that painted her with dappled light, revealing all of her to him. Or maybe it was the urgency and forbidden

238

quality of having to move quickly, before the others returned. He didn't know. Whatever it was, it felt like nothing he had experienced before, almost animal-like. Still standing and kissing, he withdrew his lips from hers and they both wrestled needed air into their lungs. He swung her gently around and she instinctively placed her hands on the trunk of the tree, holding them high.

The kisses he left on her neck sent chills through her and within seconds he had unbuttoned her shorts, slid them off her feet and widened her legs into an upside down V as she arched her back. What followed was passion only witnessed in their dreams, or on the screen of a movie theater. Fast, furious, almost surreal.

When done, Evan whispered, "Sorry, I couldn't wait any longer."

Katie replied, "I couldn't either."

How such a brief encounter could provide so much physical pleasure, and emotional closeness, tugged at both of their minds the rest of the day.

Each successive act, whether the moon or the sun watched down, seemed to increase in intensity and they found themselves looking for every opportunity to be alone without, of course, causing suspicion. There were long walks along the cliffs, expeditions for food and water, and more encounters within the arms of the baobab tree. They made love atop sun-drenched boulders that cooked their backs. And standing up until their legs screamed. And leaning against trees with prickly bark, and even under the cover of water. Neither had felt such compelling thoughts, or acted upon them with such craving and urgency and complete abandon of self-control. Their bodies ached and a soreness settled within their bones which was somehow exquisite, like the tenderness experienced when one has worked out the day before, the awakening of forgotten muscles causing pain yet feeling good at the same time.

There were fleeting moments when each felt almost ashamed, as if some animal instinct had transferred from the beasts roaming about them and into their very own souls. Or that an addiction had formed that neither could, or wanted, to control. But upon reflection both knew it was more than this, for their conversations were equally intense, equally rewarding.

"It's as if we've known each other all of our lives," Evan said one day while walking along the shore. He continued more softly with shining eyes that pierced her, "I'm afraid I'm falling in love with you, Katie Ryan."

"And I, you," she blushingly whispered back.

And when he later pointed out that the water had almost

retreated to the point at which they could probably drive out, assuming the Land Rover could be started, she sighed loudly and almost started to cry. For days she had watched the water disappear and more bridges to the village rise from the earth—bridges back to her real life. She knew that each ounce of moisture yielding to evaporation or gravity drew her closer to reality, closer to leaving this breathtaking land, and this breathtaking man. If it not for wanting to get Megan back to safety, she'd just as soon have the ashen, muddy skies return and the flooding downpours of days past.

PART SIX

CHAPTER FORTY

The flights from Louisville International Airport to Atlanta's Hartsfield-Jackson, then on to Amsterdam, had been smooth and uneventful. A movie, a meal, a couple glasses of wine. The layover in Amsterdam was three hours, enough time to visit a normal-size bathroom, eat an over-priced meal in the terminal, and buy a Heineken and a newspaper. When the last boarding call came, David boarded Delta flight 9585 for Nairobi, Kenya, and soon the 747 was taxing across the tarmac toward a long line of aircraft with blinking lights waiting to take off. Eventually the line of planes crept forward one at a time as the one in front of the pack prepared to takeoff, rocking to and fro, driven by the thrust of engines winding up.

It was then that the speaker came on over David's head, "Ladies and gentlemen, I'm afraid we'll have to turn around and head back to the gate. We have a warning light indicating a cargo door isn't sealed properly. We're hopeful that we will be able to fix the problem and get you on your way to Nairobi, Kenya as soon as possible. We apologize for the delay and inconvenience. Please keep your seatbelts fastened, and we'll keep you apprised of the situation once we are at the gate. Thank you."

Eight hours later, after David had finally landed at Nairobi Kenyatta International, he felt like he'd been beaten and drugged. What was supposed to be a three hour layover in Amsterdam turned into six hours, for another 747 had to be brought in, cleaned, fueled, and loaded with baggage and stainless steel carts of something resembling food. The only good news, free drinks for everyone's trouble.

David's only clue to where Katie and Megan might be is a phone number scribbled on a piece of paper in his wallet. Katie had given him it at the end of their last conversation, the call from Dora and Chamba's house in Nairobi. He assumes they wouldn't still be there, since they were planning to leave for Tsavo the next day. But with any luck someone could tell him where, exactly, they were headed.

Downtown Nairobi. The noon sky beats down at David as he walks along a street paved with people, cars, and buses. Noise everywhere. The concierge at the hotel had told him he wouldn't have to take a taxi. "Just look for the sign in front, Kituo Cha Plisisi," he had said then wrote the words down for David to carry along. "The police station is just down the block."

David finds the police station and enters through a large metal door. Inside are rows of faces along the wall as if people are at a fancy restaurant waiting to be seated. He feels dozens of eyes on him as he makes his way to a tall desk with two uniformed men perched behind it.

"Do you speak English?" David inquires of one of the men.

"Yes, sir. May I help you?"

"Yes, thank you. I'm trying to locate my fiancée and her daughter. I haven't heard from them in two weeks and—"

"Two weeks and you are just now looking for them?" the taller of the two men asks. One of his teeth, with gold around its edge, catches the light above and sparkles.

"Yes," David answers, then shifts his attention back to the shorter officer whose expression is fractionally more understanding. "You see, they headed toward Tsavo. I wasn't supposed to hear from them for a while, but they definitely should have checked back in with me by now."

"Tsavo is a big park," the man with the gold tooth says as he shuffles papers.

"Sir," the shorter one says, "why don't you come over here and sit down. Okay?" he asks, then smiles ever so slightly.

"All right."

They walk toward a window with streaks of light beaming in and settling on a metal desk stacked with papers and three coffee mugs. A fly is buzzing frantically above, apparently looking for a clear spot to land.

"Please sit down, sir."

"Thank you."

"Now, when did you last speak to your fiancée?"

"The eighteenth."

"I see, I see," he says as he writes this down then looks at a calendar pinned to the pockmarked wall to his right. "And you are sure they should be back from Tsavo by now?"

"Yes. I'm positive."

"Were they staying here in Nairobi before departing?"

"Yes."

"What hotel?"

"They weren't at a hotel. They stayed at the private residence of Dora and Chamba Musangu. All I have is this number," David says as he pulls out the piece of paper, slides it over the desk.

The officer's eyes aim down as he says, "That's a Nairobi number all right."

"Can you help me find the address? I tried calling the telephone company but they wouldn't give it to me. They said I'd have to come here."

"Indeed, Indeed. Yes sir, I can get the address. It will take me a few minutes."

The officer stands and starts to walk toward a closed door but pauses, then approaches with a tender expression.

Extending his hand, the officer says, "My name is Yaman, Lieutenant Yaman."

"I'm David Hubbard. My fiancée is Katie Ryan."

"Don't you worry Mr. Hubbard. I'm sure your fiancée and her daughter are just fine."

David nods, trying to believe his words.

Ten minutes pass and the officer returns with a friendly, broadened smile. "I have it," he says, holding a card in the air. "Here you are."

David takes the card and looks at it.

"It's, oh, only about five minutes from here by taxi. I tried to call the number and no one answered, but the house is in a very nice area of the city, an affluent suburb called Karen. Most of the homes there have guards and staff on duty. Maybe they can tell you something."

David rises to his feet. "Thank you. You have no idea how much this helps."

"It is no problem, Mr. Hubbard. No problem whatsoever. If you don't turn anything up, come back here and we'll see what we can do to help you. And in the meantime, I'll file a report, okay? A missing persons report."

"Thank you." David gives the officer Katie's and Megan's full names, heights, weights, hair colors, then heads quickly for the police station exit.

Forty-five minutes later a taxi comes to a stop in front of a long rock wall. David's heart is beating furiously. No lights are on in the rambling home on the hill but he sees a gatehouse a bit further up. He tells the taxi driver to wait for him and doesn't give him any money, just to make sure he sticks around.

A sleepy-looking guard emerges from the tiny gatehouse as David approaches. He yawns and says, "Habari za jioni."

"Uh, hello. Do you speak English?"

"Yes, sir."

"Is this the home of Dora and Chamba Musangu?"

"Yes."

"Are they home?"

"No, sir."

"This is very important. I came from the United States to see them. I—"

"They are not home," the guard interrupts. "I'm sorry, sir."

"Do you expect them back soon?"

The guard's shoulders elevate as he says, "I don't know."

"When did they leave?"

"Last week, or maybe two weeks."

"Look, my fiancée, my girlfriend, was at this house right about then and—"

"With a young girl?"

"Yes, yes. You saw them?"

The guard nods then says, "They left with Mr. and Mrs. Musangu."

"Where did they go? This is very important. Please..."

The guard's eyes become nervous, darting left and right as if he's being tested.

David's voice becomes louder, with a tone of urgency. "I have to find them. Please tell me where they are."

The guard hesitates, for Chamba had told him to never tell anyone where they go, or when they will be back. It was just good security practice in a neighborhood coveted by burglars. "Sir, I can't—"

"You won't get into any trouble, I promise. That girl you saw is very ill. Do you understand?"

The guard swallows hard and says, "They said they were going to the village."

"What village?"

"They just call it the village, sir."

"Where's it at?"

"It's in Tsavo."

"Where in Tsavo. East? West?"

245

"It is near the Galana River, between Kathuya and Hatulu Bisani. That's really all I know."

"Thank you, thank you very much." David shakes his hand as if he's pumping water. He asks the guard to write down the names of the places he said as precisely as he can. And as he starts to walk back to the taxi he stops in his tracks, then turns around and asks, "Can you take me there?" He holds up the piece of paper.

"I can't leave, sir."

"I know. Not now, but when you get off?"

"Well, I—"

"Please, I need your help. I'll pay you. Two hundred American dollars, how's that sound?"

David doesn't know it but he has just doubled the guard's entire salary for the month.

"I'm off tomorrow morning," the guard says with a smile.

The lights of the city, neon blues and electric pastels, are descending through the translucent sheers hanging in front of a window as David enters his hotel room and promptly locks the door's two locks, a brass chain and a deadbolt. He had been warned not to stay out on the streets after dark. Still dead tired, he tells himself he has to get some sleep before leaving at the break of dawn to go find Katie and Megan.

He walks over and draws thick drapes across the bustling town below him, then pops open one of his bags sitting on the bed. He searches its depths for his leather overnight case, a gift from Megan last year.

A shower, that's what I need.

He starts the water running. Only cold comes out. He hears someone in the room next door, a pulsing sound and water splashing at a fiberglass or iron tub. He looks up and sees some sort of shower massage nozzle and immediately realizes where all the warm water is going. The guy next door is probably well into a thirty minute water massage. Then he hears a male's voice, and the laugh of a female.

Great... Just great, David thinks as he gives up on the idea of a shower. *A bed, that's what I need.*

He strips to his underwear and peels back the covers, fluffs up two of the thinnest pillows invented by man. As he reaches over to turn off the lamp he notices a piece of paper lying on the floor, near the barricaded door. Someone has obviously slipped it under the door. He walks over and picks it up. It says: *Mr. David Hubbard. Please call your office immediately.*

David's head begins to throb, for he had given the number of the hotel just to Barb at work and told her only to call if there was an emergency, or if Katie and Megan checked in. His mind spins as he contemplates what may have happened.

A car crash on one of these insane two-lane pot-holed roads? An accident of some sort out in the bush? Or maybe it's a message about Megan, collapsing and getting flown to a hospital. Relapse?

Hands shaking, David grabs the phone next to the bed and dials out. Barb doesn't pick up. It's too early back in Kentucky. So he hits 0 twice, his extension and then password. He wants to check voice mail.

"You have three new messages," the computerized voice says.

A beep then, "David, this is Robert. I know you've already left but I wanted to tell you to not worry about having to get back here to work soon. We'll be fine. Just do whatever it takes to find Katie and Megan. Leave me a message if there's anything I can do to help."

Another beep, and David just hears static and someone hanging up.

A third beep. "Mr. Hubbard. This is Ms. Thompson at the NBMP. I'm sorry to call you at work but I couldn't reach anyone at your home, and knew you would want to get the news. We've turned up a match for Megan! It's a good one, five antigens. It just came up on the database today. I'll keep trying your home, but if you get this first please call me as soon as possible. I'm thrilled for all of you. God bless."

Two steady streams flow from David's reddened eyes as he replays the message four times, making sure he's heard correctly. He finally hangs up, walks toward a window and pries open the drapes, the sliding glass door, and steps out on the balcony. Standing here, with his pale skin and white underwear reflecting a rainbow of colors from the city lights below, he feels like bursting. He looks up at the darkened sky, silently shaking his fists in victory, then drops to his knees. Another glance at the sky and he yells, "Yes...yes! Thank you. Thank you, God."

He hears sliding doors screeching open all around him, business travelers and tourists with leaden eyelids shuffling out onto their balconies to see what all the commotion is about.

CHAPTER FORTY-ONE

Floating over waves of heat near the escarpment to the west, Chamba sees ten to fifteen rhinos making their way across an area where nothing had moved since the flood. *There is only one conclusion*, he thinks as he holds a hand above his eyes to block the sun. *The water level has dropped far enough for everyone to try and head toward the village.* He walks over to Evan and says, "Look," and points off to the distance.

"Rhinos?"

"Yes."

"Well, it may finally be time, huh Chamba, it may be time," Evan says slowly, calmly. "Come on, let's have another look at the Land Rover."

The day rolls on, heat worsening.

After two hours of fiddling with the carburetor and cleaning off spark plugs, cables, and a rusty alternator, Evan twists the key in the ignition. Nothing.

"Go ahead, try it," Chamba urges.

"I am. I'm afraid she's definitely dead, old friend."

Disappointment fills both their faces; chins drop. Evan places his forehead on the warm rubber-coated steering wheel, contemplating options, as Chamba folds the hood and sits on top, feet resting on the tubular front bumper. He, too, drops his head, stares at the changing earth, slippery brown mud becoming cracked reddish clay with each hour that passes.

Finally Evan says, "I've got it."

Chamba swings lazily around, his eyes dragging across the hood, "Got what?"

"There may be one more thing we can try. Come on," Evan says as he gets out of the Land Rover and starts walking in the direction of the truck the poachers had left behind days ago. He and Katie, as agreed when they found the piece of junk and its gruesome cargo of tusks, still hadn't told the others about it.

And now, as Chamba's confused face angles at him, Evan explains why they had kept the secret. "We didn't want to worry anyone, you know, that the poachers might still be in the area. And Katie didn't want Megan to see, or even hear about all those tusks, for obvious reasons."

Chamba nods, "I understand," then asks, "Did you try to start the poacher's truck?"

"No, I just assumed that it wouldn't start. When Katie and I first saw the two men, they were working on the engine. Then they just took off. I figured that if they were leaving all that ivory behind, the truck must be broken beyond what they were capable of repairing out here. I'm sure they went to get another truck and will come back to transfer the ivory. In any case, we should go take a look at it and see if we can fix it. It's worth a try."

They reach the dilapidated truck. An oppressive stench—much worse than before—circles the vehicle along with what must be thousands of flies, which appear as an undulating cloud of gray smoke that never rises. Chamba peeks in through the canvas draped over the tailgate and quickly comes up for air, gagging. He says nothing and only shakes his head at the sight of just one more little piece of Africa dying before his weary eyes.

Evan has to place a knee on the side of the cab, for leverage, as he jerks the driver's door open while batting flies. He ascends to the tattered vinyl driver's seat, springs showing through in several places. Then he moves his attention to the ignition switch and says under his breath, "All be damned, they're as stupid as their actions. They left the key behind." He twists the rusted key clockwise. The starter makes a horrendous noise, as if a spinning electric grinder is being held to metal. The engine stumbles and backfires miserably for several seconds. Evan releases the key.

"Want to take a look at the engine?" Chamba inquires, already popping the hood open and shoving a stick in place to hold it up.

Evan climbs down from the truck's cab. He gives a roving, intense stare to the prehistoric diesel engine then looks up at Chamba's curious eyes and coolly says, "Yep, that's the engine all right."

Chamba smiles and shakes his head.

"I don't really know where to start. How about you?"

"No idea, Evan, no idea. It's a piece of shit, in my opinion."

This elicits a solid chuckle from each of them as their frustration finds a way to manifest itself, relieving some tension. It's a laugh or cry moment.

As Evan regroups, he reaches in and makes sure the spark plug wires and anything else he recognizes look okay. Another hop in the cab and twist of the key yields the same results. The truck won't start. So they decide to head back to camp.

As they near the rocks where he and Katie had slipped several nights ago, with her falling into his arms and atop his lonely body, he smiles to himself, soothed by the memory of touching her for the first time. Then, as if someone's tossed a barrier in front of his path, he stops and says, "Let's go back to the truck, Chamba."

"What, why?"

"The battery! We'll take it out of the truck and stick it in my Land Rover. Why didn't I think of this sooner..."

They both turn around and walk back toward the truck. Evan continues, obviously thinking out loud, "The starter cranked over, right, so we know the battery is good."

Chamba nods, "Yes, it might work." Then he stops, just as abruptly as Evan had seconds ago. "Uh-oh, look."

Evan raises his eyes from the sand. In the distance he sees the two men, the poachers, making their way along the cliffs. They are clearly headed back to the truck. He slowly says in a coerced, calm voice, "This isn't good, Chamba, dammit this isn't good."

"Should we head back to camp?"

"No, no, too late, they've seen us. Just keep walking. Don't say anything about our finding the truck, okay? Don't mention the ivory, or elephants at all."

"All right."

They watch as the men walk by the truck and head toward them, head on.

"One of them has a rifle," Chamba says.

"I know, I know. Don't worry, just stay cool."

"But if they know who you are—"

"Yes, but maybe they won't. I'm sure that I don't exactly look the same with this beard I've started growing out here," he says as he strokes his chin with his thumb and forefingers. "I look like a mess, I'm sure."

As if they were representatives of an army cautiously approaching the front lines of a battlefield to discuss a possible truce, Evan and Chamba walk slowly toward the two men, who seem equally hesitant.

Evan, wanting to put a positive spin on the encounter, says with a smile, "God, we're glad to see you guys."

One of the men, wearing khaki pants and a tank top, stops and says with a South African accent, "We've been lost in those hills for days." He turns slightly and points. "There's no way out that direction," he continues, looking weary and sun-battered. His face is bronze and his lips are as cracked as the dried mud he's standing on.

Evan moves two steps closer, "You got caught in the flood too,

250

huh."

"Yes," the man replies with bloodshot eyes now coming into view. "We barely made it to dry ground. Didn't know it would be a dead end though," he says as he glances up at the cliffs.

Evan nods. "We just came around the rocks over there, and noticed the truck. We were going to head over and see if anyone was around. Maybe see if we could start it and get out of here."

"You haven't tried yet?"

"No. Is the truck in good enough condition to drive, now that the waters have recessed?" Evan asks with innocent, wide eyes.

The two men look at each other, then shift their attention back to Evan. "No, it's pretty screwed up actually, right Adisa," he says to the other man, who appears just as scraggly and filthy as he does.

His partner nods obediently and says, "The damn thing won't start."

"Want us to have a look at it?" Evan asks, then glances over at Chamba who looks like he's about to explode. Evan had never seen him so nervous.

"No, no. It would be a waste of time. The engine overheated when we were trying to get away from the flood. She's seized up for good, completely dead," the man lies.

Evan takes a deep breath then says, "That's a shame."

The man named Adisa moves forward slightly and asks, "Say, do you two have a vehicle nearby?"

Shaking his head a few times, Evan replies, "No. Not anymore. It's broken too. We were out hunting and it died on us. So we're thinking of hiking out of here tomorrow. That is, if the water is down some more over in the valley." His eyes move to the horizon for a couple of seconds, and then lock onto a flock of white-backed vultures circling overhead as if they are waiting for their next meal, which makes the encounter with the ivory poachers seem even more ominous.

As Evan turns back to the men, he continues, "You two could probably walk out right now, though, from the looks of it."

CHAPTER FORTY-TWO

A nervous evening settles in, for the run-in with the poachers still lingered in their minds. After ten minutes of small talk, Evan and Chamba had left the two men and their truck full of ivory, seemingly without incident. But Evan was still concerned. He told Chamba on the way back, "If they have half a brain between them they'll see the fresh footprints around the truck, left by us when we tried to start the engine. Of course, they might think that we are poachers too. I purposely told them we are here for hunting, to make them think we might be poachers. But in retrospect, if they think we have seen the tusks, they might consider us a threat no matter what. I guess there's no use worrying about that now though."

Chamba clears his parched throat. "Well, at least the men didn't follow us back here, to the baobab treehouse."

In the morning they planned to see whether the men had left the area, perhaps deciding to walk out and come back later with a replacement truck to pick up the tusks.

"And if they do leave," Evan says, "we'll go back for their truck's battery. If that doesn't get my Land Rover started we'll just have to hike the hell out of here, though I don't want to put the ladies through that if we don't have to."

Twilight turns to pitch-black. "Aren't you going to start the fire?" Miss Emily asks as she walks over and sits in her typical spot, an area of dirt scooped out to match the curves of her rear.

"No, not tonight," Evan replies, then clears his throat as he stalls to come up with more of an answer. He doesn't want the poachers to see the flames. He continues, "I want all of us to hit the sack early tonight, and get some good rest. We might try and walk out of here in the morning."

"Walk?" she says, then seems to mentally measure the distance to the village, a mere speck of light on a faraway hill.

"That's right, unless Chamba and I can get the Land Rover started."

Miss Emily just rolls her eyes, shakes her head. Her expression says, *Yeah, right*. She turns as Megan, Katie, and Dora approach. "Did you guys hear? Evan says we might walk out of here tomorrow."

"Really?" Katie inquires, her voice not lending even the slightest clue as to whether she is happy or sad about the possibility of leaving this place, this private sanctum separating her and Evan from reality and their normal lives. She and Megan plop down.

Evan nods and says, "I think the water has receded far enough. If we don't try now, and it rains hard again, we could be stranded here for another week, maybe more."

Katie's eyes lower and she looks at the burned rocks where a fire would normally be. Her face mingles a strange combination of sadness and relief. She knows she and Megan need to get home. But part of her, the part Evan now holds, doesn't want their time together, their adventure, to come to an end. As she stares at the blackened ring of rocks and the muted fire pit, it becomes something of a symbol. What was once warm and bright the past nights is now cold and dim. It's almost too much to contemplate, not being able to share with Evan the syrupy black African skies and soft moonlight each and every night while being serenaded by invisible creatures, rustling leaves, and trickling water. It was all coming to an abrupt end. As everything good in her life this past year.

An hour or so of subdued conversation flows between tired faces. Megan stands and yawns, "I'm heading up to the platforms. I'm tired."

"Okay, honey. Good night." Katie gives her a hug and a kiss.

"Good night, Megan," everyone chimes in.

As they watch her climb the ladder, Miss Emily says, "She sure is a sweet girl. You should have seen her near that baby elephant today. She climbed up an acacia tree and snapped off as big of branches as she could, then left them in a neat little stack. We watched Daisy chomp them down in seconds. But Megan wasn't fazed. Up another tree and, ten minutes later, another stack of food."

Katie smiles, "She is a good kid, isn't she."

As Miss Emily says, "Yes, the best," Evan nods his concurrence and turns to Katie and says, "Heart of gold. I've never met a teenager with such composure, and, well, selflessness. Come to think of it, I can't think of many adults with such qualities."

There is silence for several minutes as the galaxies above become

253

the main attraction, which are more brilliant than usual since there's no competing light from a fire. Eventually Katie says to Miss Emily, "I can't believe I haven't asked you this. Did you and your husband have children, when you were married?"

"No, I'm afraid not. I planned to with my third husband but when he—"

Miss Emily stops suddenly, as if someone has just gagged her mouth. She had told herself no less than half a dozen times, after hearing from Chamba that Megan was ill, that she shouldn't talk about her ex-husband, Jack, with Katie or Megan.

"What were you going to say?" Katie asks with confused eyes, only minimally veiled by the darkness. She notices that Dora, Chamba, and Evan suddenly have the urge to look away from her.

Miss Emily continues, "I really shouldn't talk about Jack. I told myself I wouldn't anymore."

"Come now," Katie says somewhat coyly, "what was it you were going to say?"

Miss Emily exhales just loud enough for everyone to hear then continues, "I was going to say that when Jack died, well, all my plans for having a family also died."

"I'm so sorry," Katie responds as a guilty breeze washes over her.

"That's okay. It's been a long time, Katie. A long time."

"How did he die, if you don't mind me asking?"

Miss Emily knew the question was inevitable. She musters up her courage and comes right out with it, as if it is no big deal. "Jack had cancer," she says matter-of-factly.

"I see. Was it a prolonged illness?" Katie asks, really wanting to know the exact type of cancer he had.

"Uh, yes. About six years."

"That must have been terribly difficult for you."

She nods. "But I wouldn't have traded the good times with Jack for anything in the world. And he was really the reason I ended up here, living out my dreams."

"What do you mean?"

"Well, to be perfectly blunt and honest, his insurance company tried to screw us over, you know, not wanting to pay for treatment toward the end."

"My god..."

"We lost nearly everything—the house, the cars. Everything," she says then pauses for a few seconds. "We even had to claim bankruptcy."

"That's terrible."

"But old Jack looked out for me pretty well. After he died, I opened an envelope which he had placed in our safe deposit box. I had promised him I would not to open it until his passing. Anyway, when I opened it, I found a note from him, telling me where he had hidden some money. If it not for him looking out for me, I don't know what I would have done."

Evan, who has been listening to the conversation between Miss Emily and Katie, clears his throat and coughs a few times as if to insert a pause and opportunity to change the subject.

But Katie presses on with Miss Emily, "So you used the money to come here to Africa?"

"Yes, and to hold me over in my twilight years, as they say."

"He must have loved you very much, to look out for you like that," Katie says, then watches Miss Emily nod and look up at the sky, apparently conveying a message to her beloved, Jack.

Without the light of a fire, it's fairly easy not to be seen. As Megan hunches down behind some bushes, she hangs on every word exchanged between her mother and Miss Emily. She hadn't planned on eavesdropping. In fact, she had only climbed down to go relieve her nectar-filled bladder in an area near some boulders that Chamba had christened, "The Ladies Bathroom," when they had set up camp. But she's heard everything—all of it—and the words are swirling in her head.

Cancer.

Prolonged illness.

The insurance company.

Lost everything—the house, the cars, everything.

Bankruptcy.

Megan begins weeping uncontrollably and has to place both hands over her mouth to stop her sobs from escaping into the night air. Everything she had heard matched perfectly everything she had worried about happening to her family. In her mind she sees her hair falling out again, sees Billy Murphy making fun of her at school, sees her mother's concerned face as she gets her chemo and radiation treatments.

Her tear-stained cheeks throb as she struggles to halt the uncontrollable flow of moisture and the equally raging thoughts that continue to race through her mind, *prolonged illness, cancer, the insurance company, lost everything, he must have loved you very much to look out for you like that...*

CHAPTER FORTY-THREE

Katie had resolutely, unequivocally, decided that she would drink an entire pot of coffee every morning after she and Megan returned to Kentucky, for when each African dawn arrived she craved not so much the taste but rather the steamy scent floating into her nostrils, the basting of the dry skin of her face, and the manner in which coffee coaxes her from drowsiness. The fact that those foothills on the horizon, seemingly within her reach, contain some of the finest coffee on earth does nothing to ease her craving mind and thirst. *God I miss coffee...*

As she rises she immediately senses that something is different. For one thing, she feels rejuvenated. Last night Evan had told her he wanted to stay close to camp, "And besides, we need to get some rest in case we walk out tomorrow."

With puppy dog eyes she had reluctantly agreed whispering, "All right, if I have to."

She wasn't sure at what point in the night the swaying branches high above changed to dreams of him holding her again and making love to her at the waterfall over and over. But as she lies here in the morning breeze, trying to remember every detail of her unconscious world, she still feels him atop her.

She folds herself upwards, grabs her knees, and tries to stretch her back. With the exception of Megan, who is nowhere to be seen, she's the first one up. *Amazing what a sound night's sleep can do*, she thinks as she stands and rubs her eyes.

She looks about. *Where's Megan?*

She tells herself that Megan would never get up this early, then moves over to the ladder and climbs down. Normally there would be a slight trail of smoke connecting a gray mound of ashes with the morning sky. But the hushed fire pit is lifeless as she walks around it, holding a hand over her eyes, searching for Megan.

She's not in Chamba's custom designed Ladies Room and she's not skipping rocks over the now distant water.

Maybe she's with Daisy, feeding her acacia bushes again?

Although she doesn't see any fresh footprints in the dirt, she walks along the cliffs and heads to the area where Daisy can usually be found. And sure enough, the cute lump of light gray is chewing on what's left of some branches Megan had thoughtfully placed yesterday afternoon. But there's no sign of Megan anywhere.

When she gets back to the baobab platforms Evan is climbing down. Out of breath, she says in an urgent tone, "Evan, I can't find Megan."

"She probably just went for a walk, couldn't sleep perhaps."

"This early? It's not like her."

"Did you look around?" Evan asks, then gazes anxiously down at the ground. "Are these your footprints?" He already knows they aren't hers.

Katie's focus moves to the dirt and mud, and she sees evidence of two small feet traveling in one direction amid a jumbled intersection of overlapping tracks. "No," Katie answers, "they must be Megan's."

"Okay, don't worry. We'll find her. I'm sure she's just out looking for small branches or something for Daisy. Let's wake the others and then we'll follow her footprints. All right?"

Katie nods and then runs a hand over her forehead and through her hair. "Evan," she says, then pauses until he looks at her, "the poachers..."

"I know," is his only response. A few seconds pass. "You better get some shoes on," he continues, glancing briefly over his shoulder.

She follows him up to the main observation platform of the baobab treehouse.

Chamba and Dora, jarred by tense voices, are awake, sitting up. "What's wrong?" Chamba inquires.

"Megan has apparently taken off," Katie answers. She frantically slips her shoes on, no socks, and her fingers weave laces into loose knots.

Evan throws a tee shirt over his head and moves toward the ladder. He turns to Chamba and says, "You, Dora, and Miss Emily stay here. If Megan shows up, get the fire going, okay, real smoky so we see it, and Katie and I will head back right away."

Chamba agrees and offers a conciliatory half smile.

Evan starts climbing down the ladder. "Wait, we better take some water with us. Katie, grab the canteen."

She walks over to the table Chamba fashioned in the middle of the main platform. She reaches forward, then sees a piece of paper folded neatly, leaning against the canteen. Angled rays of light, from the tree canopy, are slicing it into moving shadows and stripes. "What's this?"

Blank faces. No one says a word.

258

She unfolds the paper and sees that it is a water-stained page torn from the copy of *Out of Africa* Miss Emily had given Megan, which she had found buried, along with a moldy pack of gum and three pens, in a layer of mud under one of the Land Rover's seats yesterday. Katie begins to read the note.

Dear Mom,

I'm so sorry for getting sick and causing everyone so many problems. This is so hard for me to say. I just wish—

"What is it, Katie?" Dora interrupts.
"It's a note from Megan."

I just wish everything could be different, and that our family could be together still. But things haven't been the same since Angela died. I should have died. Not her. Because I am going to die anyway. Please don't forget me. Remember that I love you with all my heart for what you have tried to do for me. I heard you on the phone when we were at the hotel, so I know why we came to Africa. You came for me. But now I don't want to drag things out any more. I don't want things to be bad for you and David because of my prolonged illness. Thank you for everything you have done for me, and for what you tried to do for me. You will be better off without me. I love, love, love you, mom. Goodbye. Megan.

Katie turns toward Evan, who is standing behind her now. With tears pouring out of her she hands him the letter with her left hand and places her right over her mouth, which is quivering. She tries to speak but can't.

Evan takes the letter and reads it, then wraps himself around her trembling body.

"It's okay, Katie, I'll find her. It's okay."

She finally remembers to breathe and suddenly takes a stuttering intake of air, like a young child weeping after a nightmare. She runs her eyes over the letter once more then manages to say, "Prolonged illness? Do you think Megan heard—"

"I'm afraid so." Evan nods while reading the note again. He had already made the connection. He says softly, "She must have heard Miss Emily talking last night, about Jack's prolonged illness and the problems it caused for their family."

How she could be scared after everything she had been through was the thought that most troubled Megan as she walked through the night. At first her mind was quiet, at peace. The decision she had carried on her shoulders for months was finally made. And it was her decision, no one else's. How could anyone know how she felt?

But as she ambled on she heard things move in the bushes, climb in the hollows of trees, and cry out at her. She even thought she saw the outline of a lion standing firmly on a hill. Yes, the decision was made, but the thought of being eaten alive made her almost want to turn back, sneak up that frail treehouse ladder and huddle close to her mother again. Pretend nothing ever happened.

But the decision was made.

She had aimed herself toward a pallid yellow light in the village, perhaps Miss Emily's comforting front porch with those big wicker chairs and rose and ivy patterned cushions that sank and blew stale air when she sat on them. Beyond the village, see could see the snow-capped humps of Kilimanjaro shining brilliantly silver under a bright sky. At times, when she felt extremely tired, she would gaze up at them and dream she was there, looking down.

Only once did she interrupt the walking to get some rest. She dropped to her knees then rolled over on her back. The smooth earth felt cool as she remembered a winter day, before she became sick, lying in her backyard making snow-angels. The sky was swirls of blue, like blueberry yogurt, but small flakes fluttered at her and she caught them with her tongue until it became numb. A lot had happened to her family since then, she thought as she peered at the stars blinking furiously at her.

When the sun flowed over the cliffs behind her, over the thorn trees, and over the scattered baobabs, she felt renewed energy. For a change, the floodwater, which she had skirted along through the night, was her friend. She stopped occasionally, once every hour or so she guessed, to have a drink. At first it grossed her out. She assumed that the microorganisms most certainly swimming about could probably keep Mr. Doyce's biology class occupied for a month, everyone staring through microscopes at glass slides until they are blue in the face from squeezing shut their left eye. She'd probably have some type of worms within hours, she told herself as she drank, but such a calamity would be superfluous at this point. Maybe the vicious little cancer cells would kill the worms too?

For some reason she didn't feel sorry for herself. Whatever sadness that washed over her in the darkness and dawn was founded in the regret she felt for putting her mother through so much agony the past year. She couldn't ask for a better mother, really. Taking her to chemo and radiation treatments. Escorting her to school. Explaining everything to teachers and Mr. Manning, the principal. The only positive thing was that her mother was still young. Maybe she could start over, have a couple more kids. Maybe she could finally have the family she deserves.

The only other thing Megan worried about was Daisy. She had piled up several days' worth of branches, reaped from trees further and further away from the baobab platforms. Evan had told her that Daisy would probably start fending for herself once she stopped doing all the work for her, and once a few more channels of dry land emerged. Nevertheless, she felt sorry for leaving her. And as she walked through the dark night and early morning light, the idea had crossed her mind that she had some sort of spiritual connection to Daisy, a connection that was, perhaps, founded in tragedy. Daisy didn't deserve to have her mother killed by ivory poachers, especially right before her big glassy eyes. But at least it was over quick, Megan thought, unlike her lingering paralysis that tortured everyone around her each day, each night.

But now the decision was made.

Everyone would get on with their lives, and she'd finally get out of the way of their happiness.

The sputter of an engine, coughing and hacking, fills the otherwise still morning air. As Katie folds the note Megan had left, Evan says, "What the hell?"

The platform shakes as he runs to the ladder and flings himself downward, missing every other rung and slowed only by the friction of his hands on the bamboo. The burning sensation hits him just as his feet touch the ground. Swinging his body in the direction of the sound of the engine, he sees black puffs of smoke being tossed to the air with each sputter of the Land Rover's V8.

"Those sons of bitches!" he yells, then looks up. "Chamba get down here and—"

"On my way," Chamba's voice interrupts, emanating from one of the platforms above.

They run as fast as they can. Evan's face catches fire and his lungs swell and heave. He sees two men in the Land Rover. One of them has a cowboy hat on.

"It's. Those. Damn. Poachers," he manages to say between breaths.

Chamba doesn't respond. He only stares at the ground, as he isn't wearing shoes and the soles of his feet are being incised by sharp rocks, sticks, and thorns.

About halfway to the Land Rover they see it start to move. The engine's sputtering dissipates, changing into a chugging sound. The heads of the two men rock back and forth, then become steady as the vehicle picks up speed.

They watch as the Land Rover gets smaller, then disappears entirely.

CHAPTER FORTY-FOUR

"Almost there," Megan says aloud to herself, and to the zebras grazing further ahead in an undulating moiré of black and white. Beyond their whipping tails and drooped heads and necks, she sees Miss Emily's house take form out of the hazy spread of the village, everything still and golden in the light of daybreak.

Her legs are burning, and she can feel her thighs and calves getting tighter with each step forward, each step toward her decision. *It's just my luck*, she thinks, *to finally get into the best shape I've ever been in. And it's all for nothing.*

She wonders how many pounds she has lost eating all that baobab fruit and drinking only water. As she walks, she rubs a hand over her stomach. It is perfectly flat. Then she checks her sides. She is the closest she has ever been to having an hourglass figure. Probably the best figure of anyone she knows.

Just my luck...

She sees the zebras raise their heads in what seems like an orchestrated unified movement. They stare in her direction for a few seconds, then explode into dust. When it settles they are gone.

Her attention moves to a flock of some sort of birds, white with long necks. *There must be a million of them*, she thinks as they shoot to the sky and become one noisy mass, the billowy cloud shifting left and right and then becoming invisible. The eerie silence that follows is replaced by something she tells herself can't possibly be. She stops, tuning her ears to the wind like a cat. She swings around. The sound gets louder and she detects that it is emanating from the direction of where her tracks follow her in the sand and mud. She turns and runs away from the sound.

Within seconds she sees, over her shoulder, the green front grill of a vehicle and its shimmering windshield. The animal-like headlights of the grill grow larger. Sprinting as hard as she can, she wants to scream. All this work. All this way. She had almost started to feel free. Just her and the wild animals. Just her and the stars. Just her and the leukemia.

Stumbling, she falls to her knees. They sting and some blood seeps from her left leg, which is now caked with grains of sand. As she struggles to get up, the Land Rover slides to a stop beside her and its front tires sink several inches, like a horse's hoofs brought to a halt, the weight shifting forward.

Megan hears a voice, tinged with an accent she doesn't recognize.

"Well, well, what do we have here? A *white* girl in the middle of the *dark* continent," the man says slowly.

As Megan looks up she sees two men with rays of sunlight framing their dark faces, dark hair. The only features of their faces she can make out are their toothy grins, as if they've just tracked down a kill that will soon find its head mounted on burled walnut, hanging in someone's ostentatious den. Out of breath, chest rising and falling, she straightens her sore knees, then her back. She tries to speak but can't hold the air in long enough to form words.

"Looks like we caught us some nice ass," the man with the hat says. He jumps from the passenger seat and continues, "Hello there, pretty lady. What the hell are you doing out here?"

The other man also climbs out, leaving the engine running. He walks over to the left rear tire of the Land Rover, unzips his pants, and relieves himself as he says, "Probably one of those rich Americans, got left behind by her air-conditioned safari bus."

"Yeah, probably. But I don't know..."

"You don't know what?"

"She's a little young, don't you think?"

"Maybe, but she's old enough for me. Look at those breasts. What size are those anyway?" He shakes himself, zips up, then walks over as he draws a wad of spit and lets it fly ten feet.

Megan backs away as they both approach her. Trembling, she says nothing.

"Those C's or D's, honey?"

No response. She looks down.

"You're a shy one, huh. What's your name?" he asks, trying to smile through lips draped with rusty, dirty facial hair. "Mine is Adisa, and he's Robert."

"Stay away from me!" Megan finally yells as she walks backward and trips. She falls. "Get away!"

"You want to go first Robert, or shall I?" he says then drops to his knees and crawls toward Megan with an evil grin. Just as she jerks her legs away he grabs an ankle, drags her over the sand until they are face to face.

Megan cries out, "Let me go! Please—"

A hand slams over her mouth and she sees his dark eyes look her over.

"You must be a virgin, huh? I like virgins," he says as his face becomes reddened and saliva drips from his mouth. He moves toward her, sticks out his tongue, and moves it up one side of her face and down the other.

Megan screams, pries his filthy hands from her, and somehow manages to roll away and stand. She starts to turn and run but the other man grasps her right arm and says, "Get in the Land Rover."

"Just let me go, please," Megan weeps frantically.

The man called Adisa rises and dusts himself off. He coughs and spits again then says, "Why not just take her, you know, right here?"

The calmer of the two looks at the Land Rover, which is still running, albeit roughly. "No time," he says. "You want to take the risk this piece of junk starting up again? And we're practically out of gas as it is."

"Okay, you're right. We'll save us some of this tight ass for dessert tonight. God it's been a long time."

Megan feels her rear getting slapped twice and a hand sliding briefly between her legs. The men open a door and shove her inside the back seat. Her mind reeling, she looks at her bruised arm through blurry eyes as she hears gears grinding, then the Land Rover backfires and starts moving.

"They stole the Land Rover," Evan tells Miss Emily, Dora, and Katie as he and Chamba near the treehouse, almost panting.

"They who?" Dora asks.

"Two men, dear," Chamba answers.

Evan takes a drink from the canteen, hands it to Chamba, then looks at Katie. She has finally stopped crying, though her face appears sunburned and her breaths are shallow and rapid. She starts to speak, but pauses to wipe her nose, eyes.

Chamba takes a sip of water then says to Evan, "What now?"

"We'll follow Megan's tracks on foot. As long as it doesn't rain and wash them out, we'll find her. Skies look okay," he says as he peers out.

"Do you want us to go, or stay here?" Miss Emily asks with

concerned eyes.

"You three," Evan answers, "better stay here, in case Megan comes back."

"I'm going with you," Katie says firmly, then coughs.

"Katie, we can move faster if—"

"There's no discussion, Evan. I'm going."

"Okay, okay. Get down as much water as you can. Eat something so you have some energy. All right? It could be a long walk, and in the heat of the day. I'll be back in about ten minutes to get you and Chamba," he says as he looks at her bloodshot eyes.

Katie walks over to him and asks, "What about those two men? What if they run into her out there."

"If Megan has been walking all night," Evan answers, "she may very well be to the village by now, if that's where she was going. She'll be all right. Now drink some water. A few more minutes before we get started won't make a difference, okay?"

Katie nods then asks, "Where are you going?"

"I want to take care of something."

"The poacher's truck?" Chamba asks softly as he walks over.

Evan answers, "Yes."

Chamba takes another step toward him, "What if they come back?"

"It'll take them at least a week to get parts or find another truck and get back here. Right?"

"Yes, I suppose."

Evan wipes his face on his shirt. "Okay then. All be right back," he says then walks over to the ladder. He stops and turns around, "Actually, you two can get going when you're ready, and I'll just run and catch up, okay?"

"All right," Chamba says softly.

Katie picks up the canteen and starts taking in as much water as she can. She watches as Evan climbs down the ladder. Within seconds he is running alongside the cliff, and disappearing behind faded rocks.

When Evan reaches the truck, the thick layers of flies are now joined by three vultures, which are sitting on top of the canvas top and trying to peck their way in. The stench is almost unbearable as he rushes around to the cab and opens the hood. Sure enough, the battery is gone. The men put it in the Land Rover just as he had planned to do. He drops the hood, then opens the passenger door. There's nothing inside except a map of Tsavo, a flashlight that's been taken apart and tossed aside, some matches, a half-smoked pack of cigarettes, and a plastic bucket with what looks like sugar cubes inside. There's also a DC power cord for a laptop. He takes the matches and map, puts them in his pocket, then pours out the sugar cubes. He takes the plastic bucket and places it under the truck's fuel tank, which looks like a rusted barrel strapped below the left side of the cab. One flick of his pocketknife through a yellowed plastic tube and the fuel begins seeping into the bucket. It fills faster than he expects, splashing onto his arms and feet. The diesel smells terrible but it's almost pleasant compared to the elephant flesh and tusks in the bed of the truck.

Although he had done this three times before over the past few years in his run-ins with poachers, Evan's hands are shaking somewhat. There's no fear though, just anger laced with urgency. He picks up the bucket and makes his way over to the tailgate area where he heaves the fuel over the tusks.

First match. A dud.

Second match, and it flares brightly and flickers with each movement of his unsteady fingers. He starts to toss the match to where the fuel landed, but changes his mind and walks around to the tank again, which is still dumping yellowish liquid on the sand. It is here, at the edge of the puddle of diesel fuel, where he places one end of the map he found. He curls the map into a hollow stick of paper—a makeshift fuse. And it is here that he lights the map, then runs as fast as he can away.

He hears the explosion.

Then echoes, mimicking the first blast, eerily ricochet off the nearby cliffs like fireworks.

About a fourth of the way back to the baobab tree, he looks over his right shoulder and sees black smoke ascending the cliffs. The thought strikes him that the last ivory poacher's truck he had cremated, also a diesel, hadn't exploded. But this time was different.

He keeps running toward the baobab tree.

After the crackling of the explosion dissipates, he again looks over his shoulder. He sees more smoke billowing. Then it suddenly shoots upward, catapulted by a fresh burst of flames that ruffle the air then settle into smoldering yellow and gray-blue haze. Soon the tusks will crack and crumble and transform into charred rubble, the ivory becoming worthless.

And, Evan thinks as he is running, *Maybe they'll rejoin lost souls of elephants somewhere above.*

CHAPTER FORTY-FIVE

Megan stays as far away from the men as she possibly can, plastered to the door behind the front passenger seat. She considers yanking the latch, opening the door, and running away, but the Land Rover is almost flying over the rock-strewn terrain. She has little choice other than to stay put.

There's no dignity, she tells herself, *falling out of this thing and tumbling into unconsciousness, then lying helplessly on the sand as these assholes—these vultures—do whatever they want to me.*

The image in her mind sickens her.

Her only consoling thought is that they are getting closer to the village. *They'll have to at least go through it*, she thinks as she tries to keep from flailing about the interior of the Land Rover. The seat beneath her squeaks with every downward thrust of her body and her knees push at the seat in front of her, which she notices is ripped vertically from floorboard to headrest in one massive incision. It is this that makes the connection in her mind—this is Evan's Land Rover. She tries to piece together why these men have it, and how they got it started when Evan and Chamba couldn't.

Peering between the two front seats, she searches for clues, just as the jerk who had wanted to rape her turns around, "You want to come up here, honey?"

She doesn't answer.

He smiles with yellow teeth which struggle to push his crackled, dry lips apart, then returns his attention to the dirt road.

Megan tilts her head to the side a bit, looking around the seat in front of her. Her heart rate quickens as she sees two rifles. They are lying side by side in front of the passenger seat, the barrels propped up on the raised area of the floor. One is shiny black, with no scratches. The other is brownish-red, like sandpaper, and is nicked in several places.

It must be them, the men who shot Daisy's mother.

She scoots toward the door as far as she can. In her mind she sees Daisy's mother being shot, over and over. She shudders and squeezes her eyelids tightly shut, trying to rid the image from her thoughts.

It must be them, it must be...

Just like on the first day she and her mother had arrived, the village is overflowing with people as the Land Rover slowly approaches. Three safari tour vans are parked near the market and bar. One says, Tsavo National Park, and the others, Tsavo-Kilimanjaro Tours.

This might be my only chance, this might be my only chance, the voice in her head repeats. *If they don't stop I'll have to just jump out, no matter how fast we're going. I have to get away from them, here in the village...*

She moves her left hand closer to the door latch. Just as she starts to reach for it she feels the Land Rover slowing, then hears the man driving say, "We better grab some supplies while we can."

A few seconds later he yanks hard on the steering wheel and pulls in near the tour vans, about a hundred yards away.

As he turns toward her he says, "If you make any noise, I'll kill you. Understand?"

Megan nods twice, looks away.

His attention shifts to the other man as he says, "Grab one of her wrists and hold it until I get back. If she tries to leave, hit her, and I mean hard. Knock her out. Got it?"

"Okay, just hurry up. There's a hell of a lot of people around here." He cocks himself sideways and reaches behind the seat and takes hold of Megan's left wrist.

She winces as he squeezes, the skin of his hands feeling like cracked leather.

As the other man walks into the market, Megan says, "Please, just let me go. You stopped him from raping me back there. I promise I won't say a thing to anyone. Please..."

No response.

"Please...you have to—"

She feels his hand tightening about her wrist then, with serious eyes pushed down by thick eyebrows, he slowly says to her, "You heard what he said. I suggest you keep your mouth closed."

Megan turns and looks through the dirt-coated window to her right, at the row of meager buildings and huts. Down a ways, she sees Miss Emily's house, the white washed front porch standing out amongst dark green trees and their shadows. Megan's focus shifts to three men walking by the Land Rover with backpacks and expensive-looking cameras dangling from their necks. One of them smiles at her then turns to the others and says something that sounds like it is in German. She wonders whether he is making fun of her short hair, or wishing to use her like the two men she's with want to.

Within minutes the more evil of the two men returns with two bags in his arms and a six-pack of what looks like beer. Two cigarettes are dangling from his mouth, both lit and sending spirals of smoke that eddy around his head in an almost perfect vortex. He opens the door opposite her and places everything on the seat.

Her wrist is released by the other man. Seconds later, the engine roars to life with the swift push of a large black boot on the accelerator pedal. It backfires three times and then settles down. Gears grind as a tattooed arm wrestles the stick shift into reverse. Megan again moves her hand closer to the door handle, but has to pull away as the man driving runs his eyes over her chest yet again, while somehow managing to back up the Land Rover. Without even looking forward, he slams the shifter into first and seems to pop the clutch several times as he watches her bounce. Grinning, he finally turns and focuses on the dirt road.

It's now or never, Megan tells herself as they pull away from the market and creep by unfamiliar faces in the street.

She yanks the door handle and pushes hard with her left shoulder. It doesn't budge. As the men jerk their heads toward her in unison, she reaches to the windowsill and pulls the door lock up. Frantic.

"Get her!"

Two hairy arms fly behind and between the front seats as she takes hold of the latch once more, yanks it hard. The door swings out, ground rushing by below. No time to think. She leaps into a cloud of dust as she hears one of the men yell, "Stop!"

As she tumbles over the dirt road, she catches glimpses of the village spinning, an old movie real flashing frame after frame. She settles to her knees. Some locals approach with curious faces, mouths open. Gazing down at her, they say something but she doesn't understand them. Then she sees the blurry red tail lamps of the Land Rover as they pierce the dust and move quickly closer, the vehicle backing up. Rising to her feet, she turns and runs toward Miss Emily's house.

Almost there. Almost there. Megan's left leg wants to drag behind her but she keeps moving at a good clip. Having been taught in track never to look back, she aims only toward that white front porch until she reaches the gate to Miss Emily's rose garden. She lashes out at the latch, and finally looks over her shoulder. The Land Rover is sitting in the middle of the dirt road and the man who had held her wrist is running toward her.

Hands shaking, she flings the gate open and flies up the steps of the porch. She feels a slight bit of relief as she sees that only the screen door is closed. Before she can stop herself, both palms have ripped through it.

"Help!" she screams. "Help me, I—"

She hears her name, "May-gone?"

As her eyes focus through the mesh of the screen she sees Toma Zho, Miss Emily's housekeeper, walking toward her.

With an alarmed intonation he says, "What on earth?"

He opens the screen and is nearly floored as she leaps at him. He looks over her head and sees a man near the gate, out of breath and face boiling. Behind him, a vehicle is backing up. It comes to an abrupt stop and Tomo Zho sees another man emerge with intense, infuriated eyes. Toma Zho tugs Megan out of the way and closes the door, sets all three locks. He then rushes over to the fireplace and grabs the rifle resting on two iron hooks. He cocks it and walks over to one of the front windows. The two men have now been joined by half the village. Their faces standout in an undulating black sea of concern, and anger.

The men get back into the Land Rover which, within seconds, is dodging villagers and kicking up dirt, moving swiftly away. Toma Zho swivels from the window, places the gun back above the fireplace, then walks over to Megan.

"Your leg is bleeding," his confused face says softly. Questions then leave his lips faster than his breaths, "What happened, Megan? Where is Miss Emily? Who were those men?"

She wipes her face on her sleeve, trying to move the dusty grit in her eyes to one side, then says, "I don't know. They picked me up. Thank god you were here."

"Where's Miss Emily?" he repeats.

Still breathing hard, she stands and walks over to a window, pulls the drapes aside. "See those cliffs?"

"Which ones?"

"Straight ahead," she points. "Right on the horizon. They're kinda pink."

"Yes, I see them."

"She's over there. They are all over there."

"The flood?" he says as he looks down at her.

"Yeah. We couldn't get out."

"Is everyone okay?"

"Yes."

He glances at her knee again, walks over to the kitchen, then pulls open a drawer. He returns with a cotton towel. Dropping to his knees, he blots her leg and studies the cut.

"It doesn't look too bad," he says, then ties the towel in place. "Is that too tight?"

"No. It's fine. Thank you."

He rises. "Why did they send you, all by yourself? It is too dangerous here for a girl your age to wander alone. Why did they send you?" he says again, his voice gaining an octave.

Megan turns away, wipes a loose tear onto her shoulder.

"It's a long story Toma Zho."

Confused, he shakes his head and goes to get her some water.

She asks, "Can you send someone to pick them up?"

"I will try, Megan, I will try," he answers as he fills a tall glass.

As he returns she continues, "I need to use the bathroom for a moment."

"Of course."

A modicum of calmness finally washing over her. She walks into the bathroom and closes the door. Her mood improves somewhat when she sees a toilet, something she had taken for granted all of her life. And now, as she sits down, it may very well be at the top of her list of things she has missed. She leans forward and places her brow on the palms of her hands, shaking her head. "God, I can't even run away right," she says quietly.

Weaving herself through a tangled mess of thoughts, she begins to cry again, then raises her eyes to the windowsill where a fly is buzzing and trying to get out. Finished with the toilet, she washes her hands, whispers, "Soap...real soap."

She opens the window and lets the fly out. Her eyes follow its path until it vanishes and becomes, as she focuses in the distance, what has spoken to her each day since she arrived in Tsavo—the snowcapped peaks of Kilimanjaro, dyed orange-yellow by fading sunlight.

There's no reason to change the plan, she tells herself. *Nothing is different, nothing has changed...*

When she exits the bathroom, Toma Zho has prepared a tray with bread, berries, and a glass of milk. Before she can say a word he hands it to her on a bamboo tray, "Please Megan, sit down and eat something."

"Thanks," she replies to his kind smile. Her mind is on anything but eating, but she doesn't want to hurt his feelings. The cushion of a carved black chair near the kitchen feels good to her rear as she sits down and forces a few pieces of food into her mouth. The milk, though, is a refreshing change from water and baobab nectar.

Worried that she'll change her mind and perhaps settle into the front porch among the rose-tainted breezes, she stands and moves toward a front window, sends a glance down the street. Everything is back to normal. Villagers are lolling about, some carrying buckets. Others are balancing baskets on their heads. A regular African rush hour.

When she sees that one of the tour vans—with Tsavo-Kilimanjaro painted across its side—is still parked at the market, her mind is made up. She'll stick with her original plan. *After all, how can I go back after leaving that note for mom...*

She studies the tourists around the market. Some are taking pictures of a lady sitting Indian style with two chickens in her lap and a basket shaped like a beehive on her head. And others are sitting on grass, cheerily picnicking.

Everyone looks so happy, Megan thinks as she stares through the wavy glass window before her. Even their clothes look happy, bright neon-colored parkas and windbreakers, and tee shirts with the names of African cities and sights emblazoned across them.

She turns to Toma Zho and asks, "Do you think Miss Emily would mind if I borrowed a coat?"

"Of course not. They're right over here," he says as he opens a closet.

She walks over and brushes her hand across a rainbow of sleeves. "May I take this one?"

"Certainly."

His eyes tell her that he thinks something is wrong. She hopes he doesn't ask any questions. She removes a red down-filled parka from a hanger and slips her body into it. It's vastly too big, more like a tent really, but it covers her well, she thinks as she shuts the closet door. She assumes those two men are miles away by now, but with her luck she'd run into them again no matter where they are. At least she would stand a chance of looking bigger and older with the coat, especially with the hood over her head.

As she walks toward the front door, the bookcase she had studied when she and her mother arrived at the elegant house calls out to her. With Toma Zho's eyes following her, she goes over to it and her right hand seems to move with a will of its own to *The Snows of Kilimanjaro* by that Hemingway guy Miss Emily talked about, then to a guidebook, *Mount Kenya and Kilimanjaro* by someone she's never heard of.

"I'd like to borrow these two books," she says as she turns around.

Toma Zho nods confusedly. He wants to inquire why but has been told in the past to respect the privacy of Miss Emily's guests.

Megan plants the small books in one of seemingly dozens of zippered pockets in the parka, then heads over to the bathroom once more. Out of range of Tomo Zho's bewildered stare, she grabs a roll of toilet paper under the sink and tucks it into a big pouch on her left side. She's convinced that if she has to wipe her rear one more time with a wad of filthy leaves she'll scream.

Toma Zho's eyes seem to survey the bulges of the parka as she approaches him. "Thank you for the food," she says as she looks up at him. "You promise me you will send someone out to find the others?"

"Yes, Megan."

"Well then, I'll be on my way," she says as she walks quickly to the screen door, trying to outrun any questions. She exits Miss Emily's house almost as fast as she had entered.

Before she makes it down the porch steps, Tomo Zho calmly asks her, "Where are you going, Megan?"

She stops but doesn't turn around as she searches for something to say to this kind man, without lying. She slowly faces him and says, "I'm going to see the leopard," then gives him a quick smile without showing her teeth.

"The leopard?"

"Goodbye, Toma Zho."

"Goodbye, Megan," he replies with narrowing eyes, trying to avert the light reflecting at them from the stone path.

Within seconds the white gate is swinging on its old hinges and Megan is moving toward the market and tourists.

Long shadows fall horizontally from the necks of six giraffes wandering nearby. They gracefully stretch and chew at thorn trees with fresh leaves borne of the recent rains. Above, a pale blue sky unleashes the first faint stars of the approaching evening. The day is slipping by, Chamba thinks to himself. He, Evan, and Katie have been following Megan's footsteps for hours.

Evan is the first to see where tire treads intersect the trail Megan has left, but he can't seem to find the words to tell Katie. And by the time he does, she's already figured out what has happened.

"They may have just taken her to the village," Chamba says with watery eyes that betray his typically reassuring manner. "I'm sure she is all right."

Katie stops dead in her tracks as if the life has been sucked from her. She turns to Evan and before she can say a word he wraps his arms tightly around her.

"We'll find her Katie, I promise," he says softly. "*I'll* find her."

PART SEVEN

CHAPTER FORTY-SIX

As Megan makes her way quickly toward the market and the tour vans parked out front, her head moves up and down every couple of steps, her attention split between reading and walking. Near a crowded café with tables sitting outside and tourists downing sandwiches and sodas, she pauses to focus on the guidebook from Miss Emily's house, a section on Mount Kilimanjaro.

From the Tanzanian and Kenyan basins below, and the Indian Ocean framing the horizon, Kilimanjaro appears as two rounded humps, as if a huge camel has decided to take a rest, placing its belly on the cool earth while sunning its back. Kibo peak, the hump that has snow on top, is the highest summit at 19,341 feet. There, the snow never completely melts. Eleven kilometers away, across a sweeping saddle, lies Mawenzi peak at 16,893 feet, which seasonally sheds its snow.

Since its discovery, Kilimanjaro has inspired curiosity among all who have witnessed these broad shoulders stubbornly standing within reach of the equator. In first century AD a Greek merchant noted the peaks during a trip that brought him through Kenya. Later, Ptolemy placed the mountain on his early maps of Africa, locating it at the head of the Nile River. And when sixteenth century Spanish explorer Fernandez de Encisco passed through he wrote: "West of Mombassa stands the Ethiopian mountain, Olympus, which is exceedingly high, and beyond it are the Mountains of the Moon, which are the source of the Nile."

As word spread of Kilimanjaro and the vast surrounding territory with its raw materials, land, and supply of slaves, European colonial powers arrived. Some sought wealth, others came to build missions and save savage souls they thought were lost. Johann Rebmann and Doctor Ludwig Kraph, members of the London-based Church Missionary Society, landed on the coast in 1846 and established a mission near the town of Mombasa. Soon they traveled to the mountain, which natives said was protected by evil spirits.

Upon hearing the reports of snow, Europeans debated whether, in fact, this could be true, given that Kilimanjaro rests at the equator. Not until German explorer Baron Von der Decken and Doctor Otto Kersten climbed beyond the forest zone, waking up one morning covered in snow, was the issue put to rest. Indeed, there was snow near the equator.

Ascents to the 'Saddle' between Kibo and Mawenzi were commonplace by 1890. And in the 1930s, when hotels were built in Marangu and tour operators began offering guided climbs to adventurous travelers, an industry was made of the mountain. An industry ready to exploit yet one more aspect of Africa.

Megan raises her eyes from the guidebook and tucks it back in her hip pocket as she approaches the market. The two tour vans, which were present when she arrived, are now sandwiched between six others. People are streaming in and out of the market's doorway like ants somehow managing to flow through one hole in a fragile mound of sand. Beers and sodas and chips fill their hands. Many wear tee-shirts, hats, and sweatshirts with pictures of big game animals, and some have words without pictures—*I climbed Mount Kilimanjaro*, or just *Africa*.

Megan waits behind a van that says, Tsavo-Kilimanjaro Tours. There's no one on board. Walking with her chin buried three inches deep in the down-collar of Miss Emily's parka, she snakes through the narrow aisle between vans and quite matter-of-factly, as if she's boarding school bus number 5 back in Kentucky, ascends the two steps into the van. Her pulse throbs in her neck as she makes her way to the very last row and sits down, telling herself to stay calm.

What do I have to lose, anyway?

She decides to pretend she's asleep. So she places herself in a fetal position, prone on a vinyl seat with her head near a window.

Covered in sweat and wanting to shed the parka, she eventually feels the van jiggle, hears feet stomping up the metal steps. A boisterous crowd soon follows the initial quiet travelers and within minutes she hears the engine turn over. Only now does it hit her—is the van going *to* Mount Kilimanjaro or coming *back* from Mount Kilimanjaro?

Toma Zho had managed to get his friend's Jeep started, and after two hours of scouring the valley in the general direction Megan had told him that Miss Emily, Evan, Katie, Chamba and Dora were, he saw five pairs of arms waving frantically atop a sun-drenched hill. It was them. Tomo Zho drove as fast as he could and picked everyone up.

"What do you mean Megan sent you?" Evan asked Tomo Zho as everyone crammed into the Jeep.

"She said you needed help and so—"

"Where is she now?" Katie interrupts.

"I don't know. She left."

Evan's face gushes with redness as he says, "You just let her take off?"

An unspoken apology rises to Toma Zho's eyes.

Katie moves forward and touches Evan's arm, sending a signal for him to not get angry at Toma Zho, just as a wife would do with a husband. It just feels natural to her, yet instantly reminds her of the time she did the same thing to David a couple of years ago. He had ignored her, jerked away, and didn't speak to her for two days. But now, in this moment, Evan just looks at her and nods ever so slightly to acknowledge and agree with her. His reaction comforts her. She had heard and read about those lucky few individuals who had partners who just "got them," understood them even without words. She had also heard friends talk about how their boyfriend or girlfriend, husband or wife, father or mother, or a grandparent always had their back—no matter what. You just knew they were on your side, always. And when friends would even mention having "chemistry" with someone, Katie would cringe and change the subject. The feelings they described were too foreign to her. But back at the baobab treehouse and the waterfall, Katie had finally figured out what her friends and family had been telling her. She felt chemistry with Evan, something she never thought existed, yet was envious of when others discussed having it in their relationships.

Katie clears her throat and then says, "Toma Zho, did Megan say where she was going?"

"Yes, I asked her and she said, to see the leopard."

"To see the leopard? What on earth did she mean by that?"

Miss Emily raises her hand and covers her mouth slightly. "Oh my god..."

Katie turns to her. "What, Miss Emily? What's wrong?"

"I think I might know what Megan meant."

"The leopard?" Evan asks, twisting his head toward her.

"Yes," she replies softly then pauses, looking away. "You see, a few days ago I told Megan about *The Snows of Kilimanjaro*, by Hemmingway, and how the story begins. There's a description of a leopard that was found at the summit."

Miss Emily pauses again, looking downward.

"Please, it's not your fault," Katie says as her eyes become teary. "Please go on."

"Well, I remember Megan asking me why the leopard went up the mountain."

"What did you tell her?" Katie asks, and then wipes her tears on the back of her right hand.

Miss Emily's eyes move to the velvety dusk, which seems to pull the words from her quivering mouth. "I told her that the leopard probably went there to die. To die with dignity—perhaps closer to heaven."

CHAPTER FORTY-SEVEN

Megan's mind lingers between sleep and daydreams as the drone of the tourist van's engine fills the air and a soothing vibration migrates from the tires, to the chassis, to the seat, and finally to her sick and tired bones. Floating through her mind she sees images of Angela's funeral, then words she had read no less than twenty times in a dusty, aged book with a poem by Lydia Huntley Sigourney. Grandma Ryan had given her it after the funeral, telling her it was over a hundred years old and was her favorite book of poems. She said it had to do with being reborn, and she wanted Megan to have it and always remember that she'd see Angela again someday.

> *A butterfly basked on a baby's grave,*
> *Where a lily had chanced to grow:*
> *Why art thou here with thy gaudy dye,*
> *When she of the blue sparkling eye*
> *Must sleep in the churchyard low?*
> *Then it lightly soared through the sunny air,*
> *And spoke from its shining track:*
> *I was a worm till I won my wings;*
> *And she whom thou mourn'st like a seraph sings;*
> *Would'st thou call the blessed one back?*

Megan runs the words through her mind three times, then turns her lazy thoughts toward home and school, picturing what the people in her life were doing right now. Grandma and grandpa are glued to their couch watching TV, probably *Wheel of Fortune*, or maybe out square dancing with plaid clothes on. David is at work and has his eyes too close to his computer screen, or he might be out riding one of the horses. Cindy Jacobs is probably painting her fake nails or combing her long silky hair or gossiping about Billy Murphy, or maybe stuffing that lacy bra she borrowed from her mom. Principal Manning is giving Billy a lecture, or telling his parents to come pick him up, give him a good talkin' to. And Doctor Carlton is probably poking a long needle in someone's arm—This won't hurt a bit—or adjusting his funny glasses on the end of his nose while he reads something important on a clipboard.

Or maybe everyone is asleep, Megan thinks as she lifts her head and finally gets a look at the backs of dozens of strangers inside the tour van. Some heads are bouncing side to side, trying to stay upright. Others are leaning against partially closed windows which can barely be seen through, the sliding panes covered with dirt. The seemingly indefatigable and riotous group which boarded have been replaced by mute deadheads who appear as if they have just left the front gate at Disney World and have now surrendered to the parking lot shuttle ride late in the evening.

Megan yawns and is drawn toward fresh air that washes down upon her from the window above. She soaks in the scent, which reminds her of the smell that rises from the felled leaves on her gravel driveway at home after a brief autumn shower. Crisp and clean, with a taste of approaching winter. As she looks out the window next to her she sees a blur of tall trees and lush green plants that look healthier than the brown, gnarled ones she had left behind in the valley. Staring straight ahead, she notices a sign through the large windshield of the van. As the van gets closer she sees that the sign says, *Kilimanjaro National Park, Marangu Gate*. She's feels a sense of relief, that somehow she had managed to pick a van taking people to the base of the mountain rather than bringing people back from the mountain.

A man wearing a tan uniform, black boots, no smile, wanders out and says something to the driver, then waves an arm forward as he walks back inside a building.

The van chugs upward through a narrowing road until it pulls into a dirt lot with a dozen other vans, cars, and large buses.

"Please stay seated," the driver says as he stands and faces eager faces. "I have to pay the entrance fee, and then we will get started."

Megan watches as he steps down to the ground, makes his way around the front of the van, then walks over to a wooden building with a red roof. When he disappears inside, she stands and scoots between the two aisles of seats as curious faces angle at her.

"We're supposed to stay here, young lady," she hears a man's voice call out as she nears the front exit. It sounds just like Mr. Wilson from history class who had just moved over from London last summer to marry Miss Lockhart, the school nurse. But Megan ignores the voice and moves like a gazelle through the bi-fold glass doors. Within seconds she is enveloped by a group of French-speaking women, several having a really bad hair day, she thinks as she makes her way. Each is carrying a colorful backpack almost as big as their body, as if they are moving to the top of

Mount Kilimanjaro permanently. Megan tells herself she should fit in just swell with her lovely chemo-inspired hairdo and Miss Emily's glowing red parka.

Traversing a stone path that leads from the parking area and winds around the park building, she keeps her head down and tries not to make eye contact with anyone, for fear that they might start asking her questions in French or something and give her the boot once her American mouth opens. For good measure, she pulls out *The Snows of Kilimanjaro* and studiously scans a few pages. Maybe they'll leave her alone.

As the group nears an iron gate, one of the ladies steps forward and hands a burly park ranger a piece of paper, which is promptly returned. Like orderly girl scouts everyone files through the gate opening, Megan sandwiched somewhere in the middle between a large woman with red hair that dangles below the bottom of her backpack and two slim-looking, athletic cheerleader types.

As everyone makes their way up a gravel path, Megan contemplates the odds of her linking up with a troupe of pleasant French women climbing the Marangu route of Kilimanjaro today.

Eventually she drops back from the group, mingles in with three others, goes it alone for an hour, catches up with two more, and eventually drifts off on her own as the trail winds through a dense forest with scattered green light spilling through to a carpet of creeping vegetation. In several places she sees what one man says are blue monkeys, and when she again catches up with the group of women, she sees one of them getting her camera ripped right out of her hand by one of them.

Further ahead, the monkeys stare at her with piercing still eyes which yank her mind back to the day her mother dropped her off at school and the boys threw stone-faced glares her way. That these rogue monkeys remind her of the manner in which Billy Murphy and the others treated her, lightens her mood somewhat, but doesn't make her feet, which are beginning to ache, feel better.

With darkness comes a glowing moon that seems to grow magically out of the rutted trail. It casts featureless silhouettes of legs and arms swinging rhythmically to the chatter of nighttime creatures. And eventually it places a muted gray light on what she hears several climbers refer to as "Mandara hut."

As she pauses and catches her breath, she notices that no one is going further. Backpacks are sliding off slumped shoulders, sleeping bags are rolling out from dangling arms, and small tents are rising like grave markers across what is now a barren clearing of grass bordered by a perimeter of trees and small A-frame huts.

CHAPTER FORTY-EIGHT

When Evan approached the market earlier there were just two tour vans parked in front. "Have you seen this girl?" he had asked the owner of the store as he held up a picture of Megan that Katie had given him.

"No," the man replied as he dragged a yellow fingernail up and down his long nose while studying the photo, "But I have been very busy today, six vans."

Evan nodded and said, "If you see her, please send someone to Miss Emily's and tell her right away."

The man nodded and Evan walked outside and rejoined Katie and Chamba, who were asking everyone the same question. The replies were all the same, "No, I haven't seen her, sorry."

"Any luck?" Chamba inquires as they make their way toward Miss Emily's house.

"No," Evan replies, "the owner said he hasn't seen her."

Katie peers downward and stares at the tire-engraved ground, telling herself, *Don't lose it. Don't break down and make things even worse. I have to be strong.*

She fights back the tears that had only stopped flowing minutes ago. Once again, she was the strong one. She was being tested. Why, she didn't know.

As Evan drapes an arm over her shoulders and pulls her close, they head silently down the middle of the dirt road, passing curious villagers. Have you seen this girl? No, sorry. This girl, have you seen here? Hapana, samahani.

Halfway to Miss Emily's house, an old man emerges from a hut as a flatbed truck rolls by and a cloud of dust settles slowly. Evan holds up the picture as he looks down at the creased, thin skin of the man, who promptly says he has indeed seen the girl. He even remembers the bright red parka she was wearing, which Toma Zho said she had taken.

"Did you see where she went?" Katie asks.

The man raises a bamboo cane and points toward the market.

"Did she go inside?" Evan inquires.

"No."

"Then where did she go?"

285

"I don't know."

"Please, sir, this is very important."

"She walked near the lorries," he continues, "and then was gone."

Upon returning to Miss Emily's house, Evan paces back and forth in front of the fireplace. "She had to have gotten on one of the tour vans. There's no other explanation. She probably saw one of the Tsavo-Kilimanjaro ones, and just snuck on to it."

"You need to go after her right away," Miss Emily says from her kitchen. "I'm sure you can use the Jeep, Evan." She pours Katie a glass of water. "Toma Zho hasn't returned it yet," she continues.

Evan nods once, scratching the nape of his neck, pacing.

As Katie gulps down the last drops of her glass of water, she turns to Evan. "What now? Do you know where those tour vans go?"

"Yes. We'll go to Marangu. That's where most of the Tsavo-Kilimanjaro vans go from here."

"But what if she got on another one, headed somewhere else?"

"Well, I—"

"If she's going to see the leopard, as in the book," Miss Emily interrupts, "she would have chosen one of the vans headed to Kilimanjaro, over the other ones, don't you think?"

Evan nods his head yes, "It's the best shot we've got right now." Five minutes later he, Chamba, and Katie drive toward Marangu.

They finally, about an hour later, hear the rare sound of tires on pavement. Evan slows as they come into the village of Marangu, which flanks the road on each side. As he nears the one and only intersection, near the post office and Capricorn Hotel, he twists his head to Katie and says, "Did you notice the paved road?"

"Yeah, first one I've seen in weeks."

"This is where most of the money from tourism comes in. If Megan came here, she'll have plenty of people around her, you know, if she needs anything."

Katie nods as she looks at all of the buses and vans lined up like dominoes at the intersection. One by one they move forward, smoke pouring from their exhausts.

Evan pulls up to the Marangu Hotel. On his previous trips to Mount Kilimanjaro, he stayed in the hotel for a night, before climbing the next day.

"Why are you stopping?" Katie asks.

He slows and drives up to the unloading and registration area amidst people swarming around, most laden with bags or backpacks.

"Let's just go on to the park entrance," Katie continues.

He hesitates, knowing he's in for a battle. "Look, Katie, it's dark and—"

"I don't care. We need to keep moving before she gets even further ahead of us."

He speaks softly, purposely. "But there's nothing we can do tonight. She'll be fine, Katie, she has Miss Emily's coat, she'll be warm. And this is the safest and fastest route on the mountain. There are huts along the way and lots of people, if she needs help."

Chamba leans forward between the Jeep's front seats and in a calm, measured voice says, "Katie, we may not even be able to see Megan. We might walk right by her and not know it. It would be much wiser to wait until sunrise."

Katie says nothing at first, then blows her cheeks outward and emits a steady stream of air, faintly shaking her head. "I, I don't know what to do."

No one speaks for almost a minute. The idle of the Jeep is the only sound.

"Would you feel better if I continued on?" Evan eventually says as he reaches over and wipes her cheek with the back of his fingers. "You and Chamba could stay here tonight, then get started on the trail first thing in the morning. If I find her before dawn, I'll bring her back here."

"And if you don't?" Katie asks.

"I'll keep heading up the mountain until I do. Actually, the more I think about it, splitting up will actually be better. I can climb faster alone. And tomorrow you two can hike to the first hut area, Mandara. Okay?"

Another long pause then Katie says, "Yes, all right."

"Now, I want you two to stay at Mandara. Don't keep climbing."

"Why?"

"You might see her coming back down. Plus, you can ask everyone who passes through whether they've seen her, and where. And if, or rather *when* I find her, we'll need a place to meet you. Okay? I'll bring her to Mandara Hut," he continues as he turns to Chamba. "It could very well be a couple days, or more, but don't leave there. Got it?"

"Yes," Chamba responds.

Then Katie answers, "All right."

"Good. Now, I'll stop at the park entrance and tell them to keep a lookout for her, and ask them to notify local authorities. And I'll pay them so you can stay in one of the huts. But you better buy some food and water in the morning, enough to last several days. There's a store around the corner where you can buy everything you need, including backpacks, sleeping bags, and flashlights." He pauses, glancing down the street which is still bustling with traffic and people. "I'm going to head over there now and buy some things. Well, I guess that is it. Remember, stay at Mandara Hut."

Katie's eyes say thank you as she leans across the void between the front seats and hugs Evan so hard he has trouble taking a breath.

A whisper leaves her half-closed lips, "Be careful." She places a quick kiss on his cheek, then gets out of the Jeep and goes with Chamba into the hotel lobby.

CHAPTER FORTY-NINE

Daybreak. Mount Kilimanjaro. Megan pries her eyelids open and is startled, not knowing where she is. At first she thinks she is back at the baobab tree platforms. But there aren't any branches above, just crystal blue sky, and there aren't any leaves under her body, just dirt and rocks. As she raises her head she remembers. The mountain. The hike. The reason she is here—the decision.

Last night, the brightest stars she'd ever seen had sailed across a canvass of inky sky and she was so tired, and her legs were so sore, she scarcely dwelled on her predicament three minutes before plopping down behind one of the A-frame cabins at Mandara Hut, her mind quickly wandering off to sleep. Dreams soon followed, and she soared like an eagle around the snowy summit of Mount Kilimanjaro, staring down at the parade of humans making their way higher and higher. She flapped her wings and made circles in the thin air, rising and falling, rising and falling. Then she gazed toward Tsavo far below, the elephants, the thorn trees, the giraffes, the remaining flooded valleys, and finally she saw her mother, who was upset and had Evan by her side comforting her. *He would ease her mind, wouldn't he? He would take care of mom, wouldn't he?*

Megan had gotten up only once during the night, as some loud-talking nocturnal hikers descended a path nearby, guided only by flashlights. But she hadn't been scared. There were people everywhere. For some reason she had expected she would make this journey, this spiritual journey, alone, for it was a private matter between her and her God. No one else could possibly understand what she had gone through the past year, what she had ahead of her, or the decision she had just made. These were the thoughts she had last night, as she yanked the hood of the parka over her head and closed her eyes.

And now, with the rising sun slowly warming the mountain, there is more climbing to do. She hadn't expected that the climb would take so long. In fact she rather assumed that by this time she would be making snow angels at the summit, maybe with Angela by her side. Or perhaps she would be seeing the leopard from that Hemmingway book that had made the same decision she had made.

May as well get started, she thinks as her stomach grumbles and she sits up, yawning. All around her there are climbers stretching their lean arms and legs and chewing their protein bar breakfasts. She turns and looks up at the summit, which is still a gray and white blur in the distance, then ties her shoes more securely and aims herself skyward on the nearby trail.

She winds her way through a short stretch of forest and skirts the lip of Maundi Crater, traverses a meadow, then crosses a stream with thick, damp woods that remind her of Kentucky, though the trees look and smell very different. A sweeping grassland soon follows, then a series of moorland ravines. A voice calls out as she crosses one of them, an unfamiliar voice. "Hiking alone?"

Megan stops, looking up. A man, thirtyish, with a short blonde beard, smiles as he approaches. He is panting profusely. She puts her guard up, doesn't respond. Shoulders back. Chin up. Then she decides that he seems safe enough to talk to.

"You shouldn't climb by yourself," he continues as he slows to a complete stop.

"Well, you are," Megan replies.

"Yeah, but I'm a guy."

Great, Megan thinks as she studies the nerdy chauvinist. Why couldn't it be someone like that guy—what was his name, Philip?—at the pool in Johannesburg. Over the course of the past couple weeks she had often daydreamed about him while staring at the sky, sunning herself on smooth rocks back near the tree platforms. In her mind Philip would traipse through the bush in that red speedo of his, buy her drinks, put cool lotion on her back, flex his muscles, and run his eyes over her like she was a movie star.

"Man...I'm worn out," he continues.

Megan notices that his shoes look brand new, as does everything else he is wearing and carrying. A backpack is stuffed like he's Santa Claus out on Christmas Eve.

"You're going to have a heart attack carrying all that stuff," Megan tells him.

"Yeah...maybe. You should have seen me going up. I had even more to carry."

She waits for him to either stop huffing and puffing or to keel over, whichever comes first. "Is this the right way to the summit?" she asks.

"Which summit?"

"There's more than one?"

"Yes."

"Well, which one is higher? That's the one I want."

"Kibo. And yes, this will get you there," he says as he glances up the trail, then adjusts his round glasses. "You're kinda young to be out trekking on one of the world's tallest mountains, aren't you?"

"I'm younger than I look, I mean I'm older than I—"

"Hey, cool by me. Whatever. What's your name?"

"Megan."

"I'm Luke," he says as he transfers a shining walking stick from his right hand to his left, then shakes her hand. He eyes the parka, which looks more like a bright red bedspread wrapped around frail legs, and a tiny head sticking out at the top. "Where's your backpack and supplies? Is this all you brought?" he continues.

"Yeah, except for a couple of books. I have a guidebook," she says proudly as she pulls it out.

"And you don't know that this is the right trail for Kibo?"

"I haven't really read it all yet."

"Uh, huh, I see." He shakes his head, "Man, you better head back down. You gotta at least have some food with you, and water. Or you'll dehydrate."

"I know," Megan says in an overconfident tone only possible from a teenager's mouth.

"Here," he says as he slips off his backpack, "let me give you a couple of things to take with you."

"No, that's okay. I'm fine, really," she insists, not knowing how to tell him that she won't need anything where she is going.

"I insist. Please."

Somehow he knows exactly what zipper to pull and within seconds he removes three protein bars and a couple small cans of apple juice. "Here, take these."

"Don't you need them?"

"I have plenty more. Please," he says as he hands them over. "You'll be doing me a favor, take some weight off my back."

"Well, thanks. I appreciate it."

"You're from the U.S.?" he asks.

"Yes, Kentucky."

"Cool. I'm from San Francisco. I'm supposed to fly back in two days. That's why I'm a bit out of breath. I'm moving faster than I should."

Megan nods.

"Well, I guess I better get moving," he continues as he hoists the backpack upward then sort of runs under it before it comes down. "Like I said, I wouldn't go up there alone and without supplies. Are you sure you don't want to come back down with me?"

Wanting to make sure he doesn't' think she's completely lost her mind, and that she will be safe, she answers, "No, I'm meeting someone at the summit." She pauses for a couple of seconds, thinking, and then continues, "I'm meeting my sister Angela."

"Oh," he says with incredulous blue eyes, "I see. Well, bye then. You be safe. Don't overdo it."

She nods twice. "Goodbye," she says as she walks away, placing what he gave her and the guidebook in a pocket on her hip.

The sun is almost directly over the summit, balanced like a beach ball on the gray nose of a giant seal. Megan thinks it is Kibo Peak but she isn't sure. As she winds her way higher and higher on the trail, a few cotton-looking clouds grow nearer and larger, as if she can almost touch them. Some are round and seem as if they will burst. Others are more like streaks, or smears of white paint on a baby blue background.

She enters a rocky valley with colorful groundsels that glow in the bright light, then sees a wooden sign that says, Horombo Hut. Legs throbbing, she pauses and pulls out the guidebook and finds a map.

There it is, Horombo Hut. And there's where I started, Marangu Gate.

According to the guide's description, she should make Kibo Hut in another five hours, and then head up to Kibo Peak. But she's not sure how long that will take, hours or maybe even days.

Easy, no problem, I wonder how many feet 5,895 meters is, she asks herself, not knowing whether to laugh or cry. *They should put one of those aerial tram things in, like the one down at Gatlinburg, Tennessee that mom and David took me to a couple of years ago. Before I got sick.*

She pushes on and enters the Horombo Hut area, which looks just like where she spent last night. A chill shutters through her as she contemplates the notion that perhaps she has simply made a loop around the mountain and is at the exact same place. But then she sees a stream and a camp area, unlike Mandara, and she even finds restrooms. Restrooms! With toilets that flush, and sinks to wash her sunburned face, her tired arms, and her tired legs. Her whole body has been itching from whatever Miss Emily's parka is made of.

She exits the restroom dripping wet, carrying her shoes, socks, and the parka. A few men sitting near a campfire stare and snicker and laugh slightly, but she ignores them. She is used to stares and snickers and laughs. She suddenly thinks about school, and how far away from home she is.

Feeling refreshed, she puts her socks—her incredibly dirty and smelly socks—and shoes back on, then heads through much better scents of lunch, or is it dinner, floating across the lonely trail that ascends from the huts. At the moment, she seems to be the only person going higher up Mount Kilimanjaro. Just a couple obscure dots can be seen ahead, descending toward her.

What's the big deal. Even I can keep hiking...

CHAPTER FIFTY

Climbing the mountain under the soft pale moonlight was refreshing, not too cold, and gave Evan a chance to clear his mind. And then fill it with Katie. Where were the two of them going? Was what happened between them, while stranded for days in Tsavo, simply a one-time thing driven only by their circumstance? Would he ever see her again once she and Megan went back to the U.S.? This, and not much else, occupied Evan's mind last night as he climbed toward the stars, looking for Megan.

But the sun and his worries rose as one this morning. Still no sign of Megan. It isn't that she is alone, or that she might not have any food with her that worries him as he traverses a vast moorland area. And it isn't the fact that she has leukemia, and may also be weakened by the last two weeks of a relatively unbalanced diet. What worries him most are the problems that could occur from Kilimanjaro's high altitude, which are often the result of climbing too high, and too fast. Rather than cause more worry for Katie, he hadn't mentioned this to her when he left the hotel at Marangu village last night.

There are no hard and fast rules about the type of individual that might be affected by high altitude. Evan had heard of guides with years of experience taking people to Kibo summit with no problems whatsoever who were suddenly stricken and had to be carried all the way down to park headquarters at Marangu Gate. Yet there are thousands of first timers—young, old, fit, fat—each year who climb the mountain with no signs of trouble. One season several climbers reported that a half dozen men in their early twenties, several with University of Vermont sweatshirts on, tried to sell and smoked a sizable inventory of marijuana essentially their entire way up to Mawenzi Peak, which they somehow managed to find in just over two days. Not even one of them reported altitude problems to park authorities when they were arrested. Evan thought, at the time he heard of the hikers, that maybe they were just too stoned to know that they had altitude sickness.

The vast majority of climbers who do encounter problems usually experience Acute Mountain Sickness. AMS can happen at any altitude but is most common in the first thousand meters of elevation gain, which also happens to be the period in which novice climbers ascend like Swiss mountain goats. The more severe symptoms generally occur at eight thousand feet, though Evan had once seen an older man evacuated from the mountain after reaching seven thousand. One of the worst symptoms of AMS is Cheyne-Stokes breathing, which causes a victim to either breathe deeper or shallower, or at night suddenly awake gasping for air. The most susceptible climbers to AMS are the ones who fly in from a low elevation city and begin their ascent too quickly, before acclimating to the region.

Yet another condition, High Altitude Pulmonary Edema, results from an accumulation of fluid in the lungs. It can come on very quickly, and kill a climber within a matter of hours. As can High Altitude Cerebral Edema, which occurs when the small and large arteries in the brain dilate so that they can carry more oxygenated blood, which results in the brain swelling. Evan had heard of only two such cases, but they both resulted in death. Regardless of which high altitude problem that may occur, the best treatment is immediate descent.

Megan is surprised to see that the trail is, for once, well-marked. There is even a small sign that tells her that the water at Maua River is safe to drink, so she pauses and cups her hands, drinking the frigid water as if it is the last on the planet. Continuing on, she's struck by how desolate the landscape appears. It doesn't look anything like the mountains back home, not a bit similar to the Appalachians or the Smoky Mountains further south where grandpa had rented a chalet a couple of years ago on her birthday, or the Blue Ridge Mountains they visited near that big old mansion, the Biltmore Estate, she thinks it was called. Those were happy times; leisurely drives through winding roads with pretty pine and maple trees that smelled fresh, and scents from wild flowers that tickled her nose. Staying in hotels with heated pools and Jacuzzis and workout rooms and pay-per-view movies and room service. Stopping at fast food restaurants every few hours, or shopping with mom. Such happy times.

Lost in memories, she finally raises her eyes from the muddy path. There's another sign, Last Water.

Last water?

She looks up at the white peak which is still incredibly far away.

At least I'll be able to eat snow, she thinks as she takes in the spectacular view carrying her higher.

And I still have the apple juice that climber gave me.

She checks her pocket for three bulges; everything is still there. Her throat dry and wanting, she again gulps down what she can, washes her face, then regrets doing so as it grows colder with the wind hitting it.

She enters the Saddle—this, according to the guidebook she studies briefly as her feet move forward without her direction—and within minutes a sign confirms her location, *Saddle*. She was getting good at this climbing thing. On one side of her is Mawenzi Summit and on the other is Kibo Summit.

Kibo, that's the higher one, she remembers.

A junction in the trail presents her with two options, either taking the South Circuit Path, or staying on the Marangu route. Telling herself not to screw up after making it this far, she again whips out Miss Emily's guidebook. It tells her that the South Circuit Path leads to the southern glacier routes, Rebmann, Kersten, Heim Glaciers, and Decken. And continuing straight on Marangu route will take her across the Saddle to Kibo Hut then, via the Normal route, to something called Gillman's Point and finally Kibo, also known as Uhuru, Peak—the highest point on Mount Kilimanjaro. Bingo. She's getting close.

With reborn energy she moves swiftly across the Saddle and reaches another group of huts. Compared to the previous ones there are far fewer people milling about, and only four small tents sprinkled amongst numerous dead campfires. But three of the pits are spitting sparks at the deep blue sky, and calling her to wander over and warm her hands for a few minutes. She approaches one, abandoned yet still smoking, and holds her arms out from her body like a zombie. A long sigh. She soaks in the heat and pretends it is all over her goose pimpled skin.

It's an odd fire, she thinks as she lowers her eyes to the charcoaled earth. *No logs, just a small wedge of that fake wood they sell at supermarkets, the stuff grandpa Ryan says is a waste of money. I wonder what grandpa is doing right now? I bet he'd be proud of me,* she muses as she looks at the mountain she has almost beaten. She knows, however, that he definitely wouldn't like her taking off like this, not one bit. And he surely wouldn't understand the decision she had made.

She could very easily dilly-dally around this fire until it coughs up its last breath of hot air, but she convinces herself that she needs to keep moving. So she meanders through the huts and the sparse number of curious faces and eventually finds the trail marked Normal Route/North. She makes her way across gentle terrain until she arrives at Hans Meyer Cave, but the trail steepens as it turns abruptly to Gillman's Point on the crater rim. Oddly, there are scads of people now. Most funnel toward her as if poured down the path by a god sitting at the summit. Languidly, they file by with sun-strained faces, corners of mouths curled down, feet flopping forward as if only pulled by gravity.

What's everyone so depressed about? They made it up Mount Kilimanjaro for godsakes.

Or maybe they hadn't, she wonders as she studies each set of eyes for a trace of encouragement. Only a few people say "Hi" or "You're almost there" or "How's it going." Ahead, one climber, a blonde hunk who glistens in black spandex that coats almost every inch of his body, finally emits an equally lustrous smile and says, "It's beautiful at the summit today." As if he does this each afternoon, rain or shine.

"Great," Megan responds as he moves by smoothly, nothing like the herky jerky arm and leg motions of the others, the grumpy bunch making their way back to civilization.

Eventually she is relieved to detect that the pathway is temporarily descending slightly, giving her tingling legs a chance to recover before the next ascension. But soon the mountain takes over again and she is leaning forward, climbing.

She follows along the crater rim and what the guidebook refers to as the knobs of Hans Meyer Point.

Who is this Hans Meyer guy anyway? she thinks, breathing hard and pushing down on each knee, step after step.

CHAPTER FIFTY-ONE

Snow. Everywhere, snow. It collects and cakes inside the little rubber grooves and knobs of Megan's shoes as she walks across what she thinks is the summit of Mount Kilimanjaro.

There it is. The summit!

She slips three times as she ascends what seems to be the last hundred yards or so, plodding across a giant bald head. Not a soul around. Everyone has followed the sun down into the valley. Only frail light remains of the day, but all the white-covered earth before her seems determined to shine through the night. A rush of adrenaline flows through her veins as she pulls her eyes slowly over three hundred sixty degrees of horizon, from dreary darkness to pallid blue and subtle shades of twilight. Having stared at each step directly in front of her mud-covered boots, the image of the world before her is overwhelming.

I'm standing on top of the world, she thinks as the accomplishment settles on her tired mind.

She realizes she is breathing hard, and that the intake and egress of air between her lips is the only sound present, separated by exquisite pauses of silence she has never experienced before. How can such roaring beauty be so quiet?

More steps. Higher, and higher.

As she contemplates the exact point that seems to rise above all other areas, she notices a pile of rocks just ahead, a marker of sorts.

That's got to be it, she thinks, *that must be the highest spot.*

She moves toward the rocks but suddenly feels dizzy and has to stop, gasping for air that stings the inside of her dry nose. As she stands here, close to her goal, she pulls out one of the minuscule cans of apple juice she had been given, pops it open, and raises it to her mouth. The aluminum can sticks to her lips, so she painfully pries it off, half expecting to see her lower lip dangling from the rim of the can. She holds a hand over her mouth, but isn't sure whether her palm is any warmer than the can. She coats her lips with warm saliva and again raises the apple juice, tilts it back as she stares at the moon. Nothing comes out. Shaking the can reveals that it is as solid as the stones stacked before her, which she continues moving toward.

I did it. I really did it...

Breathing hard, small clouds develop from each of her breaths, each exhale. She drops to her knees, reaches out with both hands, and touches the highest stone stacked before her. Holding her palms to the chilled surface, she squeezes her eyes shut and soon feels warm tears leak from their corners, slide down her numb cheeks, then stop abruptly near her angled chin. She moves her fingers to her face and feels tiny frozen streams, like the wax runoff of a candle whose warm flow gradually hardens.

She swivels herself about, facing the brighter sky in the distance, and sits down. The snow crunches beneath her rear, settling a few inches, as she twists herself into a cross-legged Indian pose.

Her eyes move to the sky. The moon.

Everything is so clear. It's like I can reach up and poke my fingers at the moon's craters. It's so clear. Like I can wrap my hands around it, pull it down, take a bite out of it.

As a gust of wind prompts her chin to move lower, she suddenly feels sick to her stomach. She feels like vomiting, but nothing comes up when she coughs and convulses.

It'll go away, she tells herself. *I'm just hungry, that's all.*

She opens a little velcro flap on the parka and pulls out a nutrition bar, peels the foil wrapper off, and sticks it back in the pocket. As the chocolate meets her tongue she can't detect any taste whatsoever. But down it goes, in between breaths that remind her of her grandma's dog panting after she chases a chipmunk, deer, or wild turkey back home in Kentucky.

But within seconds, up it comes.

She has to tilt sideways as she throws up. Shocked, she quickly moves her eyes from the steam that rises from the snow.

So much for dinner. Just my luck, she thinks as she shakes left and right.

She assumes that the leukemia is rearing its ugly head again—the nausea, the throwing up, the dizziness.

Just my luck... Oh well, it doesn't matter now, her mind rambles. *It doesn't matter a bit.*

She scoots away from the mound of rocks and the pieces of nutrition bar strewn near it and places her back against the snow, stares up at the salt and pepper sky.

"Hear me!" she tries to yell. "It doesn't matter! You win, cancer! I give up, I give up..."

Chest heaving, she sobs uncontrollably until there's no moisture left in her, no tears able to form. She even feels her eyelids sticking to her eyes, as she struggles to blink in the frigid, dry air.

An hour passes. Stars become brighter. It's getting colder. Much colder.

Her thoughts turn to her friends.

Or were they my friends?

Most had acted like she was contagious or something. Avoiding her like she was the devil himself. Or like she had leprosy or something.

If only everyone at school could see me now. The poor little sick girl with the terminal disease, sitting here on top of the tallest mountain in Africa. All by myself. No one helped. I did it all myself, every step. If they could just see me now...

CHAPTER FIFTY-TWO

Excuse me, have you seen this girl? Evan said to every face that approached him while he ascended. She's wearing a large red parka. No, sorry, most of the replies came. I'm looking for this girl, have you seen her? She has a bright red coat. No, afraid not. Sorry to bother you but have you seen this young girl? No sir, not that I can recall anyway. It was the same routine as down in the village—no sign of Megan.

At Horombo Hut, Evan approaches a climber, a professional-looking climber with all the right type of gear, expensive gear.

"I'm really sorry to bother you, but have you seen this girl?" Evan asks.

Once again he holds up the picture Katie had given him of Megan. The man pinches it between his thumb and forefinger, holds it close to his mirrored sunglasses and says, "Yes, I believe I have. Did she have a red or orange parka, several sizes too big?"

"Yes, yes," Evan replies, then exhales a misty breath of relief. He had almost arrived at the conclusion that Megan had chosen another trail, maybe to Mawenzi or Shira. Or that she had somehow taken a tour van to another part of the mountain, or somewhere else altogether. For all he knew, she could be anywhere within a hundred miles, in Kenya or Tanzania.

As Evan's eyes fill with hope he asks, "Where did you see her?"

"Let's see," the man responds as his face angles upward and searches the sky for an answer. "I think it was somewhere between Hans Meyer Cave and Gillman's Point."

"The Normal Route?"

"Yes, I'm almost positive."

"Look, can I ask you a favor?"

"Sure."

"Would you please stop at Mandara Hut on your way down and find a lady, long reddish hair, very attractive. She should be staying in one of the huts, and tell her that you saw her daughter and that Evan will bring her down soon."

"All right."

"It's very important."

The man nods three times. "I understand."

"Thanks. Thanks very much," Evan says as he starts to walk away. But then he pauses and asks, "Did she look okay to you?"

"She seemed fine, but I didn't talk to her for long, you know, as I passed by."

🌱

As the moon floats by her against a black sea of stars, Megan wanders between sleep and muddled wakefulness. She is still dizzy but doesn't feel sick to her stomach as long as she keeps her body in a prone position, seemingly strapped onto a massive roller coaster that has ceased moving at its highest crest.

A cruel wind has been spitting bits of snow at her for over two hours. She can't feel her face, she can't feel her feet. She can't feel the pain in her heart or the diseased marrow in her bones. Only the moon, the silvery smiling face above her, keeps her company.

Cold, so cold, she says to herself as her body shakes violently within Miss Emily's parka. Earlier in the day, and lower on the mountain, the parka had seemed like such a bastion of warmth, undaunted by everything Kilimanjaro could toss at its thick feathery lining. But now it feels that it is helping to keep the cold in, rather than away from her body. *Maybe it's the moisture from the snow? I wonder what it feels like to freeze to death?* she asks herself. *I guess it can't be worse than dying from cancer...a little each day.*

Suddenly her head throbs, the pain racing across her forehead, like one of the three shooting stars she had seen since sunset.

I feel dizzy...

Once again, disjointed thoughts skim across her mind—prolonged illness, cancer, the insurance company, lost everything, he must have loved you very much to look out for you like that...

🌱

And then everything was quiet. No wind, no snow, no world spinning below her. The dizziness transforms itself into perfect clarity, feelings of control, feelings of being content and loved. She is in a dreamscape from which she doesn't want to return. Warm. Full of light.

Sweet breezes fanned by sugar maples. Gentle streams full of colorful fish that fly, not swim, through crystal water. And then the snow is back, kinder snow, big flakes of finely chiseled white. They sprinkle on her and melt into her warm skin, lost forever. When she turns her head to see the ghost of them running down the bare skin of her shoulder she instead sees a faint light that grows into tiny legs and tiny arms and a lovely face that glows as it nears her, calling her four times in hushed tones.

"Megan, Megan, Megan. Is that you, Megan?"

Partially obscured by the snowflakes, the face and tiny body fly around her and she struggles to catch a better glimpse.

"Angela?" Megan replies.

"No, it can't be you. You're dead. It can't be you."

"Yes, Megan, it's me," the voice floats gently into her ears then continues, "Why, why are you on this mountain, Megan?"

Megan tries to raise her head, to move closer to her baby sister, "Because I want to be with you. That's all I want in the whole world now, Angela, just to be with you," she says as Angela's face dissolves into the fuzzy image of the moon, then back again. She senses her heart stopping in her chest, and tightening hands squeeze at her as she whispers, "I just want to be with you Angela," as the moon continues to interrupt the image before her.

Then Angela moves closer, eclipsing the moon, kisses her cheek and softly says, "I'm with you every minute of every day, Megan. I'm with you every second."

And with the warming touch of Angela's silenced lips on her cheek, the moon suddenly becomes bright again.

"Angela, where are you?" Megan begs at the sky but no reply comes, though she feels something touch her right arm. It feels just like Daisy's trunk, she tells herself as she searches the sky for her gray not-so-little friend.

"Daisy, there you are. What are you doing on top of Mount Kilimanjaro?" she asks as she watches the dome of Daisy's head gently dangle and drag the long trunk up and down her arm. Again the moon interrupts the image before her, stealing away the big kind eyes and fluttery lashes of Daisy. Giant flapping ears become crater-strewn valleys of the moon. And then she hears a voice.

"Megan, Megan, are you all right?"

Angela is that you again? Megan asks. She sees Angela's face again, but within seconds it becomes Evan's face.

"Megan, are you okay? Megan, wake up, honey." As Evan

303

caresses her arm through the thick sleeve of the parka, he sees her eyes darting about in the moonlight. "Wake up, Megan. You're going to be all right, honey. Please wake up."

He lies down beside her and unzips his jacket, lifts his two shirts and pulls her head to his warm chest, then tries to wrap his body around her. He says to himself, *Please God, let her be all right. That's all I ask. Please...*

CHAPTER FIFTY-THREE

The sun casts long shadows as it begins to sink into the India Ocean. It is late afternoon. Over the past few hours, Evan had watched fog rise from the valley, enveloping the specks of brown that were the park headquarters at Marangu Gate. And soon the gray mass of fog crept toward the slightly larger specks of Mandara Hut and then paused. He can see it there, now, waiting ominously as if to take this responsibility from his tired shoulders.

Since leaving the summit, he had only stopped when he absolutely had to rest. Each time was for water or to sleep for a couple of hours. Initially he had to sling Megan over one shoulder or the other, which was awkward and soon began to hurt his lower back. Eventually he made it to an area with some debris, broken tree branches and twigs. He also found an abandoned sleeping bag which was all but rotted, yet the area where the zipper attached was strong enough to remove and use as a rope for tying the branches and twigs together; he also removed the piping stitched around the bag, which had nylon cord inside. He fashioned a rudimentary sled and placed Megan on it as best as he could, which enabled him to drag her down the steeper sections relatively easy, gravity assisting most of the time. There was a point in which Megan didn't seem terribly heavy; his back, his entire body had essentially gone numb during the descent. Maybe it was because he had to concentrate on the trails, and where he placed his feet in the shadowy darkness that was the long nights, and the blinding sunshine that was the equally long days. Or maybe it was because he desperately wanted to get her quickly to a lower elevation, and somehow extracted energy from the sense of urgency.

Whatever it was that drove him, it is all but gone now. He can barely move his legs, and his spine feels like it's about to break. When his eyes finally see the blurry, ill-defined shapes of humans at Mandara Hut, he feels a sudden rush of energy. He wonders whether Katie is one of them, probably scared to death and waiting for him to bring her Megan, God willing, alive and in good condition. As he approaches, Katie's face becomes clear, then Chamba's, and a man standing next to him who he doesn't know. Suddenly, all three run toward him, arms pumping.

"Is she okay, is she okay?" Katie yells, in a voice that is more a scream.

Evan replies as loudly as he can, "Yes, I think so." But even he barely hears the words coming from his parched throat.

Of the three running, Katie gets to him first, her face mingling a degree of relief with concern. "How is she?"

"She should be all right. It's probably altitude sickness," he says, trying to calm Katie.

As he says this, Chamba also reaches him and says, "Thank God, thank God," then helps pull Megan from his shoulder and back. "Gently now, gently..."

The other man also approaches and helps prop Megan's head up with his jacket.

As Evan tries to straighten his tired back, which seems permanently stuck in a shallow arch, he notices tears streaming from the man's colorless face.

The man says, "Megan, honey, are you all right?"

Evan looks at the man, confused. *Who is he? Why is he calling Megan honey?*

"Wake up, baby, it's mom," Katie joins in as she strokes Megan's forehead then stands and raises her glassy eyes to Evan's. "Has she been awake at all since you found her?"

Evan tries not to appear alarmed. "Yes. She was able to take water, and ate a bit. But she's been out most the time. I asked numerous climbers along the way to try and call for a helicopter or other help, but no one came. So I just kept descending as fast as I could, night and day."

Katie touches his arm. "You look exhausted. You need help too."

Evan nods, stretches is back and winces in pain. "We better keep moving, and get her down to the gate." As he says this he hears an engine, and over his shoulder sees something move.

"It's the ambulance," Katie says. "They've been waiting with us. We tried to get them to go higher but they said they couldn't."

Evan nods as a Land Rover pulls up, a red light flashing on its roof. Two paramedics climb out and open a pair of rear doors, then grab a plastic medical case. They approach and ask everyone to back away, "Please, we need some space."

As they tend to Megan, Katie begins to weep uncontrollably. Evan walks toward her, wanting to comfort her, hold her in his weary arms. But before he reaches her the man, who was waiting with Chamba and Katie, says, "It's okay, honey. It's okay."

Evan stops dead in his tracks and his eyebrows raise slightly, mouth drops.

Evan watches as the man envelops Katie with his arms, rocks her back and forth, then holds her face with both of his hands and kisses her lips.

"She'll be all right, Katie," he says to her, then wipes her face.

She rubs the nape of her neck and gives a faint nod, feels yet another kiss, this time on her forehead. She turns away, toward Evan, and sees him looking on with confusion. She wants to melt into the mud and disappear but she says to him, "Evan, this is my fiancé, David."

As David releases her he extends a hand and says, "Thank you for bringing Megan down."

Evan's throat suddenly feels even drier and his head begins to ache as he reaches across a chasm of something his mind can't seem to define—fear, guilt, or shock. He shakes David's hand and then turns to Katie. She is now hovering over the paramedics' backs, watching them place an oxygen mask over Megan's mouth. As she glances back over to him, he realizes that she seems to avoid looking directly into his eyes. He turns and looks at David once more, but doesn't know what to say.

David continues, "I'm sorry you had to go after her. It's a miracle that you found her, and were able to bring her down by yourself."

Evan nods.

"If Katie hadn't dragged her down here, to Africa of all places, she wouldn't have been—"

"It's not her fault," Evan interrupts. "This is really all my doing. I'm the one to blame, not Katie. And not Megan."

"What do you mean?" David asks.

Evan pauses, gazing over at Katie, then answers, "It's, it's a long story..."

Their attention shifts to Megan, as she is secured on a gurney.

Katie, knowing that Evan has to be thoroughly confused at this point, wondering why David is there, approaches and says to him, "One of Chamba's guards at his house in Nairobi brought David to the village. And Miss Emily told him what happened."

"I see," is all Evan can muster.

And then it hits her. She hasn't told him the news. Her face suddenly lightens as she steps forward, finally looks Evan in the eyes and says, "They've found a donor for Megan."

"What?"

"Isn't it great," she says as she again breaks down in tears.

"When?"

307

"Just days ago. David got the call. They want us to fly back to the states as soon as possible for the transplant."

"My god, that's wonderful," Evan says as he turns somewhat away. His eyes also become wet. "That's absolutely wonderful," he repeats under his breath.

"She's going to be all right, isn't she," Katie whispers just over the sound of the wind and the ambulance's engine.

Evan nods and fights back the urge to take her in his arms.

David turns toward them and says, "I think the paramedics are about ready." He walks toward the ambulance.

"Okay, all be right there," Katie says to his back.

Waiting for David to get out of range of her voice, she then says to Evan, "Why don't you go into the hut over there, get some water, and I'll be there in a second. Okay?"

"All right." Evan turns and walks over to the hut and goes inside.

Katie watches as they slide Megan into the Land Rover, then tells David, "I want to thank Evan. I'll be right back."

"Okay, but you better hurry. They are almost ready to go."

"I'll just be a minute." When she enters the tiny hut, Evan is standing with his back to her, near a jug of water. Light is filtering through his tangled hair. She moves toward him and realizes he is shaking. Placing the palm of her right hand on his back, she says, "Thank you for finding Megan, and bringing her down. You saved her life, Evan." As he slowly turns toward her, she sees how upset he is.

He tries to speak but nothing comes out.

"It's okay, it's okay," she whispers, then reaches up and touches his damp cheeks.

He clears his throat and manages to say, "I'm sure she'll be fine. They'll take her to the main hospital in Nairobi."

As he says this, Katie shakes her head, "David's lined up a medical evacuation jet, with a doctor and nurse aboard. It's waiting for us at Kilimanjaro Airport. Assuming they say she can fly, we're going to take her back to the states immediately. The transplant may occur in days, if she's strong enough."

"I don't think it's wise to put her in an airplane right now."

"I know, I'm concerned too. If the doctor says it's not all right, we won't. But David is adamant about not checking her into any hospital here," Katie says as she looks nervously over her shoulder, through the doorway she entered. She continues, "Looks like they're almost ready to leave."

"Yeah, looks like it."

There is a long pause as she stares at the floor boards. When she finally looks up her face is red and she is obviously aching inside. She sniffles and asks, "Where does this leave us, Evan?"

"I was hoping you'd tell me."

"I'm so confused, I—"

Evan looks outside—the paramedics are tying down the gurney and Chamba is talking to David—then pulls Katie close, kisses her forehead. Everything in him wants to tell her how he is falling in love with her, how much he doesn't want her to leave, how much he craves her each day and each night. How just the thought of her had kept him climbing down the mountain hour after hour. He feels her throb in his arms as she begins to weep loudly.

"I'm falling in love you, Evan. The time spent down here, all this time with you, I just feel—

"It's going to be okay, Katie."

"What am I going to do?"

"Megan is the priority right now. Go take care of your daughter. Everything else will fall into place..."

He takes a deep breath, raises his hands to her shoulders, and stares deeply into her eyes. "You're going to go home, and you're going to put the pieces of your family back together," he says as his knees weaken, and he feels something breaking inside his very soul.

Her face afire, she tries to control herself.

"Everything's going to be all right, I promise. Everything will work out, Katie. We have to be concerned with Megan right now."

As he says this she nods and frantically wipes her eyes. Her breathing returns, shallow and frail.

When they exit the hut together they both appear reasonably normal, but Evan stops and lets her slip away. No words can explain what he feels, or convey to her anything more than what his eyes reveal at this moment. So he doesn't say anything.

And she too says nothing. She just slips away.

"Come on, Katie, let's go," David yells out.

She nods and runs toward the ambulance. As she climbs in back, she first checks on Megan. No change, but her pulse is stronger, according to one of the paramedics adjusting an IV. Then she looks out at Evan who is framed by the Land Rover's rear opening, poised sadly against the backdrop of Mount Kilimanjaro. She motions for him to come and get in.

The two doors silently swing closed.

Two doors swing open. Megan awakens and sees men, the paramedics, folding the doors back on the sides of the ambulance. Her head is throbbing. She glances down at her right arm and sees a clear tube connecting to an IV bag which is hanging on a chrome hook.

Where am I?

The two men climb into the ambulance and lift her upward, then out the ambulance's back doorway. It's dark, very dark, yet she sees her mom, David, and Evan approaching from a vehicle parked about thirty yards away.

"Mom, mom..." she yells out. She tries to rise from the gurney but can't move.

Katie runs toward her and, once beside the gurney, cradles her face with both hands then kisses her forehead three times. "It's okay baby, it's okay."

"Where am I? I don't remember any—"

"We're at the airport in Nairobi. We're flying back to the U.S., honey. A donor has been found for you."

"What?"

"A match finally turned up. You're getting the bone marrow transplant," Katie repeats, the words trembling from her mouth. She had dreamed of saying this to Megan every day, every night.

Megan stares up at her mom with disbelieving eyes and the first thought that strikes her is that perhaps her mother is just telling her this to make her feel better, help her recover from Mount Kilimanjaro. She simply doesn't believe her. She lifts her head and looks around, and quickly sees an aircraft nearby, which convinces her that her mom is telling the truth. She looks back at her mom, as tears begin to stream from her eyes. "I'm going to be alright?"

Katie rubs Megan's forehead and answers, "Yes, you are going to be fine sweetheart."

Katie notices Evan and David approaching, an image that startles her. Here was the man she was engaged to—though she had wondered for months whether David considered them still engaged—walking side-by-side with the man she was falling in love with and felt closer to. As she begins to contemplate all this, her predicament and feelings for both David and Evan, she forces herself to put the entire mess aside, knowing

310

she needs to focus on Megan.

David walks over and places his hand on Katie's lower back, pulls her close. A second later his cellphone rings, and he releases Katie and answers, "Hello. This is David."

"Yes, Mr. Hubbard, this is Doctor Carlton. I'm afraid I have some bad news."

David feels his heart sink into his stomach. He turns away from Katie, Megan, and Evan, and takes a few steps away. "Bad news?"

"Yes, I don't know quite how to say this. But the donor has backed out of the transplant."

David walks several more steps away, and moves around to the other side of the ambulance, staring at the aircraft waiting for Megan. "What do you mean they backed out? How can they—"

"This doesn't happen very often," Doctor Carlton interrupts, "but it does happen occasionally when someone signs up to be a donor, has their mouth swabbed thinking nothing will ever come of it, and then they get the call months or years later."

"My god. I can't believe what you are telling me. We are about to put Megan on an air-evac plane right now. She was just told that we found a donor."

Doctor Carlton takes a deep breath then says, "David, I'm so sorry. I'm sure we'll find another donor and—"

"No, that's bullshit. This donor needs to step up and do what they said they'd do. This is bullshit. I want to talk to them, and tell them about Megan and—"

"David, you can't talk to them. The entire donor process is set up to protect the identity of all parties until such time that they agree to exchange names and contact information. The only way to interact with a donor is through email processed by the registry, with names and locations removed. A year after a transplant, the parties can, if they mutually agree to, communicate directly."

David is speechless. He reaches up and rubs the back of his neck.

"Are you there, David?"

"Yes, yes. Can't we send a message to the donor-match and explain the situation, you know, tell them about Megan and how serious this is?"

"I've sent a communication to the registry and called them, too. They told me that they have already communicated with the match and were told that she changed her mind and is vehement about not proceeding. Something about her getting married and converting to the husband's religion. That's all I know, David. I couldn't push any further, and the person I spoke to really shouldn't have even said that much. The system operates under careful policies which protect identities."

"So what now? Megan is thirty feet away from me, about to be transferred to an aircraft headed to Istanbul, then changing planes and going to the U.S. What the hell am I supposed to tell her, and Katie?"

"David, all you can do is convey what I've told you. And stress that I'm sure we will turn up another donor. As you know, there are over 10.5 million registered donors in the U.S. alone on *Be The Match*. The registry worked. We're just unlucky this time. So stay calm and positive and tell Megan we'll find a match...after all, they do about 6,000 transplants each year."

"I know, doctor. But I also know that over twelve thousand patients are told they'll need a transplant each year, and there are almost fifty thousand new leukemia cases each year. Do the math." David clears his throat and, just as his phone emits a beep indicating a low battery, says, "Okay Doctor Carlton. I don't know how I'm going to break the news. But I better get back over to them."

"All right, David. I'll be praying for all of you and I know we'll find a donor eventually. Goodbye."

"Goodbye."

With that, the line goes dead. David wipes his brow on his shirtsleeve, looks briefly up at the sky, trying to compose himself, then walks over to Katie, Evan, and Megan.

As David approaches, Katie sees a change in his face, which is now deflated, void of expression. "Is everything all right, David?" she asks.

David pauses about twelve feet away, motioning for her to come over so Megan can't hear him tell her the news. He takes a deep breath, pauses as he looks down at the pavement, then answers, "There's some bad news, Katie."

"What? What is it?" she asks, her forehead wrinkling down slightly.

"The transplant is off, for now."

"What? What do you mean it's off?"

"The woman who signed up to be a donor backed out. I'm sorry Katie, but—"

"Are you fucking kidding me? Backed out? How can—"

David reaches up to her left arm. "Katie, stay calm. Don't let Megan see you getting upset."

She nods, realizing he is right, then lowers her voice and

continues, "How can someone back out of saving another person's life? What kind of person would do that? Can't we contact her and see if we can convince her to go forward?" As Katie says this, she already knows the answer; you can't contact donors, or prospective donors, unless they agree.

"Doctor Carlton said the only thing we can do is be patient and another donor should turn up."

"Should?"

"Katie, what else can we do? I'm sure they will find another and everything will be okay."

Katie glances over her shoulder, looks at Megan on the gurney, waiting patiently to be carried onto the plane nearby. *How am I going to tell her?* She then looks at Evan and senses that he already knows something is terribly wrong. With her index finger, she motions for him to come over, feigning a smile for Megan's sake.

Evan reaches Katie and David and asks, "So is everything okay?"

"No," Katie replies, "the donor backed out."

At first, Evan doesn't say anything. He just shakes his head slowly left and right, not knowing what to say. "I'm, I'm sorry. I've heard that that happens sometimes."

"It is what it is," Katie says as she swallows hard, tries to calm herself.

David turns to Evan and says, "We'll just have to keep looking. If one blood marrow match can turn up, there will be another."

"David," Katie cuts in, "I'm not waiting to find another match."

"What do you mean? What, don't tell me you're going back to your crazy idea of giving birth to a clone of Megan...for the transplant?"

Katie's face turns noticeably red, as if she's about to knock David's head off with one blow. "It's *not* crazy, David. It's a baby. A normal baby. A twin of Megan. A child I'll love as much as Megan. Not some alien creature. Jesus—"

"Calm down, calm down, Katie," he interrupts, knowing that once again he had pressed the biggest button possible, one which had resulted in countless arguments with David over the past year.

David shakes his head and rubs the back of his neck. "So, let's say you can successfully clone Megan's DNA into one of your eggs, and give birth to the perfect bone marrow match. Katie, you'll then have to wait how many years before you can safely remove bone marrow from the child and transplant it into Megan? Four years? Five? How long, Katie?"

"I've read that it has been done within the first few years."

313

"That's a long time to wait, Katie. Megan needs a cure now."

"David, she's in some degree of stabilization, according to Doctor Carlton. And hopefully she didn't make things worse, climbing, and will recover from all this." She pauses, trying to find the right words. "Look, I'm not saying I'm giving up on finding a match through the program, but I want a plan B. We've discussed this a million times."

David nods. "Yeah, I know. I know." He suddenly realizes that there's no use arguing the point. He knows full well that Katie will do whatever is necessary to help Megan.

Evan, who has taken a couple steps back from Katie and David, moves forward again and says, "What about cord blood?"

"What do you mean?" David asks.

"Cord blood, you know, from an umbilical cord after a birth. It's become increasingly used to treat cancer patients, since it contains blood stem cells. Some doctors—I believe one of them was Broxmeyer, Hal Broxmeyer—published a paper on cord blood use a while back. Some mothers, after the birth of their baby, even have the cord blood frozen and stored in a medical bank, in case they need it for their child someday."

Katie's face brightens as she says, "That's it. That's it. We may not have to wait years for a bone marrow match and transplant. That's it!"

David tilts his head slightly, "Well, you don't have your cord blood banked. So how is this going to help, Katie?"

"David, best case, Megan's treatment could start immediately after I give birth—nine months to a year from now."

"So you would *still* need to successfully use her DNA and implant the egg, or eggs...and give birth to a clone of her?"

Katie begins breathing harder and her eyes widen. "Yes." As she says this, she sees a door open on the medical evac aircraft nearby and an onboard nurse stepping out and waving her right hand, motioning for the paramedics to bring Megan to the plane.

David turns to Katie, looks her squarely in the eyes. "They're ready to go. I think we should take Megan back to the states. Take everyone home. And then decide what to do."

Katie moves her focus to Evan, who has again stepped away from her and David. In his eyes she sees something different; she sees understanding, finally.

Evan steps forward. He knows Katie is looking for some sign from him, some sign that he will help. He gets the sense that she doesn't want to push, or even ask him to help again. That maybe she'll get on that plane, head home, and just go try and find another expert in genetics and cloning and ask them to help. Evan realizes that it will either be him helping her and Megan, or it will be someone else, some stranger probably far less qualified than he is. She'll never give up.

David repeats and raises his voice, "Katie, they're ready to go. We need to *get* Megan on the plane and *go* home." He says this with the tone of a father speaking to a first grader who is kicking the back of a car seat at the end of a long drive—Don't make me turn this car around, sort of tone.

Katie backs away slightly, rubs her forehead, thinking, then looks at David, at Evan, David, and back to Evan where she finally says, "I don't know what to do." She sees the paramedics rolling the gurney with Megan toward the plane.

Evan moves his hand to her upper back, then suddenly feels uncomfortable as David observes. He immediately withdraws it. "Katie, this is really something for you to decide. But I want you to know that, if you do want my help, I can't promise anything, but I'll do whatever I can."

"You mean...you're willing to try the reproductive cloning procedure?"

"Yes."

As Evan says this, a chill runs down Katie's spine and a sense of relief washes over her. She doesn't say anything for several seconds and then continues, "Evan, you understand how high profile this will be if we succeed—or fail for that matter—and how many people will condemn you for being involved either way?"

"I understand, Katie. A lot of people will have a lot of opinions, I'm sure of that. Many of my colleagues, or peers rather, won't understand. And that's their problem. I'm sure if they had a child with a terminal illness and could save their life by reproductive cloning—giving birth to a healthy, normal baby—they would probably make the same decision that you are making. *I* would make the same decision that you are making." He turns and looks at Megan. "I've grown fond of that kid of yours."

Katie smiles without showing her teeth and nods twice. "But you had said no. Why the change?"

With this question, Evan's eyes become softer, noticeably glassy. He wants to tell her how he feels about her, and Megan, but David is four feet away and listening. "I've just given it some more thought, is all."

PART EIGHT

Johannesburg, South Africa. It has been three weeks since Megan's rescue from Mount Kilimanjaro. The decision had been made back at the runway that Katie and Megan would stay in Africa to complete the medical processes she'd decided on, beginning with extraction of four to ten eggs. David had flown off in the air evac jet to Istanbul, Turkey, and changed to a commercial airline for the return trip back to Kentucky. The air evac jet had already been paid for in full by David and the company refused to process even a partial refund. So, David decided, there wasn't a reason for him not to use the charter plane for a portion of his return trip.

When Katie said goodbye to him, it hadn't gone well. He disagreed about Megan and her staying in Africa, even in a major city, Johannesburg, and he continued to be against both the reproductive procedures required to extract eggs from Katie, and the cloning attempt. Katie couldn't fathom how David could be against at least trying the procedures. Even if he had strong feelings about the cloning effort, she felt that he should have been more supportive—that in the end it was her body, her eggs, and her daughter who needed saving. And her decision. And Katie reminded David that she didn't even need his assistance in conducting the reproductive cloning procedures, since cloning takes sperm out of the equation altogether. She didn't need David's or Megan's biological father's help to move forward with her plan. She just needed one of her eggs, at least, and one minuscule, harmless cell from Megan containing her DNA blueprint—and of course Evan's help and a whole lot of luck.

Just prior to David's departure, Katie tried once more to convince him that what she was doing was the right thing to do, the moral thing to do. The discussion became heated, with David storming off, and not even hugging or kissing her goodbye before boarding the plane. She respected his right to an opinion on the matter, but she didn't respect that he wasn't supporting her decision. There comes a time, she thought as she watched his plane take off, when the people closest to you simply need to support your decisions and respect them, even if they disagree with them.

In their last conversation, Katie reminded David of his sister,

Sabrina, undergoing in vitro fertilization in order to start her family with her husband. Sabrina had tried for four years to get pregnant naturally, to no avail, and finally decided to have a "test tube" baby. The process was identical to what Katie would go through in preparing for the cloning work. In a procedure called mild in vitro fertilization, Sabrina took injections of ovarian stimulating drugs which resulted in the production of nine eggs. Then, in a technique called transvaginal oocyte retrieval, an ultrasound-guided needle pierced the wall of her vagina to reach the ovaries. The fluid extracted was sent to a lab where the eggs were stripped of surrounding cells in preparation for fertilization in-vitro, Latin for *in glass*—meaning that the fertilization occurs in a "test tube" or petri dish. David's sister ended up going through two cycles of IVF with no luck getting pregnant. On the third try, the doctor put in four eggs, and Sabrina considered it her last go at the IVF process; she couldn't take any more of the painful drug injections, which were made to her lower abdomen by her husband, or the stress of going through the process any further.

Katie still remembers when the call came from Sabrina, informing David that she was, finally, pregnant—and with twins. Like Katie, David shed a few tears when he got the news, knowing what Sabrina had gone through to start her family. Now, years later, Katie wondered how David could be so against the same procedure, with the difference being that the egg, or eggs, would be infused with Megan's genetic material. It was more complicated than that obviously, Katie knew, and there were people who had even been against Sabrina's in vitro fertilization, believing that she had intervened in the natural process of reproduction, which some considered "against God's will" or unethical, since a number of eggs don't survive the retrieval, freezing, and the implantation process. Also, sometimes fertilized eggs are left over after a couple has the number of kids they desire; they are usually donated for research or to women desiring a child. For Sabrina, she had come to the conclusion that giving birth, giving life to a child, was what was important. As in natural reproduction where a woman loses one egg per month through menstruation, there is, as Sabrina's doctor had told her, a degree of waste, or loss, in artificial reproduction techniques too. But since the first test tube baby was born in 1978 in England, society had largely decided that the process was ethical, and over five million "test tube" babies, many of whom were frozen for months or years, had been born to welcoming parents.

In the end, David's sister gave birth to two beautiful little girls, Sasha and Hayley, who without man's intervention and technology, wouldn't have existed otherwise. Katie did her best to drive this point home to David, as she knew how much he loved his sister and his nieces. But none of the discussion had helped. He left Africa upset and not offering an ounce of compassion for Katie's decision.

On May 27th doctors at Netcare Kingsway Hospital in Amanzimtoti, South Africa, which is about a five hour drive south of Johannesburg, removed fifteen eggs from Katie. The doctor told Katie that this was actually the optimum number to retrieve during an IVF cycle; that if more eggs are taken there can be risks associated with over-stimulation of the ovaries during drug treatment such as blood clots and oxygen starvation. In Katie's case, the procedure had gone smoothly, no complications whatsoever. Evan had researched and picked the hospital because they have an in vitro fertilization center, and the hospital was located over on the coast not far from where his mother, Diane, lived. This provided Katie and Megan with a place to stay, while Evan remained in Johannesburg to get work done at the labs which had fallen behind due to his being stranded in Tsavo for so long during the storms. Evan also thought that this would keep Katie at a distance from him. He wasn't sure where things were going to go with Katie, relationship wise. But he knew that perhaps some distance and time would help give her the space needed to think about what had developed between them in Tsavo and decide whether to try and erase it, or embrace it. Part of Evan also knew that he couldn't trust himself to be around Katie. He knew he wouldn't be able to conceal his feelings for her, or keep from wanting to touch her if they stayed together as she awaited the egg extraction procedure. So his mother's house in Amanzimtoti was just far enough for him to run down and check on Katie and Megan and yet far enough to keep him away in moments when he yearned for her.

To Katie, the fact that Evan allowed her and Megan to stay at his mother's home reinforced her perceptions of him, and what kind of man he was. That he would introduce her and Megan to his mom, and ask his mom to look after them, told her what she already knew. That Evan was truly someone she could trust and who would support her decisions, now and probably forever—if she let him. Katie was grateful to have a place to stay, too, even though she felt a million miles from the United States, practically on the opposite side of the world. She told Evan on one of his visits down to Amanzimtoti, "This feels like the end of the world down here, sitting on the Southern tip of Africa on the coast. I guess that makes perfect sense. End of the world. And end of my rope…" Evan didn't comment when she had said this. He knew how much she and Megan had gone through the past couple of years, with chemo and radiation treatments and, most recently, the events in Tsavo—the storm, run-ins with poachers, and Megan's giving up and ascending Mount Kilimanjaro to try and end it all, for everyone's sake.

In Amanzimtoti, the only problem that came up was when Evan and Katie, who pretended to be a couple desiring to start a family, informed the in vitro fertilization center at the hospital that they only wanted to utilize their services for harvesting the eggs and then freezing them, which was unusual since most patients would normally proceed with fertilizing the eggs, implanting a few immediately while they are fresh, and then freezing the remainder for subsequent pregnancy attempts if the first failed. Evan convinced them that Katie wasn't quite ready for kids yet, but wanted to make sure she had eggs available when she was ready—the "my clock is ticking argument."

Evan and Katie were then faced with where to actually conduct the cloning procedures. Cloning had long been made illegal in many countries, or at least condemned. In March of 2005, unable to reach a consensus on a binding convention to ban cloning, the United Nations had adopted a non-binding Declaration on Human Cloning calling for a ban on all forms of human cloning, both therapeutic and reproductive. In the United States, Evan's research found that there were no federal laws which ban cloning completely, but that thirteen states prohibit cloning. Numerous attempts, at the Federal level, to ban cloning had failed in the U.S. The Human Cloning Prohibition Act of 2007 was introduced in June of 2007, but was defeated in the House of Representatives. In Europe, the European Convention on Human Rights and Biomedicine prohibits human cloning, but had not been ratified by all countries. In most other countries, the issue of cloning was either still under contention, or clearly defined and explicitly banned, such as in Canada. As Evan researched the subject, he was stunned at the varying opinions on human cloning. Sure, he had been somewhat immune to the issue, having focused on the use of cloning for bringing back populations of endangered species. After all, who could be against that? But it seemed that the issue of cloning humans, even to help save another person's life, was a hot area of discussion. He told Katie, "It seems that a quarter of the world, including most doctors, believe that cloning a human is completely unethical. And a quarter believes that *not* using cloning techniques to save lives is unethical. And the last half simply haven't thought about it, or they avoid the discussion altogether."

"So where do you want to perform the procedure," Katie asked the night after the egg extraction. She and Evan were sitting on the front porch of his mother's house, having just finished dinner, and Megan was inside watching TV.

"Well, I'd feel most comfortable, and probably have the highest chance at success, at my lab," Evan answered. "But I'm still waiting for someone to get back to me on the current state of cloning laws in South Africa."

A look of confusion swept over Katie. "Waiting for whom?"

"A lawyer. She's a professor of law at UNISA, the University of South Africa. I met her a few years ago, when the lab had some legal issues moving animals in and out of South Africa and between countries."

"I see."

"Regardless of what she says about the legalities of it all, I might still do it at my lab. I just want to know where things stand, in a worst case scenario where people find out. But don't worry, we'll find someplace to do it. She's supposed to call me back tomorrow morning."

Katie nodded then reached over and touched his hand, which was resting upon the arm of a rocking chair.

"I just don't want you to get your hopes up too high, Katie."

"What do you mean?"

"I mean that, even with the success my lab has had with animal cloning, we still have a pretty high failure rate. Sometimes we are successful in cloning with a couple of eggs. Sometimes it takes months and a hundred eggs. I'm sure that the thoroughbred cloning you do up in Kentucky has had similar results, right?"

Katie again nodded and remained silent for several seconds. "I know it's a long shot, Evan. I know too well. But it beats sitting around and waiting for a donor to turn up again for Megan. At least I'll be doing something that might work. At least there's a chance that one of my eggs will survive the procedures, and implantation."

Prior to Doctor Doyce, the head of women's reproductive medicine services at the hospital in Amanzimototi, removing Katie's eggs, six weeks passed excruciatingly slow at Evan's mother's house nearby. Megan would spend her days hanging out at the nearby beaches with a fourteen year old girl who lived down the street. They would head out in the afternoon and watch the surfers and on several occasions they visited Arbour Crossing, a huge shopping development, a nearby arcade, and a water park. Megan also learned about the culture and history of Amanzimtoti and South Africa in general. She learned that, according to local legend, the Zulu King Shaka led his army of men on a raid against the Pondos, back in 1828, and that King Shaka had paused to drink some water from a river and said, "Kanti amanzi mtoti," meaning the water is sweet. Within a week of arriving at Evan's mother's home, Megan had fallen in love with South African culture and the town which, she quickly learned, the locals simply called "Toti." She even learned some Afrikaans and Zulu words, though most people in the area spoke English.

As for Katie, she also grew fond of Toti. She spent most of her days reading and going for walks, helping Evan's mother with her garden and chores, and relaxing. She also visited the Japanese Gardens in Toti, finding it to be almost a spiritual, calming space for her to just clear her mind and connect with nature, as she had back in Tsavo. Aside from the shots she had to take, to prepare as many eggs as possible for retrieval, she enjoyed the beach life in Toti as much as Megan did. And it gave her time to learn more about the procedures Evan would soon conduct in an attempt to clone Megan. She already was well aware of the procedures, due to her experience at Kentucky Thoroughbred Center, but she wasn't aware of the history surrounding the issues of potentially cloning humans.

Katie learned that back in 2001 a consortium of scientists planned to clone a human within two years, and she read reports of wealthy parents paying exorbitant sums of money to fly-by-night scammers proclaiming to be capable of cloning deceased relatives. One couple had spent half a million dollars to try and clone their deceased baby, without success, by using the DNA from the child's tooth.

There were also reports out of South Korea that human embryos had been cloned, but later a panel at Seoul National University concluded that none had. The more Katie read about the issue of reproductive cloning—duplicating an existing person—and therapeutic cloning—cloning cells to treat diseased organs—the more comfortable she became with her decision to give it a try. After all, the procedure they'd conduct was the same procedure used in 1997 by Doctor Ian Wilmut and colleagues to create Dolly the Sheep. And it was the same procedure that researchers back at the Kentucky Thoroughbred Center were using to clone horses successfully today, and with increasing reliability.

The process is called Somatic Cell Nuclear Transfer, SCNT. Somatic Cell Nuclear Transfer begins when doctors remove an egg from a female donor and take out its nucleus, creating what's referred to as an enucleated egg. A cell, which of course contains DNA, is then taken from the person who is being cloned. Then the enucleated egg is, amazingly, fused together with the cell using electricity, thus creating an embryo which is implanted into a surrogate mother, just as in the process of in vitro fertilization. To Katie, there was no doubt that the process could work with a human. Her main concern was how many failed attempts there could be before success. With Dolly the sheep, there were 277 failed attempts before success. But a lot of years had gone by since 1997 and biotechnology had progressed exponentially since then. Recently the Kentucky Thoroughbred Center was achieving success about 50% of the time, with horses anyway. And, Katie thought, Evan was far more experienced than anyone back at the Center.

Katie also, while in Toti, read up on cord blood transplants, as if worrying about the cloning procedures wasn't enough. Assuming Evan could create at least one healthy embryo, and assuming it would implant normally, and assuming she'd give birth to a healthy baby in nine months, there was still the challenge of timing the use of the cord blood with the chemotherapy treatment and radiation Megan would need just prior to the transplant. She also confirmed, as Evan had told her when the idea of using cord blood instead of a bone marrow transplant came up, that the umbilical cord blood would be from the baby and a perfect HLA match for Megan—since it would literally be identical to Megan's blood, but void of the leukemia that had turned her life upside down. There was, however, a potential drawback to this; the fact that it would be an exact match also meant that there would be a chance of leukemia developing again, perhaps years later, if the leukemia was due to a defect in Megan's DNA. Although unlikely, if this would turn out to be the case, Katie could eventually end up with two daughters with leukemia, Megan and the identical twin of her.

Katie read that a patient for cord blood transplantation must be "conditioned" in order for their body to accept the graft, the cord blood; the conditioning is required to destroy the diseased cells, but it also destroys the patient's immune system. Without these methods of lowering the immune system's defenses, it will later attack the incoming cells from the transplant. This struck Katie as ironic. That in order to heal the human body it was necessary to almost kill it. In order to begin a new, healthy life, Megan would need to be taken to the brink of death. Although Katie read that such bone marrow and cord blood transplants had been made safer in recent years, the thought sent chills down her spine each time she contemplated the procedure. But Katie knew that it was the only way to eliminate Megan's leukemia and for her to have a chance at a normal life.

And so Katie's mind was made up. It was all worth the risk. On the day of the cord blood transfusion, doctors would thaw the collected umbilical blood which would be in a plastic bag similar to the ones used for IV medication or blood transfusions, then infuse the blood into Megan through a tube inserted into a vein in her neck or chest. In thirty minutes or so the procedure would be over. Megan's cancer nightmare would be over. The awkward stares and walking-on-eggs encounters with relatives and kids at school would be over. And the healing would begin. The blood-forming cells would travel through Megan's body and settle into the marrow of her bones and create marrow cells, which in turn would create blood cells. Megan would get a new immune system—from her cloned twin baby sister.

One scientific paper which Katie read, which she found in the Proceedings of the National Academy of Sciences, made it clear that timing was critical for the cord blood transplant; the donor cells from the cord blood have to be ready to give to the patient exactly after the patient's conditioning is done, as the patient's body is so weakened by the chemo and radiation it needs the cord blood right away, or the patient will die.

Johannesburg, July 8th. Evan rents a Volvo sedan and drives to his mother's house to pick up Katie and Megan, and their precious cargo—fifteen eggs.

As Evan pulls up to the house, Katie comes running out to the car before he can turn off the engine. He opens the door to get out of the Volvo and Katie swings it all the way open for him, smiling broadly and wearing a bright yellow sundress she had purchased yesterday at the mall with Megan. He gets out of the car and Katie immediately throws her arms around him.

"I thought this day would never come," she says as she squeezes tighter and rests her head sideways against his chest, then pulls herself away about a foot and looks up at his eyes. "How was the drive down?"

"Fine. Not much traffic. That's why I'm a bit earlier than I thought I'd be." He looks over at the front porch and sees his mom and Megan walking out the doorway, then moving down the steps to the path that leads to the parking area. His attention moves back to Katie and as he pulls some strands of her hair from her eyes he asks, "So, how are you feeling? Any problems after the extractions?"

"No. I feel fine. I'm glad it's over. I definitely won't miss the injections of that follicle stimulating drug."

"Yeah, that's pretty rough. I'm proud of you for going through that, and especially being able to give yourself the injections in your stomach. Uh..." He shakes his head, wincing from the thought.

Katie steps further away as Megan and Diane approach. Diane hugs Evan and he kisses her forehead. She then turns to Katie and Megan. "Well, girls, I have to tell you that I've really enjoyed your stay with me. It gets a bit lonely around here and I'm going to miss both of you. I hope someday you'll come back and visit."

Katie smiles and says, "We will, Diane. I can't thank you enough for letting us stay here. It was really over the top gracious, especially for two people you've just met."

"Well I know good people when I meet good people. And like I said, I really enjoyed meeting you two and spending time with you. I'll be praying for you, Megan. I know you will be alright very soon. Someday I'm going to come dance at your wedding. Deal?"

Megan nods twice and answers, "Sure. It's a deal. But you'll have to wait a long time. I'm not getting married until I'm at least twenty-five."

"Oh, I can wait, honey. I can wait."

Twenty minutes later the Volvo leaves Diane's house, as she waves from her front porch at Evan, Megan, and Katie. There's no time to waste. Evan's prepared everything at his lab in Johannesburg and told most of the employees to take the day off, such that he can focus all of his attention on the fifteen eggs which are in a container situated safely next to Megan in the backseat.

As they enter the N2 national highway, Evan turns toward Megan and asks, "So, how's it feel to be sitting next to what may become your twin baby sister?"

Megan looks down at the container, which has a seatbelt wrapped around it and is padded with a towel, and answers, "It feels pretty weird. Actually I'm sitting next to fifteen baby sisters, right."

Katie now flips her head toward the backseat, "Lord, let's hope not. One will do."

By 10:30 AM they arrive at Evan's lab in Johannesburg. Evan immediately takes the container with Katie's fifteen eggs inside and hands it carefully to his most experienced and trusted employee, Juanita Porter, who had moved to South Africa three years ago specifically to work with Evan. She had been a professor at the John Hopkins Institute of Genetic Medicine and had obtained her MD at UCLA, specializing in bioinformatics and genomics, and worked on their DNA Microarray Core Facility and Genotyping Core Facility. She had moved to America with her mother and father from Spain in order to enter UCLA at the age of just seventeen and quickly created a name for herself in genetics.

Today, Juanita is one of only three employees on hand, all picked by Evan, to help with the cloning procedures. He had briefed all of them extensively over the past several days, but they had been through the same procedures many times. They all agreed to keep confidential what they were about to do. And although Evan had never heard back from the attorney regarding the legalities about cloning a human in South Africa, none of the employees expressed any hesitation as long as it was to try and save a life, to try and save Megan. To Evan, it didn't really matter what the consequences would be. He knew that the best chance of success for the procedures was right here in the labs where he had created literally thousands of embryos. He knew the lab inside and out, every nuance and every procedure. And he knew that he had some of the best, most experienced geneticists in the world surrounding him. And so they got to work.

As the big hand and small hand passed over the 12 on the clock in one of the lab's conference rooms, Katie realized that it was now after midnight and Evan hadn't been in to provide an update on how things were going since 9:00 PM. She begins to worry. *Maybe some of the eggs didn't survive thawing. Maybe all of the eggs didn't survive. Maybe they're all dead.*

She takes a deep breath and looks over at Megan, who is sleeping contently on a leather couch over in the corner, a television still blaring ten feet away from her. Earlier, when Evan had dropped them off in the conference room, he had turned on the TV and given Megan a few bags of chips and a couple bottles of lemonade Vitamin Water from the lab's lunch room. He also brought in a couple of blankets. Megan had flipped through the channels and landed on *Jurassic Park*, which she had already seen at least five times. To Katie, it was a surreal moment, watching Megan glued to the TV as characters in Michael Crichton's 1993 movie were shown presentations of how dinosaurs could be cloned and brought back from extinction. If only Michael Crichton were alive today, Katie had thought to herself, to see the miracle Evan was working on at that very moment.

At 1:30 AM Katie rises and paces back and forth. *Where is he? They should have been done hours ago.*

She walks over and picks up one of the bottles of lemonade and takes a few sips. Her lips are dry, and her stomach is growling but she isn't hungry. As she sets the bottle down, the door to the conference room swings open slowly and Evan steps in, looking exhausted and shiny-faced.

"We're finally done," he whispers, not wanting to wake Megan.

Katie quickly walks over to him, locking her eyes on his, trying to ascertain whether the cloning procedure was successful, but his expression doesn't telegraph success or failure and she senses that he must be tempering either his enthusiasm or sadness. "You mean, you did it?" she asks.

With one hand, he holds the conference room door open and with the other he softly touches her lower back and ushers her out of the room, so they can talk away from Megan. "Let's talk out here," he says under his breath.

He quietly closes the door behind them and finally says, "Yes, we did it."

Tears immediately emerge from Katie's tired eyes and she hugs Evan so tight he has to struggle to take a breath.

"How many eggs survived?" Katie asks, knowing that statistically they'd be lucky to have even one healthy egg after inserting Megan's genetic material. She had even told herself for weeks that she may have to go through another IVF cycle, perhaps several, to get additional eggs. And if that's what she needed to do, she would do it.

Evan continues, "After thawing, we had twelve healthy looking eggs. Then, after removing their nucleus and the fusing process it dropped to two eggs which look viable."

Katie raises her eyebrows slightly. "Just two?"

"Katie, two is spectacular. You know that. It's a miracle...really."

She takes a deep breath and says, "I know, I know, Evan. Thank you so much. I can't believe we did it. I just can't believe that—"

"Katie," he says then caresses her cheek with the back of his hand, "you know that this isn't over yet. At least one of those eggs has to implant and then be monitored carefully to make sure it is dividing normally. Let's be cautiously optimistic but be prepared for the worst, okay? And the worst is that you'll go through one or more IVF harvesting cycles and we keep trying."

"I understand. I'm just going to pray and, and...try and turn it over to God. We've done everything we can. *You've* done everything you can, Evan."

Evan backs away from her slightly and takes off his white doctor's smock and a hair net, then the blue elastic booties covering his shoes. He wipes his face on the smock and then tosses it into a bin nearby. "Okay, well then, we need to get you over to the hospital. I've already called and they are ready. It's just five minutes away. Let's get those two precious eggs back into you. I think we hit the timing perfectly for them to have a chance at implanting."

"Okay," she says as a peace seems to sweep over her. They had indeed done everything humanly possible that they could do. She tilts her head and leans forward, kisses Evan's cheek. "I'll go wake Megan."

CHAPTER FIFTY-FIVE

Katie was never good at saying goodbye, whether it was ending a relationship with a boyfriend in high school or college, or leaving a job and colleagues to move to another company. She much preferred, as her mother used to tell her, to go down with the ship and wait until the other person said goodbye first.

As she and Megan stand on the other side of the airport security check at O.R. Tambo International Airport in Johannesburg, waiting for their carry-on bags to pass through the X-ray machine, Evan can still be seen through the glass dividers separating the drop off area from the passenger security screening section. Moments ago, Katie and Megan had said goodbye to him, waiting until the last moment to get through security.

"Well, I guess this is it guys," Evan says as he hugs Megan. "I bet you are ready to get home to Kentucky after your adventure in Africa."

Megan shrugs her shoulders then says, "I don't know. I'm kinda sad to be leaving."

Katie pulls her closer and swallows hard before speaking. "Evan, I can't thank you enough. I can never repay you for what you've done for us. I mean, the whole thing with me just showing up on your doorstep, and saving Megan not once, but twice. And all the while risking your life back at Mount Kilimanjaro and, now, risking your career and reputation." Her eyes become wet as she continues. "Now I know why the locals in Kenya call you the Miracle Man. Thank you, thank you so...much, Evan."

"You're very welcome...and you've already thanked me a million times, I think. Honestly, it was an honor and a privilege, it really was, meeting both of you." Now his eyes appear glasslike, reflecting the taxis lined up at the passenger loading area and people rushing in and out of the doorway to the terminal. "Now, I want you both to call me and keep me up to date on the baby, okay," he says, then gently places the palm of his hand on Katie's lower stomach for a couple of seconds. "I'll be praying that everything goes well for the pregnancy and that in nine months Megan here will have a new sister, an identical sister, and some much needed healthy cord blood."

Megan and Katie both nod, holding back the tears that they can.

"Katie, I want to see pictures of your beautiful baby, okay." Evan suddenly feels like he is struggling to find the right words. He wants to take Katie in his arms and kiss her, tell her he's fallen in love with her, tell her he wants to be with her, forever. But deep down inside he knows that this isn't the time. Everything needs to be focused on having a successful pregnancy and birth. Everything needs to be focused on curing Megan. And everything else needs to be put aside, including his feelings.

Nearby, Katie can see the line for the security check point getting longer. She knows that she and Megan need to get going. She turns to Evan and says, "Of course I'll send you pictures of the baby." She pauses, tears streaming down her cheeks once again. "I, I feel as though this is as much *your* baby as it is mine."

This statement hits Evan hard, and he feels his stomach tightening as he tries to contain his emotions. He wants to tell her that he feels the same way, but he simply nods and looks down at the ground for a few seconds. When he looks up again, he tries to lighten the moment a bit and continues, "So what are you going to name her?"

Katie looks at Megan, then quickly returns her attention, "I'm, I'm not sure. I've thought about it, but no decision yet."

Megan cuts in, smiling as she says, "How about Megan the second?"

Katie laughs, somewhat nervously. "Well, we have nine months to think about names, don't we," she continues. Again, she looks at the line over at the checkpoint. "I guess we better get moving."

Suddenly her mind is filled with images of what they all had been through the past few months. Gone were the starry nights and shooting stars which were painted across the inky canvas above the baobab treehouse. Gone were the majestic animals grazing over wide savannas. Gone were the walks with Evan to the waterfall, the shimmering light of the moon on his wet shoulders, and the feel of his skin next to hers.

As Katie reaches up to kiss Evan's cheek, she can't help but wonder whether she will ever see him again. So much had gone unsaid. So much needed to be said. Part of her wanted Evan to tell her he loved her and that, after the birth, he'd fly up to America and whisk her away and they'd all live happily ever after. And part of her respected him more for keeping the focus on the reproductive cloning procedures and on Megan.

And then there was David, waiting back at home. Once David heard that Katie and Megan would be staying with Evan's mother in South Africa, he stopped communicating entirely for several weeks, and then just checked in once a week with Katie in polite but awkward conversations which left both of them wondering where their relationship stood, where their relationship was going. David would spend most of the time talking about the breeding activities and work related issues at the Kentucky Thoroughbred Center which, Katie came to believe even more at this point, was his real true love. Horses. Growing the business. Managing employees and investors. All of this seemed to be what he needed most. The only thing he really needed.

As Katie and Megan walk toward the baggage screening area, Katie begins to cry hard. She can't help herself. She keeps her head down and doesn't look back at Evan until she has made it through the screening area and is slightly more composed. Megan just looks on with worrisome eyes, not saying anything to her mother, and reaches for her hand to comfort her. In this moment, Katie realizes that her little girl is growing up—that Megan doesn't want to force her to explain why she is crying, after leaving Evan. Katie knows full well that Megan understands exactly why she is crying. And that it is okay.

PART NINE

Over nine months had passed since Katie and Megan returned to Kentucky, and to David. The pregnancy had gone smoothly, aside from the typical morning sickness and nausea. On June 26th, on a beautiful day with bright blue, clear skies and warm temperatures, Katie gave birth to a 7 pounds two ounces healthy baby girl which she named Morgan. A baby girl who looked exactly like Megan's baby pictures and came out screaming with life the same exact way as Megan had fourteen years ago.

8:30 AM, Saturday morning. Usually Katie would hear the sound of the TV downstairs playing one of Megan's favorite teen shows, but today the house is quiet. The past week had been the hardest week since learning of Megan's illness. The hardest week of chemotherapy. The hardest week of radiation. Yesterday, Megan had refused to eat, except for a bagel early in the day, which she promptly threw up across the kitchen floor. Her immune system was at the weakest point possible. The cord blood transplant had been scheduled for Monday morning. Katie had already given the approval to thaw the cord blood and have it ready. Everything was locked in place, with Megan's body conditioned to receive the healthy cells. Doctor Carlton had told Katie that once the cord blood was thawed it would only be good for two or three days max. The transplant had to happen Monday. And Megan had to have the transplant to save her life from the chemo and radiation at this point, let alone the leukemia.

Katie yawns and turns to her side, stares at the alarm clock for a moment. She then pulls the bed sheets off and puts on slippers. She makes her way toward Megan's room. The house is tranquil and eerily quiet. She can't even hear the typical morning chatter of birds feeding their young. Even the baby is sound asleep, as she peaks her head in to check. Ahead, Katie sees Megan's door just as she left it last night, after kissing her goodnight. It is open just a few inches, just enough to keep the nightlight in the nearby bathroom from being too bright.

Katie places her hand on the brass knob of Megan's door, and quietly pushes it open. Her heart immediately begins racing as she sees Megan strewn across the floor of her bedroom, her arms and legs in a contorted image she'd only seen on those CSI crime shows, where police have chalked the outline of a body. There is vomit projected in three different directions around Megan's body, and it is still dripping from her mouth, which is partially filled with the brownish red liquid. Katie's first thought is the worst thing possible, Megan choked on her vomit. Doctor Carlton had told Megan numerous times to try and always sleep on her side, in case she threw up in the middle of the night. That way the vomit would hopefully pour out and not cause any choking.

"My god. Megan. Megan!"

Katie drops to her knees, which become soaked. She reaches up to Megan's neck, trying to find a pulse.

Megan feels the wheels of the gurney wobble across the smooth vinyl tile, sending a vibration to her back. As she tilts her head to the left, looking down one antiseptic and unending hall after another, she sees three stripes painted on the floor. Red, blue, and yellow. She also sees busy-looking people wearing wrinkled green and white smocks, all following the stripes as they split off, fork, come together, and lead through mysterious closed doors.

Yesterday, when they told her she would have to go through one more chemo and radiation treatment, her eyes welled up and she almost begged to be taken back to the top of Mount Kilimanjaro. Just let her rest there and fall into unconsciousness between the snow and the moon, playing with the ghost of her late sister Angela, and with Daisy the baby elephant. But, they told her, "We need one last, brave effort to get rid of the bad cells and weaken your immune system so it will receive the good cells from the cord blood. Unfortunately," Doctor Carlton continued, "you may become weak, irritable, and nauseous from the drugs...as usual."

"What else is new," Megan responded. She had almost choked to death and asphyxiated on her vomit after the previous treatment session. He was telling her what she had been told probably twenty times the past year.

Just minutes ago the hospital ran a final battery of tests to make sure her heart, lungs, kidneys, and other vital organs are ready for even more trauma. Once again Megan feels like a human guinea pig, poked and prodded, assessed and diagnosed, all in preparation for the big event— the cord blood transfer.

"We have to have a baseline against which we can compare post-transplant results," one of the nurses tells her which, to Megan, means that she will be going through all of the tests yet again, after the transplant.

As she is pushed down another generic hospital corridor she stares at the ceiling tiles above her, a blurry sky made of white puzzle pieces. She's thinking of what her mother had gone through to get her to this moment. *There couldn't be a better mom in the world*, she tells herself as the gurney slows, and a nurse caresses her head a couple of times.

Her ride through the hospital complete, she is transferred from the gurney to a firm bed with chrome rails on one side that are almost too cold to touch.

"This will be the easy part," Doctor Carlton says as he finally enters and begins verifying and preparing the cord blood, which Megan responds to by averting her eyes, turning toward the amber light drifting in through the one window in the room. A feeling of peace and contentment seems to wash over her.

Within minutes the healthy marrow is flowing intravenously into her weakened body. No surgery. No pain. No complications. And she is struck at how simple the procedure is that she has dreamed about every day and every night.

As red drops of life slowly make their way into her tired veins, her eyes follow the descending sun, which lowers itself gently onto the hushed tones of the city and then disappears altogether. She envisions the cancer cells that had silently invaded her body, her soul—her entire family—also vanishing. For the start of healing to be so peaceful, so discreet, somehow seems fitting.

Alone now, almost to the top of another mountain, her heart lightens. For she knows in time her hair, her sense of humor, and her friends will all come back.

CHAPTER FIFTY-SEVEN

Summer arrived in Kentucky seemingly all at once. The spring rains were choked out and in their place came temperate breezes that said goodbye to the tulips and welcomed an even more colorful palette of perennials rising from the garden. Bright colors and bright scents.

By all accounts, the transplanted cord blood had engrafted successfully, but since Megan was susceptible to infection she was kept on antibiotics. She also had to endure numerous transfusions of platelets to prevent bleeding, and received immunosuppressant medication to control graft-versus-host disease.

For Katie, the weeks following the transplant became an ever-changing blur of euphoria mingled with several bouts of mild depression, which her gynecologist had told her was probably just the typical hormonal, post-partum variety. When she focused on Megan and the baby who had saved her life she was fine, but when her mind wandered back to Africa and to Evan's arms she felt out of place lying in bed next to David each night. They hadn't made love since she returned from South Africa. In fact, she couldn't even remember the last time they had been intimate; she knew it had to have been several months before she left with Megan for the trip. It was as if they both had some sort of tacit understanding, a mutually agreed upon need to start from scratch after almost two years of turbulence in their lives. Yet the fresh start was elusive, never making itself known. Often waking up in a cold sweat, Katie would turn and stare at David's face, hoping for some answer to take form, something to either ease her guilt over what had transpired with Evan or to give her the courage to make a decision that would surely change her life, and the lives of everyone around her, forever.

She still loved David, this she had no doubt. But the yearning inside that she felt for Evan was making her crazy, an urgent crying of her soul that was only tempered by the words she heard him say that day in the hut on Mount Kilimanjaro as he raised his hands to her shoulders, and stared deeply into her eyes—"You're going to go home, and you're going to put the pieces of your family back together."

The message couldn't have been clearer. It was over.

She had only talked with Evan two times since leaving South

Africa. She placed the first call from the waiting room at the hospital, within minutes following the cord blood transplant. "Everything went perfectly," she said as David sat next to her in the waiting room. Then, a month later, she called Evan from home when David was at work. Megan was asleep on the family room couch downstairs, television blaring the teen show of the hour. With her hands shaking so hard she could barely enter Evan's phone number, and her mind filled with ten different versions of what she would say to him, his voice came on.

"Hello. This is Evan Drake."

"Hello, Evan, this is Katie."

The line went silent for a couple of seconds and when he finally said something his voice seemed to break. "I, I wasn't sure I would hear from you again."

"I'm sorry... I'm sorry I haven't called."

"How's Megan?"

"She's fine, doing great. Doctors say that the engraftment has taken."

"Thank God. That's wonderful news. Please tell her I said hi, and I'm glad she's doing so well."

"I will."

Evan soon changed the subject and told Katie what he had been up to since she and Megan had left South Africa. He said Chamba and Dora had recently brought up Rosie, the elephant she had seen in Johannesburg in the lab facility, and had successfully set her free near the baobab platforms. Three days later Evan saw her bathing in a nearby water hole with young Daisy; Rosie had taken Daisy as her own. He also told her of three more run-ins with poachers, and that one of the encounters was with the pair who had picked up Megan. They were now in a Nairobi jail. It turns out that they were also responsible for a high profile case which had garnered international attention, the poisoning of over 300 elephants, lions, and other animals in Zimbabwe. Investigators found their fingerprints on canisters which had contained cyanide, left behind near ponds in Zimbabwe's largest game park, Hwange. Evan went on to say that just fifty rangers patrol over five thousand square miles of the park, and until ivory export and import penalties are increased there was little hope in stopping all poaching activities; there's simply too much demand for ivory, especially in Asia and the Middle East. The dilemma was still the same. Areas banning all trade in ivory, and which don't have solid tourism revenues, had little money to spend on preserving what few elephants remained. And the decreasing supplies of ivory was having the effect of increasing its value. Poachers willing to take risks were being well compensated for obtaining even just one or two pairs of tusks, even from the national parks.

The conversation had ended without Katie or Evan bringing up what had happened between them at Tsavo during the flood, though they both had the same questions, fears, and unspoken desires. Evan didn't want to push Katie into saying or doing something she might regret once her family was completely healed.

As the months rolled by, after he said goodbye to Katie and Megan at the airport in Johannesburg, he fully expected Katie's and David's relationship to get back to normal. Without the stress of Megan's illness, and with time slowly healing the wounds left by David's car accident and Angela's death, he assumed Katie would simply file away all memories of him and of Africa. Just erase the passion they had experienced altogether, or tuck it away into a corner of her mind, never to be contemplated or acted upon. And though he thought of her each night, whether at the baobab tree platforms in Tsavo or at his home in Johannesburg, he told himself he would have to do the same.

And so he did.

For a while anyway. He threw himself at his work in typical male fashion, putting in eighteen hours a day until, on a bleak stormy August afternoon, he walked into Michael Jenkins' office at the facility and said with weary eyes, slumped shoulders, "I need to talk to you."

Michael asked him to sit down and close the door. "What's on your mind?"

"I'm burnt out," Evan said as he ran his fingers through his hair, rubbed the back of his neck.

"Gee, I hadn't noticed."

"Is it that obvious?"

"Yes, I'm afraid so. Over the past few weeks I've thought about asking you what's wrong several times, but didn't want to put my nose where it doesn't belong."

"You could never do that, Michael."

"Do you want to talk about it or—"

"I think I just want to take some time off, maybe head up to Tsavo for a few weeks. No work, just relax a bit. Can you manage without me for a while?"

"Of course, whatever you need to do..."

The next day Evan flew to Jomo Kenyatta International, rented a truck, and drove to the village. He stopped and chatted with Miss Emily, giving her the last update he had on Megan, then bought some supplies at the market. By noon he had arrived at the baobab platforms. His mood improved as he saw the speckled light filtering through the branches, moving over the ground and the bamboo framing. With the bag of supplies tucked under his right arm, he climbed the ladder and, looking upward, couldn't help but think of Katie. In his mind he could see her long legs making their way up the ladder rungs, her hair dangling back and forth across her shoulders.

When he reached the main platform it was like no time had passed at all. Everything was in good shape still. There were even a few dried leaves left where Katie slept each night, over near the trunk. He could see her there, lying on her back and looking up at him with wide, glistening eyes.

When darkness fell he built a fire in the pit they had abandoned. The rocks were still in place, except for two or three which had somehow been dislodged. And as he held his feet near the warmth he stared at the moon, just as he had with Katie by his side each night at the waterfall. He wasn't sure he could handle hiking up there again, seeing the naked ghost of her standing under the shimmering water.

The next five days passed as one. He would sleep in as long as he could, before yielding to the chatter of birds, then he would go for walks along the cliffs, or read one of the paperbacks he had brought with him. He was never one for taking naps, but found himself doing so each afternoon when the sun slanted at just the right angle through the branches and the platform's slight movement rocked him to sleep.

But if his goal was to stop thinking of Katie, he was failing miserably, he told himself one evening. Yet deep down inside he knew he had come here for exactly the opposite reason, to be close to his memories of her.

An ocean and a continent away, things had turned from bad to worse between Katie and David. Whether it was the lingering guilt over the car accident, or his anger toward Katie for putting Megan into danger in Africa, or the stress from work, Katie didn't know. Katie even wondered whether David held some sort of animosity toward her for being right about not waiting for a bone marrow match, and instead pursuing the reproductive cloning and cord blood transfusion. Or perhaps David, who had always been hyper competitive in almost everything in his life, couldn't cope with being wrong? Katie couldn't imagine how he could feel that way given the end results. But whatever the cause, David slipped deeper into his old routine with each week they were back together.

Letting things go around the house. Taking too much time off from work. Moping around. Never touching her or providing any other form of affection. Katie couldn't fathom how he could be so depressed, with Megan doing so well, and with a beautiful, healthy baby joining the family. At one point Katie actually talked him into seeing a psychologist with her, but he only went twice then said it was a waste of time and money, "I don't need a damn shrink." It was soon thereafter that he told her he thought it would be good if they had some space, "Just a couple of months to sort things out." He rented a condo and moved into it two days later. Though he had visited at least once a week since then, playing with the girls, he rarely spent ten minutes with Katie, and as the days and weeks went by she realized he was, without a doubt, happier without her around. Just as when she had gone to Africa.

So summer moved by in Kentucky, humid days and sticky nights filled with the incessant clicking sounds of cicada insects. Katie wondered whether David's scars had just grown too thick—or whether he had sensed a change in her. Or maybe he had asked her to marry him, which was almost three years ago at this point, just because it seemed like the next step. On more than one lonely night, Katie even wondered whether he was seeing someone else, but dismissed this each time it crossed her mind. The one thing that she couldn't dismiss was the uneasy feeling in her gut that perhaps he really didn't love her—at least not as she wanted to be loved.

The few weeks off from work, the labs, turned into two months. Evan had sent word via Chamba that he needed a "leave of absence." He felt guilty for changing what he had told Michael, but he couldn't bring himself to leaving Tsavo. In actuality, he wasn't just relaxing anymore. In fact he would spend at least half of each day tracking and replacing animal tags and radio collars, which had needed to be done for six months. He was also collecting and freezing sperm and eggs from various large game animals when the opportunity availed itself, and sending them back for freezing and storage. And though he didn't expect support from the Johannesburg facility, Chamba would bring him fresh supplies each week. Michael and all of the co-workers seemed to understand that to keep Evan inside a lab all day was like keeping a wild animal in a cage for too long. He needed to be outside, and free.

The baobab platforms were now an elaborate treehouse, one that could, with certainty, instill envy even in the eyes of Disney imagineers. Evan had added slanted tin roofs, safety railing, and a couple walled rooms for nights when the wind was strong. There was even a kitchen of sorts, with a metal camping stove, a bamboo work counter, and cupboards. A barrel, suspended with ropes, collected water from one of the roof panels which had a hollowed piece of split bamboo for a gutter.

As for bathing, he decided the waterfall was indeed the best solution, though the first few trips up the canyon he had opted to just sit on the smooth rocks nearby and let the mist baste him while he dreamed of his time with Katie there. On one such afternoon, which was unbearably hot, he meandered up the path to the falls and dangled his feet beneath the water, then slowly kicked at his reflection. Upon feeling his skin redden beyond comfort, he walked back down to the baobab, and climbed lazily up the ladder. Time for a nap.

At first he thought he was seeing her ghost again, for the horizontal light was draped all around her and his eyes were sun-strained such that they made everything dull and gray. The aberration said nothing to him as he squinted and walked toward it, but he could see her smile come into focus, then her eyes.

It can't be, he told himself, it can't be. "Katie?" he said softly, as if not wanting to scare the image away. "How on earth did you—"

"Chamba dropped me off," she finally spoke in barely a whisper.

"My god," he said as he opened his arms for her, "I can't believe it's you!"

"I know, I know. I've missed you so much."

They held each other for several minutes, swaying back and forth, touching fingers to faces, and eventually lips to lips.

"I was worried about you," she said as her eyes filled with compassion.

"Why?"

"Every week I would call the facility in Johannesburg, and they told me they didn't know when you would be back. I finally got through to Michael and he said you had come up here."

And so they rambled on like teenagers catching up on each other's lives after summer break. Megan finally returning to school, with long shiny hair, and boys calling the house all the time. David moving out and eventually dating a secretary from work. Katie taking a leave of absence, focusing on raising the girls, and working on the novel she had put off for too many years. She also rode horses every afternoon over long stretches of Kentucky blue grass. She talked of how she had reached an epiphany of sorts—that she could follow someone else's dream, or she could follow her own. The sparkle in her eyes made it clear to Evan the choice she had made.

Before they knew it the sky was only filled with their voices and stars and an opalescent full moon that seemed to have been waiting for their return. Hand in hand, they followed it once again to the waterfall.

The End

Note from the author

First of all, thank you for reading *The Miracle Man*. I appreciate it. In the beginning of this book, I dedicated *The Miracle Man* to my daughters Emily, Hayley, and Sasha. Now that you have read the story, I thought I'd share something with you. My daughters actually helped inspire this novel. Emily and Hayley are fraternal twins, and were created via a long heart-wrenching process involving the ups and downs, successes and failures, of genetic reproduction procedures (in vitro fertilization). They—Emily and Hayley's embryos—were amazingly frozen for two years before being implanted and nine months later being born. And during that period, Sasha was adopted from an orphanage, which was also a challenging process in itself. All of this, overcoming obstacles to create a family and have kids, proved to be helpful to me when writing scenes about how parents will do anything to have children, and protect them. Plus, with all these girls running around the house, I had a pretty good feel for how to write about Megan in the story, and her perspectives and behavior.

Not everyone will agree with all of the genetic engineering activities described in this story, and that's fine. Some will say that I attempted to put forth a message condoning reproductive cloning, if it will save another person's life. But my real mission was simply to tell a high concept, "big story," which would make people think about some of these issues while also entertaining the reader. So paramount in my writing process was…would I like to read this story, or would I like to see these scenes in a movie theater? Nevertheless, for my family, medical and genetic reproductive technology was beneficial. As I write this, there are two incredibly cute ten-year-old twin girls sleeping in beds thirty feet away from me who would not be there if it weren't for some of these technologies and procedures.

Where society draws the line on such issues will no doubt be debated in the coming years. Is it ethical to clone a human in order to save the life of another human? Is it safe? Whatever the answers are to these questions, one thing is for sure. Whether it is ten months, ten years, or a hundred years, a human will eventually be cloned. It may be someone wanting to give birth to a baby to help save another's life, as in this story. Or it may be a woman wanting to give birth to a clone of someone who has died. Or it may be some eccentric billionaire or leader who wants to live forever, in essence, by replicating himself or herself. In the end, society will need to determine what the appropriate uses of reproductive and therapeutic cloning procedures are. In the meantime, these technologies are already being applied to the animal population and there are efforts to bring back endangered species—an exciting process referred to as *de-extinction*, as portrayed in this book. Some scientists have already considered bringing back the Mammoth, for example. In 2008, seventy percent of the mammoth's genome was decoded and this, combined with the fact that today's elephants share very similar DNA, sparked interest in possibly bringing a hybrid version of the mammoth back to life to once again roam the Arctic...or at least a zoo.

Aside from the inspiration provided by starting my family and time since spent with my daughters, I was also inspired by other writers, such as the late great Michael Crichton, the master of high concept big stories, each driven by careful research. I only wish that he were still alive today to witness these activities in genetics, many of which he envisioned in his now iconic *Jurassic Park* novel. Knowing Michael, he has probably figured out a way to do this, and is looking down now. I was also inspired by some of Hemingway's work, including *The Snows of Kilimanjaro*. And I recall reading *The Horse Whisperer* in the late nineties by the extremely talented Nicholas Evans, which garnered a widely publicized six million dollar+ advance for the book and movie rights to Robert Redford. I was impressed by the writing and intrigued by the mother's quest to help her daughter, and inadvertently finding romance and adventure in the process. I also liked the atmospheric settings, and use of animals as a backdrop to a story. Having lived in Kentucky for eight years on a small farm, before returning to the San Diego, California area in 2004, I can relate to the beautiful horse settings and the draw of nature, all of which I believed helped me with this story's scenes in Kentucky and in Africa.

In a way, after spending thousands of hours writing and rewriting, and making what must have been a million decisions on plot and relationship direction, the characters in *The Miracle Man* almost became real to me, essentially becoming members of my family too. They sort of took on a life of their own, creating a responsibility on my shoulders to look after them. They filled many of my days as I guided their adventures and relationships, and often also filled my dreams at night. I will miss many of them—young Megan, Katie, Evan, Miss Emily, Chamba, and Dora. And I hope you will too.